P9-DBO-426

EAGLES AT WAR

EAGLES AT WAR

WALTER J. BOYNE

CROWN PUBLISHERS, INC.   NEW YORK

Copyright © 1991 by Walter J. Boyne

All rights reserved. No part of this book may be repro-
duced or transmitted in any form or by any means,
electronic or mechanical, including photocopying, recording, or by any information storage and retrieval
system, without permission in writing from the pub-
lisher.

Published by Crown Publishers, Inc., 201 East 50th
Street, New York, New York 10022. Member of the
Crown Publishing Group.

CROWN is a trademark of Crown Publishers, Inc.

Manufactured in the United States of America

Library of Congress Cataloging-in-Publication Data

Boyne, Walter J., 1929–
  Eagles at war/Walter J. Boyne.—1st ed.
    p. cm.
    1. World War, 1939–1945—Fiction. I. Title.
PS3552.0937E24 1991
813'.54—dc20   90-2691
                                                    CIP

ISBN 0-517-57610-4

10 9 8 7 6 5 4 3 2 1

First Edition

*To my inspiration,
my wife Jeanne,
and children Molly, Katie, Bill, and Peggy
—plus Max and Minnie
and Duke and Spike
—pets are family, too.*

PROLOGUE

Over Germany/April 24, 1944

The B-17s came from the northwest, locked in formation as precisely as migrating geese, their target the Dornier aircraft factory neat Friedrichshafen. There were no escorting fighters and the bomber crews sweated with fear, their nervous young gunners probing the hostile sky for bogies, seeking cold comfort in the heft and wicked oily smell of their guns.

The Bomb Group Commander repeated his call to close up the already tight formation. He had flown Flying Fortresses through the blood baths of Schweinfurt and Regensburg and knew the chilling odds against them.

The crews crouched in their frozen aluminum tubes, swaddled in zippered leather suits, bodies kept barely mobile by electrically heated garments, deafened by the unremitting roar of slipstream, the prairie-fire crackle of their headsets, the pounding of propellers and engines. Their fingers itched to add to the din with the reassuring thunder of their .50-caliber Brownings, to *do* something other than passively wait for a random burst of flak or the quick slash of a fighter.

From the southwest, a single North American P-51 fighter turned parallel to the distant bombers, its pilot watching the flickering images of B-17s projected against the towering silver cumulus clouds behind them. The Mustang was free-lancing, briefed to seek out and strafe anything moving—a train, a truck, a wagon, even a soldier on a bicycle. One of its mates had been shot down, the others were somehow missing. Now the pilot was headed home alone, low on fuel and ammunition.

From the east there came a dot, a single speck that quickly changed into a speeding shark, moving in and out of the line of clouds more swiftly than any airplane he had ever seen before. It banked sharply, an arrow shape curving around the bomber's flank. The American pilot checked his instruments and dove. This was a predator from a new technology, something special that must be reported—after he killed it.

The German pilot focused on his attack. He knew how many hits it took to hurt a B-17 and how savagely a formation of them responded. In the old piston-engine Messerschmitts, he'd had to fly long, tenacious attacks, trying to concentrate twenty or thirty cannon shells in a vital spot, aiming and shooting amid a virtual bath of machine-gun fire from the bombers. Fearful and inexperienced pilots would fire from a thousand yards out, fanning their shells into a pattern through which the bombers could slip.

Keeping his turn wide, the German pilot banked around the northern edge of the bombers, wisps of moisture curling from his swept-back wings. He wanted to pass through the formation diagonally, preventing all the guns from being trained on him at once, curving constantly, masking his own plane with those of the enemy. He knew that most of the gunners would fire behind him, unprepared to compute the lead necessary to nail a target moving at his jet's 850 kilometers per hour.

Turning in, he selected the B-17 at the northernmost corner of the formation, noting its graceful shape, the green diamond mark on its vertical surfaces, and the brush-bristle stippling from the machine guns studding it. He didn't see the name *Rebel Rose* on the nose or the copilot crossing himself.

In three seconds his six cannon hurled ninety-six pounds of lead, the tight cluster of shells impacting near the inner port engine, shredding the aluminum bridge-truss structure of the spars and ribs. The unleashed gyroscopic forces of the overspeeding propeller ripped the engine from its mounts, wrenching the wing apart, sending the *Rebel Rose* reeling, the dead crew members at peace, the living to face long tumbling moments of terror before the impact. The lone German plane skimmed over the dying B-17 like a track star leaping a hurdle, cutting to the formation's center. Its pilot pressed the trigger again, pouring a terrible fire into the bomb bay of a B-17 named *Cloud Duster*, the crew on its thirtieth and—truly last—mission. Plunging through the red-black explosion of metal and body parts, the pilot hoped that the jet engines would not suck in the debris.

Exactly ninety degrees from where his first victim still spun toward the ground, he put the formation leader in his sights, a touch of rudder sliding him to the left to rake its forward fuselage. It was the *Minnesota Mauler*, its crew proud to be carrying the Bomb Group Commander on its twentieth mission. The young colonel commanding was alert, aware of the intruder in his flock, unable to deal with it. The cries of "Bogie at six o'clock" and "B-17 going down" had squirted adrenalin through him, changing everything. A moment ago the mission had been but a stepping-stone to his stars. Now the mission was survival.

The German jet shuddered as it fired, destroying the bodies, minds, and ambitions of the two men at the controls. The dying colonel convulsively hauled back on the B-17's control column, pulling the bomber up into a violent stall, tumbling the remaining crew like dice in a cup and trapping them in the spinning wreck.

Inside the other bombers, the eager gunners were calling off the jet's position, firing randomly.

The German pilot climbed, a hawk circling panicked rabbits. Invulnerable, he glanced down at the black strings of gunfire still erupting futilely in all directions from the formation. Enough fuel and ammunition for one more run, he thought, then home for a drink.

The single American fighter pilot hurled his aircraft toward the battle, ignoring the fires buzzing from the desperate bombers. He roared toward the German plane at top speed, but the distance seemed unchanged as he watched the German plane tear up the bombers. In dreamlike slow motion, though his nose was thrust down, his throttle full forward, he couldn't close and stop that lethal green-black shark from tearing bloody chunks out of the formation.

His Mustang quivering like a reed, he deliberately fired from too far to distract the enemy. All six of his .50-caliber wing guns were firing at first, then four, then three, as the ammunition was exhausted. As he dove through the formation the bombers' gunners fired frenziedly at him, not recognizing him as a friend, riddling his fuselage with hits. His radio suddenly went dead.

He didn't see the Messerschmitt break off its attack, climbing insolently, the raw power of its jets lifting it faster than any piston-engine plane could follow, the pilot only mildly annoyed at the interruption.

The B-17s clustered together again, closing up the gaps torn from the formation, guns silent now, the Deputy Group Commander's voice coming over the air hesitantly, repeating "Close it up," and then, plaintively, "See any chutes?" There was a quick gabble of responses; no one had seen any chutes. Finally a quiet Alabama voice asked, "What was that that come through us? A rocket?" There was no answer.

Far below, the normally docile Mustang hurtled down toward the green German countryside, controls locked solid by air squeezed to compressibility, battering at the speed of sound, airframe porpoising and shuddering as if it were flying through boulders instead of clouds. The pilot had chopped the throttle and tried to roll the airplane to safety, but the ailerons were as locked by speed as he was by fear as he plunged vertically, insane aerodynamic forces tucking his nose under, ripping control away from him. The rate-of-descent meter pegged as the altitude melted away, clouds whipping past. He placed both feet on the bottom of the instrument panel, leveraging his grunting heave on the stick. It didn't matter if he bent the wings or pulled them off; the alternative was to punch a big black hole in the earth. The ground was looming up, no longer just colors, but now flecked with roads and lakes, crossed by fences and tree lines. He was horsing back on the stick and the houses were getting bigger and bigger, straight beneath him, the landscape scroll was not rolling, he was going to go straight in, bore down thirty feet, become fused with the engine in an amalgam of flesh and oil and fire.

Yankee Stadium, New York/October 9, 1938

The score was 4 to 3, Yankees, but the raucous Cub fans were roaring with expectation—the series wasn't over yet. In the McNaughton Aircraft company box, halfway down the third-base line, four people were gamely trying to stitch together the relationships ripped by the morning's arguments. A fifth person, the man who had done much of the ripping, was oblivious both to the situation and the game. Colonel Henry Myers Caldwell was totally engrossed in the good-looking woman sitting next to him.

Looking a decade older than his forty-one years, with thinning hair and smoke-yellowed teeth, he was an unlikely match for such a pretty lady. Years of squinting out of open cockpit planes had given his broad, high-cheekboned face the look of old leather. At West Point, he'd earned the cruel, accurate nickname "Hank the Hawk," in part because his hooked nose curved down toward an upturned chin, in part because of the bird-of-prey way he constantly swiveled his long neck, quick brown eyes missing nothing.

But now the Hawk's gaze was riveted on Elsie Raynor, drinking in the silky red hair bobbing around her oval face, seeking out the meaning of every expression of her green-flecked eyes, recalling how delectable he found her creamy skin.

The colonel moved with the vigor of a much younger man, despite a paunch that bourbon and a wretched officers' club steak-and-potato diet had added to his wiry five-foot seven-inch frame. A born organizer, he seldom needed to raise his voice, but when provoked he could bring an awkward squad to a halt from a block away. Sometimes his presence was *too* powerful—the energy channeled into his table-drumming fingers and tapping toes frightened less driven people. It had this morning.

Thirteen years younger and much more worldly, Elsie Raynor was still trying to ease the tension by playing up to Caldwell. She laughed at his jokes and even made him laugh, too—he hadn't laughed often in recent months. The young woman had a full-figured, well-toned body, and she carried herself with the silky grace of the dancer she had once aspired to be, seeming taller than her five-foot four-inches.

The chorus line would have been easy for her—she had succeeded on her own terms in a far tougher arena, the rough male world of aviation. Despite her father's wishes, she had not become a pilot. Instead she'd worked hard to learn what made aircraft factories tick, in the process discovering how to control the men who ran them. At the morning meeting in Troy McNaughton's suite at the Waldorf, she'd shown clearly that she was a person to be reckoned with. Her official title was "Personal Assistant to the President," but Troy McNaughton had not only depended upon her this morning for facts and figures, he'd looked openly to her for guidance at some of the tough management questions he'd been asked. And she had twice saved the meeting from degenerating into a fistfight.

Caldwell, sure of his position and anxious to impress Elsie, had started the Waldorf meeting with an abrupt announcement that Frank Bandfield was being recalled into the Air Corps, with the rank of major, and that Hadley Roget would join him at Wright Field to head up a new program he was calling "Operation Leapfrog."

Caldwell had reason to be sure of himself with Bandfield. He had arranged a commission for him as a captain in the Air Corps reserve

and in 1937 sent him under cover to fly with the Loyalists in the
Spanish Civil War. Flying fighters supplied by Russia against the
German Condor Legion had taught Bandfield much, and he'd
become an ace in the process. When the war ground down to the
bitter end, he'd escaped by flying from Guernica to France, after
one last dogfight that still haunted his dreams. Caldwell knew very
well that Bandfield was bored with running his aircraft parts factory
and was dying to get back into the Air Corps, and had simply
presented him with official orders.

It was different with Roget. He was a civilian, and Caldwell had
no hold on him—except the job offer of his dreams. Roget was an
intuitive engineer—an "imagineer" he called himself—and Caldwell was giving him a chance to run a program intended to force the
development of a line of radical new aircraft. It all seemed cut and
dry to Caldwell, and he'd moved immediately to discussing
McNaughton's new fighter, the Sidewinder, without giving either
Roget or Bandfield a chance to comment.

Roget had blown up.

"Goddamnit, Henry, you can't treat me like this, especially not in
front of Johnny-come-latelies like Troy McNaughton and his girlfriend."

McNaughton, six feet tall and crackling energy from every pore,
was Arrow-collar handsome except for a big nose broken in college
boxing. His voice had a soft, cajoling quality, and he normally had
the professional grin and easygoing manner of a first-rate salesman.
But Roget's gibe—not his first—made McNaughton's neck veins
bulge, and he moved around the table to confront Hadley. Elsie had
stepped smoothly between them, straightening the narrow knot of
McNaughton's paisley tie with one hand and thrusting a cup of
coffee on Roget with the other.

Later there had been another outburst, over the Sidewinder's
design. McNaughton had brought plans and illustrations. It was a
beautiful little airplane, its shape obviously derived from his 1936
racer. Small, with a sharply pointed nose and tapered wings, the
plane's innovations alone were enough to justify a contract from
Caldwell. Unlike any other pursuit in the Air Corps, it had a novel

tri-cycle gear. The liquid-cooled Allison engine was equally innovative, mounted in the fuselage *aft* of the cockpit and driving a three-bladed propeller via a shaft running under the pilot's seat. A big 37-mm cannon fired through the propeller hub, the heaviest armament for any fighter in the world. McNaughton waved four-color drawings that looked like pulp magazine covers, each showing the waspish little fighter shooting down formations of "enemy" bombers.

McNaughton glowed with pride. "It's going to be a world beater! It's plenty fast—four hundred miles per hour, and it's got long legs—it'll fly Nashville to Washington, nonstop."

Roget snorted and planted his gnarled finger on the plans where the fuselage connected to the wings, growling, "Four hundred miles an hour my ass! Goddamnit, Troy, you've made a hell of a mistake with this crate. Everything you gain in drag reduction by putting the engine midship, you lose at the wing-fuselage intersection. You've built a goddamn barn door in there, and you can't even see it. If you get three hundred out of this dog, I'll be surprised."

McNaughton responded savagely. "Look who's talking. You never did design an airplane anyone would buy, and you're telling me how to build them? We've got ten thousand wind-tunnel hours on this airplane, hard data, and I don't have to stand here and listen to your off-the-cuff bullshit."

Bandfield pulled Roget back as Caldwell dressed them down in his drill sergeant's voice. Even Elsie sat back, respectful and expectant.

"Shut up! There's a war brewing, and I'm going to need all of you. We're three years behind the Germans now, and I'm scared to think what a first-class outfit like Messerschmitt has in their shops. They're experimenting with everything over there, crazy planes and engines I can't talk even to you about."

Everyone was silent, cowed by the power of his conviction as he went on.

"I've been given responsibility for the procurement of aircraft for the new production programs. I've practically got carte blanche, as long as I take care of the Congressional sacred cows. Arnold,

Spaatz, and Eaker are all tied up with developing the combat organizations—they're giving me a free hand in procurement. Bandy, you're one of the few people around who has both combat and manufacturing experience. I want you to be my right-hand man, to act as liaison with the field. You'll test-fly the airplanes, find the fixes, smooth out the red tape. Hadley, if we're going to try to catch up to Germany we've got to try some new ideas, stuff that's only been on the cover of *Popular Science*—flying wings, buried engines, rockets, tail-firsters, all sorts of crazy stuff. You are the *only* man for the job. And Troy, I need a company that will take chances and build unconventional aircraft. I need all of you, and I need you to get along. So stop your goddamn bickering and get serious!"

The rest of the meeting passed in an embarrassed haze as Caldwell ticked off the assignments for each of them for the next few months. At one point he pounded the table and said, "One thing for sure! We're going to fly every airplane we've got, and operationally, too. We're not going to sit back at Wright Field seeing the war through some goddamn file of reports."

"Hap Arnold will never let you fly operationally, Henry. You're too valuable to him."

"Wrong. We've already discussed it and he agrees. He's a smart guy, even if he is irascible as hell. He saw what happened after the last war, when guys who couldn't even fly walked all over Billy Mitchell."

At the meeting, in a severe black suit and white blouse, Elsie had been the hard-eyed executive, tracking the discussion carefully, quietly making points, keeping Troy out of trouble. After the meeting, Elsie had changed her clothes and her persona. Now, she was the genial hostess, making sure everyone had plenty to eat and drink, occasionally joking in a fake Southern accent. But all the while, she kept Caldwell in focus, seizing on his comments like a duck snapping at cracked corn, then passing them back moments later with a humorous twist.

Caldwell eased back in his seat for a moment, just to enjoy her freshness. God, he thought, what a perfect woman! Brains and beauty! And so wonderfully alive. The word "alive" brought Shirley to mind. A fleeting sense of guilt passed quickly as, involuntarily, he reached out to brush back a lock of hair that had strayed across Elsie's forehead. Desire crackled through him and he glanced around with embarrassment, aware that the pretense of their being "just friends" had long since been compromised. He called, too loudly, to his old pal.

"This your first World Series, Hadley?"

Baseball didn't mean much to Roget: it didn't have an engine or wings. He stood up slowly, stretching, his tall, rawboned frame creased with muscles tempered by long years of hard work. A Lincolnesque face crowned by a mane of silver hair ironically gave him, devoutly unreligious as he was, the appearance of an Old Testament prophet. His hair was his only vanity—he combed it constantly and would let no one but his wife, Clarice, cut it for him.

"Naw, I saw one once. It was in 'eighteen. The Cubs were beat then, too, by the Baahston Red Sox. Bandy's old man and me only went to see Babe Ruth pitch; he won two games that series. We didn't even know he was a big hitter back then."

Roget had worked for Caldwell at Wright Field long ago and later designed airplanes for sale to the Army, staying good friends even though Caldwell didn't buy many Roget airplanes. Caldwell hoarded the Army's money as if it were his own, spreading it out among as many competing manufacturers as possible. He was totally dedicated to business and to taking care of his poor wife, who after an agonizing illness had died last year.

Roget watched cynically as Caldwell's eyes wandered back to Elsie. Roget felt sympathy for her. He'd known her father—spare, sour Jack Raynor. Jack had scraped out a meager living for his wife and two children by barnstorming Jennies around the country. He had taught his son to fly, but the boy died at sixteen, a victim of typhoid fever picked up in a farmyard well. Jack then tried to make a pilot out of Elsie. She was too young and too scared, so he gave up, using the little influence he had to get her a job at the old Hafner Aircraft Company. Since then she had grown from a novice secretary, almost too frightened to answer the telephone, into the confident young businesswoman she was today. As she had learned the business, she had become "close" to Bruno Hafner—Roget assumed that she was probably just as "close" to Troy McNaughton. He wondered if McNaughton was jealous of Caldwell, or vice versa. It was an interesting, multifaceted situation, revolving around a unique woman. There certainly weren't many around like her; flyers were notoriously tough on females. But, he thought, Caldwell won't stand much of a chance with her—who would?

He wiped the rim of the silver flask Caldwell handed him and took a throat-filling swig before offering it to Frank Bandfield. Bandy sat next to him, the stubble of beard on his chin smeared yellow with mustard as he wolfed his third hot dog of the game.

Roget was virtually a foster father to Bandfield, their relationship forged in the fire of years of collaboration in building aircraft that were always just a bit ahead of their time. They'd worked and played hard, arguing and raising hell with each other in the way that only old friends could achieve.

Munching the now stone-cold hot dog, Bandfield was thinking about the lovebirds sitting in front of him. A hot-blooded man himself, he readily understood Caldwell's feelings. Elsie exuded a cheerful sexuality. On another woman the plaid dress she wore might have been conservative, but on her it was provocative. Ever the movie fan, he saw her as a mix of Ann Sothern and Rosalind Russell, softly seductive but diamond bright. She was vibrant—and Caldwell was lonely.

Yet he wondered how much Caldwell knew about Elsie—or how much he cared to know. The man had worked too hard all his life, and Shirley had become ill just when they should have begun to enjoy themselves. It was time that Caldwell had a little fun—even at the risk of being involved with a contractor's employee.

The Yanks got down to business, with Lou Gehrig and Joe DiMaggio scoring to make it 6 to 3. With two outs, the Cubs sent Dizzy Dean in to pitch, past his Cardinal prime but still a crowd-pleaser. When Dean finally retired the side, the score was 8 to 3, and the Yankees were assured of their third straight World Series win. Roget stood up.

"Excuse me, folks, this here beer has persuaded me to go see a man about a dog."

Bandfield joined him. Roget didn't speak until they were standing in line within the dark, odorous confines of the stadium restroom.

"He's really besotted! I've never seen him behave like this!"

"No, but I'm glad he's having a good time—he's suffered enough."

They moved over to the row of dirty washbasins, where Roget became engrossed in combing his hair. It was a harmless vanity, one of the few things Bandfield didn't dare tease him about. Staring into the mirror, Bandfield dabbed away the mustard on his chin. At six feet, he was two inches shorter than Roget, but sturdier, with broad shoulders and a barrel chest that tapered down to a thirty-inch waist. His square face was creased with lines from long hours of flight—the airman's squint—but his curly black hair showed no signs of graying. His tanned skin was roughly textured from chicken pox in his childhood, but his brown eyes sparkled with humor and good health.

Bandfield glanced at his own reflection again, running his finger around the smooth welt of a scar that ran across his forehead and down the side of his left cheek. He'd picked it up the last time he'd worked for Caldwell, crash-landing his fighter on a French beach, and it still bothered him when he shaved. Shrugging off the memory, he moved toward the door with the quick, tight grace of the natural pilot. Still in pretty good shape for an old man, he thought. Haven't gained a pound or an inch around the middle.

Outside, Roget resumed their conversation. "That must be a forty-dollar suit Caldwell's wearing, and a ten-dollar Stetson—pretty hot stuff for a guy who always shopped at Monkey Ward. And did you see his manicured nails? No Hupmobile grease on him nowadays!"

"He's driving a supercharged Graham now. And Elsie's changed, too, like she's been to some fancy finishing school. She's sure got Caldwell's number, you can see that. Did you ever think you'd hear somebody calling him 'sugarbaby'?"

Roget grimaced. "Well, old 'sugarbaby' is moving in some pretty fast circles nowadays. He was a major when I first knew him."

"Yeah, and next month, he's going to be a brigadier general. He's jumped ahead of a lot of big shots in the air force."

Roget shook his head. "Well, no matter how mad he makes me, he deserves it. If it hadn't been for the smart way he spread the money around, there wouldn't be any Air Corps worth talking about. The way I hear it, if it wasn't for him, Hap Arnold wouldn't be running the Air Corps today."

It was true. The once rough-hewn Caldwell had become a superb politician, smoothing over the differences that his mentor Billy Mitchell had had with Congress, while still managing to promote Mitchell's concepts on air power. After Mitchell's court martial, Arnold had been sent into oblivion, but Caldwell, at real career risk, had labored behind the scenes for him. Even the Navy brass liked Caldwell—a virtual miracle. Caldwell always cooperated with them, keeping them abreast of all the engineering developments the Air Corps had under way at Wright Field and once even testifying to Congress on the value of carrier-based aviation.

"What's his secret, Bandy? When I was working for him back at Wright Field, I always thought he was a grouch, no sense of humor."

"You haven't seen him operate! He's a real smoothie when he's working with the White House or Congress. Congressman Dade from Tennessee runs the military appropriations committee, and he's thick as thieves with Caldwell. They cut a sweetheart deal; Dade agreed to buy the four-engine Boeing bombers Caldwell wanted, if Caldwell would give McNaughton a contract for his new fighter."

Roget slapped his forehead. "Shit, so that's it. The McNaughton plant is in Nashville, Dade's home district."

"Sure, it's just a political quid pro quo."

Troy McNaughton had appeared on the aviation scene in 1936 with a stub-winged racer that had won enough money in the Cleveland Air Races to let him buy the remains of the newly defunct Hafner Aircraft Company. He hadn't gotten much—a few designs, some machinery, and the services of Elsie Raynor—but he'd moved the operation to Nashville and was beginning to prosper.

Roget reached out and touched Bandfield's arm. "I'm sorry about this morning, Bandy. I just got mad when that goddamn McNaughton bragged about getting a two-million-dollar contract from the French purchasing committee. Can you imagine it? A two-million-dollar order for a plane that hasn't even flown!"

"Hell, with Europe boiling over, it will help us—we can build parts for McNaughton just like we do for Douglas and Boeing."

Bandfield and Roget had finally given up trying to build aircraft in competition with the bigger manufacturers, turning instead to making aircraft parts and tools. For the first time in their lives they were a roaring commercial success, with orders coming in from all over the country as the defense buildup began.

Bandfield went on. "But you were right to be angry. Caldwell should have held two separate meetings, one to get us back on board, one to talk about McNaughton's new projects. I don't blame you, I was pissed off myself."

The game—and Elsie's efforts—had gone a long way to soothing tempers. Even Roget was feeling conciliatory when he and Bandfield finally got back to their seats. McNaughton moved aside as Elsie and Caldwell rose.

Elsie, simulating a little shiver, said, "I'm sorry, boys, this cold is just too much for me."

Caldwell took time to shake each man's hand warmly, and said, "I'm going off to Germany next month—it'll be my first official trip as a general officer—and I'll feel a lot better knowing you guys are firmly on board."

As McNaughton and Roget edged uneasily into a neutral conversation about the game, conscious that each had probably made an enemy of the other, Bandfield watched the other two leave, holding hands. Yesterday, life had been relatively simple for him. Now he tried to tie all the new developments together—his new job, Roget's argument with McNaughton, Caldwell's infatuation, the war that Caldwell seemed to think was certain. Things had become very complex. He wondered how it would all end.

En route to Hankow, China/October 10, 1938

James Curtiss Lee's father had drummed it into him that the Lees were many things—leaders, Southern aristocrats, Democrats—but above all, they were *survivors*. Well, he'd probably need to be in China. It had been a rough day, flying from Hong Kong to Chungking in a Chinese National Aviation Corporation Douglas DC-2 crowded with Chinese officials. The only other English-speaking person on board was one of the pilots, an American.

Now they were bumping across a range of craggy mountains, east-northeast toward Hankow. The Yangtze River twisted and turned below, a better navigational aid than a railroad, its yellow roiling waters a vivid Chinese Mason-Dixon Line dividing the huge country into North and South. The scenery reminded him of the rugged foothills of the Rockies, rough mountains interspersed with valleys where little farm villages nestled against the side of the hills. The whole landscape was painted in a single dirty gray, save only where the river's yellow streak flashed in the sun.

He was just out of flying school, carrying a reserve commission as a second lieutenant in his back pocket. Normally he would have been assigned to some dull stateside base, flying Boeing P-26s or Martin B-10s. Instead, his father, broke but still with political influence, had pulled strings to get him a special detached duty. He was to work for an old family friend, Claire Chennault, now tasked by Madame Chiang Kai-shek with rejuvenating the Chinese Air Force.

Lee remembered that he'd been sixteen years old when his father had driven the family to Langley Field to watch Chennault lead the "Three Men on a Flying Trapeze," the Air Corps' premier acrobatic team. Flying little yellow-winged Boeing P-12F fighters linked together with ropes, they put on a dazzling routine of loops and rolls. After a literally tied-in-tight landing, Chennault had popped out of his plane like a genie from a bottle, his nickel-Indian face cordovan-leather tan, flying suit streaked with oil stains, and a grin as wide as his black, bushy mustache. The image had never left Lee, and he determined on the spot to be an Air Corps pilot.

Lee was half dozing when the DC-2 stood on its wing and plunged like a dive-bomber. The transport leveled out to race along the side of a mountain, jinking back and forth, its left wing just missing the boulder-strewn surface, its right poised over the void. The DC-2 rolled up on its wing again so that Lee stared straight down at the mountainside. Behind the shadow of the transport, distorted as it raced across boulders and crevasses, he could see two smaller images in pursuit and thought, Man, they're not paying me enough for this!

Machine-gun fire slashed through the right side of the cabin; an officer, big for a Chinese, slumped over in his seat, his head torn apart like a dropped melon. Seconds later, the DC-2 abruptly leveled out and began to climb. Lee jumped out of his seat and leaned across a screaming Chinese businessman to peer out the window opposite. Two Japanese fighters—low-wing monoplanes with fixed landing gear—were disappearing into the sun. Must be out of fuel or ammunition, Lee thought.

He unbuckled his seat belt and went forward to see if the pilots were okay. He stepped through the cockpit access door and splashed into blood.

The American pointed to the copilot slumped against the control wheel, blood pouring from wounds stitched across his chest. "He's dead. Pull him out of the seat, and fly copilot for me. I might need you if those bastards come back."

The rest of the flight into Hankow was uneventful; Lee sat in the blood-stained seat, queasily aware of the gore oozing through his trousers. The roads outside the city were jammed with people leaving, most walking with their possessions slung on poles, a few lucky ones with carts piled twice as high as they stood.

The pilot pointed. "Refugees evacuating. We're expecting the Japs in a week or so. These people don't want to stay here for a replay of the rape of Nanking."

The runway was a disaster, pocked with holes, its margins strewn with the wreckage of crashes, the pennons of their tattered fabric showing that some had been there for years. When they taxied in, he could see a Packard staff car pulled up to the flight line. Chennault himself was driving, no mustache now, but his face as craggy as ever.

"What the hell happened to you, son? You hurt? Trying to start your own war even before I get a chance to tell you what's what?"

Chennault's Southern-accented bellow betrayed his deafness. Lee saluted and Chennault, relieved to see that he wasn't wounded, grinned. "That's right, play it military with your ass dripping blood like a stuck gator! Don't think you're going to ruin the seats of my car."

Throwing Lee's bags in the trunk, he commanded, "You stand on the running board next to my window here, and hold on. I'll try not to scrape you off against a rickshaw."

Chennault drove with flair and his horn, sending pedestrians scrambling, talking continuously and doing little listening.

"They don't like me to drive myself, they say I lose face, but my Chinese drivers are too dangerous."

Lee hung on as the Packard wheeled into the arched entrance of Chennault's compound, squealing to a halt in front of a mass of servants.

Chennault waved expansively, saying, "Manpower's the one thing there's no shortage of in China. You go get a bath, and come down for drinks and some home cooking. Civvies will be fine."

The big old house was cool and silent as Lee and two servants padded down teak-paneled hallways to a huge room overlooking the central atrium of the compound. A garden was at one end, with fruit trees now losing their leaves and well-tended flower beds; at the other end the kitchen, laundry, and garage ran haphazardly into each other.

There was a tub of hot water in his room; Lee bathed, changed into wrinkled shirt and slacks, and went downstairs. As he entered he heard the welcome clink of ice dropping into glasses.

"J.C., you look just like your daddy—he's about five-eight, too, isn't he? And the same red hair and freckles. By golly, the apple doesn't fall far from the tree."

He gestured at his brimming drink. "I just have two a day. You probably need one after your flight. Tell me all about it."

Chennault listened intently to Lee's account of the attack.

"Yes, the bastards are getting bolder. You're right about them being out of ammunition; that's the only reason they let you go. I'm surprised they didn't try to fly you into the ground. Hankow's about the limit of their range; they were probably short on fuel, too."

He swallowed with the lip-smacking appreciation of a man who knows he likes to drink too much.

"For a while, they weren't shooting at CNAC planes, but now that they're almost in Hankow—and we don't have any air defense—I guess they're starting up again."

"No defense? How many planes do you have?"

"Damn few. The Chinese busted up all their Curtiss Hawks in landing accidents. Let's eat."

The food was served in endless steaming trays, delicious but successively spicier. Lee could see that Chennault was teasing him, seeing how much he could take; as they ate, he watched Lee closely, all the while popping little red and green peppers into his mouth like after-dinner mints.

It was almost two hours before they were served the traditional last dishes of soup and rice; Jim, exhausted and burning up inside, wanted Chennault to excuse him.

"You did okay, son, your poppa would have been proud of you. I'm sorry things have gone so bad for him financially. He always helped me out."

"Things are bad for most people. As soon as my tour is up, I'm going to go back and help him get back on his feet. We Lees don't like living like poor white trash."

"That you could never be—but you should help your poppa."

Eyes squinting from the smoke of the Camel cigarette that hung like a growth from the corner of his mouth, he took Jim by the arm and led him into the living room. It was decorated simply, in Chinese style except for an enormous Wurlitzer piano in the corner.

"I want you to study this book on the little fighter Madame Chiang bought for me. She paid fifty-five thousand U.S. for it."

Lee glanced at the photo of a Curtiss Hawk 75H on the front of the red velvet-covered manual Chennault handed him.

"Looks like a fixed-gear P-36."

"That's just about it, son. Fastest thing in China right now; I use it for reconnaissance mostly, but it's got two machine guns, if I need them." He tossed over a loose-leaf folder, filled with crude three-view drawings and hand-lettered tables of specifications.

"These are the best I can do for identifying the Jap planes. You don't have to worry about the biplanes, you can outrun them. But they've got some damn fast bombers, and a little Nakajima fighter they call the Type 97. Probably what hit you. Looks a lot like my Hawk, but it's smaller and lighter. Anyway, you get familiar with these tonight; I've marked the performance estimates down beside them. I've got a job for you tomorrow."

Lee was pleased that Chennault was not wasting any time.

"I'm meeting with the mayor of Hankow in the morning, so I'm sending you out to the field to preflight my airplane. The car will take you and wait for you. Just give the ship a walk-around and run it up. All you need to know is in the manual there."

As Jim left the room, Chennault's voice boomed out behind him, "The water on your dresser is boiled; the Bromo-Seltzer is in the dresser drawer."

He slept better than he expected to, and the breakfast of tea, rolls, and noodle soup was just what the doctor ordered. Hankow woke up around him as he rode to the field, peddlers pushing carts with huge wooden-spoked wheels and tiny narrow flatbeds, beggars sitting mutely on the corners, hands outstretched, women scuttling along with back-breaking loads. The air was miasmic with human waste, poverty, and death, as if the bacteria had no more room to breed on the ground and were invading the atmosphere.

He'd come to China with the Charlie Chan stereotype in mind, expecting the Chinese to be oval-faced and paunchy. Instead he saw all about him a universal leanness, a crowd of scarecrows with sallow, emaciated faces, their rib-etched bodies grunting under loads he couldn't have budged on his best day. Most were barefoot, clothed if they were lucky in a worn tunic and trousers, a few wearing the traditional straw hat. Gaunt children squatted in groups around little hooped baskets; he couldn't see what they were selling. Hunger clasped their gaunt bodies like a jockey riding a horse; their feet were long extrusions of dirty flesh, slender toes snaked into the mud like tendrils of a vine.

And through all the hustling humanity trooped the bearers. They wore nothing but a cloth twisted across their middle as they balanced a bamboo pole across their shoulders, huge baskets of goods suspended at each end. Moving at a trot, heads bobbing, they threaded their way through the thickest crowd. The narrow streets were lined with tile-roofed mud houses leaning drunkenly together for support; down past them the bearers tramped, converging like runs of herring at narrow points, never colliding or upsetting a basket.

Two fierce-looking soldiers stood guard at the Curtiss Hawk, their long Mauser M1899 rifles unslung. The chauffeur barked at them and they moved sullenly to the side.

The Curtiss was a beautiful little airplane, mint-bright, as if it had just come from the factory, and Lee felt immediately at home in it, the familiar scents of leather, oil, and metal a relief amid the stink of China. The chauffeur stood at the side of the engine, holding a huge American fire extinguisher he had pulled from the Packard's trunk.

The Wright Cyclone engine caught on the first crank of the starter, and Lee slowly went through the engine run-up drill, enjoying the aircraft's sense of leashed power as it leaned against the chocks, vibrating with energy.

He felt rather than heard the first explosion and looked up to see a stick of bombs walk across the field, blasting holes and rearranging the wrecks. A flight of twelve Japanese twin-engine bombers passed overhead in immaculate V-formation. They looked like the Mitsubishis shown in Chennault's notes; supposedly they were fast but lightly armed.

The chauffeur understood his signal—thumbs thrusting outward rapidly—and pulled the chocks. If Lee had been planning to fly, he'd have worn a seat-pack parachute and be sitting six inches higher; now he was sunk almost below the rim of the cockpit and had to strain against the shoulder-harness to see over the instrument panel. He was airborne after a four-hundred-yard run. The Hawk was simple—no gear controls to worry about—and the power settings were just full forward. Scanning the sky, he sorted out the arming and firing switches. A second group of bombers was in the distance with a copper-toned glint of reflected sun above them—a fighter escort.

I hope it's one of the bastards that shot us up yesterday. At fourteen thousand feet he was level with the bombers but still well below the fighters. He warmed his guns with a short burst.

Lee accelerated, running a triangular check between the fighters and the bombers. Squinting, he saw that there were nine fighters, probably the Nakajimas again, monoplanes with fixed gear and a closed canopy.

They were diving now, slanting over the bombers, trying to cut him off. It was going to be close. The bombers' nose guns were already opening up, little red dots reaching out toward him as they closed at five hundred miles per hour. Lee hunched forward in his seat, raising himself to aim through the simple fixed sight. He fired a quick burst, then dove under the bombers, using them as a shield against the escort fighters while he zoomed back to altitude.

The lead bomber went straight down, the dead pilots slumped over the controls. The other bombers scattered when their own fighters dove through them.

The Nakajimas bounced up, silver propeller discs twinkling in the early morning sun, wings moving skittishly as they jockeyed for firing position, their V-formation untidy and strung out. He turned into them, diving down, guns already chattering. The Japanese broke up into two sections, turning right and left. The Hawk was by far the most maneuverable plane Jim had ever flown, but he saw at once that the Nakajimas could out-turn and out-climb him. He broke for the bomber formation, the Japanese fighters whipping in behind him.

If Chennault's right, if this is the fastest plane in China, I'll outrun them.

Chennault was wrong; the Nakajimas were faster. When he swiveled his head he saw that the lead planes were already firing, the decking forward of the canopy alight from their 7.7-mm Type 89 machine guns.

Lee ducked down in his seat, trying to make himself as small a target as possible and still be able to aim. He streaked across the rear of the bomber formation, ignoring the tail guns, firing as he went. One bomber's wing lit up as his tracers flamed its unprotected tanks; it began a gentle arc, a dying bird seeking the ground.

The Hawk shuddered as it took hits from the rear; there was a sudden roar as his canopy was blown off. Jesus, he thought, if I'd had a parachute on, my head would have gone with the canopy! He aileron-rolled the plane on its back and pulled hard on the stick.

Can't out-turn or out-speed the bastards; maybe I can out-dive them.

The Hawk roared vertically down, wind shrieking around Lee's unprotected head, picking up speed every foot till it hit terminal velocity, near five hundred miles per hour, a mass of plunging metal butting up against compacted air, neither power nor gravity able to make it move faster. The starch-stiff control surfaces fed pressures back to him through the stick.

The Japanese planes fell back, unable to dive as steeply or as fast, heading individually for the bombers that were distant spots in the east. A hunger for revenge replaced Lee's fear. He reefed back on the stick as hard as he could, forgetting about speed, G forces, and structural limits, popping his ears as he sent the little Hawk ricocheting skyward, converting speed and energy into altitude, soaring up into the sky like a silver-tipped arrow.

Above the unsuspecting Nakajimas, Lee booted the rudder and snapped the stick forward, selecting two targets, one slightly above the other. The Japanese pilots were concentrating on rejoining formation, making the classic combat mistake of not checking behind them and about to die for it.

Ammunition must be low, can't fire yet, he thought. He let the dainty little fighters grow in size. Silver with red cowlings and a red arrow stripe down the fuselage, they were flying slightly nose high as they slowed to join up. He could see the helmet and parachute straps on the nearest pilot, who was intently making the tiny control corrections, nudges of rudder and aileron, that would bring him into tight formation. Lee's bullets ripped into the pilot of the first Nakajima, then without interruption into the cockpit of the second. He was through them in a flash, both Japanese pilots dead, their fighters spinning drunkenly away, their comrades still unaware of an attack.

Neck twisting, shoulders hunched, Lee scanned the sky behind him; it was as empty as his gun belts, as he turned back to the airfield.

Chennault was leaping up and down on the flight line, swinging his hat in an arc. The engine was still running when the grinning, eagle-beaked colonel leapt on his wing.

Lee switched off the magnetos, to hear Chennault yell, "God-damnit, Lee, that's the way, dive and zoom, dive and zoom! You fried four of the bastards! I'm never going to let you go home!"

Lee squeezed his nostrils tight with his fingers and forced air into his eardrums.

"You let them shoot the canopy off! Who the hell told you you could use my airplane? Madame Chiang will be furious!"

"Wish you'd been up there with me, Colonel."

"If I had been, we'd have gotten them all, just like the old bull and the young bull. Dive and zoom!"

Salinas, California/October 16, 1938

Clarice Roget didn't know or care about Hadley's business in New York any more than she knew or cared about the war in China. She pressed the head of the just awakened Charlotte Bandfield against her breast, blissful with a love that made up for all the children she had never had herself.

How smart she'd been to lure Patty and Bandy into living with them! It gave her the family that Hadley's devotion to work had denied her, even while it gave Patty the free time for her reckless flying career.

Clarice forgot all of the frustrations and anxieties of a lifetime of self-denial in the sheer pleasure of changing the baby's diapers on the sink drainboard. The simple domestic act made her feel like a real mother at last, making up for the disappointments in Hadley's ill-fated business ventures. He and Bandy had always been too far ahead of their time, building airplanes so technically advanced that they couldn't find buyers for them.

The two men, fiercely loyal to each other even as they argued and fought, were a financially disastrous mixture of brilliant engineering and almost zero talent for business. Hadley was usually too enthusiastic to bother to patent his inventions and, strangely enough, didn't seem to resent it when someone else would steal an idea and commercialize it. Bandy trusted everyone, including an accountant who looted their firm.

Only in the last two years, after Clarice had at last asserted her innate business sense, had they done well. Hadley had invented some special machine tools and Bandy had designed some generic structural aircraft parts—oleo struts and oil coolers. Clarice saw their commercial value and insisted on patenting both tools and parts. She then took it upon herself to hire production managers, honest accountants, and a hardworking plant manager on a profit-sharing basis to run what was left of Roget Aircraft. Hadley and Bandy were too obsessed with flying to interfere in such routine manufacturing operations—how could you test-fly a drill press?— and so they prospered. And none of it mattered to her except that she now had the time and the means to lavish her love on the Bandfield baby.

But there were hazards—she knew that Patty felt a mixture of relief and resentment at the way Clarice had taken over. Her own feelings were mixed. On one level, she wanted Patty to quit flying, to avoid the risks that seemed to grow with every new venture and to stay home and care for her baby. On another, more primitive level, she wanted Charlotte for herself! Such were her thoughts when Patty came bouncing in, glowing from her regular morning horse-back ride.

Clarice thought for the hundredth time that Patty was the image of her mother, baby Charlotte's namesake. She had the same long blond hair, full bosom, and mischievous grin. Her amethyst eyes, one slightly rounder, one slightly longer than the other, gave distinction to her beautiful face.

"Good, you've cleaned little 'Pestilencia' up! Hand her over."

Charlotte shrugged her mother away and clung to Clarice's neck. Patty flushed, annoyed and embarrassed.

"Can't say I blame her, Patty. Let me show you something."

A Coca-Cola calendar hanging on the wall showed both Patty's passions and her faults. It featured a glamorous shot of Patty climbing out of the dark green Seversky P-35 racing plane in which she had won the Los Angeles Air Derby. The older woman flipped back to August, saying, "I've x-ed out the days you've been gone." Counting rapidly she said, "You've been away thirty-two out of the last sixty days. It's no wonder Charlotte is shy with you."

Patty flushed with resentment because she knew Clarice was right—and she knew that she couldn't change. She was her mother's daughter, locked in a campaign to breach the male monopoly on aviation, to open the door to women flyers everywhere. She was willing to risk her life in closed course racing or testing new aircraft to get the public forum she needed.

Little by little, she was succeeding in filling the vacancy left when Amelia Earhart crashed in 1937. In the last year she had set a women's land speed record, an autogiro altitude record, and an endurance record. But she knew her career was in crisis. Only the week before she'd been halfway across the country, averaging 270 mph in a Northrop Gamma racer leased from her friend and archrival, Jackie Cochran. A new transcontinental speed record was a certainty until the engine blew up. She'd managed to put the plane down in a cornfield, ripping the wings off in the process, wrecking her career almost as much as the airplane. It was the fourth time she'd tried and the fourth time she'd failed. She knew that the men would be saying, "She's bad luck—and she doesn't understand airplanes."

Patty knew that records in themselves were meaningless—but

without them she'd have no base to work from. And she knew very well that but for Clarice her flying career would have come to a halt. Now Clarice was going to use this last accident as a weapon to make her stop flying.

Clarice went on. "You know how much I love taking care of this baby, but I don't want her thinking I'm her mamma! That's your job and your privilege. You've got to stop trying to kill yourself!"

As if on cue, Charlotte reached out for Patty. Clarice handed her over, then gently pushed Patty down on a kitchen chair.

"Sit. And listen. It's bad enough that her daddy flies and might get killed. Losing her mother would be just too much. You of all people ought to know that."

Patty bridled. Her mother used to say that "only the truth hurts"—and it was so. But Clarice had no concept of doing something for a cause, no idea of what Patty's larger aims were.

"Let's not talk about my poor mother."

Clarice, indignant now, said, "Let's *do* talk about her. Let's talk about how she insisted on flying the big Hafner bomber, how she was going to break all of Amelia's records, how—"

"Damnit, Clarice, Mother didn't just crash. Bruno Hafner killed her, he sabotaged the airplane, you know that."

Just saying the name "Bruno" made Patty feel sick; he'd married her mother and used her to promote his airplanes, then, when it suited him, snuffed her out.

Clarice took advantage of her silence to say, "You know what that baby in your arms is? She's a bridge, a lifeline, between three families and two generations. She ties your family—what's left of it—and Bandy's family and ours together like no one else could. And she needs you to take care of her."

Still shaken by the thought of her stepfather, Patty said, "Don't be cruel, Clarice."

"I'm trying to be kind and you won't let me. Men are different. You'll never get Bandy to stop flying, no matter what you do. You could tell him you were divorcing him, taking the baby away—he can't help himself, he'd let you, and just keep on doing what he's doing. Men are idiots."

Patty knew that it was true. Bandy loved her and the baby with all his heart—but flying was an integral part of his life. He could not live without it.

"I don't know what you're flying for, except to prove that a woman can be as stupid as a man. And let me tell you something else. If you do kill yourself, the real victim will be Charlotte."

Clarice paused, her eyes filling with tears. "When the phone rang last week, I knew something had happened, I knew you were dead. I couldn't believe it when I heard your voice. I love you and I love this baby, but I'm old and I'm not so sure I'm well. I won't be around to take care of her. And even if something happens to you, Bandy won't stop flying. What if he got killed, too? Who'll take care of her?"

Concern flooded Patty's face and she rose to embrace Clarice. She loved this woman deeply. "Is something wrong? Have you been to the doctor?" she asked.

"Don't start on me. We'll talk about that another time. Right now we're talking about you stopping flying."

"All right, Clarice, you win. I'll start cutting down."

"My God, Patty, this is not like quitting smoking cigarettes. You can't just taper off, not if you can get killed in the process. I could be holding the baby at your funeral today, damnit! You won't always get away with it!"

Patty heard the sound of the mail truck pulling away.

"Let me check the mailbox, Clarice, please. I hear what you're saying, and I know you're right. Let me work on this." She kissed her and ran from the room.

Clarice, upset with herself, upset with Patty, turned back to straighten the countertop. They'd remodeled the house last year— new bathrooms, new cabinets in the kitchen, and a wing added on for the Bandfields. In a way the house was a homecoming for Bandy. His mother, Emily, had inherited a huge property that bordered on the Rogets' land, and his wastrel father, George, had mortgaged it all off before skipping town. Two years later, poor and bitter, Emily died of a broken heart.

The Rogets had stepped in back then to serve as surrogate parents.

Hadley always said that George Bandfield was the finest machinist he'd ever known, and he passed most of his talent along to young Frank. Hadley had been tough on him, driving him almost as hard as his father had done, trying to teach him everything he knew.

As she mopped up the sink, Clarice sighed, wondering if she'd gone too far. She knew that Patty was really a good mother even if she was career-crazy. And Bandy smothered the baby with love when he was home, but he was often gone, too.

At least Patty and Bandy were talking about having another child. It would be good for the parents and Charlotte, and perhaps soothe whatever devils were driving them. Bandy was not satisfied just being in the airplane business anymore. Something had changed him—the fighting in Spain, probably—and he was clearly restless.

Patty walked in waving a letter, Charlotte slung under her arm like a sack of potatoes.

"At last, word from our *wandervogels*, postmarked Dayton. That old Henry Caldwell has really latched on to them."

She opened the letter and a snapshot of a huge rambling three-story brick house fell out, a big red X marking a room on the second floor.

On the back Bandy had written, "Our new house; X marks the spot where we're going to make our next baby."

Patty tossed the picture in the wastebasket and began reading aloud:

"Dear Patty. Surprise, surprise! Old Caldwell's called me back to active duty; I'm going to be working mostly out of Wright Field. But that's not the best part!"

There was a coffee stain, and the ink had run, but Patty could make out: "Hadley's coming, too! Tell Clarice to pack her glad rags and both of you get on the next rattler coming East. Bring the baby, too, ha ha. Hadley's got a really important project, and he says to tell Clarice that she'll love it—"

Clarice broke in. "I'm not going anywhere, especially not to a hole like Dayton, Ohio."

Patty boiled with anger, clenching her fists and stomping her boot on the floor. First the dressing down from Clarice, and now this.

She crumpled the rest of the letter up unread, tossed it in the wastebasket with the photo.

"God, he's done it again. This is the last time. I'm not going either, Clarice, he didn't even discuss it with me." Her voice trailed off as the thought crashed down. How could he be so insensitive to ask me to go back there, where my mother was murdered?

She turned and ran from the room as Clarice picked up the baby and danced her around the room, whispering, "Nobody's taking you from me, honey, not your daddy, not nobody, nobody. She'll go—but I'll be coming with you."

2

Berlin/November 10, 1938

Caldwell felt ill at ease in the ballroom of the Italian Embassy, the
only American amid the crowd of German, Italian, and Spanish
officers, diplomats, and their guests. After all Bandy had told him of
the horrors about the Spanish Civil War bombings of Guernica,
Madrid, and Barcelona, he had expected them to look like thugs.
Instead they were very ordinary. In American uniforms and with
American-style haircuts, they could have been officers at any U.S.
Army base.

His Luftwaffe escort in Berlin, Captain Helmut Josten, had
jokingly made wearing his uniform a condition of his invitation.

"Come along, Henry, but you have to wear your uniform. Franco's peasants never get to meet a real live American general."
Caldwell had accepted instantly, more than glad to wear the insignia of his new rank. He'd spent twenty years toiling in the
procurement trenches, expecting that he'd retire as no more than a
major. He was entitled to enjoy his new stars.

It was an anniversary party. Two years ago, the famous Luftwaffe
Condor Legion had made its clandestine journey to Spain to fight in

the civil war. They had traveled in civilian clothes, and their airplanes had been shipped in crates marked FURNITURE. Although they came in far fewer numbers than the Italians, they had been of decisive help to Franco. Now, the men who fought in Spain were busily shaping Goering's Luftwaffe in the light of their newfound knowledge. Most of their old theories had been proven wrong. Hard fighting had hammered out new concepts on bombing, ground support, and formations for air combat.

Instead of introducing him to the combat pilots, Josten had been busy dancing around the flower-heaped room with a beautiful White Russian held tightly to him. We used to call that doing the fish, Caldwell grinned to himself.

As the pair approached, the woman whispered to Josten and excused herself. The twenty-four-year-old captain was a walking Luftwaffe recruiting poster, almost six feet tall, with a swimmer's build, broad shoulders, and narrow waist. His engaging face was framed with close-cropped curly hair over his broad brow, wide-set eyes, and strong jaw. Earlier Caldwell had watched him, surrounded by fellow pilots, telling in German too fast for Caldwell to follow a flying anecdote that involved lots of hand movements and sound effects. Josten had kept them captivated, and at the last moment everyone burst into laughter—one woman who was listening had turned away holding her sides. At an American lawn party it might have been ordinary—in the stiff society of the German military, it was worth noting.

Josten reminded him in so many ways of Bandfield. They both had the pilot's confident manner, and the ability to listen intently and absorb what was being said, then ask key questions. They were both quick technically, able to explain engineering problems easily. Josten's fluent English derived in part from his omnivorous reading—Caldwell was amazed at the depth of his knowledge of history. He was obviously a voracious reader in both English and German. More interesting, Josten managed to tie his views of history into today's events without seeming either pedantic or political.

Unlike most pilots, the man was dazzlingly versatile. In 1936 he had swum in the Olympics, then later that year set half a dozen soaring records at the *Wasserkuppe* in a glider of his own design. During the Spanish Civil War he was credited with four kills—but according to some of the people Caldwell had talked to, had actually destroyed several more than that. Remarkably, his whole demeanor reflected an inner peace and self-assurance not found among many of the German officers Caldwell knew. He carried himself with a perfect military posture, but he did it easily, gracefully, unlike most of the stiff-necked "heel-clickers," as Bandy termed them. And Josten's candor had convinced Caldwell early on that he was a man of integrity and good will.

A voice asked, "Will you introduce me?" and Josten turned to introduce Caldwell to his companion.

"Lyra, may I present my friend and fellow pilot, General Henry Caldwell. General Caldwell, Countess Illeria Gortchakov."

She extended her hand, and Caldwell fumbled for a moment, trying to recall if you were supposed to kiss the hand of an un-married woman. He played it safe, holding her hand for a long moment as he stared at her. Lyra was stunning, fair-skinned, wear-ing little makeup. An emerald necklace—expensive if real—matched the color of her wonderfully intelligent eyes. A simple white gown clung to her tall slender figure, a perfect foil for her thick black hair which shimmered with an iridescence so dazzling that she dared to wear it unfashionably long. It took all of Caldwell's self-control to keep his eyes on her lovely oval face, away from her startling cleavage. Caldwell felt that for the first time he truly understood the word "aristocratic."

They chatted and he was surprised at how well informed she was about current events, like the scare Orson Welles had given Amer-ica only ten days before with his *War of the Worlds* broadcast.

"Countess, how do you know so much about American affairs?"

"Not by reading the *Voelkischer Beobachter*, I assure you. I work at the Foreign Ministry, translating key articles. I get to read most of the American, French, and English periodicals. And I must say, General, I'm amazed at the technical information in American magazines. You seem to have no secrets."

"We have a few, but a free press can ferret them out."

She smiled, "Your point is well taken."

Something in her manner told Caldwell that this woman was different and might be useful to him. He pressed his luck. "Isn't it a little unusual for a foreign national to work in a key German ministry?"

"Not in these busy times. I certainly didn't raise the issue. I needed a job."

Work was the key to survival in Europe, crowded with fragmented families trying to survive the Depression-reinforced disaster of the 1914–1918 war. No matter how much one might dislike Hitler and the Nazis, he had solved unemployment and even created a labor shortage.

Yet it was hard for Caldwell to believe that a White Russian woman was employed in the Nazi Foreign Ministry. Lyra saw the skepticism in his eyes and, lowering her voice, said, "Helmut won't be offended if I tell you that most of the leading Nazis are snobs. They think employing a White Russian countess—a victim of the Bolsheviks!—is chic, and I won't disabuse them."

"Well, you are chic to me as well, Countess. You are the first royalty I've ever met."

"My family is not royal, not at all. Did you know that your American Civil Service organization was copied from the old Russian system?"

Caldwell shook his head in surprise.

"But there was one big difference. If you did an outstanding job in the Russian government, so that you reached the very top, the good Czar Nicholas could ennoble you. I don't think President Roosevelt can do that."

"No, but the Republicans claim he wants to."

"In any event, my father was one of the fortunate ones, an engineer. He had a major role in building the trans-Siberian railway. He did so well that the Czar gave him a hereditary title and a modest estate."

A frown passed over her face. "Unfortunately, after the Revolution, the only thing we could take with us was the title. I don't even remember the place, but my father misses it so. You should hear him tell of the fruits that we grew there, the wines that we made."

"Is your father still living?"

"Yes, and my mother, too, in Riga. He is struggling with a timber export business there, just able to make ends meet. I came here to give them a little relief, a chance to have a life of their own without worrying about me."

A tall, serious-looking woman rushed over to Lyra, took her arm and pulled her aside to whisper in her ear. Caldwell could tell by their manner that she was a trusted friend.

A look of intense concern shadowed those wide green eyes, and Lyra said softly to the two men, "Will you excuse me?"

Puzzled, Josten watched them leave, then turned to his duties as a host. "I don't know what this is all about, Henry. I hope it's nothing serious."

Caldwell picked another snifter of brandy from a passing tray, thinking how much Elsie would enjoy a party like this—and how little Shirley would have. As much as he had loved his wife, her death had turned out to be a surprising deliverance for him. Since meeting Elsie, he'd grown far beyond his old world of work and family. He'd become far less inhibited and had come to relish a sense of danger in his new freedom. To his surprise late in life he discovered that he was a born gambler at heart, eager to calculate odds and take chances.

Two floors above, Lyra was locking herself in a tiny foul-smelling bathroom used by the servants; the larger facilities downstairs were crowded with laughing women, and she was no longer in a laughing mood. Turning off the light, she leaned back against the door, her stomach contracting, her throat tight, suffocating in apprehension.

It was happening at last; the Nazis were dropping all pretenses and taking direct action. The day's papers had been full of indignation about the assassination of a minor official at the German embassy in Paris by a seventeen-year-old Jewish boy. She had just learned that a pogrom was under way. Jews were being beaten, a synagogue was burning in the Fasanenstrasse and shop windows of Jewish stores were being broken. It was horrible in the abstract, and a personal catastrophe for her. She was so stupid to have become involved with a German Luftwaffe captain, to let her physical desires overcome her common sense. Twenty years of wandering about Europe had taught her nothing! She wondered what her father would say if he knew she was involved with a Nazi.

It had begun innocently enough. She'd been introduced to him at a party, and they had hit it off immediately, dancing close, holding hands, laughing at everything. He was a gorgeous, healthy animal, with a sense of humor rare among German men. At first she had shrugged off the fact that he was a Party member by reasoning that the romance would die aborning. Then, when it was evident that they both felt strongly about each other, she had asked him about his political beliefs. It was evident that Helmut had a complex psychological adaptation to a Germany controlled by the Nazis. He regarded the Nazis as just a primitive first step in Germany's political rehabilitation. He was using the Party as he believed Hitler to be using it, as a means to an end. His voice had been passionate with conviction when he told her, "You don't think a man as brilliant as Hitler can be taken in by the likes of Goebbels or Streicher, do you? He's just appealing to the dark side of the German soul until he can get the economic situation straightened out. When that time comes, he'll jettison the whole crew!"

He was ingenuously convinced that the only way he himself could effect any changes when that time came was to rise to a leadership position in the Luftwaffe. He was not ashamed that his beliefs coincided with his overwhelming desire to fly.

Josten tried to pass his philosophy off as pure pragmatism—she knew that it was a submerged idealism. He told her, "Lyra, as a civilian, I'd never have a voice in anything. As a senior officer, I'll be listened to—I'll be able to make a difference. But I'll never get to be a senior officer if I fight the system now."

"But what if you're wrong—what if Hitler doesn't 'jettison' the others? What if he keeps on demanding new territories?"

His reply had been brusque. "If Hitler doesn't stop after the Sudetenland, the *Wehrmacht* will stop *him*."

She had heard that before. Many of the career diplomats in the Foreign Ministry were predicting a coup, with a return to free elections, and perhaps even a restoration of the monarchy.

Lyra had questioned Helmut closely about his admiration of the Fuehrer. There was no doubt that he identified Hitler with his own father, who had served in the Imperial Navy—he had even slipped once and said *"der Vater"* instead of *"der Fuehrer."*

Helmut argued that even Hitler could only do so much in just five years—tearing up the treaty of Versailles and bringing Germany out of the depths of the Depression. Threatened militarily by France and even by weak states like Poland, Hitler had transformed Germany into a powerful force. He felt it was too much to expect that Hitler could cure all the social evils at the same time, even the ones within his own party.

Yet Lyra knew from her work at the Ministry that Helmut was terribly wrong. Her father had called Hitler the Antichrist early on. He was right.

In the last few weeks, Lyra had sensed that her counter-arguments were having some effect, and that Helmut was beginning to have some doubts. It was enough to let her rationalize the situation and allow their romance to go on. But even now in her anxiety the familiar burning feeling overcame her and she was ashamed of her insistent, overriding physical need for him. It was an addiction! Just the thought of his hands touching her body filled her with longing, a reaction impossible to ignore. There was certainly more to it than sex—he was completely charming, a man she'd have been proud to bring to her parents as her husband—if he were not a German officer.

But she was a realist, and she knew they had only a brief, precarious time to love—a life together was clearly impossible. It was so unfair. In the few months that she had known him, Helmut had proved himself to be as truly good as any man she had ever met—kind, courageous, forthright. Her opinion was not just based on observation. She had checked on him with her new network of friends and talked to his comrades. He was known to be honest to a fault, a hard worker, fiercely proud of family, and totally reliable. But with that went the inescapable fact that he was a loyal German, ready to fight for Hitler.

She let the tears flow. Circumstances had entrapped her in a web of lies, at the Ministry, with Helmut, with her parents. Even tonight, when General Caldwell had inquired about her work, she had not been able to tell the whole truth—that she owed her job to a powerful political connection.

The week she had arrived in Germany, she had been invited to a charity ball sponsored by Magda Goebbels, the wife of the Propaganda Minister. As powerful as Madame Goebbels was in Nazi social circles, she tried to ingratiate herself with the patrician families of the old regime by surrounding herself with members of the German nobility.

Lyra's father was distantly related to the ancient Field Marshall von Mackesen. Dressed as always in the Imperial uniform of his beloved Second Death's Head Hussars, the skeletal old man had presented her to Magda Goebbels formally, as if they had been at court. Magda had taken an instant liking to Lyra, inviting her to yet another benefit the following night. Lyra, anxious to eat well and to meet people who might help her, gladly agreed to come. Within days she had a job and had joined the circle of German and foreign aristocrats Magda cultivated.

It was Joseph Goebbels himself—"Mahatma Propaganda" as the wits called him—who had arranged for her instant employment. After Magda introduced them, he had stood in the doorway, his piercing dark eyes probing the room like searchlights, sifting through the crowd of women the way a miner sifts the gold from the sand. Under his gaze she had felt a sudden chill. He nodded curtly, turned, and left. The next day, there was a call from the Foreign Ministry, and she suddenly had work. Goebbels had not called since, but she knew that she had incurred an obligation.

Lyra flicked on the switch, squinting in the dim light to check her wristwatch. Twenty minutes had passed. It was time to go back and tell Helmut the truth, to end this comedy of errors.

Josten was waiting patiently with champagne and plates of food, quite accustomed to the idea that someone as beautiful as Lyra might sometimes be capricious. They walked silently to the French doors, which led to a covered balcony overlooking the garden.

As they moved toward a corner ledge where they could rest their plates, Josten sensed the dramatic shift in Lyra's mood. Josten knew that she constantly fought some inner battle; it was part of her charm for him, a man who had no doubts about himself.

"Helmut, we've got to talk. I haven't been honest with you."

Josten wondered if she was bothered that she had not been a virgin. He had never said anything, never asked. And what did it matter in Germany, in 1938?

"My mother is a Jewess. Under your stupid racial laws, I am *mischlinge*, half-Jewish. If I am found out—and I will be, of course, with all the gossiping informants that crowd your country—it will ruin your career."

He stepped back involuntarily, for once speechless.

She went on, her tone changing swiftly from anger to sadness. "I'm sorry. I had no idea that we would become so involved, or that I would love you so much. With this pogrom going on, I realized that tonight I had to tell you. I'll have to leave Germany."

"It's not a pogrom, there are just some disturb . . ."

"It *is* a pogrom. But I don't blame you for being angry. I should have told you at once, before we made love." Then she snarled, furious again, "Before you defiled your precious Aryan blood."

Josten was stunned. His life had been one of orderly progression, from *Gymnasium*, to learning to fly with the Gelsenkirchen flying club, then joining the new Luftwaffe. Each successive challenge had been something predictable, to overcome with effort, eye-hand coordination, and training. Lyra's announcement was devastating, forcing him to make a decision that meant not progress but regression. To keep her he would have to give up all that he had worked for.

Her voice broke as she continued. "I didn't expect us to fall in love."

"Please be still for a moment." Josten's voice was harsh, betraying not anger but stress. "First, before I say anything, let me tell you that I love you, and we will find a way to do what we have to do."

She looked at him, unbelieving. "There is nothing *to* do."

"Of course there is. I'll do whatever is necessary."

"That's what you say now. Just let them say, 'No more flying' or

'No more promotions' or 'Off to Oranienburg,' and you'll sing a different tune."

Josten controlled his anger. "You have a pretty picture of me, don't you? Thank you so much for your confidence."

She had a far prettier picture of him than he could have imagined. The deep physical love she felt for him was overwhelmed by her admiration for him. They shared so many passions—reading, music, walking in the mountains. He was the brightest man she'd ever known, able to talk convincingly and at length on any subject. He would have been unique anywhere; in Nazi Germany he was an anomaly, a biological phenomenon.

He took her by the hand. "Lyra, you've given me a surprise. Let me give you one. I am going to marry you, and no one, not the Party, not the Luftwaffe, no one, will stop me."

"I might have something to say about that."

"You might, but you don't. Enough of this nonsense. I'll resign my commission. We can go to Argentina or China. We'll be married within the month!"

Lyra stood with her hand to her mouth; the years of flight and survival had taught her that wanting anything too much was dangerous.

"I'm sorry, but I can't believe you."

"That really offends me, Lyra! What do you think I've been doing, using you as if you were some sort of whore? Did you think we were just having an affair, a few quick romps in the meadow?"

She was standing close to him, drowning in the physical sensations he called forth, suddenly quite passionate, anxious to kiss him here, then take him home to bed.

"What would they do to you if they knew your lover was a Jewess?"

"Nothing—and my lover won't be a Jewess, my wife will. What do you think about marrying a horrid Nazi?"

His arms were around her, the heat of his body pressing against her. She buried her face in his neck, her tongue greedily licking his perspiration, desire rushing through her.

She moved back and took his face in her hands. "It doesn't matter what I think. It doesn't even matter what you think tomorrow, in the cold light of day. Right now I just want you to hold me."

They were kissing deeply when a hand tapped Helmut on the shoulder.

"Captain Josten, I'm sorry, but you have been recalled to base. Apparently the disorders are spreading."

Lyra watched in amazement as the cloak of military responsiveness fell over Helmut. He glanced at her apologetically and said, "I'm sorry. I'll ask General Caldwell to see you home."

Stunned at his abrupt reversion to form, she could only say, "Go ahead, Helmut, call me in the morning. I'll walk home—it's only a few blocks, and there surely won't be any problems here, near the embassies."

As they reentered the ballroom through the French doors, Josten nodded to Caldwell, who hurried over and offered to see Lyra home. She refused curtly. Caldwell followed her out, watching her stride like a proud young lioness. He turned in the opposite direction toward his car.

Lyra walked swiftly, oblivious to the chill or the unevenness of the pavement beneath her high heels, her mouth dry with fury that she had believed even for a moment that Helmut would actually give up everything for her. The events of the past few moments had driven the truth home to her, enabling her to make a clear-cut decision. Marriage was out of the question—she realized that she had always known it would be. But she would be his lover as long as time and circumstance permitted. The future had always been uncertain, and now with the increasing talk of war, there was no assurance that either one of them would even be alive in a year.

The decision was an immense relief. Lyra knew that there was no reconciliation possible in their political differences. He was simply as incapable of giving up flying, or of betraying his father and his fatherland by leaving with her, as she was of changing her own heredity.

They would just have to take what they could from life, enjoying the moment. The time was coming soon when she would have to end the affair, with regret, but without compunction.

An Opel *Blitz* truck packed with brown-uniformed SA storm troopers rumbled by, the men waving and shouting with the truculent boozy humor of bullies on a spree.

As she neared the corner, she heard the sound of breaking glass and the wavering high-pitched scream of an old man. Lyra sprinted ahead to find the storm troopers using clubs to smash the windows of a jewelry shop. In front of the store, four of the men were kicking the source of the now diminishing screams; others were picking at the glittering but inexpensive items that had been left in the window for show. Enraged, Lyra burst among them, grabbing an uplifted club and jerking a surprised storm trooper backward to the ground. She screamed, "Stop at once, or I'll report you to Goebbels!" She glanced down in horror at the old man, his head crushed and bleeding.

The Nazis reacted as if on maneuvers, quickly circling to surround her, weapons at the ready. The obviously intoxicated leader, built like a howitzer shell, all bullet head and sloping shoulders, paused to appraise her.

"*Kameraden,* maybe there's something better to do than teaching dirty old Jews a lesson."

Lyra backed away step by step as the SA leader moved forward. The other storm troopers formed a rank around her, smiling and joking with each other now, the injured man forgotten on the pavement.

Suddenly, headlights illuminated the group against the shattered remnants of the storefront. Henry Caldwell jumped the curb to plow among them, the chrome bumper of his Buick staff car shoving them apart like an icebreaker, separating them from Lyra. One man ripped off the American flag that flew on the right front fender, while another pounded on the cover of the fender-mounted spare with his club, knocking the rearview mirror off. The storm troopers were obviously confused, uncertain as to how far they could go, wanting to destroy the car, afraid to do so, but still not willing to back down.

Caldwell reached back and opened the door behind him.

"Get in, Countess."

The SA leader stood weaving at the front of the car, his truncheon slapping against his hand. In slurred, broken English he said, "Clear out, Yank. You've no business here."

Six of the troopers had their guns aimed at the car. Rifle bolts clicked and Lyra screamed—she knew too well what the sound meant. The troopers, some Great War veterans and some dough-faced hooligans from the street, were clearly anxious to shoot, waiting only for a signal or a threat. Caldwell knew that the situation had gone critical; he had seen men like this before, angry strike-breakers coming to the mines, preferring to kill rather than argue.

"Don't say anything, don't make any sudden movements," he cautioned her. Calling to the storm troopers' leader he said, "I'm General Caldwell, United States Army. I'm with the American Embassy. Let me proceed at once."

"I don't care if you are President 'Jewsevelt.' I want that woman for interrogation. Turn her over and clear out before I break your head."

Caldwell eased out the clutch, rolling the Buick's big front wheel over the SA man's foot, sending him screaming in pain back toward his truck. Caldwell burned rubber accelerating into the street as the troopers fired.

On September 1, 1939, a new world war proved that *everyone* could be wrong. The English and French believed they could appease Hitler, and were blindsided by the infamous Ribbentrop/Molotov pact. The Poles so believed in their own strength that their colonels boasted about how quickly they could take Berlin. The Russians believed they could buy time by sending Hitler tributes of raw materials and foodstuffs. The Germans believed that the English and French would not honor their guarantees to the Poles. And the United States believed that it would remain neutral, as the law required.

The Allies watched Hitler like a frog watches a snake, hypnotized by impending doom, allowing him to split the war into two distinct halves, each with time and events moving at vastly different rates. In the East, Germany savagely liquidated Poland in a war of blazing swiftness. In the West, nothing happened except for loudspeakers blaring propaganda messages and bombers dropping leaflets.

In America, President Roosevelt was preparing to run for an unprecedented third term, pacifying the isolationists by stressing U.S. neutrality and issuing an embargo order on the sale of arms to belligerents. At the same time he began an unprecedented peace-time military buildup, spending that helped pull America from the mire of its ten-year Depression.

In the face of the nightmare, individuals tried to live "normal lives."

Dayton, Ohio/January 15, 1940

Frank Bandfield had never felt more helpless, somehow an intruder at Patty's bedside in the ward where other women also labored. She lay asleep, vulnerable, her fragile beauty marred by deep circles of fatigue and pain, her mouth, normally so sweetly shaped, slack and open as she gasped for breath.

A small radio, its fractured brown plastic case friction-taped together, was quietly vibrating to the tune of "Pennsylvania 6-5000." The tired night nurse, sprawled in the chair, her uniform rumpled and hair straying out from under her cap, sat tapping a thermometer in rhythm to it.

Patty was in her eighth hour of labor. Bandfield had stopped patting her hand, not wishing to awaken her. She groaned as another contraction hit her, his own insides grunting and compress-ing in sympathetic reaction.

Her eyes opened and she grunted, "What does the doctor say?"

"He wants to wait another few hours; if nothing happens, he'll do a Caesarean."

"Stretch marks or scars, not much of a choice, eh? I'm about ready to give up; I'm pretty tired."

She lapsed back into sleep. He sat watching her, torn between admiration for her courage and utter relief that she would never have to undergo a similar agony. This was it; two children were enough.

With Charlotte, Patty had started labor about three in the after-noon, and the baby was born at eight. Now that worried him; if the first olive out of the bottle had been easy, the rest should be even easier.

He'd missed Charlotte's easy birth and had almost missed this one. He had just come back from observing the outnumbered Finnish David bringing the Russian Goliath to a halt in the Winter War, and Henry Caldwell had already cut orders for him to go to Brazil, where the quasi-Fascist government was in the market for some new airplanes.

Bandfield knew he was fortunate to have the confidence of the most important man in the American aircraft industry. Caldwell's genius was keeping a dozen balls in the air at a time. He had the Curtiss P-40 production line rolling. Boeing was cranking up B-17 production, and Consolidated had flown their XB-24 at December's end. And that was just the current stuff; for the future there was a competition for a whole series of fighters and for a huge superbomber that could bomb Germany from the United States!

Caldwell was even more deeply involved with Elsie—he'd told Bandy privately that he wanted to marry her. He was talking about having children and Elsie hadn't even consented to an engagement. Bandfield worried that Caldwell was going to trip himself up. It was stupid to have an affair with the "personal assistant" of the president of an airplane company he was doing business with, yet Caldwell seemed to feel he could manage it. Bandfield was certain that Elsie would exploit the relationship.

Caldwell needed to be careful. The Air Corps was growing, bringing in young, ambitious hotshots eager to make general. And it was no different than any other organization—there would be sharks circling Caldwell, especially now that his influence had spread so far.

Recognized as Hap Arnold's right-hand man—although his help getting Arnold his position was not generally known—Caldwell had a moral authority far beyond his rank, gained by his knack for reaching across organizational boundaries. Caldwell had not just done people favors—he'd gone out of his way to create situations where he could do them. He had markers from the right people everywhere, and he used them judiciously as he imprinted his personality on the entire Air Corps. Perhaps his infatuation with Elsie was good, a sign that he was, after all, a mere mortal, not like the comic strip guy, Superman.

Patty groaned, and he picked up her hand.

"I felt something move, Bandy—you'd better get the doctor."

Two hours later, a baby boy was born, six pounds and four ounces of red-faced fighting fury. Bandy loved the sight of him, his little features compressed into prunelike wrinkles, tiny blue eyes peeping out at the strange new world, lungs loudly protesting the strange new order of things. Bandy had already picked out a name for his son: George Roget Bandfield—George for his father, whom he still loved deeply despite his desertion, and Roget for his best friend. Later, he sat again at Patty's bedside as she slept, happier than he'd ever been, aware of just how lucky he was.

Cottbus, Germany/July 13, 1940

Captain Helmut Josten felt that he was the unluckiest man in Germany. The woman he loved wouldn't marry him, and he was being dragged down a gravel path by a fat little Nazi to a meeting for which he didn't even know the reason. Behind them, the entourage of staff officers were struggling out of the convoy of flag-decked Mercedes sedans to stretch their legs.

Honorary SS *Obergruppenfuehrer* Kurt Weigand was almost running to stay ahead of Josten's crisp military stride. From the back he looked like a gingerbread man, so short that the tip of his SS ceremonial sword dragged in the crushed gravel of the path. Weigand's hand continually caressed the Hitler-duplicate mustache underneath the bobbed fleshy knob that was his nose. In 1916, during the first attack on Fort Douamont at Verdun, a French trenching spade had smashed into his face, breaking his nose and cheekbones, and knocking out his front teeth. The spade had provided the only angular relief to an otherwise perfectly round head and body. Almost bald, his remaining hair close-cropped, Weigand was essentially featureless—except for his eyes, which hinted at the complexity of his personality. When he spoke, their pale blue gleamed with the expectant happiness of a new puppy. Yet those same eyes were never still, always moving and recording, continuously assessing the value of every person and every event to himself.

Josten tried to get a feel for the meeting. "Sir, you flew with the Director in the World War, did you not?"

"Yes. After Verdun I was no longer fit for duty in the trenches, so they let me train as a pilot. That's the way they did things in those days—they felt you didn't need to be well to fly. We flew in the Richthofen *Geschwader*, through the great early days of 1918—and the sad last days, too. I've not seen him since. What unit are you with?"

"*Jagdgeschwader* 26; we're stationed on the Channel coast."

"You know the Director?"

"We flew together in Spain. He's a man of great vision."

They were early for their appointment. Traffic had been light on the drive from Berlin, and there had been no delay at the gates of the Focke-Wulf factory. Josten was infuriated that it was Saturday, and everyone was off. Here they were, a full year into the war, and an aircraft factory was closed for weekends like some routine business. He knew that it was in part the labor shortage, but it was also a national attitude. Germany had not yet become serious about the war; perhaps the victory over France had come too easily. The guard on the gate was a symptom, casually waving them through the gates with only a cursory glance at the driver's identity papers.

Weigand paused to catch his breath, surveying the flat countryside. A few years ago it had been farmland; now there was an aircraft factory and, on the opposite side of the runway, their destination, the Hermann Goering Aerial Weapon Establishment. It was a perfect spot for an airfield, but a study in contrasts. On the Focke-Wulf side, sunlight reflected off the tall windows of the long manufacturing building; below, shadows enfolded the low-set engineering offices arrayed alongside. The buildings were laid out in the new German style, well separated to avoid bomb damage, with plywood shutters to cover the windows if the RAF ever got that far. Even though the factory was shut down for the weekend, it had a purposeful military look, with fire hydrants well spaced and clearly marked and directions to bomb shelters posted every hundred yards.

In contrast, the Aerial Weapon Establishment area looked like a small city park, well landscaped and with gravel-covered paths curving through the pine forests. After a sharp right turn in the path, the plant lay before them, submerged in a shallow meadow so that it was invisible from the road. It was startling. The two men had both expected to see another aircraft factory, sawtooth roofs of steel and glass buildings, chimneys smoking. Instead, they saw a rambling wooden complex, a gigantic spiderweb of frame hangarlike buildings, all connected to a central administrative office by covered walkways. At the far left was a huge, grass-covered hillock, two hundred meters long and a hundred meters wide, studded with artificial trees.

They were greeted at the door of the administrative office by a primly dressed woman of fifty, her hair pulled back in a tight bun, a white lace blouse buttoned to the neck.

"Greetings, gentlemen. I am the Director's personal assistant, *Frau* Schroeder. He sends his apologies; he is taking a physical therapy treatment and won't be able to see you for a few moments. You know, his injuries . . ." Her voice trailed off apologetically.

Josten found a chair and assumed the approved position, hands on his knees, gloves folded in his hat. He kept his mouth shut. It was one thing to chat with Weigand as they walked along the path, quite another to speak to him in front of a third party.

Weigand walked around inspecting the walls, covered with photos of most of the Nazi leaders. In the place of honor was a huge, silver-framed photo of the Fuehrer, personally signed, the ultimate gift in the Third Reich. He whistled to himself—his old comrade was obviously well thought of. The trip might be worthwhile after all.

Frau Schroeder returned with a silver tray laden with real coffee, white rolls, butter, and cherry jam, luxuries even at this level in the Reich. Weigand ate greedily, piling on the butter, licking his fingers. With his mouth full he said, "A handsome portrait of the Fuehrer."

"Yes, *Herr Obergruppenfuehrer*, but let me show you some other important photos."

She led him to the far wall. The knotty-pine paneling was hung with a red suedelike fabric covered with smaller photos of ordinary German working-class people—machinists, secretaries, welders.

There was pride in her voice. "These are what the Director calls 'the real people,' those he knows do well—secretaries, adjutants, the aides, foremen in the key factories, workmen on the assembly line. The Director remembers them all, and they appreciate it. The Director always says that knowing the right sergeant is sometimes better than knowing the right general."

There was a crackle of static and a husky, familiar voice came over the speaker. "*Frau* Schroeder, please tell my guests that I'll just be a few more minutes."

Inside the inner office, the Director was stretched out on an operating table, the lower half of his body covered by a sheet. A massage by the Buddha-like Dr. Felix Kersten was an incredible experience. His fingers seemed to be driven by tiny vibrators, demonically delivering an electric yet muscle-soothing pulsation. And that was only part of it. The real pleasure came from knowing that Heinrich Himmler thought enough of you to lend the services of his own personal masseur.

It was legend that in their very first session, Kersten had massaged away Himmler's increasingly troublesome stomach cramps. The *Reichsfuehrer* had peremptorily taken the doctor from his clientele of wealthy industrialists and royalty, forcing him to stay at home on his farm at Harzwalde, seventy-six kilometers from Berlin. As compensation, Himmler saw to it that the farm was transformed with the resources of the Reich into a magnificent estate.

Kersten knew that he and his family would live very well as long as he soothed Himmler. Yet to his credit he did more than that. The rumors that Kersten was a benevolent Svengali were true. He could hypnotize Himmler with his hands into an occasional act of mercy—the release of a Jewish prisoner from a concentration camp, or an agreement to permit emigration. The greater Himmler's pain, the greater favors he would grant.

Kersten said, "A few more minutes, *bitte*," and moved the sheet so that he could work on the scarred and twisted legs.

The Director went limp as Kersten's magic fingers lured the pain away. Kersten was a decent fellow, and his ministrations reminded the Director of the massages his wife had given him years ago, after he'd come home from a long flight or a hard day at the factory. Strangely, he rarely thought of her or of his factory in the United States. Any thoughts he had of those times were only of the bastard who had brought him down with a trick over Guernica, the man who had started him on this *via dolorosa*. He groaned involuntarily.

It was incredible that his own son-in-law, that *Grünschnabel*, a greenhorn knowing nothing of combat, could have been able to do it. Hafner had outflown him in Peru, and outsold him in the marketplace. Oddly enough, they had many interests in common, might even have become friends if Bandfield had not been so independent, so arrogant.

The Guernica dogfight was always in his mind, an obsession. He'd made a mistake he'd never make again—toying with an enemy. He should have killed Bandfield when he had the chance— then the rest of his life would have been different. The man had been at his mercy; he could easily have shot him down. Instead, he had tried to extend the pleasure of the moment. But Bandfield had tricked him, ramming the propeller of his Russian fighter through the rudder of his Messerschmitt.

Hafner closed his eyes, wincing as he recalled the violence of the wild tailspin that trapped his legs in the cockpit as he struggled to bail out, one of the few times in a danger-filled life that he had been truly frightened. In desperation, just a few hundred feet from the ground, he had pulled his parachute ripcord and let its opening canopy yank him from the cockpit like a cork from a champagne bottle. As he left, the jagged metal of the dying Messerschmitt had knifed great chunks of muscle from his legs and buttocks. The pain had been incredible, yet he had never lost consciousness, not once, until the first operation.

At the field hospital, the doctors told him with casual brutality that he would not live. After the first operation, they congratulated themselves, deciding that he would live but be completely paralyzed. Now they only said he wouldn't walk again. He would prove them wrong about that, too, no matter how long it took. He *would* walk again, and he would fly again as well, and to hell with them all!

Kersten gave him the customary three gentle taps on the back that signaled the end of the session, shook his hand, and left. In the outer office Kersten chatted briefly with Weigand and Josten while Hafner dressed. Then the intercom crackled: "Please ask my visitors to come in."

Weigand was impressed beyond measure by meeting Kersten. Only a very important man would have both Hitler's silver-framed photo and the services of Himmler's masseur. He self-consciously checked the shine of his boots and straightened his tie before moving through the large mahogany double door.

They hurried into the immense, pine-paneled office. The polished hardwood floor, glistening with wax, reflected the battery of lights suspended from the high ceiling. Hafner's enormous desk was half paperwork and half machine shop, covered with folders, aircraft models, cannon shells, and odd bits of machinery—gears, valves, and unidentifiable bits of metal. Behind the desk were the Reich battle flag and the flag of the Luftwaffe. On the wall opposite the desk hung an enlargement of a photograph of Hermann Goering, showing him at his desk, the President of the Reichstag. Stuck in the lower left corner of the frame was a smaller, candid photograph of Goering, this time with helmet and goggles on, seated in the cockpit of his Albatros fighter, Hafner standing at the aircraft's side, handing him a map. Both photos were signed.

The outer wall of the office was half an octagon, each division having large French doors opening to a ramp leading to a separate factory building. At the center of the complex, in the middle of his office, crouched over his desk like a malevolent spider, sat Bruno Hafner.

"Forgive me for not rising, Kurt. You rascal, you were early."

"If you're always early, you're never late, Bruno. You used to say that, back in the Great War. You are looking very well; *Frau* Schroeder says you have shoulders like Max Schmeling."

Weigand peered at Hafner's face, and in his usual blunt fashion said, "Your airplane burned, I take it?"

"No, these are scars from the parachute risers." The lines of the parachute had made one quick twist about him as it opened, abrading the flesh on the right side of his face so that his cheekbone stood out sharply above a tight and twisted mouth.

"Helmut, it's good to see you again. It's been a year, at least."

Weigand saw immediately that the two were friends, and his opinion of Josten rose sharply.

As the two older men ran a conventional roll call of remembered names, Josten sat quietly, examining the extraordinary pair of portraits of Hafner on the wall to the left. One, obviously painted from a photo, was Hafner as Josten remembered him in Spain. Hafner, helmet in hand, stood tall, looming over the cockpit of his Messerschmitt fighter. His blond hair was askew, as if the helmet had just been pulled off after a combat sortie, and he was gesturing with his hands in the familiar fighter pilot style. The artist had taken some liberties—Josten didn't remember that Hafner had been as lean and fit in Spain as he was portrayed here. But he had captured the face, the broad forehead, thick eyebrows, wide-set eyes, shown with the fire of combat still burning, and the thing Josten remembered most, the captivating grin, the smile of a boulevardier. There had been an absolute procession of women through Hafner's quarters in Spain— local Spanish ladies, visiting German women, foreign women photographers and journalists—and they all seemed to cherish the experience, judging by their return visits.

The other portrait was a painfully exacting reproduction of Hafner's current twisted state, crouched behind a desk, his face scarred, his left eyelid drooping, hatred implicit in his stony gaze.

Hafner noticed him looking at it, and said, "I keep that to remind me that I was not always this way. I don't know whether it's vanity or penance."

Even Weigand was embarrassed by the conversational turn, and asked, "Well, what exactly are you building here, Bruno? I was expecting a Hermann Goering Works, and all I find is a spiderweb of frame sheds."

"This is far more important than the Hermann Goering Works, even though it won't make me the money 'der Dicke' makes from that. This is a working model of the new German industrial base.

You're seeing in miniature what German industry must become by 1942. We've got to get started producing on a monumental scale."

He spun his chair around and glared at them. "Do you know how many changes were made in the Ju 88 before they finally began production?"

Protocol demanded silence from Josten, and Weigand said, "I have no idea."

"More than thirty-five thousand!" Hafner launched into a diatribe, a catalog of the mistakes Germany was making in their war effort. Josten felt a cold shudder of apprehension as Hafner ticked off the errors—making too many kinds of aircraft, too many types of engines, too many parts. "Everybody thinks Germany is one big Krupps; it's not, it's just a group of toy factories, almost what they call 'cottage industries.'"

"That's America talking, Bruno, just like your rogues' gallery of welders and secretaries out there. This is Germany."

"Yes, it's America talking, and Germany better listen or we will get our arse kicked, just like in 1918."

Weigand's nose and mustache quivered as he sensed opportunity like a fox sniffing chickens.

"So what are we to do, Bruno?"

"This 'spiderweb of frame sheds,' as you call it, is a model for a central German industrial complex. I've gathered some of the best practical engineers in the country, not a pack of selfish academics wishing to write papers for each other, but people who can *do* things. And I've filled it with operating machinery and staffed it with experienced factory workers, people from that 'rogues' gallery' on the wall, men and women who know what they are doing, without worrying about the red tape that clogs up Udet's offices."

Weigand nodded. Udet had made a shambles of the traditionally efficient German bureaucracy. At last count the Inspector General of the Luftwaffe had forty-three major departments reporting directly to him; he couldn't manage even one of them.

Hafner's scarred face glowed with animation as he grew more excited. "The first step is to rationalize what we are producing now, standardize all of the fasteners, the tools, the jigs; then we decide on what's the best, not just from performance considerations, but from availability. It doesn't make any sense to call for chrome piston rings that will last for a thousand hours in an engine that won't run for two hundred before it's blown up. Put in pig-iron rings and forget it."

"But why this spiderweb?" Weigand asked in bewilderment. "Why not do it all on one site like the Russians do, like Ford did in Detroit?"

"First, efficiency; second, dispersal. I want to build five or six complexes modeled on this one, spread all over the east and south of Germany, away from the RAF. They'll be mutually supporting, like a bridge truss; if a ball bearing plant gets bombed out in one complex, we'll be able to supply it from another."

"And what do you want from me?"

"I don't want *from* you, I want *for* you. We are going to need someone to supply labor on a scale we've never conceived of before."

"But Bruno, everybody wants labor. You know we are near full employment now. That's why most factories are only running one shift—no workers."

"Full employment! What a joke! We have damn few women in industry. And we've got six hundred thousand Jews in this country, most of them professionals or in retailing."

Josten felt his attention focus sharply as he thought of Lyra; this was getting close to home.

"They would yield at least three hundred thousand good, smart workers. Instead of talking about sending them to Madagascar, we ought to build ghettos around factories and let them put in twelve hours a day helping the Reich they've exploited so long."

Weigand nodded. "But even three hundred thousand is a drop in the production bucket."

"You're right. But there are almost two million French prisoners of war. Should we just feed them, or let them go back to Paris to drink wine? They can work, too. Mussolini has been pressured into sending Italian laborers. And that's not the end of it."

Weigand knew what was coming. "The East?"

"Of course, Poland, and when it comes, Russia. The bodies are out there. All we need is someone to press-gang them into service, like the British navy used to do. You are that someone."

"I do know how to organize such a campaign. But I don't know anything about allocating the workers."

"That will be my job."

Weigand gestured to Josten. "And, may I ask what all this has to do with Captain Josten? I'm a little surprised that you would speak so frankly in front of a junior officer."

"Ah, Weigand, I should have explained. Josten was in my squadron during the war in Spain; I trust his judgment. I'm going to need someone on operational duty to work with me, to be my legs, to tell me the truth about what they are saying in the front lines. Josten is that man."

"One of your 'right sergeants,' according to *Frau* Schroeder?"

"Exactly, except he is a 'right captain' now, and it won't be long before he's a 'right major.' I want his help for the other part of this establishment's mission, the visionary half."

"Visionary?"

"Exactly. Do you think we can take on half the world and win with inferior weapons? We are going to have to win with ingenuity, with weapons the Army High Command hasn't even dreamed of."

"Like what?" Weigand's Berliner accent dripped doubt.

"Come, let me show you."

Hafner opened a door and rolled down the polished hardwood path at a speed faster than the other two men could run, spinning twice like a top to wait for them at the entrance to the building.

"Let's look at solutions to the production problem first. This is my fastener section. Nobody thinks about it, but fasteners are one of the most important elements in building an airplane. They determine how large a section you can build at a time, how strong you can make it, how you can put it together."

They went inside. The machine shop was lavishly equipped, and in a large jig was a section of an aircraft fuselage, mounted next to a stub of a wing.

"Let me show you how Junkers designed the wing attachment for the Ju 88."

He pointed to the two sections. "You see these bolt holes? They are so precisely drilled that you have to use a jig to install the wing; it's like fitting a gear in a watch. Wonderful craftsmanship—but it takes twenty man-hours to do in the factory, and can't be done at all in the field." He turned to a burly machinist, lovingly wiping the turning metal on his lathe with an oily rag.

"This is an old comrade, Fritz Ihelfeld. Fritz, show the gentlemen your wing attachment fitting."

"*Jawohl, Herr Direktor*. It's quite simple—you bore a large tapered hole in the fuselage fitting, and slide the bolt in easily. Then you use a squeeze plate to take up the slack with the nut. Three mechanics can replace a wing in forty minutes with hand tools. And it's stronger than the original."

Both Josten and Weigand nodded approval. All that Hafner said had made sense; this sort of thing added to the force of his argument. If you doubled the work force and reduced the skill requirements, you could increase production enormously.

Hafner sped them around the peripheral track from building to building. The first four had dealt with solutions to production problems: quality control, interchangeability, standardized specifications, training techniques, determining how to make things good enough—but not too good. Weigand saw a sign saying, IF THINGS CAN GO WRONG, THEY WILL GO WRONG—DON'T LET THEM.

Waffen SS sentries scrambled to rigid attention at Weigand's approach. Hafner said, "Now let's see what we are dreaming up next for the Luftwaffe."

Wheeling his chair faster than they could follow, Hafner took them on a whirlwind tour of the long wooden buildings, showing them new tools, new weapons, rockets, fire control systems, and torpedoes. They were breathless when, in the last building, he paused in his chair before a canvas shroud that concealed the rear of the room.

"Now what you see here, you leave here, understand? This is most secret; the Fuehrer has given orders that no one is to be allowed in without my personal authorization, and that *no one* is to talk about it."

As soon as they entered, the lights went out and a film projector clattered. The words *"Ernst Heinkel Flugzeugwerke"* appeared and there followed company test photographs of the Heinkel He 176 rocket plane and the He 178 jet. Josten had seen the films before— the flights had been made in the summer of 1939—but Weigand was startled that the two planes could fly without any propellers.

When the lights came back up, Hafner said, "There is the future, gentlemen, turbo jets and rockets."

Weigand said, "Very impressive, but I thought Heinkel was persona non grata with the Fuehrer—too many promises, too many demands, too many problems."

"He is—and that's why I want to show you these drawings."

Hafner opened a cordovan leatherbound portfolio marked MES-SERSCHMITT A.G. Inside were stylish drawings of a twin-engine jet fighter.

Josten whistled. "Whew. When are these going to be ready?"

"That's what you two are going to tell me. If we leave it to Messerschmitt, it will be three years before we get any airplanes, because he can make more money turning 109s out in quantity than by experimenting with these. But if we develop the airplane here, ourselves, we can get it in operation within eighteen months."

"What are you talking about, Bruno? You don't have production facilities here."

"Wait and see. I have one more thing to show you."

The last spur of the web of walkways led them to the grass-covered hillock. A shallow ramp led down almost thirty meters to a door at the bottom.

"Don't let go of my chair; I'd pick up speed in the dive and crash right into the concrete wall."

He led them inside the cavernous manmade cave.

"Labor from prison camps built it for me. We scrape the ground level and pour the concrete first—ten meters thick, one hundred meters wide, two hundred meters long. Then we excavate beneath it and put in walls and floors. It makes an instant factory; you can build them cheaply, as big as you want, and they are bomb-proof. I'm going to bring in raw materials at one end and fly jet fighters out the other."

Weigand looked at him with admiration. "Bruno, you're either mad or a genius. Which do you think, Captain Josten?"

Josten shook his head. "Both, I hope. It took a madman to conceive of this, but it will take a genius to get it in operation. Does Professor Messerschmitt know that you intend to 'help' him?"

"No. Only the Fuehrer knows what I intend, and he told me specifically *not* to tell Goering about this; he doesn't want him to take it over. This is *my* project. It will win the war for us."

Back in the octagonal office, Hafner said, "Now, Weigand, the most important thing I've shown you is the jet fighter. We have to get them into operation before the British do."

"Do the British have one yet?"

"Not yet, but we know they are doing research. A young RAF officer named Whittle has been working on a jet engine for years."

Weigand stood up, obviously impressed and ready to go to work. "Well, Bruno, you've convinced me. The only thing that worries me is the expanded work force. How will we feed two or three million more workers? You know they've already cut fertilizer production because of the demands for nitrates for munitions."

"That's a problem I'm working on personally. It has a lot of interesting variables. I'll let you know in a few months what I find out."

Hafner sat at his desk long after the two men were gone. He knew he could depend upon them both, but he knew that was not enough. He was going to have to do more than take Himmler into his confidence if he was going to be able to get the raw materials and the personnel he needed. He was going to have to play upon his obsession, the perverse black streak of racial hatred that Kersten so deplored. Whatever he asked Himmler, it would have to have the appearance of assisting in the solution of the Jewish problem.

It would be easier if either Hitler or Himmler had a real idea of the true potential of the United States—it was a vast, untapped cornucopia of material, labor, and ideas. At present it was probably using less than 40 percent of its latent strength. Poor Germany was already operating at 95 percent of its capacity, straining at the seams, forced to use ersatz materials, scrambling for labor wherever it could be found. There was room for expansion, too, but it could only come out of the substance of the nation, from its very bone and fiber. One could almost plot the curve. If a maximum effort was made in Germany, ruthlessly exploiting everything in Europe and quickly overrunning Russia, it would be strong enough in 1944 to face the United States and England. But unless vast changes were made in its methods, by 1946 it would crumble from within, exhausted, out of food, manpower, and critical materials.

Hafner shook his head in both hope and dismay. Hitler was a gambler, willing to bet all on the throw of the dice with Russia. But it was just possible that they could pull it off. If they did, and they really reformed their research and production methods, Germany could win a war against England and the United States.

Caffiers, France/September 14, 1940

Josten was vastly relieved to be away from Cottbus and back on active duty. After the day's three missions in miserable weather over England he was bone-weary, but a month of heavy losses had chopped the pilots' roster in half, and it was his turn for alert again. It was late in the day, though, and there was little chance that they'd be ordered to take off. He sat in a folding beach chair, a little apart from the other eight pilots at the well-camouflaged Luftwaffe *Einsatzhafen*—operational base—at Caffiers.

The pilots, encumbered with emergency life vests, flares, and sea-dye packets, sprawled in front of austere, hastily built hangarettes. One was built to look like a typical French barn; the rest were covered with camouflage tents or netting. Each was just large enough to house a Messerschmitt Bf 109E, the trusty "Emil." The alert aircraft, fully serviced and ready to go, were protected by sandbags stacked between sawed-off tree trunks. The planes were parked a sprint away under the apple trees along the grass runway, parachutes in the seat, straps hanging out of the cockpit. If the loudspeaker commanded, they could be airborne in less than two minutes.

Josten pulled his sunglasses off to allow the sun to shine redly through his closed eyelids. Little dots moved in front of his retina; he knew they were blood cells in some tiny capillary, but he played that they were British fighter planes and he had to keep them in his sights. The dots were as shifty as Spitfires, and just the thought of combat squeezed enough adrenalin into his system to sit him bolt upright, eyes wide to scan the field.

The third *Gruppe* of *Jagdgeschwader* 26's airfield was bustling with activity even after the day's forty sorties. At the edge of the runway, mechanics were swarming around the almost new Renault tow truck they had "requisitioned" from Paris, tugging at a battle-damaged fighter that had belly-landed into the green-scummed pond at the end of the field. In one of the tents, a 109's wings rested on tripod jacks as a retraction check was run, the slow, un-synchronized lifting of the gear evoking the image of a novice ballet student practicing at the *barre*. In front of it, a new Daimler-Benz DB 601A engine dangled precariously from a homemade A-frame. Other fighters sat with the mechanic's legs sticking out of the plane's entrails like a half-digested fish from a pelican's beak.

The improvisation was marvelous, a fine by-product of the Luft-waffe's discipline, so much easier than the Army's. Left to them-selves, the men could do almost anything.

And overseeing everything was the *Kommodore* of *Jg* 26, Major Adolf Galland.

Galland's devoted ground crew joked that he looked like the personal insignia painted on his airplanes—a big-eared Mickey Mouse. His brow reached high into jet-black brilliantined hair, brushed closely back. Extraordinarily large black bushes of eyebrows clung to the bony ridges over his deep-set dark eyes. His once classic nose had been pounded by crashes into an irregular beak that was punctuated by a smear of a Hitler-style mustache. His mouth, generous enough in size when he smiled, seemed small as it perched over his jutting jaw. Taken individually, his features were not handsome, but they were stitched together in a way that made him seem larger-than-life and extremely attractive to women. Galland's ordinary expression was intent, almost obsessively serious, but he smiled readily, and he could explode into riotous laughter.

His headquarters were at Audembert, but he maintained a room at Caffiers as well. Rumor had it that he also maintained some select and lovely women at each place. Galland knew all of the *Jagdgeschwader* personnel by name and always spoke to them of some personal element—their families, their hobbies, their escapades. Yet Josten found him to be the most focused man he'd ever met.

In ordinary conversation—or in combat, over the radio—Galland spoke clearly and distinctly. But in a serious man-to-man discussion, his fast-working mind compacted his speech pattern, changing it into short, brittle, information-laden fragments studded with blanks that one was supposed to understand. Usually what he said made sense, but sometimes Josten had to stop him to fill in the clipped code, and *that* made Galland impatient.

Josten closed his eyes and was content. His father would be very proud of him, here at the very knife's edge of combat. Gerhard Josten had been an officer in the Imperial Navy, one of the old school. He'd been absolutely nonpolitical and found it easy to weave the high ethics of his service into the stern fabric of his Lutheran faith. A gunnery officer, he had survived Jutland, only to have his faith and dignity destroyed by the ignominious scuttling of the German fleet at Scapa Flow.

But his father had developed admiration for the discipline of the Royal Navy, drilling into Helmut the importance the British attached to smart appearance so that he was always "ready for inspection." Unlike most of the pilots, who would slip a flying suit over everything from pajamas to dinner jackets, Josten always flew in the prescribed uniform, boots polished to a high luster. And just as he dressed to please his demanding, long-dead father, so did he believe in his father's code of ethics and love of country. Josten's youth had been spent listening to his father's patriotic catechism, railing against the injustice of the Versailles treaty, and emphasizing the need to make Germany strong again. These were ingrown beliefs to Josten, as were the other things his father had taught: absolute honesty, compassion, fairness. Josten had protested when

Lyra had accused him of equating Hitler with his father—but he knew it to be true, because the Fuehrer so closely fulfilled his father's political requirements.

Josten was Galland's *Katschmarek*, his wingman, and he wanted to be liked by his leader. They'd gotten off to a rough start the very day he'd shot down his sixteenth aircraft and was tapped to fly on Galland's wing. After the decision had been made, the major had invited him to go bird shooting.

"No, thank you, *Herr Major*, I don't like to shoot birds and animals."

Feeling rebuffed, Galland had stiffened, his eyes looking Josten up and down in contempt. Then he had laughed abruptly, without humor. "Well, now, you're a real Nazi, aren't you, Josten? You just like to shoot people!"

Although they flew well together, their friendship developed slowly. There were formidable differences. Galland was an iconoclast, railing constantly against orders he considered stupid, recklessly challenging the party line to anyone, even Goering himself. His sarcastic request, "Please reequip my wing with Spitfires, *Herr Reichsmarschall*," was already a legend in the Luftwaffe. But Galland's forty kills and Knight's Cross gave him cards that few men could play.

There is no place like combat to measure a man. It was obvious that Galland was a genius in aerial tactics, a hero as well as a patriot, and day by day he had eroded Josten's orthodox beliefs.

They had gone to supper after the alert was terminated. Later that night in Galland's quarters they had nursed the one cognac they allowed themselves before an early morning mission. Galland was only twenty-eight, but the strain of the day's missions was still as evident on his face as the marks of his oxygen mask. He sat with tunic unbuttoned, cigar constantly going, unburdening himself in a torrent of words.

"You know, Josty, Germany's been lucky so far; we're like some postal clerk that breaks the bank at a casino."

It was a challenge. "Lucky, yes, but inspired, too. We've soaked up Europe from Norway to Spain like a blotter, and Hitler hasn't made a mistake yet."

"He's made dozens, and the biggest one is Goering, no joke intended."

Josten brushed back his blond hair, looking nervously around the room, glancing at the light fixture and the bookcase. Galland smiled.

"Don't worry, we can talk. I have my radio man check this room carefully—there are no listening devices. Just watch what you say over the telephones, though; Goering has taps everywhere."

He stubbed out his cigar and lit another. "Dolfo" Galland's cigars were as much a part of him as his nose or his ears. Big, black, and deadly, with a distinctive acrid odor, they were gifts from admiring countrymen. The *Voelkischer Beobachter* had run a lead story on Galland's Knight's Cross, awarded after his thirtieth victory, and had mentioned his fondness for cigars. A week later, the mail room began to bulge with cigars from all over, so that Galland was able to select his favorites and give the rest to the men. Even his plane was equipped with a cigar holder; he smoked before a mission until he clipped his oxygen mask on. After landing, as soon as the canopy was lifted open, he lit up again.

"Your reaction is part of our problem. We don't have any trust because we are not trusted. I tell you again, so far we've been incredibly lucky." He drew at his cigar as if it were a vital source of inspiration. "Now our luck is running out. We've got the wrong fighters, the wrong bombers, and worst of all, the wrong leaders."

Josten started to speak but Galland went on.

"Look at this big bloody ditch they call the Channel, waiting to soak us up when we come back, like Rudi and Gunter today. No wonder the pilots get *Kanalkrank*—Channel sickness! If we had drop tanks we could range all over England and fight for an hour or more! We had them in Spain, why not here?"

"I don't know, Dolfo—it must be material shortages."

Galland's smoldering intensity seemed to compress him like a rubber ball, concentrating his strength and his will and at the same time threatening to release it in an explosion. His closely set black eyes burned hypnotically.

"Nonsense. They're made out of plywood and we have tons of that!"

Josten rallied. "But look how magnificently we improvise; this strip is a perfect example of our strength."

Galland snorted with contempt. "Perfect example of our weakness! We're not some gypsy raiding party, trying to steal a few cows from the Bulgarians! We've started a world war."

He took a sip of cognac, calmed himself, then leaned forward.

"And this is just the start. Do you think America will see England go down the drain? Do you think Russia will stand by and let us prepare to attack her?"

Josten said nothing.

"Germany has to get serious, build ten times as many planes, ten times better planes." He paused, then almost shouting, yelled, "*Serious* planes, not criminal short-range pea-shooters."

"Criminal" was the current omnibus Luftwaffe slang for anything terribly hazardous or terribly wrong.

Josten felt the time was right. "I think there's something that can be done about it. You know Bruno Hafner, of course?"

The gravel voice came back, clipped, funeral tone, pell-mell pace. "Of course, Richthofen *Geschwader*, *Pour le Mérite*, industrialist, wounded in Spain, and perhaps a madman. I know Hafner; what about him?"

Josten spilled out the details of his visit to Cottbus, emphasizing both the production improvements and the radical weapons. Galland sat in silence absorbing what he said.

"I don't know, Josty. I'd like to believe it. But Hafner has a murky past; you've heard the rumors about his leaving America?"

"Some nonsense about killing his wife by sabotaging an airplane? You don't believe that, surely."

"Perhaps not—but he's supposed to love to kill for the pleasure of it."

"I don't give a damn about that if he has the right formula for building airplanes. If he can produce five hundred jet fighters for us next year, airplanes that could fly across the Channel, wouldn't you accept them?"

A great grin lit up Galland's face. "If he can do that, I'll personally kiss your ass in front of the chancellery on Hitler's birthday!"

"That won't be necessary. But to work with Hafner, I may need to take leave at odd times, just to keep things going. Are you willing for me to help these projects along?"

"Of course—as long as you keep me posted—and as long as you let me fly the new planes."

They toasted silently with the last of the cognac.

Northolt, England/September 15, 1940

Galland and Josten were crossing the French coast heading toward England as Frank Bandfield sat perspiring in the cockpit of a Hawker Hurricane fighter of the Polish Kosciuszko Squadron 303.

Bandfield was an outsider thrust upon them. Caldwell had sent him to England to follow the progress on the RAF's jet engine, and to get in some combat experience if the British would let him.

He glanced wistfully around the primitive facilities at Northolt, mentally questioning why he was there even as the hot anticipation of combat rushed through him. A tiny corporal, his uniform rank with the body odor of unbathed weeks of toil, leaned across Bandfield to strap him in.

"At least you can understand the briefing, sir, better than these bloody Poles."

In the short pre-takeoff briefing, Squadron Leader Keeler had told him that their task was simple: attack the bombers. If there were Messerschmitt fighters in the way, they would simply ignore them.

"Leave the Me's for the Spitfires, Bandfield. If we can get the bombers to jettison their bombs, we've done our main job. After that, any we shoot down are just icing on the cake."

Bandfield did not think of dogfights as being quite so tidy, but perhaps things had changed since Spain.

The young squadron leader had the face of a choirboy and the voice of an experienced commander. He had turned away abruptly, then come back and shouted, "You've had a few hours on the Hurricane, I expect?"

Bandfield said, "Yes, twenty-three," and Keeler smiled broadly, hoping that the Yank would not be a total loss. Bandfield had found the Hurricane to be a delightful airplane, with its broad thick wing, deep fuselage, and handsome lines. It was heavier on the controls than the Spitfire or the American Curtiss P-36 but the visibility from the cockpit was wonderful as the fuselage curved down from the cockpit to the spinner. The wide landing gear track made for easy landings. The only difficulty Bandfield had was in mastering the Dunlop pneumatic brakes. You had to use a lever on the control column spade grip, pulsing air as you moved the rudder pedals—a bit dicey. He'd damn near ground looped on his first taxi-out. Anyway, they obviously didn't expect too much of him, knowing that he was there to pick up experience for the Air Corps. They probably figured that, with luck, he'd get killed and maybe create some additional pro-British sentiment.

Bandfield was number two in Natty Flight, four Hurricanes sitting at the edge of a frame shack-studded grass strip on the western outskirts of London. As he plugged his radio in he could hear Squadron Leader Keeler bawling over the radio, "Come on, get your bloody fingers out, Natty Flight!"

A month ago twelve aircraft would have scrambled, three flights of four each. Attrition had cut them down, and on this, 303's third mission of the day, only four Hurricanes rolled, khaki-colored storks, kicking dust up behind them as the pilots carefully kept the measured balance between lifting the tail off and keeping the prop tips from digging in. Northolt fell rapidly behind them, disappearing into the neatly mulched greens and fading brick reds of the garden allotments surrounding suburban London. From the corner of his eye he saw at the field's edge the main road that ran from London to Oxford, a good checkpoint if he had to come back by himself.

The Hurricanes climbed hard, gray-black streams pouring back from the exhaust stacks and staining the camouflaged fuselage sides. The fires from last night's raid had largely been contained by London's exhausted fire companies, but this morning the Luftwaffe had returned. Flames and smoke grew from the dock area in huge tiered stalagmites that ran together at the top, a long greasy gray string against the teal-blue sky.

The myriad cries of the ground-to-air radio chatter formed a chaotic stream: "Operations calling, operations calling, Beta squadron scramble, hello Long Mike, hello Rugby Leader," a thousand directions, questions, and sometimes salty observations, all done in accents ranging from cockney to Oxbridge to Australian. The controlled panic was at first a jumble to Bandfield, but he was beginning to be able to sort it out as he glued himself to Keeler's wing. When he got to the scene of the battle he'd know what to do. He had done it often enough in Spain, against the same enemy.

Keeler led them in a curving climb at 170 mph, flying in two tight elements. The Hurricane was fun, a study in contrasts. Modern-looking, its performance suffered because the propeller was just a big wooden club, no different in principle from props used in the Great War. Top speed was supposed to be about 320 mph; yesterday Bandfield had not been able to nudge his past 300 mph in level flight. The obsolete propeller was just another one of England's pennywise economies that had cost them bitterly on the continent. Engine power was everything in modern combat; without it no airframe was worth anything. That's why the sheer power of the jet was going to be so important.

The other two planes stayed glued to him and Keeler. He had met the pilots at the bar the night before. They were older men, majors in their own air force, but like all the gallant Poles in the RAF, they had to start with the most junior commissioned rank, pilot officers, because of some stupid bureaucratic concern about seniority. One—Bandfield thought his name was Pisarek—spoke English fairly well and had that very morning taught him rather more about Kosciuszko's role in the American Revolution than he had wished to know.

Bandfield concentrated on keeping his position, close in on Keeler's wing. It was a bad formation for combat; they should be more strung out, letting all four pairs of eyes comb the sky rather than depending upon just Keeler and Pisarek.

He smiled to himself, "There I go again—I'm here to learn, not to teach." But he recalled his last combat flight, in Spain, in 1937, and how he and his old comrade Lacalle had flown farther apart, able to fly formation easily and still scan for the enemy. It was at times like this when he wanted to believe in an afterlife, to think that Lacalle was somehow looking down at him, preparing to take care of him, just as he had in the old days.

Above the English Channel/September 15, 1940

Josten squinted into the bright blue afternoon sky, searching for the little dots that would appear from nowhere and try to kill him. His eyes traversed the horizon from north of London toward Land's End, noting the changing striations of color above the cliffs' chalky smear. The variegated countryside was tan and dull green to the north, growing stripe by stripe to a viridian brightness in the far south. While he and his comrades had fought their long battle, summer had drained June's bursting green glow to the sere tans that forecast an early winter. With luck, perhaps a peaceful early winter.

The Royal Air Force could not hold out much longer according to the intelligence reports, straight from "Beppo" Schmid at Luftwaffe Headquarters. Schmid, whose unremitting optimism had destroyed his credibility weeks ago, had again pronounced that the poor "chaps" flying the vulnerable Hurricanes and the nasty Spitfires had been worn down to a pitiful handful.

And yesterday the RAF attacks on the bombers had been poorly coordinated and not pressed home, perhaps a sign that they were indeed losing their nerve. Josten eased out his right foot from the retaining strap of the rudder bar and stamped it upon the cold metal cockpit floor of his Messerschmitt, muttering, "Wishful thinking."

Below them, in an aerial staircase stacked up and back from twenty thousand feet, flew 150 bombers, mostly Heinkel He 111s with a few Dornier Do 17s mixed in. The bomber pilots were obviously tired, letting their prescribed tight mutual defense formations straggle into lengthening oblong ovals. Wearily courageous, they plodded implacably toward an already burning London.

The whole scene looked strangely different to him after last night's conversation with Galland. Yesterday the bombers had seemed lethal and purposeful; today he realized what a puny force they really were.

It was like a tug of war, he thought, each side mustering its dwindling strength, trying to make the last-gasp effort to overwhelm the other. Both sides were worn and battle weary. He wondered if the RAF intelligence was as bad as the Germans'. Maybe they'd just fight until there was no one left.

Josten reached up and ran his finger around the edge of his oxygen mask, letting the perspiration seep out. The prospect of combat made his senses more acute, and he could smell in the arid oxygen a scent of the hay stacked in neat little triangles along the strip at Caffiers.

They were flying as the staff flight in a two-ship *Rotte*, a loss-induced departure from the usual four-aircraft *Schwarm* the Luftwaffe had employed since Spain. He glanced across the 175-meter gap that separated him from his leader. The yellow nose of Adolf Galland's Messerschmitt Bf 109E fighter glistened vividly in the hot afternoon sun. The Emil, capable of 570 kilometers per hour, was loafing along at 450. It banked slightly as Galland ceaselessly checked for enemy aircraft, and on the gray-green fuselage side, beneath the canopy, Josten could see his leader's personal insignia, the bloodthirsty Mickey Mouse, smoking a cigar and holding a battle ax in one hand—paw?—and a pistol in the other.

The pair of them were lucky, on a free chase while the rest of their squadron mates below were still confined to a close protective weaving orbit over the slow bombers, per the embarrassed *Reichsmarschall* Goering's orders. Just one month ago, on Eagles Day, he had promised the Fuehrer a victory within five days.

It had been easier said than done. At each attack, the Hurricanes and the Spitfires were positioned correctly to defend their territory, the beneficiaries of expert radio detection. The enemy fighters were hacking the German bombers out of the sky, five, ten, twenty a day. And despite their own losses, the RAF kept coming.

For a change, the radios were silent; this, too, was simple fatigue, well earned in months of endless warfare. As soon as the first glints of the British fighters appeared, the usual quivering, yipping cries would begin to jam the channels. Luftwaffe radio discipline was appalling; Josten realized that it was one of the many changes that had to be made if they were to win the war. He wondered if the bomber crews talked as much as the fighter pilots. He didn't know because they were on totally different frequencies, another planning fiasco. It wouldn't have taken too much brainpower to figure that the bombers might like to talk to the fighters!

The pleasure he took in the almost mutinous thinking surprised him. It opened up a whole series of possibilities beyond the daily dogfights. He could help both Galland and Hafner—and really make a difference. It was one thing to shoot down a few airplanes; it was quite another to have an effect on the war!

Josten was jerked back into his cockpit by a sudden waggle of Galland's wing. He caught a glimpse of his rudder, the *Luftsieg* stripes of forty victories picked out, each with a date and type recorded. Josten's thoughts swung briefly to Lyra, then to the horizon, where dozens of dots suddenly swarmed, a whirling mass of lethal gnats hurtling toward the bombers.

Above Southeast England/September 15, 1940

Leveling off at twenty thousand feet, the Hurricane gained speed and its controls tightened, imparting the taut, finger-drumming feel of a sailboat placed precisely before the wind. The magnificent Rolls-Royce engine's turbine-smooth song of power inspired more confidence than the American Allison engines Bandfield had flown behind. All the compounded forces of the aircraft—the pistons flashing up and down, the gears turning, the propeller trying to tear itself apart, the suck of wind upon the wings, the invisible air battering it everywhere—all were smoothed by the airplane's harmonious lines into a single flow of power, an endless sheet of energy he controlled with the tip of a finger. Only the hammering recoil of the eight .303-caliber Browning machine guns would disturb the Hurricane's dolphin-smooth flight.

Bandfield had never felt lonelier. He thought of Patty and the children constantly and hated missing even part of George's young life, the wonderful time when he was proficient in crawling and just beginning to think about taking the first step. He wondered if even a vagrant thought of him flickered through the children's heads. Charlotte must think of him; perhaps even George, with his crooked grin and slobbery smile, might sometimes remember him.

Abruptly, Keeler's voice came through his earphones as loud as if he'd been in the cockpit beside him: "Short John, Short John, this is Natty Leader."

Short John, the deputy controller for Northolt, came back, "Hello, Natty Leader, we have some custom for you; vector one-twenty degrees, angels twenty."

Keeler's roar didn't need a radio.

"Angels twenty my bloody ass, Short John. I can see the bastards and they're at angels twenty-five if they're an inch. We're climbing to meet them."

Unruffled, Short John said, "Thank you, Natty Leader, 74 Squadron is climbing behind you."

Keeler's voice was calmer. "Short John, it's a mixed bag of Heinkels and Dorniers with a stack of 109s just above them."

Then, to his flight: "All right then, Natty Flight, line astern, head-on attack on the lead Heinkels."

Bandfield felt his muscles go through the automatic constrictions that tried to squeeze him into a tiny ball hidden by the engine and the armor plate behind the seat. The four Hurricanes had leveled off, accelerating as they swung to the attack. He felt a surge of hope as a squadron of Spitfires slammed into the top cover of German fighters, the two groups first merging in a dense ball and then separating like incompatible fluids into a series of clawing individual dogfights.

Natty Flight bored in and Bandfield eased farther to the left so that he could concentrate on the oncoming Heinkels. They were sinister-looking airplanes, full of complex curves, the sun shining on the perspex canopies and the twin cowlings, little red winking dots issuing forth from the single guns in front.

He crouched down farther in the cockpit as the Heinkel blossomed in size. Pathetic, he thought, I've got this big engine in front of me like a ton of armor plate and that poor brave bastard is sitting in a fishbowl. I've got eight great guns to hit him and he's popping at me with a little pea-shooter!

The Heinkels got prettier as they got closer, the gray-green shapes sometimes flashing a bit of blue when an undersurface was exposed in a quick formation-closing bank. A slight shudder told him he was taking hits from somewhere, nothing vital, not enough to disturb his concentration. He pushed the firing button just as the circle of the reflector sight shrank around the Heinkel like the loop of a snare. The eight .303 machine guns reached out in a harmonized pattern of ball, tracer, and De Wilde incendiary ammunition. The mass of lead converged into an arrowhead, hammering the Heinkel's perspex fishbowl into powder. The instant tornado of wind fire-hosing into the open fuselage cavity braked the Heinkel to a shuddering, convulsive stall that pitched it out and to the left. Bandfield followed Keeler into a hard turning descent to the right that rapidly changed into a prop-hanging climb to trade the energy of the dive for precious altitude. "Form up, Natty Flight," Keeler's rough voice called.

Bandfield looked around; one of the Poles was gone. Shot down? Or as the courageous Poles were prone to do, just off on some forbidden solo hunting?

The German formations had drifted to the right, extending the distance between them to almost a thousand yards. The void left by Bandfield's doomed Heinkel, now spiraling eccentrically away, had been filled by another.

"Once again, Natty Flight, line astern, attacking, go." Bandfield savored the thrill of combat, wondering at his own detachment, at his lack of concern at having killed again.

Four thousand feet above, Galland's guttural voice crackled into Josten's earphones: "Attacking."

They plunged down on the three Hurricanes, Galland fastening onto the leader. The old pro flew bucking into Keeler's slipstream, letting the brown camouflaged fuselage fill his windscreen, aiming just forward of where the huge identity letters—RF and F—flanked the blue-white-red of the cockade. He pressed and quickly released the firing button for the two cowl-mounted machine guns and the two wing-mounted 20-mm cannon. The three-second burst slammed almost twenty pounds of lead into Keeler and his fuel tanks. Swirling flames and wreckage blotted out the sky around Galland as, unable either to turn or to stop, he lunged through the debris of the exploding Hurricane.

Josten slid over to attack the number three Hurricane. He fired carefully and saw his own victim stagger, turning inverted to plunge away burning, black smoke pouring from a vicious red blot of fire. "Twenty," he thought, "now that's a decent number."

The murderous assault on Keeler forced Bandfield into a violent turn to the right.

Josten pounced on him, trying to edge the remaining Hurricane into his sights when Galland gruffly ordered, "Return to base."

Josten horsed his Messerschmitt around, glancing down to the blinking red warning light. There was just enough fuel to make it to France. He trailed Galland, pushing over in a maneuver he knew the carburetor-equipped Hurricane could not follow. Diving, he realized how right the man had been the night before. All the preparation—and then no time to fight. If they'd had drop tanks they could have finished off the other Hurricane and perhaps protected the bombers for another half hour. He thought of them, plunging toward London, prey to the fighters being called down from beyond the Messerschmitt's range limits. It was outrageous! You couldn't fight today's war with yesterday's technology! Things had to change!

Turning back to reengage, Bandfield saw the two German fighters fast disappearing. He watched them go, at once ashamed to have been beaten so soundly—losing three out of four in a single attack was inexcusable—yet suffused with the unbelievable sense of vitality in being once again a survivor.

All of Spain's old combat fears and hatred welled over Bandfield. He had scarcely known Keeler or the Poles, but to lose them in a single mission seemed incredible, especially to just two enemy fighters. He set course back to Northolt, cursing the Germans, cursing the Hurricane.

We're going to have to come up with something a lot better than this, he thought. Wonder what Roget has cooking?

Wright Field/September 15, 1940

"Holy shit!—oops, sorry, Gracie." Hadley's priceless secretary, Grace Davidson, had joined him from California, and she strongly disapproved of bad language.

"Look at these, Gracie. Have you ever seen anything so beautiful in your life?"

Grace took the pile of proposals from him and began sorting them out in preparation for the meeting.

"Very nice, Hadley, but let me get these separated and put in folders before you lose everything."

"You do that, hon, and make sure we get a new file cabinet with some decent locks. That stuff's all top secret."

Roget had never liked paperwork before; now all he did was plow through reams of it, enjoying every moment. It wasn't the usual "you stamp my drawings and I'll stamp yours" review process that had suffocated him years before at Wright Field. Caldwell's project amazed him as its details unfolded before his information-greedy eyes. Even better, Caldwell continually called him in for advice on other projects. The two men shared a rare ability to envision the flow of air over an aircraft, all of it, not just over the wings and fuselage, but over the little details—struts, radiators, even rivets. It was what Tony Fokker had meant when he said, "You've got to see the spray." Only if you could "see the spray" could you tell if a design was really excellent. Too many people fixated on an individual element—the engine, the wing—and forgot that it is the whole airplane which flies.

Gracie was filing the evaluation of the response to the Request for Data R40C—Operation Leapfrog, an innocuous-sounding government inquiry that had detonated a charge of dynamite under the imagination of American aviation manufacturers.

Everything was in the file—sleek twin-boom pushers, crazy "tail-first" airplanes, flying wings—all the things Caldwell had said should be experimented with. Impatient with her calm methodic approach, Hadley shuffled down through the pile of folders and pulled out one marked "McDonnell Aircraft Company, St. Louis, Model 1."

"This is the one, Gracie, believe me. Nobody else thinks so, but just look at this beauty."

The airplane was a twin-engine fighter, conventional in everything except for the sinuous beauty with which its wing, fuselage, and engine nacelles were melded together.

"Lookee how this thing curves together, no angles; hell, it's built better than you are, Gracie—no offense. If they get the right engine for this little hummer, it's a winner. I'll bet they'll know what to do with jet engines when we get them some. You keep your eye on this outfit, Gracie, they are going places."

"You're going places, too. You're supposed to be at a meeting with Caldwell in Building 12 in ten minutes. You've just got time to walk over there; I put a copy of the new contract in your briefcase."

"Bless you, Gracie, I'm glad someone can keep me squared away. Be sure you stick that folder on the McNaughton jet in with the others."

Bless old Henry Caldwell, too, he thought as he walked. If it weren't for him, I wouldn't be here having all this fun. But the designs he carried tucked under his arm disturbed him. They were unusual-looking, but none projected the blazing potential he'd hoped to see. Maybe it wouldn't matter—not with the North American job coming along.

The previous year, the British Air Purchasing Commission, desperate for more fighters of any caliber, had asked Caldwell if he would object if they contracted with North American Aviation to build Curtiss P-40s for the RAF. The P-40 was already obsolete, but a new plant could begin building them with a minimum loss of time. Caldwell had been inclined to agree, but in January Hadley had dragged him out to Downey, California—the site of the old Roget Aircraft plant—to talk to the head of North American Aircraft, Dutch Kindleberger, about a new design. Roget had brought with him all the data from the labs of the National Advisory Committee for Aeronautics, back at Langley, and opened the meeting with an unwelcome bombshell.

"I've got the dope on a new airfoil Dutch should use—we've got to break away from the 1930 airfoils being used on the P-40."

The NACA had developed a whole series of brand new airfoils, thinner at the front than usual, with the thickest section farther aft. They promised to add both speed and range to airplanes using them.

Caldwell, mildly irritated that Roget had grabbed the leadership of the meeting from him, objected immediately.

"I've read those same damn reports, Hadley. Building a laminar flow wing calls for production tolerances beyond the capabilities of most companies. I don't want to buy fifty of these things, I want to buy five hundred, maybe five thousand."

The big numbers stirred Kindleberger, who was anxious to please Caldwell, and annoyed with Roget's trying to tell him which airfoil to use.

"We've got a good airfoil of our own, Hadley. I don't think we need laminar flow."

Roget shook his wild white hair, rolled his eyes to heaven, and raised his voice a few decibels. "You guys aren't listening. If you build this airplane, it's going to *have* to have a laminar flow wing to get the speed and range you want. Don't tell me you can't build it, Dutch. I've been talking to your best guys, Edgar Schmued and Ed Horkey, and I know they want to use it. You can build it, you're the best in the business."

In the end, he'd prevailed. Now the XP-51 was supposed to make its first flight before the end of the month—and everybody would see that he'd been right!

Dayton was suffering one of its dry summers, and the scanty patches of grass the Corps of Engineers had tried to plant were parched brown. A single tree struggled to survive in front of the laboratories of the Materiel Division, an example to the row of shriveled shrubs gasping along the curb. To Roget's left, dust rose from the grading being done for the new hangars and the Armament Lab's gun range. The whole field was in an ordered turmoil as new roads and buildings shot up, a reflection in miniature of America's industry springing into life, shaking off the decay of the Depression.

Overhead a steady procession of aircraft spaced themselves to come in to land, all taking care to avoid the construction work going on for Wright Field's first paved runway.

Damn, a paved runway, who would have thought it? He remembered, as he always did, that it was at the far end of the same field where Charlotte Hafner had crashed and burned in the Hafner bomber.

Roget walked into Building 12 and took the stairs two at a time up to the conference room by Caldwell's office. There was a steady roar that shook the glasses on the sideboard. He ran to the window and saw the huge Boeing XB-15 turning downwind. It was a good omen, for Caldwell was waiting to talk about its even bigger successor, the Boeing Model 345, the super secret XB-29. Roget wondered if anyone could build an airplane so advanced.

Dayton, Ohio/January 15, 1941

It was as wet and cold as only a midwinter storm in Ohio can be. The wind-driven clouds, overladen with moisture gathered over Lake Erie, were beginning to glaze the landscape below with a gravely dangerous mixture of sleet and freezing rain.

Clarice and Hadley were back in Salinas to settle on the sale of some property they held, and the Bandfields were alone in the big red house on Kettering Place, glad to have the place to themselves for a change.

Little George's first birthday party had gone well; the baby didn't know or care what was going on, but four-year-old Charlotte was happy to blow the candles out, monopolize the conversation, and in general be the star of the show. When the last bedtime song had been sung, the last glass of water delivered, and the last prayers said, Bandy went down to the living room. Patty's Christmas present had been a console record-changer from Sears, and he was busy stacking it with new records—"The Last Time I Saw Paris," "All or Nothing at All," "Taking a Chance on Love"—heavy stuff, he figured. With the kids in bed, the Rogets gone, some wine and sweet music, he felt he might have a chance at a little loving. He'd built a fire earlier and now stoked it to battle the moaning winds that sucked heat from the walls and windows.

Patty came in, hair pinned up and bundled into her old pink housecoat, fuzzy slippers slapping as she walked. Bandfield's desire ebbed a little; it was clear Patty didn't have loving on her mind tonight.

She nestled beside him, slipping under his arm as he continued to poke the fire.

"Do you realize this is the first birthday you've ever been home for either child?"

He kissed her absently on the side of the head and said, "Come on, now, this is the way fights start. I know I've been gone a lot, but it's not like I have a regular job. If Caldwell says go, I have to go." There was a welcome spurt of flames from the grate, and he added another lump of "smokeless" coal, gleaming black anthracite, the best you could buy.

"And it's not like he stays at home. He's on the go himself, all the time. He's off to Europe again."

"Sure, but he's a widower and his kids are grown up. How long before you leave again?"

"I'm not sure; he wants me to take an A-20 and drop down through Central and South America, to try to see what the German airlines are up to. Just show the flag, the usual stuff."

He poured wine, and they settled down on the battered couch that Hadley Roget had insisted be brought out from Salinas. It had been his only request—demand, really, for he was serious about it—and they had reluctantly given in. It was a big wooden-framed leather couch, the kind seen in the offices of ancient law firms, and the years hadn't treated it kindly. Clarice had tried to get rid of it more than once, but Hadley had always objected. Now it sat, tattered leather concealed beneath cotton throws, creaking in every joint as Patty snuggled tight and asked, "Did you ever think about what would happen to the children if one of us crashed?"

The question was cogent. Bandy was testing the newest aircraft, fighters and bombers, and Patty was flying around the country in a "civilian" Seversky P-35. Hap Arnold had called her "the best recruiter in the business," and she was always in demand at rallies to sell war bonds.

She pressed him. "What would you do if I were killed?"

"Jeez, Patty, let's not talk about stuff like this. I was hoping to get a little loving."

"You always want a little loving. But let's talk for a minute. If you get killed, I know I'll never marry again." Patty had lost her first husband in a racing accident.

"Well, it's pretty simple to me. If I get killed, you'll have to stop flying. The kids need somebody to take care of them. But if you got killed, I couldn't stop flying, not while there's a war on. So I guess you're the one who'd better stop."

"I wish I didn't think you were so right."

He kissed her, and she pulled away.

"You know the problem with you is that you don't need anyone, not me, not the kids, no one, not as along as you have your airplanes and your job."

"That's wrong. I need you and the kids a lot. It's just that men and women are different. It goes back to caveman times—the man had to be out in front with a club, fighting off dinosaurs, while the woman stayed by the fire with the kids."

"God, your knowledge of psychology is about as good as your knowledge of anthropology. There weren't any dinosaurs by the time the caveman was running around with his club."

"You know what I mean. And how about you? How much do you need me, when you're always off flying to sell war bonds?"

"It's different—I need you all the time; when I'm away, I ache for you. When you're gone, you probably never think about us."

"How'd we get into this? I spend a lot of money for new records, dig out the last bottle of claret from my trip to England, and you want to fight about who needs you. I'll tell you what I need, and that's a little *of* you."

He tugged at the tassel-corded belt that held her robe together. It came open, and he saw that she was nude.

"You little devil. Here I've been thinking I was going to seduce you, and you're way ahead of me."

"That's the way it's been all along. You never catch on, do you?"

He was tender with her at first, but the wine, the Rogets' absence, the kids all being tucked up in bed fast asleep, and the stark beauty of her body, recovered so swiftly from George's difficult birth, excited him.

She responded enthusiastically and they drove together, moving more and more violently, gasping for breath, whispering hot endearments into each other's ears. He asked, "Are you ready?" and as she screamed yes, Roget's old couch gave up the ghost to their flailing, disintegrating in a crash of splitting leather and flying splinters.

They climaxed, laughing, amid the wreckage of the couch, then lay side by side gasping with pleasure and amusement.

"Did the earth move?"

"No, but the goddamn couch sure did!"

It was fun until they heard Charlotte's voice piping from the doorway: "What you doing? Why you wrecking up the couch?"

Stockholm, Sweden/April 28, 1941

Palms sweating with nervousness, Countess Illeria Gortchakov forced herself to breathe deeply. She feigned interest in the small white-painted steamers bobbing at the quay below, staining the harbor sky with the ugly soot-laden black clouds of smoke. The passengers, mostly countryfolk from the north, scurried busily about with their rough bundles of luggage.

Breathing deeply made her feel better, as if Swedish air was cleaner than Germany's. She had just left the German legation, located only a few hundred yards from the hotel, between the National Museum and the Royal Automobile Club. The legation had a more relaxed attitude than she was accustomed to in Berlin, and she had been pleased to find some old family friends working there.

She was in Stockholm for a secret meeting with Henry Caldwell. To make her clandestine work easier, she had long ago acquiesced to a highly placed "special friend." It had not been difficult to persuade him to send her on a bogus mission to "check on propaganda material"—he thought she simply wanted a vacation and was happy to indulge her.

In the bitter four days after *Kristallnacht* in 1938, she had grown close to Henry Caldwell, who stayed at her side, using his position to try to wrest an answer from the obdurate German bureaucracy about the identity of the SA storm troopers who had harassed them. In the process the scale of the pogrom became obvious and she had steeled herself to fight the regime. Caldwell had sensed her feelings and bluntly asked her to spy for him. When she accepted, she volunteered that she was half-Jewish.

Surprised, Caldwell asked, "Does Helmut know of your background?"

"Yes—he wants to work out something for us, he's even talking about marriage. They won't let him."

"Of course not. If he even files the necessary papers, you'll be exposed. He shouldn't risk that."

"I agree. It would be impossible."

Caldwell had taken both of her hands in his and looked straight into her eyes. "Lyra, I want you to understand that espionage carries the penalty of death by beheading in Germany. And they would accuse Helmut as well."

"I realize that."

She still loved Helmut, responding physically to him as before, but it was increasingly difficult to accept his premise that he could be both a good human being and a good Nazi officer. His vision of technology saving Germany, at the same time somehow purging it of the Nazi regime, was overcast by his inveterate patriotism. Now all he really wanted was for technology to win the war.

In the three years since *Kristallnacht* she had communicated with Caldwell on five occasions. Each time he had initiated the contact, via a coded message in an advertisement in the *Berliner Tageblatt*. It was a primitive system, but it worked. And each time he had made a trifling request for innocuous information that he must have already had, or could readily have determined from open sources. She gradually realized that it was a testing and an incriminating process; he was seeing if she were sincere and, at the same time, gaining control over her. She'd already done more than enough to be accused of treason. The Gestapo was not fussy about whom it charged, nor about the validity of the charges.

Three floors above the veranda, Henry Caldwell had left his room door ajar, then gone back to adjust the motion picture projector he had borrowed from the American legation. He had arrived two days before from an abortive mission to Finland. The Finns had been very courteous, but their burning desire for revenge was obvious even as they refused his offer to supply McNaughton Sidewinder fighters. It was obvious to Caldwell that they were planning another war with Russia—and that could only happen if Germany invaded the USSR.

In Helsinki, he'd listened to more of the wild rumors on the progress of the German jet engine program. McNaughton was developing a jet engine and aircraft of its own design but had run into enormous problems keeping the turbine blades from melting from the fierce internal heat. Caldwell had to find out if the Germans were having problems, too.

He turned as Lyra slipped into the room, pausing only to check up and down the hallway before closing the door. They chatted briefly, and Caldwell got down to business.

"First, Lyra, I'm going to show you some raw British newsreel films of the Blitz. These have never been released to the public— just too horrifying. But I want to show you what Germany is doing to England, what it has done everywhere so far. And I want to show you what *will* happen to Germany, unless this war is stopped."

He started the film. "There isn't any soundtrack. This is London, during the raids on September eighteenth and twenty-second. The buildings you see are mostly workers' housing projects."

Lyra felt as if she had a box seat at a satanic opera as the camera focused on a workers' housing district in the loop of the Thames. There were strong fires in the center of the district, the flames fanning outward like a prairie burning. The cameraman switched to a telephoto lens, and the widening flames loomed suddenly closer with a frightening clarity of detail—a pub sign, blanched white in the inferno, hung above a row of grotesquely crumpled bodies, arms charred black, reaching upward, tiny babies still pressed in their mothers' arms. Then the camera focused on the outer wall of an apartment building just as it shook like aspic and collapsed. The façade tore away abruptly, suddenly injecting an oddly human note into the film. In the layered floors, each one identical to the one below, she could see the exposed sawtooth stairwells, the remains of kitchens, sinks still fastened to the surviving wall, pictures hanging at an angle, bathtubs and toilets suspended on stubs of floor. Another explosion collapsed the building completely.

The projector clattered to a halt. Lyra leaned forward and closed her eyes, determined that she would do *anything* to end the war, no matter what was asked, no matter whom it affected, even Helmut, even her parents; it didn't matter, the war must end.

Caldwell turned on the lights, then sat down beside her. "I'm sorry, Lyra, but I wanted you to see the real effects of what the Luftwaffe is doing. It's not brave battles between young athletes—it's a systematic, squalid killing of the innocent. I hope you never experience it."

"You've made your point. How can I help you?"

His voice softened, became almost paternal. "There is one issue that I need information on above all others, one I'm sure Helmut either knows about, or can find out about." Caldwell began a technical explanation of the jet engine, and Lyra put up her hand.

"Stop. I know I can help. Helmut is directly involved in the German jet engine program, working with a man you may know— Bruno Hafner."

Caldwell rocked back in his chair—it was impossible, Bruno was dead. He hesitated for a moment, then got up and poured drinks as he struggled to get control of his voice.

"Of course I knew Bruno Hafner. I bought airplanes for the Air Corps from his company years ago. But I thought he was dead."

"He was badly wounded in Spain, but he's recovered enough to drive Helmut crazy trying to get the jet engines working."

The news was a tremendous blow to Caldwell. Hafner would be a formidable enemy, amoral, absolutely ruthless, and an expert in manufacturing sophisticated aircraft. Recovering his poise, he asked, "What do you know about the program? Does Helmut talk to you about it?"

"He talks of nothing else. Helmut's monomaniacal about the jet plane, says it will be Germany's savior. I'd far rather have a woman rival than this utter dedication to a machine. And he's still flying combat—the work he does for Hafner is all extra duty. He is burning himself out."

"What does he say about it?"

"He won't talk about what happens in combat—for some reason that's private. But he tells me about his test work. For example, he was at the Heinkel factory at Marienehe earlier this month, and saw a prototype jet fighter fly. He was not too impressed, said its range was far too short. Messerschmitt apparently has a better plane in the works."

Germany had already flown one jet fighter and had another ready to go! It was almost as unbelievable as Hafner being alive.

"Do you know when the Messerschmitt jet will fly?"

"Ah, this is tricky to explain. Helmut flew a version of the Messerschmitt—they call it the 262—about ten days ago. But it was a special airplane—the two jet engines weren't installed. Instead, they had put a piston engine, with a propeller, in the nose, just to test the airframe."

It sounded absurd to Caldwell. "The jet engines weren't installed?"

"No, and he doesn't think they'll be ready for a year or more. They are having tremendous problems—the engines keep breaking apart. They just explode and burn on the test stands. Once a piece of burning metal landed on Helmut's shoulder. It burned right through his epaulette."

Caldwell felt partial relief. If Josten preferred the Messerschmitt, and it wasn't going to be ready for a year, then he could allow McNaughton some development time.

"Do you know Hafner?"

"I've met him. He's a hideous sight, scarred and crippled, but obviously brilliant. To tell you the truth, he frightens me. When we talked he somehow conveyed that he knew *everything* about me. It wasn't anything he said; it was the intent way he stared, with his eyelid drooping at half mast."

"Hafner was always well informed. Be careful with him."

"I think there is a better way for us to communicate. I have an old family friend who works here at the Legation. He's a monarchist and absolutely hates Hitler. I don't want to involve him, but he could get messages to your Legation, if you have a man you can trust there. They could meet here at the Grand."

Caldwell agreed quickly, his mind still trying to digest the import of Hafner being alive and working on the jet engine.

Above Minsk, Soviet Russia/June 29, 1941

The greatest invasion in history surged forward in an irresistible *feldgrau* tide. The immense Axis army—162 divisions, three million men—rolled forward from the Arctic to the Black Sea, driving great enveloping armored probes to trap the massed Russian forces. Just as Western Europe and the Balkans had fallen, so would Russia, the ancient enemy of the East. Adolf Hitler's *blitzkrieg* tactics were all-conquering.

Helmut Josten led his *Schwarm* of four Messerschmitt Bf 109Fs in a tight circle, protecting the little Fiesler Storch that hung below, immobile as a hat on a wall. The slow-flying Storch, a fabric-covered high-wing reconnaissance plane, was the aerial podium from which the maestro, General Heinz Guderian, orchestrated his Panzer divisions. Guderian didn't like to fly—was often airsick, in fact—but the distances in Russia were so vast that he couldn't operate out of a tank command post as he had when he raced through France.

The calm of the escort mission was a relief for Josten and his men, who had been flying five and six close-support sorties a day since the invasion started on June 22. On that first day, thirteen hundred Luftwaffe planes had flown more than four thousand missions, striking tirelessly behind the Russian lines, destroying bridges, railways, even not sparing the trains that were trundling toward the German border, still carrying supplies for the Reich. The Luftwaffe attacked everything that would permit the Russians to escape to fight another day. Airfields were priority targets, and the first collation of reports showed more than eighteen hundred Soviet planes destroyed against only thirty-five German losses.

Josten didn't know how many he himself had shot up on the ground—forty, fifty, perhaps more, planes of all kinds, ancient Po-2 biplanes, huge four-engine ANT bombers that looked like winged moving vans, and the ubiquitous flat-nosed I-16 fighters. Each one shot up on the ground was one less to dispose of in the air. Yet it was strange—once he had sought nothing but victories, now he resented the time he spent in the air, away from the jet project. There was so much to be done and so little time. Hafner was even more demanding than Galland.

He looked at the battle below, realizing that the extent of the Russian catastrophe was possible only because of an incredible contradiction of ideas. The military buildup was tremendous, completely out of scale with any German estimate of Russian strength. Yet the Russian military had submissively presented its neck to the Germans like a pekinese to a wolf, ignoring all the warning signs of war. They had left their airplanes lined up wing tip to wing tip, uncamouflaged, with only negligible flak to defend them, letting the Germans strip their air power from them like skin from a tangerine.

Josten had shot down Russian planes even more unsportingly than Galland had popped-off pheasants back in France. The Russians were unbelievably brave, incomprehensibly stupid. Their bombers were usually the twin-engine SB-2s that had been proven so vulnerable in Spain and in Finland, or the freakish-looking single-engine SU-2s; neither plane had the speed or the guns to defend itself. It was reinforcement of the lesson he hoped his leaders had learned over England: the quantity of planes wasn't nearly as important as their quality.

Yet with it all, Josten felt a deep stirring of unease. Two days before, his unit had been shifted to the south, where von Rundstedt's armies had needed additional air support. As he had flown the two-hundred-kilometer flight, he saw the full magnitude of the German effort. For miles behind a front that ranged the breadth of

Russia there were columns of trucks, horses, artillery, all the impedimenta of war. The number of horses amazed him. The *Wehrmacht* was supposed to be mechanized, but most vehicles were horse-drawn. Still, it seemed incredible that all the tremendous quantities of materiel could have been squeezed out of a Germany so impoverished that bread was now two thirds wheat and one third bran. There was no fat left for the nation to feed upon. This first attack on Russia must not fail; there would be no second chance. The quantities of men and materiel the Germans were overrunning was enormous—but the Russians had a much larger base to draw from. Could the gigantic German war machine endure and prevail?

As Guderian's Storch was gliding in to land, he saw a flicker on the horizon and grew instantly alert. The flicker changed into dots, then crosses; three aircraft were coming, Russian fighters flying in their old-fashioned V-formation. He called, "Russian fighters, due east, altitude about two thousand meters." His *Schwarm* climbed behind him, each man mentally checking off his victory score. Josten was disappointed that there were only three; at best he could run his victory string to forty, perhaps forty-one. The thought made him laugh—a number of pilots already had scores approaching the legendary heroes of World War I, von Richthofen and Udet. Who would ever have believed it?

He led his Messerschmitts toward the oncoming Polikarpov I-16s, stubby little monoplanes that he had fought against in Spain, wonderfully maneuverable but dangerously unstable. He signaled and they dove to the attack.

The I-16s formed up in a line-abreast formation to meet the attack. Josten noted with satisfaction that the Russians began firing at far too long a range, the mark of the amateur, their cowlings lighting up with the fire from the 7.62 ShKAS machine guns, with slower bursts coming from the 20-mm ShVAK cannons mounted in the wings.

The explosion of the number three Messerschmitt killed Josten's satisfaction as it tossed his own aircraft into a vertical bank. To his left, the fourth Messerschmitt was pulling up with a huge cloud of white smoke pouring from the radiator. These Russians were sharpshooters! Stunned, Josten and his wingman flashed through the enemy formation, breaking all the tactical rules by separating. Josten dove to the left, cursing himself for letting the Russians get the advantage. He was followed by the lead I-16 as the other two Russians raced toward his wingman, Balzar, now desperately turning to rejoin.

Josten soon realized that the Russian pilot was better than anyone he'd fought since England. They danced a strange aerial polka, the Russian continuously turning, snaking his stubby nose around on a schilling to try to bring his guns to bear, Josten climbing and diving, using his superior speed to seek an advantage. He gasped with the physical exertion—the strain of the G forces pressing him into the seat, the enormous effort required to pull the stick back, the broiling Russian summer compounded by the heat pouring back from the straining engine. As they circled the sun sent dizzying semaphore flashes off a lake below each time they turned. Sweat drained from him, and he would have given his wings for a drink of water.

The Russian was elusive as an eel, using the instability of the I-16 to tumble out from under his sights, then magically reappearing in a firing position behind. Perspiration soaked Josten, and his breath came harder. Off to his right, where his wingman Balzar should have been, there was nothing but a huge cloud of black smoke.

The I-16 turned into him again, all guns blazing, and Josten squirmed down into his seat. The two planes hurtled head-on together, closing at nine hundred kilometers an hour, neither willing to give way. He tried to hide behind the engine as he pumped shells into his enemy. The round green snout of the I-16 grew larger, pieces beginning to break off it as his cannon shells hit home. A tremendous explosion drove hope from his consciousness as his Messerschmitt disintegrated around him, slinging him into space. He felt the rush of wind, saw the whirling earth and sky exchanging places, and realized that he was alive. He hesitated, wanting both to slow down and to get some distance from the battle before pulling the rip cord.

The harness straps slammed together in his crotch and across his chest as the parachute opened. As he drifted down, the green Russian I-16, streaked with oil and showing lots of battle damage, circled around him like a shark about a wounded whale. He could see the pilot's face and waved to him. There was no response, and the I-16 pulled away in a sharp turn, then reversed to bear down on him, bullets crackling from its cowl guns. What a shabby way to go, he thought, bracing himself for the impact of the bullets.

Somehow the Russian missed, and as he turned to attack again Balzar came thundering down from behind, guns blazing. The startled Russian overcontrolled and his I-16 spun out, Balzar falling behind to snap shoot at it all the way down. Josten was still watching the combat as his feet hit the ground near a German flak battery.

Aching from the jolt of the parachute opening and embarrassed at his defeat, he was gathering up his parachute when Balzar flashed by overhead, waving his wings to signify a victory. Well, he thought, I owe him a drink for this one. We'll have to have a "birthday party" tonight to celebrate being alive.

Galland came into Josten's mind again. He should have seen this. If the Russians have many shooters like this last one, we are in for a long war.

Moscow/September 14, 1941

Few observers would have agreed with Josten as the gorgeous weather gleamed bright against the pipe-organ columns of smoke and flame marking the collapsing front. The Germans were advancing from Narva in the north to Zaporozhye in the south. Even the arch-conservative Chief of the General Staff, Franz Halder, a prophet of gloom and doom, reluctantly noted in his diary that the war was won.

But in Moscow, people savored the sun-soft September as a swimmer does the air before a dive, knowing that in only a few brief weeks an endless sea of mud would divide the seasons between dust and frost. The first group of Siberian soldiers had arrived and were bivouacked in the streets, staring at a hawk riding the shimmering waves of heat that radiated from the Kremlin's bricks. Sweating in their heavy uniforms, they pointed at the bird, soaring effortlessly around the onion domes of Ivan the Terrible's wonderful St. Basil's Cathedral, never seeming to beat its wings. It was exactly like birds they had at home, the only familiar, comforting sight in the ancient city.

In a long narrow room of the Kremlin's green-domed Council of Ministers building, a different sort of hawk was trying vainly to stifle a yawn.

Henry Caldwell's struggles were watched with amusement by Commissioner Giorgi Scriabin. Scriabin, sixty-plus with a shock of silver-gray hair and bright blue eyes, ran his staff with an iron hand. Short and squat, dressed in the universal chalk-striped gray suit of an upper-level Soviet bureaucrat, his flushed face was an anomaly. Although for the most part it was pure Slavic, with a heavily ridged brow, deepset, slit eyes, and commanding jaw, instead of the usual Slavic nose, his was almost Cyranoesque, long and mottled with veins. He was unaware that he used it as a pointer, bobbing it to emphasize his remarks or to signal that someone could speak. It mesmerized the group, Russians and Americans alike, and gave control of the meeting to him. Scriabin didn't have the appearance of an educated man, but he was gifted with a talent for languages. He spoke German, Swedish, French, and English—the last with a pronounced Brooklyn accent.

Caldwell grunted and shook himself, remembering that he'd used Scriabin's negotiation ploy himself in the past. You stall all morning, feed the opposition a heavy lunch, and then close them up in a hot room. Within an hour, their eyes glaze over and their resistance goes down.

A heavy lunch was a rarity in war-panicked Moscow, but Scriabin had arranged for shashlik and potatoes, washed down with endless vodka toasts. He noted that Caldwell drank down his vodka, not dissembling like many of the Americans just pretending to drink. Then, to raise the drowsiness quotient, Scriabin had made sure that the draperies and windows were tightly closed.

The American was there as a part of an advance team flown in on Consolidated B-24 bombers, to assist the patrician Averell Harriman arrange the terms of the new Lend-Lease program. If the Germans could be held off for just a few more months, the combination of unlimited Russian manpower and unlimited American materiel could defeat Hitler.

Caldwell's task was to lay the groundwork for aviation supplies and aircraft deliveries, and the process was far more difficult than he had imagined it would be. They were, after all, offering the Soviet Union enormous quantities of everything from aluminum to zinc, from aircraft to X-ray machines, and yet the Russian negotiators acted like Teamsters just informed that hours were going up and wages going down. They were monumental note-takers, writing continuously on pads of coarse paper, a beige woody pulp that would have been rejected as newsprint in the States.

"Comrade Scriabin, could you arrange to have some windows opened? I find myself getting very sleepy after that excellent lunch."

Scriabin's nose described a horizontal arc as he shook his head no.

"I'm sorry, General Caldwell, I cannot, for security reasons."

They smiled at each other as Caldwell cursed him under his breath, wondering what security risk could be locked away in the Kremlin.

His point made, Scriabin continued. "So, my American friends, we are agreed upon the bombers. Douglas A-20s, 'Bostons' you call them, and North American B-25s, 'Mitchells.' Now back to the pursuits, P-47s and P-38s."

Caldwell leaned forward, trying to will circulation to his legs and buttocks, speaking with increased forcefulness. "I've explained to you that while our desire to be generous is unlimited, our resources are not. We will send Curtiss Warhawks and McNaughton Sidewinders as fast as we can produce them. We don't have enough P-47s or P-38s for our own training units yet."

"When can we get P-47s and P-38s?" It was the fourth time that Scriabin had asked.

"As soon as possible—I don't know when. But we will have two hundred Sidewinders ready for acceptance by the end of this month."

Scriabin leaned back. He liked this man, and he hoped that he could trust him. The Germans were flying Messerschmitts, fine, deadly airplanes; he didn't know if the McNaughton was a worthy opponent. Some of his advisors said that it was not. Yet two hundred airplanes of any sort were better than none.

His voice was pleasant as he asked, "General Caldwell, are these the same airplanes you offered Finland last April?"

Caldwell steadied himself, emptying a little of the foul Russian *makhorka* into a pipe, to give himself time to prepare an answer.

"Why yes, Comrade Scriabin. You'll recall that in those days— they seem so distant now, don't they?—we were concerned about the millions of rubles of war supplies that Russia was sending Germany; in fact, the general consensus was that the Soviet Union was going to enter the war on the German side. It was only natural that we would wish to help a possible ally. Now all that has changed, of course."

Scriabin sputtered and Caldwell continued. "We have our intelligence sources, too. I can assure you that the McNaughton fighter will be at least as good as your LaGG-3. Please forgive my pronunciation, but I believe your pilots say it takes its initials from '*lakirovanny garantirovanny grob*'—the 'varnished wooden coffin'?"

It had been the right tack. Scriabin's fair skin gleamed red as he shouted to change the subject. "General Caldwell, what our pilots say or don't say is none of your damn business. Russia is in danger. Kiev has fallen. By tonight the Germans will have cut off the Crimea. I don't believe we can hold Leningrad. I ask you how you would like it if the Germans had taken New York, Chicago, and New Orleans, and were two hundred miles from Washington?"

"We wouldn't like it. But it wouldn't change the production situation. We'll give you McNaughtons because they are excellent aircraft and they are available. More no one can do."

When the meeting had ended, most of the others left swiftly. Scriabin grinned at Caldwell like an accomplice, tacit recognition that they had taken each other's measure. "Cut the *makhorka* a little finer for your pipe. It's an acquired taste, but if you smoke it for a while it makes other tobacco insipid."

Berlin/November 21, 1941

Helmut Josten was lying quietly by Lyra in bed, the first frantic desires sated; his arm was about her as she nestled into his side, her left leg slung over his right, her toes resting on his, tapping them lightly. But something was wrong—he was angry. Did he know something?

They were on the fourth floor of a block of flats, in the "apartment" that the von Hatzfeldt family had offered Lyra on her arrival. It was tiny, no more than a bedroom, bath, and little kitchen, but it was free. The proprietors were grateful to have someone there, keeping their eyes on things, while they sat out the war in their apartment in Rome.

"What's the matter?"

Without a word, he took her hand and pulled her out of bed and along the long hallway. At the end was a window set high in the wall; beneath it was a stout table.

"Climb up here and tell me what you see."

She did as he asked.

"I see the street in front of the apartment." She realized immediately what the trouble must be. "Do you spend your time spying on me when I'm gone?"

"I didn't think I was spying. I thought I was an eager lover, watching for your return so that I could open the champagne and have a glass waiting. And what do I see? A huge big touring sedan, a Maybach, no less, pulls up, and who pops out? You."

"And what of it?"

"Well, to begin, you hadn't mentioned it. I know that if I'd been given a ride in a Maybach, I'd tell the world about it. They only make a few hundred cars a year, and each one costs perhaps fifty thousand marks. And only the most elite people have them."

She led the way back down the hall. Even though he was hurt and angry, he could not keep from admiring the delicate ease with which she walked, the symmetry of her hips and buttocks.

"Further, my little anti-Nazi *provocateuse*, I don't think anyone owns a Maybach unless he is a top Party member."

"I notice you didn't let your anger interfere with your lust. I guess you needed a quick tumble before you lectured me."

He ignored the point, a valid one. "Let me see. It couldn't be Hitler; he is above sex, and anyway, he's a Mercedes man. It couldn't be Goering; Emma wouldn't let him. It couldn't be Himmler; it's common knowledge that his secretary keeps him fully occupied in bed. So who does that leave? Our own dwarf, Joseph Goebbels."

She poured the Henkell champagne, a gift from Goebbels, angrily splashing it about, then lay down on the bed, crossing her legs firmly.

He persisted. "So, please, fault my logic. Prove to me I'm wrong about this mysterious man who owns a Maybach."

"What makes you think it is a man?"

Embarrassment flooded him; he had made a fool out of himself. Josten remembered immediately that Magda Goebbels had befriended Lyra. He stuttered, "Well, not many women . . ."

"What an evil little mind you have, Helmut. That's the real Nazi in you, believing the worst, never even giving me a chance to explain, virtually accusing me of sleeping with that disgusting dwarf. Magda is always good to me—she gave me this champagne we're drinking."

"I'm sorry, Lyra; I was stupidly jealous. Forgive me."

"Of course. It's flattering that a decorated fighter pilot can make such a fool of himself over me."

He moved up, kissing her as he went, till he sought her mouth in a deep kiss. She kissed him passionately.

"I'm sorry, Lyra, to be such a fool. It's just that we see each other so little. It's the strain of Udet's funeral, too."

Josten had been brought back to serve as a honor guard at the funeral of Ernst Udet. Officially, Udet had been killed "testing a new air weapon." The truth was that he'd committed suicide, unable to bear the pressures of being Inspector General of the Luftwaffe.

Opening another bottle of champagne, Josten said, "I've brought some Veuve Clicquot; it's in the refrigerator."

"Plenty of room; God knows there's little enough food there."

"I've brought things to eat, too; pâté, a really good salami, some bread, and some sardines. We'll have a feast."

"Later, my love. Come sing a song of love to me."

"I can't sing to you, but just lie still and let the Gieseking of the mattress play a *Klavierkonzerte*, a little sweet night music, upon you."

"Play as you've never played before, Maestro . . ."

Afterward, they lay closely together, feeling each other's heartbeats begin to subside from the racing crescendo of passion.

"Lovemaking is so wonderfully sticky, isn't it?" she asked.

"That was tremendous. Do you know, at times I felt that I was somehow out of my body, just watching us?"

"A voyeur, too, eh? That's having your cake and eating it, isn't it?"

"No cake, but salami, champagne, and a full ten hours ahead of us before we part. What could be better than that?"

"Eleven hours."

"Eleven years. Why won't you marry me?"

"God, Helmut, don't ruin this. We can't get married because I'm Jewish and you're a Nazi. That's pretty clear. And pour me some champagne."

Having just plunged through one patch of thin ice, he skirted this one.

"Sorry. Poor timing. But I will prevail. We will get married. That's the last I'll say about it."

"Good. There's nothing I want more, and there's nothing more improbable. Let's just enjoy what we have."

"I'll drink to that; not many people have so much."

Wheeler Field, Hawaii/December 5, 1941

Frank and Patty Bandfield lay on the golden sands of Waimea Beach, locked in that self-congratulatory postcoital embrace long-married couples feel when a sudden flame of excitement has swept over them and they have more than measured up to the challenge. It was long past sunset on the deserted beach, and they'd taken an illicit delight in their passion. The trip to Hawaii was in part a reward, but Bandfield's mission was to solve some engine-cooling problems on the new Curtiss P-40s that had just arrived in the islands.

The couple lazed together, watching a yellow-green phosphorescence burbling at the water's edge, more relaxed than they'd been in years. They'd arrived in Oahu in early November, surprised to find the island beautiful even in the rainy season. The trip was proving to be wonderful for Charlotte, who had become somewhat shy as George began to take attention away from her. It was good for George, too. He'd been a late walker—almost fourteen months before he was really on his own—and now he was making up for lost time, padding up and down the beach, plopping in the water.

Sometimes Patty and Bandy would steal away to explore the island in a rusty 1933 De Soto sedan the Maintenance Squadron commander had loaned them, exploring the rough back roads, farm wagon-worn ruts between the fields of pineapple or sugar cane. Other times they would take long walks around Kahana Bay. People told them that they were missing the real beauty of spring and summer, but they found more than enough to admire, from the blatantly sexual antherium to nameless tiny white flowers. And, best of all, the kids slept soundly at the other end of their spartan, lanai-style open guest quarters. At sunup, the outrageously feathered birds would begin an aria competition, birdy opera stars practicing voice exercises. The chorus would start off low, building in volume until it sounded like an explosion in an aviary. It was a lovely way to awaken, and for the first time in years they had time for leisurely, familiarly conjugal lovemaking, touching and playing affectionately, telling each other with gestures how good it was to be together, how foolish all the arguments were, building to a mellow satisfaction that still left a little edge of appetite. There were quiet talks and little courtesies afterward—getting the coffee, bringing a magazine—gestures more important than the joining. Their life took on a new domesticity; in Hawaii, twenty-four hundred miles from the States, they achieved a closeness and a sense of family that had eluded them in California or in Ohio. Patty knew that most of the problem had been her own flying career—it was time that she put it behind her.

The happy tone for the entire trip had been set at their initial reception at Wheeler Field. Bandfield had been briefed—warned—that Willie Westerfield was the commander of the 19th Air Base Group, overseeing the two maintenance squadrons with which Bandy would be working. Their last meeting had been many years ago, when Westerfield had scuttled Bandfield's flying career—or so they had thought. As tall and thin as Ichabod Crane, Westerfield had been the senior officer of the board investigating the mid-air collision between Bandfield and his fellow cadet Charles Lindbergh. Bandfield still stirred with resentment when he remembered Westerfield, in a cleft-palate Kentucky twang marshalling the "evidence," his thin-slit alligator eyes staring unblinking at the board as he recommended that Bandfield be washed out. Lindbergh got off scot-free.

What the review board didn't know, and Bandfield was too young and scared to tell them, was that Westerfield's recommendation was influenced by another matter—Bandfield's brief, chaste romance with a lovely Mexican girl named Maria. Captain Westerfield was very interested in Maria himself.

Time and Patty had long since healed Bandfield's wounds, and he had probably gone further in flying out of the Air Service than he would have in it, so he was prepared to be friendly. Still, he was a little apprehensive as he stood opposite the main barracks, Building 102, to face the row of family quarters. Like their guesthouse, the houses were of undistinguished island architecture, but the grounds were studded with impressive barrel-bottomed coconut palms and breathtaking foliage, all held together with the drafting table neatness of a white-washed peacetime permanent station. A young adjutant, Lieutenant Dunning, puppy-eager to please, escorted them through Westerfield's quarters toward the sound of ukulele music and laughter. At Army flier gatherings, the celebration—that is, the pouring of drinks—started the moment the first person showed up.

The Bandfields followed Dunning over mat-scattered polished teakwood floors toward the garden, where a forest of leis served as a backdrop for Westerfield, Adam's apple bobbing, his tanned face betraying both years of drinking and many hours of flying. Bandfield felt a little squeeze of apprehension when he realized that the woman next to him was a slightly plumper but still beautiful Maria.

Westerfield stepped forward, leis in hand, twanging, "Aloha! Welcome to Wheeler Field!"

Bandfield didn't know how to salute a major carrying flowers, so he stuck out his hand instead. Westerfield enfolded it, pulling him to him, and boomed out again, "You may remember my wife— Maria, Major Bandfield."

Maria slid toward him, throwing first her leis and then her arms around his neck, kissing him as she said, "Oh, Bandy, you've come for me at last!"

Bandfield shot an agonized glance at Patty as Westerfield burst into wild laughter.

"Got you that time, Major! You thought I'd forget, didn't you?"

The rest of the party was a little less stressful. Maria ruefully apologized to Patty for the trick.

"He made me do it. That's the sort of thing that keeps him from being promoted, that and his drinking, but I love him anyway." With a few words the two women established that they were married to equally goofy mates, always a basis for instant inter-wife friendship.

Pilot reunions are a little different than most; instead of recounting old friends' successes and failures, they tend to run to who has crashed and how, with the best stories being foolish survived accidents. Underneath lay the tacit understanding that those who crashed were somehow at fault to a degree the speakers could never be. Instead of "Did you hear old So-and-so got divorced," it was "Old So-and-so propped his old Jenny and it got away from him! He grabbed hold of the elevator, and the damned thing dragged him from Clover Field to Long Beach," or "Remember 'Downwind'

Faulkner? Always drunk? Bailed out of a B-10 over Cleveland, chute didn't open, went right through the roof of a saloon, landed on the bar! Talk about poetic justice."

When they got down to business, Bandfield found that Westerfield had invited all the key people he'd be working with. He had been worried that he might be viewed as a feather-merchant expert from out of town, but the pilots were as concerned as he was about the overheating problems of their new P-40s and welcomed Bandfield's experience. The most interesting among them was Lieutenant James Curtiss Lee, affable, ingratiating, yet somehow disturbing to Bandfield.

Lee was just back from China, where Chennault's newly formed Flying Tigers were experiencing exactly the same P-40 engine-cooling problem that Bandfield was in Hawaii to solve. Chennault, now a brigadier general in the Chinese Air Force, had directed Lee to go wherever he had to—Hawaii, Wright Field, the Curtiss plant in Buffalo—but to solve the problem. Lee was happy to have a chance to do it on Oahu and glad to work with Bandfield. Bandfield knew he needed Lee's help, but by the end of the party he had figured out his unease with the man. Like of lot of up-and-coming young officers, Lee's charm masked an implicit message: be nice to me now, because you're going to be working for me later.

Wheeler Field Flight Line/December 7, 1941

Bandfield left a pot of coffee for Patty when he went to meet Jim Lee at six o'clock—the two men were both early risers. The line chief, Master Sergeant Norman Higbee, was on deck as always; he resolutely refused to let anyone work on "his" airplanes without being present. Higbee was old Army, broad-shouldered and big-bellied, a hillbilly with sun-bleached hair that stood white against skin that burned but never tanned. He was suspicious of everyone, officers, the native Hawaiians, and especially the new troops filling up the tents between the ramp and the runway. Equally devoted to work and to booze, he divided his days and nights between them. He didn't get along with many people; he did get along with Bandfield and, to a lesser extent, with Lee.

In the last two weeks, the three men had pretty well isolated the engine-cooling problem. The task of forcing enough air through the radiator was enormously difficult. The designers always wished to minimize the size and frontal areas of the radiators to reduce drag and were always optimistic about the resulting cooling effectiveness. Then, as other factors forced changes—higher power settings, cowling modifications, operation in different climates—the engines would overheat just as they always had in the past.

Higbee had watched doubtfully when Bandfield removed the cowling and drilled holes in it. He was even more dubious when tufted strings were inserted through the holes. No one had authorized the modification, and he hated to see a flatland foreigner, even a good Joe like Bandfield, punching holes in one of his airplanes. But Bandy conned him along, and when they ran the airplane up on the ground, letting it roar at full power while the temperature indicator climbed, all three stood close together observing how the tufted flows danced, peering through the shimmering lethal disc of the propeller. Once, for comparison, they had run the engine with only a few of the strings in the holes, and the remaining tufts lay perfectly flat, with the temperature leveled off well within the normal operating range. It told them that there was some sort of pressure disturbance around the lip of the intake, one that might be cured by drilling more holes. They would test the theory this morning.

Jim Lee was holding the P-40's radiator cowling, a piece of aluminum as large and shapely as a 1941 Cadillac fender, running his fingers over the curved inner edge. "They build them strong enough to take a beating from the air pressure, vibration, everything. Firing the guns must shake the hell out of it."

Bandfield nodded. "This curve is a little airfoil, giving us lift where we don't want it. I think it spoils the airflow through the radiator by setting up a burble at the mouth. Let's drill the bejesus out of this one to try to break up the pressure area, leak it right through. Then we can fill in behind the lip with putty, tape it down, and run it up on the ground. Between smoothing the inside contour and boring holes in the lip, we should have it."

Lee nodded. "Sounds reasonable. Why don't you get the guns belted up, and I'll take it out over to the firing range and see what the effect of firing the guns is."

Higbee spoke up. "Way ahead of you, Lieutenant. I've already belted up this one, and I gotta spare standing by, fully fueled and armed. All we'd have to do is swap the chin cowlings and go."

They had finished the work and were tightening the Dzus fasteners on the cowling when Lee looked up to see some aircraft, so well remembered from his China combat experience, sliding in over the Waianae Mountains. His jaws moved wordlessly, not believing the familiar shapes could be here, so far from China—then he sputtered, "Holy Christ, here come the fucking Japs!"

Just to the left of Kolekole pass, two large formations of aircraft were outlined against the mist cresting the green haze of the range, shadowing past like fish in a shoal.

"The first group's dive-bombers—looks like Mitsubishi fighters behind them." Lee jumped off the wing and ran to the other P-40 while Bandfield threw himself in the cockpit, hands flying around the controls to get the engine started. Higbee pulled the chocks from each plane, then sprang to the wing of a third Curtiss, opening up the access plates to load ammunition.

Within a minute, the two P-40Cs were rolling straight ahead into the wind, taking off from the grass triangle enclosed by the intersecting runways.

In both cockpits, the pilots automatically went through the myriad motions necessary to raise the gear, close the cowl flaps, snap the switch to charge the six .50-caliber wing guns, and turn the reflector sights on, all the housekeeping details of preparing for battle, while at the same time tracking the Japanese, choosing a place to attack. It took Bandy two and a half minutes to lead the climb to five thousand feet, get some altitude to trade for speed, and take a moment to be sure they were properly prepared for combat. A moment of stark terror in Spain had taught him that there was nothing worse than pressing the trigger of unarmed guns. Looking to the south as he turned, he saw swirls of aircraft making magpie dives into the boiling clouds of smoke rising from Pearl Harbor.

Anger and reluctant admiration forced him to think, They're really working us over. It's one hell of a strike! For a moment he debated about flying to Pearl for his attack, then realized he'd lose time going back to rearm and refuel. There were plenty of targets over Wheeler.

Higbee was on the wing of a fourth P-40, laying in with sweating hands the belts of .50-caliber ammunition brought out to him by some grinning young soldiers, so inexperienced they were enjoying the bombing as much as fireworks over a carnival midway. He darted a glance up from his work in time to see two bombs destroy the supply building, blowing its corrugated roof into four huge waving scythes that slashed through palm trees like a steak knife through a filet. Another bomber flashed by, crew members' heads visible, black-goggled coconuts behind the glistening canopy. Higbee saw the big rising-sun insignia and made a mental note of the black tail number, EII-214, irrationally determined to put the pilot on report for low-flying.

As the Japanese bombers circled the field, a wave of Zero fighters came in low to strafe the rows of immobile aircraft, sitting-duck targets tied to the ramp. It was clear that the Japanese had practiced well, their quick bursts shifting from plane to plane. Each burning plane threatened its neighbor, and the field came alive with people trying to save them, pushing them away from the fires, even as airplanes exploded and hangars collapsed. Partly clad soldiers swarmed from the tent area like ants, frantically pitching in to put out the fires or prepare planes for takeoff. Higbee and a crew of four were able to get four P-40s and three McNaughton Sidewinders ready for any pilots who showed up, while other scratch teams were loading them with ammunition belts.

One of the Japanese Aichi D3A bombers had strayed out of formation. A beautiful aircraft, with a slender, long greenish-silver fuselage and Spitfire-like elliptical wings punctuated at each end with the rising sun insignia, it reminded Bandfield of the old Curtiss A-12 attack plane.

Bandfield had learned combat in Spain and honed his knowledge in England, and he knew that shooting at an airplane was easy but hitting it was very difficult. He held his fire, letting the Aichi fill his sights, approaching so close that he could see the rear gunner taking pictures of burning Wheeler Field with a hand-held camera. Thinking, Now there's a real fucking tourist, he pressed the control stick trigger. Only the three guns in the left wing fired, but the stream of bullets exploded the Aichi's center fuel tank, sending the pilot and his tourist gunner to oblivion.

Lee had attacked on a ninety-degree angle to Bandfield, ignoring the sporadic antiaircraft fire and shooting directly into the cockpit of the lead aircraft. It staggered and veered out of formation just as a flight of three Zeros dropped on Lee's tail. He dove away to escape.

Their pilots unaware of Bandfield's kill, the Japanese bombers roared across the field with him in formation; he fired again just before they dropped their bombs, and another dive-bomber nosed straight over to plunge directly into an ancient Boeing P-26 fighter parked at the end of the flight line. Bandfield maintained formation and was ready to shoot again when the Zeros caught him, the concentrated fire from two fighters crashing into his engine, tearing off the cowling over which he had labored so intensely. The propeller shuddered to a halt, turning from a source of power into a gigantic air brake that sent him mushing toward the ground. The Zeros resumed their strafing runs. By sheer accident Bandfield was in perfect position for a straight-in approach to runway 24.

There was no problem telling the wind direction; all of Wheeler Field was in flames, a mountainous cloud of black smoke streaming parallel to the flight line. Dropping like an elevator, he went through the P-40's complicated gear-down drill; nothing happened as the smoke-and-flame-studded field raced upward at him. He jammed the stick forward, forcing the nose almost straight down to maintain flying speed. The gear snapped down just as he crunched into the ground and rebounded crazily toward the ramp.

Got to get another airplane, Bandfield thought. Throwing himself out of the cockpit, he ran toward the flight line, now sheathed in flames billowing from the line of destroyed hangars. The ramp was heaped high with the jumbled carcasses of destroyed airplanes. A

Curtiss P-36 was burning fiercely and two of the little Boeing-Pea-Shooters had been tossed together, the wing of one draped in comradely fashion over the other.

Lee had climbed back into the battle, dropping behind a Zero that had just strafed the flight line and had pulled up to do a series of impeccable barrel rolls.

Extraordinary thing to do in a fight, Lee thought, as he watched the fire-dotted lines of his tracers intersect with the Zero just as it rolled inverted again, its gleeful Japanese pilot unaware that he had one second to live. The bullets of all six guns reached their harmonized point within the Zero's thirty-eight-gallon fuselage tank, turning man and metal into a red fireball. Out of ammunition, Lee chopped his throttle and sank into a steep approach, ingrained habit causing him to check his watch as he touched down. It was 8:42 A.M. as he turned in toward chaos.

Still working like a demented dervish, Higbee saw the next wave of Zeros moving in to strafe; he dropped under a P-40, heard the thud of bullets and roar of exploding tanks as the little silver-gray fighters whipped by overhead. When he crawled out he grunted in dismay. Only two of the fighters they had prepared under fire were still whole, a P-40 and a Sidewinder, the rest burning or badly damaged. He saw Bandfield and Lee running toward him and signaled them into the two surviving aircraft. Lee leapt into the P-40, his engine catching even as his chute harness was being cinched up. Bandfield jumped on the wing of the streamlined Sidewinder—next to the P-40 it looked more like a racer than a fighter—and climbed through the automobile-style door into the tiny cockpit.

Bandfield felt uneasy in the unfamiliar plane, his legs spread by the drive shaft that ran from the aft-mounted engine to the propeller. When the engine caught the airplane shook like a washing machine with one caster gone, vibrating so badly that his vision blurred. He'd forgotten how rough the engine-propeller coupling was at idle speeds. Back at Wright Field, he'd flown perhaps twenty hours in the McNaughton, always swearing that he would never use it in combat. The P-40 was no Spitfire, but it at least gave you the sense you could compete.

Bandfield followed Lee, heading south toward Pearl. After six minutes, he saw a formation down low; the airplanes were different than those that had attacked Wheeler.

Over the radio, Lee called, "Ah, Major Bandfield, if you read me, there's a flight of eight Nakajima torpedo planes heading toward us. I'm attacking now."

Bandfield clicked his transmitter and bent the throttle forward on the Sidewinder, trying to flog three hundred miles an hour out of it. Checking his armament, he saw that the 37-mm cannon wasn't loaded; he had to depend on the four .50-caliber wing guns.

Ahead, one of the Japanese planes blew up, and he saw Lee diving away, then zooming into a climb just as he started his own attack.

The controls on the Sidewinder were heavy, and he used brute force to turn in behind the last of the Japanese torpedo planes, inching his sight up toward the fuselage center section.

The Japanese pilot flicked his controls and darted out of Bandfield's sights to begin an intricate aerial ballet that set them drifting back toward Pearl Harbor. Even as he concentrated on the fight, Bandfield's peripheral vision registered the acres of flame and smoke at Pearl and the hundreds of isolated dots of fire around Oahu.

The Japanese pilot was good, jinking left to disappear into thin air. Bandfield rolled and turned, unable to find him, then banked back to chase the formation again. He had just picked another target when his Sidewinder bucked and shuddered as if it were being beaten by a telephone pole flail. Machine-gun fire burst through the aft section of the fuselage and spattered against his armored seat. The aircraft suddenly became very quiet, with the propeller ticking to a stop in front of him. Smoke filled the cockpit and Bandfield didn't hesitate, popping the car-door entrance open, just as the emergency manual called for, and sliding out and down the wing.

It wasn't until the chute opened that the realization hit him that he'd been shot down by a goddamn bomber! What a total failure the Sidewinder was! Or was it? Maybe it was just him, getting over the hill, no longer able to cut the mustard.

• • •

Bandfield hitched a ride back to Wheeler to find that Lee had landed, shot up but unwounded at Ewa Field. Wheeler, once the stronghold of Hawaiian aviation, was wiped out; by now there were more pilots on hand to fly than there were planes remaining for them.

Panic-stricken, he ran the mile back to the guesthouse. He was disoriented—nothing looked the same and he suddenly realized that all the palm trees had been blasted flat, and that the burning hole in the ground was where his guesthouse had stood. His knees buckled in fright.

Bandfield leapt into the hole, trying to see if there were bodies, desperately hoping that there were not. Amidst the debris, he saw some familiar items—photos of Patty's family, George's stick-horse, broken chairs, and a table cloth. Finally, he moved away from the smoldering flames. He saw a military policeman stationed at the end of the street. Bandfield raced to him and, scarcely coherent, demanded to know if there had been injuries.

The MP, a stickler for protocol, carefully perused the handwitten list on his clipboard before telling Bandfield to check the base hospital. Bandfield didn't ask him if anyone had been killed; the MP might be wrong. A Signal Corps corporal came by on a motorcycle, and the MP, friendlier now, persuaded him to drop Bandfield off at the hospital.

He prayed all the way, Hail Marys and Our Fathers cascading out as they threaded through the debris-strewn streets.

"God, if they were inside, they are gone; no one could have lived through that." Tears welled in his eyes, and when the motorcycle came to a stop, the driver had to gently tap him on the knee and point to the hospital doorway.

Still praying, he ran into the pandemonium of the receiving room, realizing instantly that it was the same medical facility he'd been taken to after his 1927 flight to Hawaii. Nothing seemed to have changed but for the addition of dozens of wounded soldiers and civilians. Amidst the chaos he found a calm, round-faced nurse seated at the reception desk, making entries in a ledger just as if it were a normal day. She recognized his name immediately and, without a word, led him down two endless corridors.

He peered around the door into the tiny room where Patty was sitting, sobbing hysterically. He closed his eyes and slumped against the wall, afraid to go in.

Gathering his nerve, he burst into the room, embracing Patty. "Thank God, you're alive."

"And you, too, darling. I was sure they had killed you."

He kissed Patty fervently, with his eyes closed, almost unwilling to ask about the children. He looked around to see young George sitting on the bed, absorbed with a toy metal dump-truck.

"You and George are okay? Where is Charlotte?"

Patty could scarcely breathe. "She's just down the hall, in the bathroom. She got a cut on the scalp, shrapnel, I guess, bled like a stuck pig."

The door opened and Charlotte ran to throw herself in his arms, her face barely visible under the huge bandage. When she leaned back he kissed her on the cheek, then held her at arm's length to look at her. She had always been an open child, though sometimes timid. She had started talking at seven months, and he could see she had something to say now.

"Daddy, are we okay?"

"Sure, honey, we're all fine."

"That's good." She was quiet but obviously wanted to tell him something more.

"Daddy, I wasn't scared a bit. I'm not scared now."

"I wish I could say the same." He squeezed her hand and kissed her.

5

Nashville, Tennessee/December 25, 1941

They sat in Troy McNaughton's oak-paneled office, a bottle of Old
Forester bourbon on the table between them, smoke floating up
from their cigars, the sound of rivet guns humming in the factory
bay below them.

"What a lousy way to spend Christmas! This has been a bad month,
Troy. You heard that Hong Kong surrendered?" Caldwell asked.

"What gets me is that the English were no better prepared, after
two years of war. Seems like they would have learned something."

There was a long silence. Elsie Raynor was on the phone with a
supplier, raising hell about prices and deliveries, her cultivated
voice reverting under pressure to its original New Jersey inflections.
As usual, neither man acknowledged her presence. Caldwell was
edgy, anxious for the meeting to be over so that he could spend
some time with Elsie. She always refused to see him until he'd
concluded his business with McNaughton, saying that she didn't
want him to be distracted when they made love.

Caldwell coldly got down to business. "We've got *real* problems.
I'm getting nothing but unfavorable reports on the Sidewinder from
the field."

McNaughton's practiced voice, an instrument he'd used to sell everything from Fuller brushes to fighters, bristled with irritation. "That's *always* the way. Nobody's *ever* satisfied."

"No, this isn't just dogface bitching. You guaranteed it would do at least three hundred and fifty miles an hour; most people are having trouble getting three hundred out of it. And the goddamn thing is useless above seventeen thousand feet. What can you do to improve it?"

"Well, slip me some funds for research. We could use some more wind-tunnel time to clean up the design. Even better, give us the dough to build a wind tunnel right here. I need a wind tunnel for the jet."

"God, I'm leery about funneling any more dough to McNaughton; people are already saying I'm too easy on you."

"Look, we're delivering what *you* ordered. You've been loading the airplane up with equipment; you pulled the supercharger off it. What the hell do you expect? It's as fast as the P-40."

"No, it's not, and you know it. Worse than that, it's got some lousy flight characteristics. You saw the report Bandfield wrote."

McNaughton snorted in triumph. "Jesus, no wonder, he lets some Jap shoot him down, he's got to blame something. He didn't sound too sure of himself; besides, did he submit a report on him getting shot down in the P-40? I tell you, there's nothing wrong with the Sidewinder that a good pilot can't handle."

"Look, if Bandfield can't handle it, nobody can. We've got green kids with maybe two hundred hours flying these planes. In the last month we've lost five of them in flat spins."

"Accidents happen in wartime flying. The main thing is we're producing a hundred airplanes a month and the rate is building. By next fall, we'll be ferrying the airplanes across Alaska to Siberia. That's what you wanted, wasn't it?"

Caldwell's tone was bitter. "Yeah, but I told the Russians I was sending good airplanes. These guys are tough negotiators—they'll scream to high heaven when they find out the airplane can't cut the mustard."

"Henry, the airplane is *fine*. We'll continue to improve it. Give us more powerful engines, Packard Merlins instead of the Allisons."

Face drawn, Caldwell snapped, "I've promised the Merlins to Dutch Kindleberger at North American."

"Come on! You know the damn P-51 is so lousy at altitude that the British are going to use it for tactical reconnaissance. And you're complaining about the Sidewinder!"

"I promised Dutch the engines, Henry. I can't go back on him."

"Why not? Exigencies of the service, demands of the state department. Ship me the damn engines and I'll get some better fighters to Russia for you. Who knows when North American will deliver?"

Caldwell felt his stomach shrink. He *might* be able to ship the old Allison engines to North American for another year or two, until Packard built the production rate up enough to supply Merlins for both the P-51 and the Sidewinder.

A wave of weariness swept over Caldwell and he slumped in his chair. He'd fought for years to get U.S. airplane companies prepared for war. Then war came and *no one* was ready; it was as if nothing had been learned since 1939.

McNaughton's voice rose. "Look, I'm not out to cheat anybody. It's just that the Sidewinder turned out to be a little overweight and underpowered. It's not the first airplane to do that, and it won't be the last. But the Russians can use them, and we'll improve them. You can't ask for more."

Caldwell reached for the whiskey bottle. He *needed* to see Elsie. The woman was more than an obsession, she was a compulsion, a darling compulsion. Well, he had everything else going pretty well; maybe they could get by for a year, until the new McNaughton airplanes were coming down the line, and there were enough Merlins for the Mustang.

"What about the jet engine? How are you coming on that?"

"I'll give it to you straight, Henry. We think we've got a good design—it runs like a charm for the first fifteen hours or so. Then the turbine blades melt—they just can't take the sustained heat. When one of the blades starts to go, the turbine wheel gets out of balance and the whole damn thing blows up. We've had some close calls down in the test cell."

"Well, you better get busy. General Electric is working hard on their version of the Whittle engine, and unless you come up with something fast, you'll be out of the jet business before you start."

The British had sent a prototype of the Whittle engine to the United States in October for G.E. to develop for Bell Aircraft.

"Don't tell me that, Henry. There's always room for more than one engine, more than one airplane. You don't want to have all your eggs in one basket."

"No, but Troy, you've *got* to start producing. The Sidewinder's iffy, and you're not making fast enough progress on the jet. If you don't come up with something soon, I'm going to start you building P-51s."

"It'll never come to that, General, believe me."

Impatiently shaking his head, Caldwell left for his rendezvous with Elsie.

Berlin/January 26, 1942

Joseph Goebbels's Maybach SW 38 sedan, custom body by Spohn, was to a Mercedes what a Rolls-Royce was to a Jaguar. A sable throw—the personal gift of Joseph Stalin himself in the palmy days of 1940—covered the backseat, and on each side of the car were Orrefors crystal bud vases, each with a single white hothouse rose. In previous drives Lyra had opened the inlaid rosewood cases in the doors; on the left were crystal bottles of perfume and makeup, a silk handkerchief, a golden comb; on the right were some miniature decanters, each hung with a golden medallion telling its contents.

Lyra's throat constricted with desire for a taste of straight vodka, but she refrained. Little Joseph did not drink very much, sipping at the champagne he plied her with, and she would need her wits about her. The affair had begun slowly; after weeks of sending her flowers and providing a car for her ride home, he had at last sent a note asking to meet her. On the first visit he had been entirely correct; on the second he had displayed some impatience. On the third she had complied. It had been an intellectual decision; with

Goebbels as a lover she would be protected and better able to work against the regime.

Each time she had to mentally prepare herself for the "seduction," rationalizing it as her private "combat duty," a price she had to pay to fight her own personal war, a battle intensified in just the last week. She'd received word that her father and mother had gone into hiding, frightened by the Nazis' roundup of Jews in Riga. She knew that they had disappeared as much to protect her as to save themselves—and she could do nothing to help them.

As sickening as it was, it wasn't the first time she'd had to compromise herself just to survive. *None* of her affairs before meeting Helmut had been for love. A few had been out of loneliness, out of a need to be needed—but most had been simply for survival. Helmut had never asked about her past; if he had she would have told him. She was not proud of the way she'd had to live, but not ashamed either—she did what had to be done.

It was the same with Goebbels. She'd do what had to be done. The real challenge would be to maintain his interest after his "conquest," so that she would not lose her source of information and protection when he tired of her body.

He was unquestionably a brilliant man, but cunning, too, and suspicious. She must not underestimate him. Vanity was his weakspot, and she played to it by assiduously reading his speeches and articles, and quoting his pithiest phrases. He was particularly susceptible to any commentary in the foreign press, and she combed the papers to find them. It was convenient that he felt that attacks on him proved he was doing a good job. But occasionally there were objective words of praise, even from the British, about a particular idea or article, and these gave him immense pleasure. She had one tonight—the London *Times* had written: "Goebbels's unquestionably imaginative propaganda was still effective" in an article examining German morale. She would save that morsel for parting, to use as a means of safe entree once again.

She wondered which would bother Helmut the most: her spying or her reluctant affair. She shuddered as she thought of Goebbels. His enemies called him *"Schrumpfgermane"*—shrunken German.

He was physically repellent, and most of all she hated his wretched square teeth, set in his broad mouth like discolored tombstones, freighting his breath with the death-scent of caries. Kissing him had been an abomination; making love to him was horrible. She drew little comfort from knowing that she was using him.

The car turned into the alley and glided to a stop, seeming as huge and silent as the Zeppelins that Maybach engines once powered. The chauffeur stepped out, transforming himself into a butler in the process.

Upstairs, a red light told Goebbels that the door had opened, and the elevator indicator began to move. He checked his sunlamp tan in the mirror, reassuring himself that he looked well for a man of forty-four. He glanced down to see that his trousers draped correctly across the mounded hump of his custom-built shoe. His deformity gave him the usual momentary sense of injustice, but he quickly put this aside, concentrating on the faultless fall of the jacket, the prosperous feel of his cream-colored silk shirt and underwear.

Moving around the room, he dimmed the lights, then turned them up again, spread the flowers to show the roses off, and started the "Appassionata" on the record player. He fussed with the champagne; two bottles of good German Henkell, no looted Dom Pérignon. That was Goering's style, like his baroque hunting lodges.

Goebbels's apartment—a long, narrow art deco drawing room, a small kitchen, and a sensually furnished bedroom—was just off the Friedrichstrasse. Berlin was a rabbit warren of tunnels, and a very convenient one of whitewashed brick ran from the Ministry of Propaganda, the old Prinz Leopold Palast on the Wilhelmplatz, directly to the elevator door in Goebbels's basement. His visitors could enter with equal discretion, via an unmarked door in the alley to the rear. The apartment was ideal for his "rest and recreation."

For that was all the affairs were, necessary restoratives to his health and well-being. He knew that women came to him because of his position, especially his power in the film industry. Emil Jannings had once told him that there was a Hollywood term for this practice—"the casting couch." An apt phrase, one he wished he'd coined himself. But the important point was that the women did not *have* to come; they came to sell themselves for their career. It was no different than the industrialists who had sold themselves to Hitler with their immense campaign contributions, or the politicians, teachers, journalists, even priests, all the "March violets" who had joined the Nazis after 1933.

He checked the motion picture projector's bulb. He'd just received the week's film shipment from Switzerland; tonight he'd show her a brand new American film, *Foreign Correspondent*. It was of course anti-Nazi, and that was the point, to illustrate his confidence in himself, his trust in her, an ideal stage setting for making love.

There was a timid knock. He opened it and stood for a moment taking in her beauty. Then, with a bow that he fancied was quite Viennese, he kissed her hand and gently tugged her inside.

Lyra enjoyed the film, especially Joel McCrea's bravado, but was unsettled to find Goebbels preoccupied and a little distant. Had he decided that she was not worth pursuing? Repressing her repugnance, she reached out to take his hand, asking if he was well.

"It's nothing—a headache. We're going to have to raise the price of potatoes, and I'm worried about the public reaction."

"What a man you are—concerned with everything from potatoes to the Eastern Front. And"—squeezing his hand—"always in danger, too." They had talked about his personal security earlier. "Aren't you concerned that the Communists, or some insane person, will make an attempt on your life?"

Preening with drawing-room bravery he confided, "Not at all—it doesn't matter what happens to me. The Fuehrer could readily find another writer like myself." He hesitated, waiting for her protest.

"But, no!"

"No, let me interrupt. My life is not important—but the Fuehrer's—*that* is everything."

His reserve dissolved and he launched into an animated discussion of Hitler's habits—the armor plate he wore in his hat, his frequent changes of schedule, the way he would suddenly, without any previous announcement, change the location of meeting places and the routes to them. It was the insider talking, the man who knew all, a great leader.

She nodded eagerly, saying nothing, drinking in the flow of words, knowing how dangerous they were to her, how invaluable they would be to her friends in the Resistance.

His voice faltered and alarm suddenly registered in his eyes, as he realized he had said too much. Without hesitation, she made herself tremble as if her passion could no longer be contained, extending her arms to him and saying, "My sweet, enough of this. Kiss me."

Le Touquet, France/February 10, 1942

Hitler, the frustrated architect, had made one characteristic contribution to the art: the reinforced concrete bunker. All over Europe, Todt Organization crews had despoiled the landscape with massive ugly structures sited half above and half below the ground, many of them taken from Hitler's own design sketches. They varied in size and function, but all were cloaked with certain dismal characteristics: the hum and grind of auxiliary power units, salts exuding from every tunnel wall, and the pervasive odor of a Parisian *pissoir*. The gloom was amplified by the dim yellow lighting pulsing to the fluctuations of the generators. The only decorations on the wall were the phantom impressions of the long-gone wooden forms that had contained the pour.

Colonel Galland, relishing his new role as General of the Fighter Arm, had assembled all of the leaders of fighter units in the West for "Operation Thunderbolt," a literal sink or swim operation for the still formidable remnants of the German surface fleet. Three of the proudest names in German military history adorned the ships bottled up in the harbor at Brest. The British bitterly wanted revenge against all three. The *Gneisenau* and the *Scharnhorst* had sunk the aircraft carrier HMS *Glorious* in 1940, while *Prinz Eugen* had escaped after aiding the *Bismarck* in sinking the *Hood*. The RAF had launched more than three hundred attacks against the ships; sooner or later they would sink them where they floated at Brest.

Josten knew no words would be wasted as Galland stepped to the podium, forcing himself to speak in slow, measured tones that compelled attention, his rich baritone reaching to every corner of the briefing room.

"The Fuehrer has directed that the battle cruisers *Gneisenau* and *Scharnhorst* and the heavy cruiser *Prinz Eugen*, with the necessary escorts, leave the harbor at Brest, and proceed"—he paused for emphasis—"*via the English Channel* to Wilhelmshaven, and then to ports in Norway."

There was a collective gasp. The British had permitted no enemy navy to force the channel since The Armada; they would certainly throw in everything they had in order to stop this effort.

"I understand your reaction, but the fact is there is no alternative. If we leave the ships in Brest, they will eventually be sunk by the RAF; if we take the other route, around Ireland and Scotland, we will be met and outgunned by the Home Fleet. If we sail the Channel"—he grinned broadly at the Navy men fuming near the podium—"the Luftwaffe can protect the Navy."

"The Fuehrer recognizes that this is a high-risk project, but has determined that the effort must be made. These ships will be vital for the defense of Norway, and to attack the convoys."

Some of the men were taking notes; others looked on in a stunned silence.

Galland swiftly laid out the plan—the ships would weigh anchor at night and steam at full speed through freshly swept minefields. Absolute radio silence was required. At noon the next day they would force their way through the narrowest part of the Channel, the Dover Strait.

"It is his view that the British reaction will be delayed long enough for us to effect a daylight passage of the narrowest part of the Channel. It is the most prudent time, even though we'll be vulnerable to air and sea attack, and even to shelling from the shore."

Galland went down an exhaustive list of requirements, detailing radio frequencies, takeoff times, and the absolute necessity for radio silence. He took a few questions, then began his conclusion.

"Gentlemen, this is one mission for which the only acceptable result is success. We must try to remain undetected for as long as possible, for as soon as the British learn we are at sea they will launch every available bomber and torpedo aircraft against us. These must be shot down at all costs."

He paused, conscious that he was beginning to speak too rapidly and that he must not lose the import of his final comment. He surveyed the room, letting his presence fill it.

"No matter what the reason—no ammunition, guns jammed, low fuel, whatever it might be—the Luftwaffe pilots who cannot shoot the hostile aircraft down will ram them."

There was another stunned silence among the Air Force men as their naval counterparts broke into broad smiles, realizing that the Luftwaffe had just accepted the ultimate responsibility for the success of the mission.

Driving back to base in his Horch cabriolet, Josten had time to digest the full meaning of Galland's briefing and to consider how it influenced his own position, already highly unusual. Galland had selected him as an airborne commander during the critical initial part of the operation. That sort of recognition would help him with his advocacy of the jet fighter. And he needed all the help he could get because time was so critical. If Russia were knocked out this year, the Me 262 could be developed at leisure. If Russia fought on, the jet would be absolutely necessary to ward off an invasion in the West, perhaps as early as next year. Then the 262 would be invaluable, perhaps even decisive.

The English Channel/February 12, 1942

Galland's plan called for a minimum of sixteen fighters to be over the fleet at all times. For twenty minutes of each hour the relief aircraft overlapped, combining to form a force of thirty-two. The squadrons were to leapfrog along the French and Belgian coasts, landing to refuel at progressively more northern bases until the job was done.

At first the term "over the fleet" was a misnomer. To avoid the

British radar for as long as posssible, they flew below the mast height of the three capital ships that steamed north at full speed, their bows diving like eager dolphins into the slate-gray ocean, rising to toss back V-shaped spumes of green-white spray. On the day's first sortie, the miserable weather forced the ships to weave in and out of the gray-white frosting that heaped the surface of the sea like whipped cream on a Sacher torte. Josten maintained a constant watch for the destroyers and motor torpedo boats that bounded around the ships like dogs nipping at the heels of sheep.

By Josten's second sortie, the clouds began to lift, and he had a clear view of the extent of the fleet. The three big vessels were in line astern, with destroyers ranging ahead and on each side, and the German E boats scampering about, crisscrossing in a watery gymkhana.

The noise of the engine receded into the background of his consciousness, and there remained only the unremitting crackle of the receiver of the non-transmitting radios. Dolfo must have impressed them; the Luftwaffe was maintaining perfect radio discipline. All of Galland's preparations had been good, from the gradual increase in jamming to confuse British radar to the flurry of Luftwaffe sorties that had been flown in the past few weeks to disguise today's efforts.

The fleet had been at sea for fourteen hours, the last four in broad daylight. It was a February blessing that little more than four more hours of daylight remained. It seemed impossible that the British had not detected them by radar or by the innumerable aircraft with which they patrolled. Was it a trap?

He knew that the fabled white cliffs of Dover were only eighteen miles away; the ships were within the range of the guns there. And where were the bombers and the torpedo planes?

Josten banked sharply as a wall of water erupted in front of him; gunfire from the coast, well behind the stern of the last ship, *Prinz Eugen*. Very well, they had been sighted, and the code words "Open visor" came over the headsets, relieving them of radio silence and low altitude flight. The Messerschmitts quickly broke up into groups flying at one-, two-, and three-hundred meters height.

The bombers would not be far behind. The relief flight of Messerschmitts had just showed up; that meant Josten had ten more minutes on this sortie, then back for fuel and a cup of coffee.

Five minutes later he saw a German E boat swing sharply to engage five British motor torpedo boats approaching at high speed from the west. Where were the British aircraft?

The British were coming, in a balls-up rivaling the Charge of the Light Brigade for both bravery and stupidity. The mighty British Empire, forewarned of the possibility of the German sortie for weeks, had so disposed its forces that only six ancient Swordfish torpedo planes were available when, after incredible delay, the first attack was made.

The open cockpit Fairey Swordfish would have looked at home on the Western Front in 1918. Encumbered with a stiltlike fixed landing gear and laden with drag-inducing struts and wires, it was nicknamed "Stringbag," after the bags made of string netting that women carried when shopping. Designed in 1934, the three-placer—pilot, gunner, and radio man—could drop an eighteen-inch torpedo. Its crews bolstered their courage by bragging that Luftwaffe gunners could never hit it because their ranging devices were not designed to fire at a target that flew as slow as eighty-five miles per hour. And, they boasted, any lucky hits would pass right through the Swordfish's wood and fabric frame without damage. There was some minimal truth to both of these whistles in the dark.

The Stringbag had already done heroic work. Operating from HMS *Illustrious*, twenty-one Swordfish had crippled the Italian fleet at Taranto in November 1940. The following spring, Swordfish from the *Ark Royal* had launched torpedoes that jammed the *Bismarck*'s rudder and set her up for the heavy guns of the Home Fleet. But those attacks had been made without fighter opposition.

Lieutenant Commander Eugene Esmonde flew the lead Swordfish. He had just made a command decision, the last of his short life. The fighter escort had not arrived at the rendezvous point; the

German fleet was getting away, beyond the Strait into the Narrow Sea. He elected to attack, knowing that the German fighters were waiting, and that few, if any, of the Swordfish would survive.

As the six Swordfish lumbered toward the target, a flight of ten Spitfires—less than a quarter of the promised escort—suddenly materialized and a brief glow of hope stirred Esmonde—there might be a chance after all.

The red fuel warning light was blinking as Josten saw a sheet of flak erupt from the destroyers on his left. All of them had been fitted with crude welded mounts for extra 20-mm automatic weapons, and the wall of smoke and flame they laid down looked impenetrable. To his amazement, six Swordfish stumbled through the curtain of fire in two flights of three, battered but on course to the main fleet. Banking to engage them he reefed back on the stick to avoid a forest of water spouts blossoming in front of him. The eleven-inch guns of the battle cruisers were firing shells right through his own line of flight to ensnare the Swordfish. He shrugged; he'd never know if one hit him.

The port lower wing of one Swordfish vanished, as if Neptune had reached up from the sea to clutch it. Its nose rose sharply, then bowed to the left before disappearing in a spray of water. Josten's own starboard wing scraped the wavetops he racked around to slow himself enough to pick up a head-on shot at a target. He pressed the trigger and saw his tracers passing behind his target as he whipped through the formation. He blinked as he did so, not believing his eyes. On the third Swordfish a madly brave gunner had crawled out of his seat and was straddling the fuselage like a horse, facing the rear, trying to beat out a fire in the fabric with his hands.

Josten throttled back, slowing down to drop some flaps; there were Spitfires about, but the top flight of Messerschmitts had already engaged them. His targets were the remaining Swordfish.

Other Messerschmitts were attacking, barracuda against bonito, getting into each other's way as the Fleet Air Arm planes lumbered forward. One of the Swordfish disappeared in a huge ball of flame— a shell must have exploded its torpedo; another simply stopped flying, to drop limply into the Channel like a dead fly in a glass of beer.

Josten gained on the formation slowly this time, aiming and firing with care. The wood and fabric of the trailing Swordfish sponged up his gunfire. Smiling grimly, he trod on the rudder pedals, walking his tracers back and forth across the cockpit until the guns went silent. Just as he ran out of ammunition, he saw the gunner throw his hands up and the pilot lurch forward on the stick. The big biplane tucked its nose into a wave and halted, swamped immediately to its aft cockpit by the building sea, then slipping without reluctance beneath the surface.

He had overflown the attackers again, reaching almost to the jaws of the *Scharnhorst*'s thundering main batteries when he threw his fighter in a steep bank to reverse his course. The amount of cannon fire roaring past him did not bear thinking about. There was only one Swordfish still flying, gamely headed directly toward the big battle cruiser, torpedo ready to be launched.

The fuel warning light was burning red steadily now. It didn't matter, for Josten knew he would never reach shore. He caught the Swordfish in his sights, the big three-bladed fixed-pitch propeller glistening in the mist, the enormous wings pushing the shell-freighted air aside like a child burrowing in the sand. He pressed the trigger, just in case, but nothing happened. The two airplanes closed. In a single fluid motion, Josten lifted his fighter over the huge upper wing of the torpedo plane, then dipped his port wing so that it sheared off the Swordfish's vertical fin. The Swordfish dropped straight into the sea, the Messerschmitt cartwheeling at its side. A geyser of water covered Josten's cockpit, turning the outside world rapidly from blue to gray to blue again as his tired fighter bobbed up and down before lurching to a halt. Jettisoning the canopy, he pulled his one-man life raft out just as the plane sank beneath him.

Battered, stomach and mouth engorged with the teeth-rattling chill of the seawater, Josten inflated the raft and struggled into it. He looked up to find the last Swordfish directly in front of him, engine sunk deep, water flowing over the cockpit rails. The gunner was dead in his harness, but another man, the radio operator probably, was dragging the unconscious pilot out of the cockpit. He had just freed him when the tailless Swordfish rolled over and plunged out of sight, as if glad to end its embarrassing agony.

Josten choked back nausea as he paddled toward the two British survivors. The radio man was treading water, holding the pilot up and trying to inflate his life jacket as the rolling sea bounced them. Josten knew that he could expect to survive no more than a few hours in his raft; the two enemy crew members would not last for twenty minutes as the chilly Channel sucked warmth from their bones.

A wave crested, dropping Josten's raft next to the British airmen. He reached out and grabbed the pilot's jacket, saying to the radio operator, "Hold on to the raft. I'll take care of him."

The radio man, too cold to be surprised by Josten's English, nodded gratefully. Josten managed to get the jacket inflated and then held his arms around the pilot's head, keeping it from bobbing forward into the water, the long blond hair slicked tight against his skull, veins showing big and blue beneath the translucent skin, deep blue eyes open with pupils fixed.

The radio operator's teeth chattered like a flak battery while his color drained to a gray-blue as, cell by cell, he gave in to the cold.

"Can't hold on, going to let go."

"Nonsense, there are dozens of E boats looking for us. Just hang on."

A decision was forming in Josten's mind as he scanned the water, praying that a German boat would spot them. The unconscious pilot was not going to make it. He could not afford to waste his strength on him. The radio man was a goner unless he somehow got out of the water. The raft was not supposed to be able to hold two people, especially in the swelling chop of the Channel, but he'd have to take the chance. He shook the radio man's arm, forcing his eyes open.

"I'm going to have to let your friend go. I can't hold on to him.

When I do, you crawl aboard. You've got to help, I don't have the strength to bring you in myself."

The radio man looked mutely at his comrade and mumbled, "No, hold on to him."

Josten let the pilot go; he bobbed away, disappearing at once, then reappearing, his head lolling back now so that his accusing open eyes stared deep into Josten's soul, seeming to say, "I have died and you are going to live." It was a sight Josten would never forget.

"Do you have the strength to get in?"

The radio man shook his head.

Josten tried and failed to haul him in the raft.

He was still holding him, arms aching with the cold and fatigue, when an E boat came alongside thirty minutes later. Rough hands pulled him on board; the radio operator, dead for many minutes, slipped out of their hands to drift in search of his pilot.

Below deck they wrapped Josten in blankets and forced *muck-efuck*—ersatz coffee—laced with schnapps down his throat. It acted like a depth charge to the seawater he'd swallowed; he vomited and at once felt better.

The E boat raced at top speed back to port, the water pounding the thin planks on which Josten lay. As warmth returned to his extremities, he had time to rethink the battle. It was incredible that the British had thrown antiques like the Swordfish against them. No matter how brave the pilots were, they couldn't overcome their disadvantage in equipment.

The true meaning of the battle dawned on him. It wouldn't make any difference how many airplanes Germany had, unless they were of superior performance. The jet fighter *had* to be built.

Wolfschanze, Rastenburg, East Prussia/March 20, 1942

No one could accuse Hitler of ostentatious living. Josten, Galland, and another fighter pilot, *Leutnant* "Bubi" Zink, waited in the paneled tea room, furnished in the varnished pine and padded pillow comfort of a Bavarian rifle club, but by far the most elegant of the buildings they had seen. Situated in the heart of a forest near the Masurian Lakes, the headquarters was a collection of utilitarian single-story wooden barracks and concrete blockhouses, each about twelve meters long and five meters wide, without paint or decoration of any sort, and grouped according to their official functions. Other bunkers, larger, were under construction, and the whole was neatly knitted together by concentric rings of barbed wire.

Everywhere except on the graveled paths there was snow; even the camouflage netting, strung on the tops of the pine trees, sagged under its weight in a pendant mouse-gray ceiling, filtering light and noise.

They had been waiting for two hours in the Number Two Mess in the *Gorlitz Kurhaus*, the dining room for the Operations Staff, thawing out from the four-hundred-mile flight from Berlin in an unheated Junkers Ju 52. Josten had spent part of the time talking to Christa Garnowski, Hitler's garrulous private secretary who had come in to apologize for the delay—the Fuehrer was in conference with Dr. Goebbels. She mixed a loving Fuehrer fervor with the desire to be recognized as a real insider, someone who was secure enough to criticize freely. Young and pretty, she warmed immediately to Galland, as all women seemed to do.

"This is the nerve center of the Reich—and the most boring place in the world. At least now we don't have the mosquitoes, but it's so cold we take turns holding the dogs, just to get our hands warm."

Josten tried to walk the line between being friendly and curious.

"How could it be boring here?"

"It's the crazy hours we keep. We follow the Fuehrer's schedule—dinner at seven, then a small social meeting with the Fuehrer later." As she spoke, her pride was evident.

"He needs to unwind, so he talks to us—sometimes it's two in the morning before we get away. We go to bed, and it might be noon before we go to work again. There are no newspapers, no radio. Occasionally there's a film, but not often, not since the Fuehrer stopped watching them. The winter was so terrible for him."

The newly promoted Major Josten was hungry. They had left Berlin before lunch and had not eaten anything since. Worse, Zink had brought along enough brandy for a platoon, and they had drunk most of it. Now his stomach was queasy and his head ached. All three men had been following the Fuehrer for almost four days, waiting to be summoned to his presence. The investiture ceremony was to have taken place in Berlin; Hitler had abruptly broken off his visit and returned to his headquarters, and they were sent after him. Galland, who had received the ultimate decoration, the Knight's Cross with Oak Leaves, Swords and Diamonds, in January, was there to debrief Hitler personally. Zink was to receive the Oak Leaves to the Knight's Cross. It was a special distinction for Josten to be told to accompany them; his award was the Knight's Cross, normally given by the local commanding officer.

"I suppose that you eat very well here."

"You're joking, Major Josten! It's virtually a starvation diet. The Fuehrer is an ascetic who eats only the simplest things. Here, let me show you the menu for tonight so that you won't be surprised."

She reached in her leather purse and handed him a small ivory-colored card. On it was written in good German script:

WOLFSCHANZE

PEA SOUP

RICE PUDDING

RYE WAFERS

APPLE PEEL TEA

20 MARCH 1942

"Keep that for a souvenir. That's what you'll be having. The rest of us will do rather better tonight, pork chops, the first time in weeks. But you get to eat with him and Dr. Goebbels."

Galland had been leaning back in his chair, eyes closed. He had met Hitler before on several occasions but had never seen Goebbels in person. Josten wondered if he should talk to the good Doctor about Lyra and Magda's friendship.

"Dr. Goebbels is going back right after supper. That's why you are eating early."

The door opened, and Colonel Nicholas von Below, Hitler's Luftwaffe adjutant, bustled in. Tall, thin, blond, his condescension conveyed the proxy power peculiar to the personal assistants of great men.

"The Fuehrer will see you . . . What's that smell?"

He walked over to the three pilots and sniffed; when he came to Zink he said, "You've been drinking and you stink like a French whore from that hair oil. You cannot be admitted to the Fuehrer's presence like this. Go back to the barracks and wash; I'll try to arrange for him to see you tomorrow. You two, follow me."

As they entered, Hitler stepped forward and clasped them both by the hand and introduced them to Goebbels and the other staff members. Goebbels felt a curious satisfaction that Josten was such a good-looking young hero. He grinned wolfishly and pumped Josten's hand, saying, "I've heard of you."

Hitler led them to a wall map where a small table held the decorations. A staff photographer came in. With each photograph, a restrained tussle occurred among the people present as they vied for a position as close to Hitler as possible. Goebbels did not. He always made sure that he stood on the extreme left of every shot so that his name would appear first in the photo caption.

Hitler's voice was firm and strong, hinting at the range and depth of tones he used in his speeches.

"Major Josten. I don't usually award the Knight's Cross of the Iron Cross personally, but this is an exception. If you had not rammed the Swordfish, we might have lost the *Scharnhorst*."

None of the conflicting stories Josten had heard about Hitler had proved to be true. He had the appearance of a correct, friendly business executive, obviously in good health, and immaculately turned out. His eyes were a deep blue, but Josten didn't sense the burning magnetism journalists attributed to them.

Goebbels, on the other hand, was exactly as depicted by the rumor-mongers—tiny, with a limp, and a hideous oversize grin that looked as if it had been forcibly stuffed in his head by a revengeful dentist. The little Propaganda Minister stepped forward to congratulate Josten again, saying, "The captain of the E Boat has reported your heroism in trying to save the British crew member. Newspapers all over the world will print the story. I thank you for a propaganda triumph as well."

As Josten replied, Goebbels continued to press his hand thinking, Well, the Fuehrer has decorated you with the Knight's Cross, and I've decorated you with horns.

The meal lasted only a few minutes. A plane was waiting for Goebbels, and the pea soup and rice pudding were equally tasteless glue, nothing to linger over. Hitler had monopolized the conversation, discussing various European opera houses, a subject neither Galland nor Josten could do more than nod about.

After Goebbels left, they went back to the tea room, and Hitler began to ask pointed questions about the Luftwaffe.

"What do you think, Colonel Galland, were we lucky in the Channel, or was it skill? Be honest with me."

"Sixty percent luck, forty percent skill. It was lucky that the British were so slow in reacting. But when they did react, the Luftwaffe stopped them. It was a good feeling."

Hitler interrogated them about the quality of their aircraft, the training new pilots were receiving, what the Luftwaffe's weakspots were, how many fighters should be built, a thousand details. He had incredible grasp for specifications, calling out the speed, range, armament of all the major aircraft, Allied and German, and even quoted them the muzzle velocities and throw-weights of the various weapons. Suddenly he seemed to change the direction of the conversation.

"You have an excellent friend in court, Major Josten. I suppose you know that."

"Yes, my Fuehrer, Colonel Galland has taught me a great deal."

"Not Colonel Galland; I'm referring to Lieutenant Colonel Hafner, the director of the experimental station at Cottbus. He speaks very highly of you."

"Colonel Hafner is a good friend."

"Do you agree with him on his ideas about expanding production by building interconnected industrial complexes around Germany?"

Galland's black eyes shifted to him in amusement; it would be interesting to see how Josten handled this.

"About expanding production, yes, my Fuehrer. And about creating a system of factories. But I think the important thing is the types of aircraft we build."

"What do you think of this so-called jet fighter?"

"It is essential. If we don't get it, our Messerschmitts are going to be as obsolete as the Swordfish."

"I agree with you in part. The problem is the time and resources the technical development for a weapon like this takes. In 1939, at Rechlin, I was shown a half dozen aircraft that were going to revolutionize warfare. It is now 1942 and not one of them has been in action. What makes you think the jet fighter will be different?"

"It *won't* be any different unless we manage it correctly. As you know, Colonel Hafner has set up a team to expedite the introduction of the Me 262. This team should have top priority over everything."

A weary smile passed over Hitler's face. "Yes, the tank men tell me about the Russian tanks, and say they need top priority to counter the T-34. Admiral Doenitz comes in and dances on my chest until he gets top priority for the submarines. And now Speer, who wants top priority for everything."

In his mesmerizing basso, Galland spoke with a quiet urgency. "You won't have tanks or submarines if we lose control of the skies over Germany. They will bomb us into oblivion."

Hitler registered no emotion at Galland's remark. "What is the one major technical problem that we have to overcome with the Me 262?"

With a movement of his bushy eyebrows, Galland signaled Josten to be quiet and said, "The engines, of course, *mein Fuehrer*. They are designed to operate at much higher temperatures than piston engines do. We still have to find the correct alloys for the turbine blades."

"Agreed," Hitler snapped. "And that is precisely the problem. The jet engines require large quantities of chromium and high-grade nickel. We don't have it. Yet. When we finish with Russia, things will be different. And we can defeat Russia with our present aircraft. Can't we, Josten?"

"Russia, perhaps, but not England *and* Russia. And if we don't finish Russia soon, before the United States gets mobilized, England will become a huge, unsinkable aircraft carrier."

"You know what Goering tells me about the American airplanes, don't you?"

"That the Americans can build cars and razor blades—"

Hitler interrupted, "No, not that old story. No, now he tells me that it is good that they are building four-engine aircraft, because when we shoot them down, it means twice as great a loss. Do you believe that?"

Galland could not restrain himself. "Sir, may I answer that? You know that the American aviation publications keep no secrets. We would shoot anyone who gave away information as they do. The Americans are continually improving the B-17s—if they come in large numbers they will be very difficult to bring down with our existing equipment."

Hitler seemed excited now, his eyes acquiring a fierce glow, expanding even as his voice did. "Exactly. I've been calling for thirty-millimeter cannon for our aircraft for years, and not one has it. At least the 262 is supposed to get them. Now I want fifty-millimeter cannon installed, and all I hear from the Luftwaffe technical staff is that it can't be done."

"The pilots would be satisfied with the thirty-millimeter, sir. We—"

Hitler stood up suddenly and put his hand out. The gesture seemed curiously constrained; he offered his hand, yet the crank of his arm told how reluctant he was to have it accepted.

"Thank you and congratulations again. I've learned a great deal from you." They saluted and Von Below led them to their rooms in a bunker half sunk in the ground, chill and dank in the cold East Prussian night.

"What do you think, Josty?"

Josten waited to reply, to make sure that the boyish enthusiasm he felt was not too evident. After a moment he said, "He is undeniably brilliant, and he knows what he's talking about. I have to say he inspired me."

As Josten spoke, Galland moved carefully around the room, checking it for microphones, his hand pressed to his lips. Then he reached over and turned on the battered record player which a former occupant of the room had left behind. The only record was a scratched one, of Furtwangler conducting the Berlin Philharmonic in the overture to *Fidelio*. As the record groaned, Galland signaled Josten to speak.

Galland whispered back. "You're easy, Josten. Yet there's something to what you say. I've met him several times before, but never like this. It gives me something to think about." He paused, then added, "Just like your friendship with Hafner does."

Josten raised his voice defensively. "What is there to think about? He is an old comrade."

"He's a dangerous man, Josty. Be careful."

Josten paused before he replied. "Dolfo, if you and Hafner combine forces, we'll get the 262 next year. He already has enormous power, plus backing at the very top. But he needs your approval, your imprimatur, for the 262. Will you work with him?"

"Now that you've asked, point-blank, I'll tell you. I'm reluctant to work closely with him as a matter of principle. He siphons off something from every deal, just like all the top Nazis, Hitler included."

Josten was troubled, almost insulted. How could he say this about the man they'd just left? "Hitler? Goering perhaps, but not Hitler. He lives very simply."

The concern about microphones had one advantage; in speaking softly, Galland also spoke slowly and distinctly.

"Don't fool yourself. He's become the wealthiest man in Germany, from the sales of *Mein Kampf*, from his royalty on stamps—and they *all* have his portrait now—from gifts, who knows what all. But I can excuse Hitler and Goering; they are certifiable. But not Hafner; he is a soldier, or he was one. For him to steal from his fellow soldiers is truly criminal."

Galland turned and went to his cubicle. Josten fingered his new "tin necktie." Every German service man dreamed of winning the Knight's Cross; it was the ultimate reward, respected by all, soldiers and civilians alike. With it you could go to the head of any line, get reservations in any restaurant, and rarely have to pay. Even the enemy knew what it meant. Yet after talking to Galland, it didn't seem significant anymore.

The Japanese were unstoppable in the Pacific. President Franklin Roosevelt decided to intervene personally in the tactical conduct of the war, to create a victory as a sop to American morale. Germany was still the main target, but he demanded a reprisal air raid on Tokyo.

On the surface, it seemed impossible. The pitifully few U.S. carriers could not be risked close to Japan, nor were there any bases from which the longer-ranged Army Air Forces bombers could attack.

Yet, by chance, the answer to Roosevelt's demands had already been realized. On January 20, 1942, six weeks after Pearl Harbor, Captain Francis S. Low had suggested to Admiral Ernest J. King, chief of naval operations, that Army medium bombers launched from a Navy carrier could bomb Tokyo. It was unheard of, but the aggressive King liked the concept, and sent Low to ask General Henry Arnold's opinion. Arnold concurred, calling Henry Caldwell in to confer. The meeting was simple. Arnold outlined the problem and Caldwell said, "There's only one man for the operation—Jimmy Doolittle. I'll back him up with some good help, but Jimmy's your man." After the meeting, Caldwell called Jim Lee on the phone and detailed him as Doolittle's right-hand man.

Despite the urgent need for materiel everywhere—warships, aircraft, men, equipment—a task force was created for this symbolic strike at the Japanese heartland. King saw to it that the Navy made the carrier and escorts available and, with Caldwell's backing, Lee saw to it that Doolittle had everything he needed. It was a tremendous learning experience for everyone—and one of the things Lee learned was that he had a talent for management.

As so often in the past, Caldwell had picked exactly the right men for the job. The diminutive Doolittle was world-famed for his record-setting flying. The public was less aware that he was a scientist and a manager of extraordinary capability. His first task was to select the aircraft to be used. The choice was simple, for only one bomber existed that had both the range and would fit on the deck of the carrier—the North American B-25. It was called the "Mitchell," for the court-martialed general who had so long ago preached the vulnerability of warships to airplanes and predicted a Sunday morning attack by Japan on Pearl Harbor.

Doolittle, given carte blanche, sent Lee to the depot in Sacramento to supervise the aircraft modifications. In the meantime, Doolittle worked out the tactics and logistics, trained the pilots and crew members, and had the entire task force on the docks in Alameda, California, ready to sail on the new U.S.S. *Hornet's* first wartime sortie. To Lee's intense disappointment, Doolittle didn't select him for a crew position. To Doolittle it was a simple decision—Lee didn't have enough multi-engine flying time. Lee took the rebuff quietly, making up his mind to check out in every damn airplane at Wright Field.

On April 18, 1942, Doolittle delivered the blow Roosevelt had called for, one that affected the war only imperceptibly but foretold its end perfectly.

Characteristically, Doolittle had been the first man off the *Hornet's* deck. No one before had ever taken off from a carrier in a heavily laden bomber the size of the B-25. There had been only 467 feet of deck between the plane and the ocean. Two white lines, one for the nose wheel and one for the left wheel, were painted as guides down the rolling, pitching deck. If the pilot stayed on the lines the right wing would miss the carrier's island by six feet. Doolittle had made it look easy. The other pilots had followed with confidence.

Each of the sixteen B-25s was carrying three five-hundred-pound demolition bombs and a single special five-hundred-pound canister of incendiaries. Sixteen planes, each with a ton of bombs, was not much of a force compared to Pearl Harbor—yet it made the Japanese blink. And much later, when Caldwell had Jim Lee compile the intelligence summaries on the raid, their planning was reinforced. The country needed the long-range B-29 if it were ever to defeat Japan.

Wright Field/July 18, 1942

Bandfield stood at the window, watching the flight line at Wright Field. When he'd been there the first time, in 1933, there had only been a handful of biplanes scattered about. Now there were more than a hundred airplanes on the ramp, everything from Ryan trainers to the huge Douglas XB-19. With a 212-foot wingspan, it was the biggest airplane in the world—and already hopelessly obsolete.

Bandfield followed Hadley Roget into the conference room and Roget nodded to the group of officers sitting around the table, muttering, "I only know a few of these guys. They're pretty big wheels to be lumped in one meeting."

"They head up all the major supply and logistic divisions at Wright and Patterson fields."

Roget, always irritable, moaned, "Well, what does Caldwell want? I've got more to do than stand around jawing with you."

"I'm not sure, but he's only called in you, me, Jim Lee, and the division heads."

Lee, recognized as Caldwell's fair-haired lad since the Tokyo raid, was sitting quietly in the corner, exhausted from his self-imposed schedule. Still furious with himself because Doolittle hadn't selected him, he'd spent the intervening months flying everything he could get his hands on, from PT-17s to B-24s.

At the same time, he knew his non-selection had been fortunate. None of the sixteen airplanes on the Tokyo raid had made it to their planned safe havens; only fourteen of the crews had survived. Jimmy Doolittle came home expecting to be court-martialed for what he considered a failure—instead he'd been given the Medal of Honor and was made a brigadier general.

The door flew open and a grim-faced Caldwell stormed in, both arms clasped around a bulging leather briefcase. Around the table the officers made halfhearted attempts at coming to attention, the mixture of movements that said, "We know what we're supposed to do, but we know you don't go for that stuff."

"At ease, gentlemen, as if you weren't already. I'm sorry to interrupt your schedule, but I want to make sure you understand my message today. Let me go through my list, then we'll have questions later."

Caldwell picked through his briefcase and picked out four manila folders, each one crammed with the crumpled onionskin carbons that poured out of headquarters and sheets of yellow foolscap with his cramped writing scrawled all over.

Looking around, Caldwell said, "Gentlemen, I've called you here to impress one thing upon you. The only way we can win this war is with the best technology. The Germans are smart—we've got to be smarter. For that reason the top priorities for the United States Army Air Forces are the following four projects."

He paused, making sure he had their attention, and went on. "First, the Boeing B-29. The program is just beginning to develop, but it takes precedence over everything, even the other priority programs. I'm going to be the point man, but you are the people who will make it happen.

"Second, the long-range fighter program. We've got to have a fighter that can go all the way to Berlin and back. Don't rule anything out—refueling, towing, parasite fighters, anything— because we won't be able to live in the air over Germany without them. Bandy, I want you to concentrate on this, especially on developing bigger external tanks. Right now I think the best solution is to put a Merlin engine in the McNaughton Sidewinder, and hang some big tanks on it."

Eyebrows lifted all around the room. McNaughton's contribution to the war effort had been marginal so far—more bad technology than high technology.

"Third, Hadley Roget's 'Operation Leapfrog.' We've got to come up with something special. We're getting back reports that the

Germans have already flown at least two different types of jet fighters."

There were surprised exclamations; these men were veterans and knew that it took years—decades sometimes—to develop a conventional engine, much less anything radical.

"And last, aircraft for Russia. We're going to send them as many P-40s and McNaughton Sidewinders as we can; Arnold is willing to waive all deliveries on Sidewinders to the USAAF, and send them all to Russia."

He looked up expectantly and asked, "Any questions?"

The lowest ranking man in the room, the just promoted Jim Lee, was the first to speak.

"General, how come we're sticking with McNaughton? I saw Bandfield here get shot down in one by a slant-eye in a Jap Piper Cub over in Hawaii."

"The McNaughton is a good plane—"

"Come on, General, you know as well as I do that the McNaughton is a big disappointment." Lee paused during the stunned silence and said, "Forgive my speaking out, but you didn't make general by being quiet, did you?"

Caldwell knew that stupid familiarity like this was the price for seeking out individualists—and for not pulling rank. He took a moment to control himself, then said, "No, Captain, but that's how I made major."

The group burst into laughter, relieved to have the situation resolved with the general coming out on top. Caldwell looked at Lee for a few seconds, realizing that his work was cut out for him.

"Stick around after this meeting, Captain Lee. I've got a little additional instruction for you." The officers around the table nudged each other and winked; nobody liked a smart-ass and Lee was going to get his. Yet most felt that he was right—Caldwell's support for McNaughton was unusual.

"Any *serious* questions?"

Roget put up his hand. "Yes, General, can you tell us what the source of your information is on the new German engine? Or at least, how reliable you think it is?"

Caldwell thought of Lyra and suppressed a smile. "Hadley, take it from me that it's a very reliable source."

He entertained a little more discussion, then dismissed them, motioning Lee to wait. Bandfield asked if he could wait outside and see him after he was finished with Lee. Surprised and somewhat annoyed, Caldwell agreed.

When the door was shut, Caldwell said quietly, "Captain Lee, you were out of line. You did a terrific job working with Doolittle, and I know you were disappointed that you didn't fly the mission. But it's not becoming for you to behave like that. And it's insulting to me."

Lee automatically came to rigid attention.

Caldwell went on. "At ease. I'm as concerned as you are about McNaughton's performance. And I think you are the man who can help. The Sidewinder has some problems, just like any other new plane."

Lee shifted uncomfortably, feeling that he was being set up.

"In about six months I'm going to need you to go to Seattle to ramrod the B-29 program. That's how much I think of you—how much I value what you did in preparing for the Tokyo raid. In the meantime, I'm getting you an assignment to the 67th Fighter Squadron in the South Pacific. It's reequipping with Sidewinders, using airplanes that the British ordered and turned back. You're just the guy to figure out how to improve them."

Lee saw immediately what Caldwell was doing. It was classic service discipline: give somebody who makes a criticism the task of correcting the problem. And perhaps there was more. Caldwell was giving him a flick of the whip, getting him prepared for the future. Well—okay. Flying even the McNaughton in combat was better than pushing papers at Wright Field.

"That's great, General. I appreciate the challenge. I'll do my best."

"You're dismissed. Send Major Bandfield in, please."

Bandfield came in and asked, "Can we talk off the record—as friends?"

Caldwell nodded, pointed to a chair, and dug in his desk for a bottle of Old Crow and two glasses.

"What can I do for you, Bandy?"

"I'm trying to do something for you. It would be the biggest mistake of the war to put Merlin engines in the Sidewinder; it's throwing good money after bad. The engines ought to go in the P-51."

"I think you're wrong." Caldwell's voice had gone up a notch, the veins in his neck were thickening, and a rosy hue suffused his face, all signs of losing control of his temper.

"There's something else, too." Bandfield was hesitant. They'd been friends a long time, but this was pretty delicate.

"It's how people perceive it, Henry. Everybody knows the Mustang is a superior plane. The P-51 program is going to need all the Merlin engines Packard can produce. If you send Merlins to McNaughton, the only conclusion people will draw is that you're favoring them."

"Goddamnit, Bandy, I don't care what conclusions people draw. I think I'm doing the right thing, and that's all that counts with me. I believe in McNaughton, just like I believe in you and Hadley. Even like I believe in that smart-ass Lee. Troy McNaughton says he can fix the problems. If he can, we can have a long-range fighter by early 1943. The *best* North American can do is mid-1943. It's a gamble, but I'm used to taking gambles when the odds are right."

The tone was final, admitting to no argument.

"Henry, I'm sorry to be such a pain in the ass, but I had to say what I was thinking."

"It's okay. I understand. I've just got so many other problems. But I've got some ideas. Sit down."

He poured and they drank, letting the masculine mixture of whiskey, anger, friendship, and stubbornness mix, then settle. Bandfield could have sworn that he saw tears in Caldwell's eyes.

"Bandy, you're about the only one I can talk to. If I went to the flight surgeon, he'd probably ground me or throw me in the loony bin."

"Sure, spill it. You know it'll never leave this room."

Caldwell drank again, then let the words tumble out. "Maybe I'm spread too thin, working too hard. But, Bandy, this goddamn woman in Nashville is driving me out of my mind. Elsie. I'm obsessed by her."

Caldwell twisted a pencil in his hand.

"I know I'm behaving like a high school kid. I go crazy if I think somebody else is looking at her. I'm jealous of Troy McNaughton, because he gets to spend so much time with her. And now I'm jealous of a dead man—or at least a man she thinks is dead."

Bandfield might have laughed if Caldwell hadn't looked so desperate.

"You know she used to work for Bruno Hafner. You probably knew all along that they were lovers."

"Well, I didn't *know* anything, but it figures. Bruno was a bastard who'd fuck anything that moved, and she was just a young kid who didn't know any better. But Christ, that was ten years ago, maybe more, and Bruno's dead. What can it matter?"

"You think he is and she thinks he is. But I've known for a long time that he is alive. Crippled, I understand, but alive."

Bandfield knocked his drink over as all the old emotions of hate and fear flooded him. Bruno Hafner! The man had haunted him for almost ten years—and now he was back from the dead! He mopped up the liquor with his handkerchief and, finally, his voice under control, said, "Incredible. I thought I killed him over Guernica."

"No, and I feel like a damn fool for not knowing earlier. We should have followed up on the fight, found out what happened. But everything was so sensitive—you being in the Air Corps and fighting for the Loyalists."

"Are you sure? How good is your source? Why didn't you tell me before?"

"I couldn't, because of the source—it's inside Germany, and I can't reveal it. And I didn't want to shake you up. But that's beside the point. Elsie doesn't know he's alive—but I'm still insanely jealous of the time she spent with him."

"That *is* nuts, Henry. You're overtired, overworked. You can't let something like this eat you up."

"Jesus, Bandy, think about it. It's bad enough that I'm emotionally involved with a woman who works for a contractor—I know everybody thinks I'm favoring McNaughton because of that. But she'd probably be considered a security risk, too, because she used to"—he hesitated, visibly torn by his choice of words—"used to screw Hafner!"

"Henry, that's the least of your problems! The real threat is that people might believe you're being influenced by love or money. You know, you're a much bigger spender nowadays than you ever were before."

Caldwell stared at him. "Jesus, Bandy, it was pretty goddamn tough for a captain to be a big spender during the Depression. I'm a general now, with no responsibilities—of course I can spend more."

"We're talking about how things look, Henry . . . and people—"

"Goddamnit, you're getting off the point. I don't want to talk about stupid bullshit like whether I'm on the take or not. I'm acting like a damn fool over Elsie, and I don't know how to stop."

"Well, I know what Patty would say. She'd say face up to it, tell Elsie your concerns. Tell her you've heard Bruno is alive. See how she reacts. You're probably just borrowing trouble. You ought to take two weeks leave and haul Elsie down to New Orleans or somewhere and just screw this out of your system."

Caldwell calmed down as he turned the idea over in his mind. "It would be great. I don't think I could get away for two weeks. But I could manage maybe four or five days. Hell, I'm entitled."

"You're entitled. Besides, the Army needs you; it can't afford to have you worrying about your sanity."

The older man was touched by Bandfield's obvious concern. "Back to business. Tell you what, Bandy. Just to be on the safe side on this long-range fighter business, why don't you see what you can do about extending the range on some of the standard fighters—you know, external tanks, fuel in the wings, behind the cockpit, whatever?"

Bandfield decided to go for the extra mile. "And how about splitting the Merlin engine deliveries between McNaughton and North American?"

"Yeah, maybe we can do that. And, Bandy, I'm sorry if I flew off the handle. I've got a lot of pressure on me. Talking to you really helped."

"Giving me this assignment will help, too—people will see that you've got a lot of irons in the fire and aren't just playing up to McNaughton."

"I hope so. Doesn't matter. I've got to do what I think is right. Fuck 'em all but six, Bandy, and save them for pallbearers. Right?"

"Right, General."

6

Leipheim, Germany/July 18, 1942

Many more than six pallbearers were needed in a Germany suffocating in bad odors. From the rank fug arising from the unwashed masses on the U-Bahn to the death-sweet stench of burned wood and crumpled bodies in bombed-out buildings, Germany reeked. On the windblown airfield at Leipheim, there was a nauseating new stink, the pestilential vapors of J2 fuel. A half-tracked Kettenkrad had towed a tank truck into position and greasy, snouted nozzles were pumping peat-yellow oil into the tanks of the prototype Messerschmitt Me 262. Its turbines could burn anything from alcohol to paraffin, but were designed specifically for J2, the dregs of the refining process and available in quantity.

"Smells wonderful, eh, Josten?" Bruno Hafner sat in his wheelchair, a woolen throw across his legs. "Don't wrinkle your nose like that—we couldn't afford this masterpiece if it burned aviation gasoline."

Josten looked at Hafner with an odd combination of fascination and admiration. He was one of the bravest men he'd ever known, fighting from a wheelchair the total war that Hitler always called for.

Absolutely ruthless—cruel was a better word—he put Germany before everything. And he knew how to get things done. Josten had once been sickened by the human cost of foreign workers systematically starved to death under Hafner's methods. But as the casualty tolls from bombing and the Eastern Front soared, he had hardened. Now he was as committed to winning by any means as Hafner. After the war, the *Frontsoldaten*, the warriors, would clean up this Nazi mess.

"This is what we need to stop the bombing. I hate to think what it will be like a year from now when the Americans join with the Royal Air Force. We've got to get some new fighters. If we win on the Eastern front, we can come back and build all the bombers Hitler wants."

Hafner nodded in agreement. "I have a meeting scheduled with Albert Speer for later this afternoon. If you have a successful flight, I'm going to try to convince him to let me bring this aircraft into immediate full production."

Josten nodded and then walked to the waiting 262, admiring the shark shape of its flat-bottomed triangular fuselage with its leopard-like mottled camouflage. Messerschmitt engineers had coated the skin with putty and water-sanded it smooth for the sleekest aerodynamic finish. The 262 was big for a fighter, with a thirteen-meter wingspan, and weighing seven thousand kilograms fully loaded—twice as much as the 109. Its conventional tail-wheel undercarriage gave the plane a nose-up stance, so that the Junkers Jumo 004A turbojet engines slung under the wing almost touched the ground. Josten knew that on engine start, flames would blowtorch out the rear of the long, tubular nacelles, and he'd have to move forward quickly to avoid burning holes in the asphalt hardstand. The tricycle gear planned for production aircraft models would eliminate the problem.

A mechanic helped him up on the wing and into the cockpit. The side-closing canopy was similar to the one in the 109, but the cockpit was bigger, more spacious. The obvious, most disquieting differences between the airplanes were the absence of propellers and the stomach-churning stench of the jet fuel.

Once settled in the cockpit, he adjusted the clipboard on his knee, then began the critical, two-handed engine-start process. In a practice session, he'd had to leap out of one burning 262 when pooled fuel ignited in the nacelle.

The jet burned fuel so fast that there was no time to waste. Josten taxied quickly to the end of the twelve-hundred-meter-long grass runway, checked his instruments again, and slowly added power. Throttle movement was critical—too fast and you would have an explosion, too slow and the engine would stall from fuel starvation.

The engineers had said the airplane would fly off at 180 kilometers per hour. He hoped they were right. If they were wrong there wouldn't be enough runway left to stop, and burning up, even in the world's fastest fighter, would be no honor.

The high-slung nose blocked out the forward visibility, so he used the runway edge as a reference as he eased the throttles full forward. The airplane was sluggish, leaden, as if protesting that the power rushing from the rear of the engines was only so much hot air. At least it didn't have the corkscrew torque forces of the 109, which still killed pilots on a daily basis by pulling them off the runway on takeoff.

The 262 dragged forward and an internal alarm went off as the runway slowly unreeled beneath him, a sensor warning, "This thing isn't moving fast enough." The airspeed passed 160 kilometers per hour and the tail showed no sign of rising. Adding more and more forward pressure on the stick, he tried to get the nose down to cut the drag and accelerate. There was no response—the airflow over the wing was blanking out the elevators. The runway could reach to Johannesburg and he'd never get off the ground.

Grudgingly, the Messerschmitt moved faster, the short runway disappearing behind it, its tail wheel still planted firmly, the airflow streaming over the wing, hitting the ground, then deflecting up to hold the low-set tailplane down.

Hafner half rose out of his wheelchair, screaming, "Jesus, Helmut, pull up, pull up!"

The airspeed indicator read 180 kilometers per hour. Josten knew that in ten seconds he would scream off the end of the runway into a line of trees, rolling Germany's last chance at victory into a ball of flames. There was no longer room to stop—it was fly or die.

In desperation he tapped the brakes; they grabbed momentarily, wrenching the nose down in a reverse rotation. It was miraculous; the elevators bit the air, and Josten instinctively horsed back on the stick to send the airplane rising like a pheasant from a hedge, the wheels clipping through the tops of the trees, speed building, the controls answering crisply. One tap of the brakes had changed death to life.

His left hand reached down and pressed the buttons to raise the landing gear. The jet was accelerating so fast he was afraid he'd tear the gear doors off; he kept coming back on the stick, the nose kept rising, but unlike any airplane he'd ever flown before, the airspeed kept increasing at a faster and faster rate. They had briefed him that power would increase with speed, as more air was forced into the engine, but no one had told him to expect that the plane would grow quieter the faster he went, in a sweet, vibrationless soaring that was more like a super-swift sailplane than a fighter.

God, what an airplane, he thought. It feels like the angels are pushing!

He glanced below—the field was already almost out of sight, and he hadn't even leveled off, the speed packing power into the engines, the engines translating the power to more speed.

He cocked the jet up in a sixty-degree bank, keeping the field in sight; when he leveled out he left the power forward. The jet fighter leapt forward to 800 kilometers per hour, faster than any fighter in the world, and on its first test flight. What a triumph for the engineers, for Willi Messerschmitt, for Germany! No matter what the Allies were doing, they couldn't have anything like this. The speed and the firepower made this a *war-winner*, and no mistake.

As he leveled off and checked the instruments, the full weight of his responsibility hit him. It was one thing to have made a successful first flight—he knew that a less experienced pilot would probably have crashed before the plane left the runway—but it was another now to affect national policy, to weld together all the competing political interests and concentrate on manufacturing this airplane, to get Galland and Hafner to work together.

The flight was only eight minutes old when Josten swooped down and thundered across the field at ten meters above the ground, the slim, trim lines of the aircraft appearing and disappearing before the crowd of engineers and pilots lining the field could even hear the roar of its engines. Josten pulled up in a steep chandelle to traffic pattern altitude and then flew a cautious approach, carrying power, making sure that he touched down on the near edge of the runway; this was no time to have a landing accident.

Bruno Hafner had watched the jet roar across the field with the certainty that he had found a solution. As a pilot, he knew he was watching history being made. As a manager, he knew that the bureaucracy would take years to get this airplane into production. Everything depended upon Speer's response, for Speer would have the last word with Hitler.

Josten managed to taxi back through the jubilant crowd lining the runway. Utterly pragmatic, he knew that he'd been lucky to survive the first flight of an experimental aircraft and that he might not survive the second. Shrugging off congratulations, Josten ran to the operations shack and put through a Blitz Priority call to Galland's headquarters.

"Dolfo, you were right about the 262—it is sensational."

"Congratulations on surviving the first flight!"

"Thanks. Let me tell you, I'm not just being carried away. I'm being conservative when I tell you that this could put us two or three years ahead of the enemy. They couldn't live in the skies with this airplane, not now, not next year, not three years from now. We've got to get it into mass production right away."

"Any problems? Besides the engines, what needs to be changed for the operational aircraft?"

"I've only flown it once, so I can't be sure. It needs to have a tri-cycle landing gear, certainly; service pilots couldn't use it otherwise. And you're right, the engines are just toys now, they need to be developed. But believe me, no matter what the problems, if we build enough of them we can establish air superiority everywhere.

The speed is fantastic, and the ground tests prove that the guns are killers."

"The engines are the only bottleneck—we've got to solve the overheating problem."

Josten agreed, signed off, and then sat slumped in the chair, the joy of his triumphant first flight fading in the light of Galland's concerns.

As the test-flight tension drained from him, he wondered why his life had to be so complicated. He was just a soldier, yet nothing was easy. It was evident that he and Lyra were drifting apart, no matter what he did. She was preoccupied with something, behaving more and more strangely. He didn't think it was another man, although it could be, of course. It was probably this stupid Jewish business. He knew *he* hadn't changed.

The war, perpetually at a crucial stage, was expanding on all the fronts, never quite achieving a final victory. Now they had the answer in hand, if he could only come up with a solution that would convince the right people. If these jets went into action in 1943—even by the fall—Germany could stop the enemy bombers.

Berlin/August 14, 1942

Her breakfast had been the usual porridge mixed with yogurt—now her stomach was rumbling, and she wondered whether the office canteen would have its standard red cabbage with meat sauce for lunch, or perhaps the tasteless but more filling stonefish patties. Lyra started to get up when, hands suddenly trembling, she saw the two items in the "Blue Sheet," the daily military intelligence summary. She quickly checked to see if her unctuous chief, Anton Rascher, was properly buried under his paperwork. Hostile when she'd come on board, Rascher was a tea-and-biscuit twit who became friendly in a smarmy way after he had sniffed out her "friendship" with Goebbels.

The thought of the little Propaganda Minister made her skin crawl. Try as she might, it was impossible to blank out the memories of her personal war, the nastiness of her physical relationship with Goebbels. Fortunately, the sessions were always short. Goebbels was an inept lover, ejaculating almost instantly. He always seemed relieved that she had no demands of her own, and believed, or pretended to believe, her protestations of satisfaction. The sole saving grace was that he always had hot water in his apartment so that she could bathe quickly.

Shuddering, she turned back to her task, thanking God for the insatiable German penchant for documentation. Short of the outright criminal activity, *everything* was put on paper, stamped SE-CRET and promptly circulated on one of the numerous interdepartment "restricted lists." Rascher was high enough on the Foreign Ministry totem pole to rate several, none of which she was supposed to read.

It was strange to see Helmut's name and an account of his successful flight in the jet. Even more interesting was a detailed account of Hafner's subsequent meeting with Speer—the diligent clerk even noted that Speer had given Hafner a dachshund puppy!

She placed the Blue Sheet in an aging manila folder for camouflage, then began to copy the salient points.

Her hands were sweating, and the steel nib of the pen scratched the cheap paper, a pad of old reports that had been reversed, then bound in another one of the department's "economy drives." The carte blanche Speer had given Hafner for his experimental center was amazing. The Messerschmitt plant at Augsburg had twenty-four airframes for the 262, standing idle because there were no engines for them. Speer had approved their transfer to Hafner, who had guaranteed bringing an operational jet unit into being within the year. He was going to freeze the airframe design and promised somehow to solve the engine problems.

There was more. Hafner had an experimental feeding program for his foreign laborers, trying to determine the minimum calorie level he could provide and still get ten hours work a day from them. One group was to get two thousand calories a day, another twelve hundred, and a third eight hundred. A phrase leapt out at her: "The workers are to draw on their present stock of fat and muscle in

the service of the Reich." A very elegant way to say, "The workers
are to be starved to death."

She decided to pass on the information about the feeding experiment to Caldwell, too. It was sickening. She could understand how
Helmut might be so loyal to Germany that he tolerated the Nazi
idea. But how could he have anything to do with a monster like
Hafner?

Guadalcanal/September 29, 1942

In the South Pacific, the Japanese, flush with an apparently endless
series of victories, were startled by the Americans in the Battle of the
Coral Sea in May. For the first time in naval warfare at sea, the
exchange was entirely by air; no ship on either side saw the enemy.
The Japanese claimed a victory, having inflicted slightly more losses
than they received, and rejoiced in the sinking of the famous
American aircraft carrier, the U.S.S. *Lexington*. But it was far from
being a victory on the scale of Pearl Harbor. The real result was that
the intended Japanese invasion of Port Moresby, New Guinea, was
postponed.

Determined to lash back, and mindful of Doolittle's Tokyo raid,
Admiral Isoroku Yamamoto decided to take Midway Island, some
thirteen hundred miles west-northwest of Hawaii. He dispersed his
fleet from the Marianas to the Aleutians. Sailing on the world's
most powerful battleship, the 72,800-ton *Yamato*, Yamamoto commanded the greatest armada ever assembled in the Pacific, 165
warships.

He himself was commanded by worms. Yamamoto loved sashimi
and had indulged himself before his ships sortied. En route, tiny
parasites staged their own Pearl Harbor in his intestinal tract, virtually incapacitating him during the most crucial moments of
battle.

Besides Yamamoto's worms, the Japanese fleet had to contend
with a U.S. force, albeit smaller, savagely hungry for revenge, and

as a result of intercepts, well informed on Japanese intentions. The American carriers were ably handled—and lucky. In the ensuing battle in early June 1942, Japan lost four carriers, more than three hundred aircraft, and the bulk of its most highly trained pilots. Precisely as Yamamoto had predicted, Japan had run wild in the Pacific for six months; now the tide was beginning to turn. Now Yamamoto concentrated his efforts on evicting the invading Americans from Guadalcanal.

Captain Jim Lee, sitting in a pool of sweat as his McNaughton Sidewinder vibrated beneath him like a Harley-Davidson with a blown gasket, was not aware of the war's new trend. He'd arrived on Guadalcanal the week before, flying in with four other pilots from the Sidewinder Operational Training Unit. They were replacements for the 67th Pursuit Squadron, part of the "Cactus Air Force," a tiny group of Army, Navy, and Marine pilots who maintained a tenuous American grip on Guadalcanal as Japanese efforts to retake the island escalated.

The battle for Guadalcanal, an obscure island until it was seen as the logical stepping-stone for a Japanese invasion of Australia, centered on the tiny airstrip the Marines had wrested from the surprised Japanese defenders. American engineers poured in, and with bulldozer and interlocking perforated steel plates—Marston mat—made it available to Grumman F4F fighters and Douglas SBD dive-bombers.

So far the fighting had been fairly even. The American planes were generally slower and less maneuverable than the Japanese, but they were far more rugged and had greater firepower. The principal Japanese bomber was the Mitsubishi G4M1, called *Hamaki*— cigar—by its crews because of its round, fat fuselage. These were large, fast airplanes, possessed of a very long range because of their huge, unprotected fuel tanks. Regularly, they flew in impeccable formation over the six hundred miles from Rabaul, New Guinea, in the Bismarck Archipelago, to bomb the airstrip. Mitsubishi fighters

—Zeros—escorted the bombers, then made their own strafing runs.

With highly disciplined hit-and-run tactics, the Grummans could combat the Zeros on even terms; dogfighting with them was fatal. But the F4F pilots loved to catch a flight of the vulnerable G4M1 bombers and light them up like torches with just a few hits.

For the thousandth time, Lee realized just how tough Caldwell had been with him—and how lucky he was for it. First he'd been sent for a month-long indoctrination at the McNaughton factory to check out the Sidewinder. Presumed to be Caldwell's friend because he came from Headquarters, he was immediately introduced to the top management—including the woman he'd heard so many rumors about, Elsie Raynor. In the process, he'd really learned to fly the Sidewinder and had concluded that, while it wasn't as good as McNaughton claimed, it wasn't as bad as most people thought.

Lee was not unaware that McNaughton had given him a specially prepared airplane, powered by a more powerful engine and cleaned up on the basis of wind-tunnel reports. Troy McNaughton insisted that if the Packard Merlin engine was installed, the Sidewinder could be used as the desperately needed long-range fighter. From the reports he gave Lee, it looked possible.

More important, Lee recognized that Elsie was extremely powerful. When people wanted things done in the plant, they went to her first. Troy obviously liked and trusted her, and he valued her link to Caldwell. Lee had done some pro forma flirting, just part of a pilot's customary routine, and was surprised by Elsie's immediate and direct response. Flattered that a younger man would be interested in her, amused that they were both redheads, she had taken him to bed within a week of his arrival.

Now, wiping sweat from his brow in Guadalcanal, Lee was watching a line of Navy Grumman Wildcats warm up. The Marine and Navy pilots had been quick to fill their Army reinforcements in on living conditions, nicknames, tactics, and survival in the miserable heat and humidity. The island, so beautiful from the air, green and clean against the blue waters and white clouds of the Pacific, was dourly distressing close up. The jungle's exuberant growth choked the volcanic soil; its rotting vegetation was laden with poisons. Even the slightest nick required medical attention to prevent rampant infection.

Situated in "Mosquito Gulch," their rain-drenched tents were spotted among the huge coconut palms of the old Lever Brothers copra plantation, between the field and the beach. There was no flooring and a shortage of cots; some pilots had to sleep on stinking wet Japanese straw mats. Each day, at the height of the rain, the cots and mats sank into the mud, to be pried out later.

Dress wasn't a problem; they had only the flying suits or the khakis they'd arrived in, their "cover" a blue baseball cap designed to shield them from the burning sun that followed the rains. They ate a miserable melange of captured Japanese rice and Spam, cooked in as many different ways as possible by beleaguered Marine cooks, who worked with spoons in one hand and rifles in the other.

The war was everywhere. Every night ships of the Tokyo Express would come down the slot to heave shells into the compound, to be followed by small two-place seaplanes harassing them with machine-gun fire. They called the seaplanes "Washing-machine charlies" in jest, but the noise destroyed their chances for badly needed sleep.

The pilots lay less than two and one half miles in any direction from the fighting perimeter held by the First Marine Division. A "banzai" charge could overrun them in just a few minutes, so most kept a weapon near at hand.

There were hazards everywhere else as well, from taxiing the fighters over the rough, watersoaked ground, to clearing the trees that surrounded the runway in an enormous green crash barrier.

The one great advantage of the Cactus Air Force—the name came from their radio call sign, "Cactus"—lay in the coast-watcher reports, the information from the patriots who hid themselves in isolated island outposts and reported the movement of Japanese ships and planes. With admirable foresight, the Australian Navy had recruited from a mixed bag of civil servants, retired enlisted men, and planters an intelligence force that radioed critical information on Japanese intentions. It saved the pilots precious fuel by letting them delay until the last minute before scrambling.

Now Lee waited, his eyes glued to the needle of the coolant temperature gauge that was hovering at its redline, as heat shimmered from the olive-drab Sidewinder. If his flight didn't take off soon, the Allison engines would cook themselves to pieces, and instead of four McNaughton fighters, they'd have four fixed-machine-gun nests to trundle into the firing line.

He grinned, recalling his last time on the firing line, in Nashville, two days before he left for the Operational Training Unit. He'd submitted a whole series of test reports on the cleaned-up Sidewinder, but General Henry Caldwell hadn't believed one of them. Caldwell was always looking for an excuse to visit Nashville, so he came down to "talk to Lee personally"—and get in a little time with Elsie.

Things had started off badly—Lee had walked into the conference to find Caldwell and Elsie yelling about someone named Hafner. They were both embarrassed at his arrival, and Caldwell was giving him a severe dressing down on the etiquette of knocking before entering, when Troy McNaughton bounced in—also without knocking.

Like a schoolboy caught with jam on his face, Caldwell tried to cover by talking about Lee as if he weren't there.

"Jesus, Troy, back at Headquarters, Captain Lee raised hell with me, telling me that the Sidewinder wasn't any good. Then I get these reports that say it can be a superplane."

"He just had to get familiar with it, Henry. It's the same with all pilots. I'll bet even Bandfield would like it if he flew it a few hours."

"Well, if these are right, you've done a spectacular job cleaning the airplane up. I couldn't believe Lee's reports—picking up thirty miles per hour in top speed, and an extra four hundred miles in range."

"He's a good man, Henry. I didn't like him at first, thought he was a smart-ass, but he did his job and he was fair."

Elsie chimed in, "He's a real good test pilot, too. He'd fly the airplane all day and spend all night writing up the reports. He kept me busy typing."

Lee broke in, trying to sound properly modest. "I was just lucky, General; all the work had been done before I got here. All I had to do was validate it."

They ignored him.

"We had our best people on it, Henry, our 'tiger team.' They went over that airplane bolt by bolt, nut by nut. It was details, just details, but they added up."

When Caldwell left the meeting to go back to Washington, he had shaken McNaughton's hand, barely nodding to Lee and Elsie. Now, as Lee sat stewing in the Guadalcanal heat, he wondered if Caldwell knew that nothing was ever as it seemed—not love, not airplanes, not anything.

The scramble call crackled through the headsets, and the four Sidewinders took off, rocking back and forth as the nosegear chattered along the rough runway. Ahead, eight Grumman F4Fs were in a circling climb, waiting for them to catch up.

Sweat poured from Lee as he urged his plane higher. The Navy pilots had agreed to level off at fifteen thousand feet, because the McNaughtons had no oxygen. They circled clockwise in two groups, the Grummans on the outside, trying to slow down enough to stay with the Sidewinders.

Ceaselessly checking his instruments, Lee began to wonder if the scramble was a false alarm. They flew for forty minutes, watching their fuel supplies creep down while the towering cumulus clouds that presaged the next rain showers crept up.

Suddenly, down below, he saw four bombers, escorted by eight Zeros, hurtling toward the line of ships offloading supplies at the beach. Lee heard the flight leader yell "Tallyho" and dive; Lee followed with the rest of the McNaughtons while a flight of Grummans immediately peeled off after them.

Lee was exultant. They wouldn't have had a chance at fifteen thousand feet against the Zeros; now they were going to be fighting on the deck, where the odds were more even.

He lined up a bomber in his sights and fired a quick sighting burst from the four machine guns. Then, his aim dead on, he lifted the nose slightly and fired the flat-trajectoried 37-mm cannon, the thump, thump, thump of its recoil slowing the Sidewinder. The left wing of the bomber tore away, its fat fuselage rolling seaward before disappearing in a salty geyser.

Lee wracked the McNaughton into a vertical bank, turning as tightly as he could, G forces hammering him into the seat, trying to clear behind him. He saw an F4F dispose of another bomber and two Zeros spinning toward the sea.

Reversing his turn, he glanced back to see two Mitsubishi fighters behind him, one on either side. He pushed over toward the sea a thousand feet below, the Zeros following, thudding 7.9-mm bullets and 20-mm cannon shells into his aircraft. Squeezing down, praying that if the weak-lunged Allison engine behind him couldn't outrun the Japanese it would at least absorb their fire, he headed for the beach, hoping to draw the enemy fighters across the Marine antiaircraft guns.

The lead Zero moved closer, wanting to finish the McNaughton off. Lee felt the airplane shudder as cannon shells slammed into the engine. The propeller disc dissolved to a slowly turning paddle before stopping. He put the nose down to maintain speed, trading altitude for distance toward the shore.

Professionals, their job done, the two Zeros turned away to seek new prey while Lee concentrated on the touchdown. He knew he wasn't going to make it to landfall, so he tried to get within swimming distance of one of the lighters offloading cargo.

With the shattered engine and stopped propeller, it was quiet in the Sidewinder until he jettisoned the car-door entrance to the cockpit. The rush of wind was deafening, and he could hear the hissing from the boiling coolant radiator. A glance at the instrument panel showed that he was out of airspeed and altitude. Cinching up his straps, he eased the shattered fighter into the water, touching down tail low. The Sidewinder slowed until the propeller struck, pole-vaulting it over on its back.

As the plane somersaulted tail first, his arm flailed out the side door and his face crashed into the gunsight. He felt a sickening crack in his forearm and a lightning rush of pain as water surged in around him. The plane sank straight down until it was resting, inverted, twenty feet below the surface. His left arm useless, Lee fumbled with his straps, trying to hold his breath when all he wanted to do was scream in agony.

Cottbus, Germany/October 1, 1942

Bruno Hafner was drowning in bad war news. Rommel was retreating in Africa, and the drive toward Stalingrad was slowing down. The old warrior was edgy, despite his satisfaction with progress on the jet fighter. The first Me 262 airframes were already assembled in the huge underground factory. Galland had readily agreed to let Hafner have them, as the best hope of getting jet engines into mass production. Even the new blades, made of the rarest metals, had a short life in the raging inferno of the jet, but now old Fritz had provided a solution.

Hafner picked up a turbine blade, a simple T-shaped fold of metal. Fritz, the master machinist, had ignored the need for rare metals and gone to the heart of the problem: heat transfer. He had taken a simple sheet of ordinary steel and made a hollow airfoil of it. Ducts permitted air to flow through the turbine blade, cooling it effectively and eliminating the need for rare metals. It was a million-mark idea—and it might just win the war. They had run one engine in a test cell at full speed for a hundred hours straight. Now they were running acceleration and deceleration tests, full throttle, back to idle, full throttle again, and the engine was chirping along like a canary bird. Production engines probably wouldn't do as well, but if they lasted even twenty-five hours, it would be enough.

And if it didn't win the war, it might be a bargaining chip afterward. A year ago it looked as if Germany couldn't lose; now the odds were shifting rapidly. Russia sprouted divisions like a hydra—was there no end to their manpower?

Hafner reached into the satchel beside him and pulled out a package of foreign magazines, sent in from Switzerland, looking for the article he'd snipped from *Aviation*. It said that a farmer in Nashville had brought suit against the McNaughton Aircraft Company because the high-pitched roar of an engine under test had caused his chickens to stop laying, and that the explosions had frightened his cows. A McNaughton Aircraft spokesman had said only that it was a necessary test of a radical new type of engine.

There had been intelligence reports that McNaughton had a jet engine under development—this confirmed it.

Hafner realized with a start that this opened entirely new opportunities. If McNaughton was having trouble with its engine, he might be able to open negotiations with his old colleague Henry Caldwell directly. They might be able to do business. Caldwell was an entrepreneur, even if he wore a uniform. He'd be willing to trade—if he thought the terms were right—and Hafner would see that they were.

He had known for almost two years of Lyra's contacts with Caldwell; perhaps it was time to play the cards he held on the pretty little Jewess.

Northwest of Tula/November 18, 1942

They were sweeping too low for his taste over the tops of the green-black pine trees, the propellers of the red-starred Lisunov Li-2 transport churning twin crystal vortices from the snow-laden branches. Giorgi Scriabin hoped that the Messerschmitts would ignore the glistening signal that a victim was at hand.

Damn, I'm too old for this, Scriabin thought. He compressed himself into a ball beneath the rough Army greatcoat, trying to squeeze warmth from his fast-pumping heart into hands and feet long gone numb in the piercing forty degrees of frost. The Russians had kept the outward form of the license-built DC-3, but their version was sadly lacking in fit and finish. The faint warmth trickling from the cabin heater valve was swept away in the cyclone of wind sieving through the Li-2's cabin.

The harsh interior didn't bother Foreign Minister Vyacheslav M. Molotov, hunched over a rough wooden desk, as icily indifferent to the cold as he was to everything but his work. With his narrow-set unblinking eyes behind a pince-nez and his unsmiling mouth under a Stalin-like mustache he was the personification of an executioner.

Within the next hour, Molotov would determine whether Scriabin lived or died. Caldwell had convinced Scriabin that the McNaughtons were sound—and he had not paid attention to the warning cues from his colleagues. Scriabin had made the recommendations, Molotov had approved them—and the planes were failures.

A mechanic leaned into the cabin and whispered to Molotov's aide, who hesitantly relayed the landing warning to the Foreign Minister as if it were a mortal offense. Molotov ignored him, picking up yet another file to scan.

Scriabin huddled on the floor where he could glance upward out the windows on each side. The leaden sky, a sump of weather-baggaged clouds, abruptly changed to green walls, and he knew that his fate would soon be decided. He could sense the Li-2 pilot's skill as they crept in at the edge of a stall, the plane hanging on the power of its engines, struggling to touch down on the very edge of the short, narrow strip hacked out of a forest. The landing was firm, and Scriabin could feel the gradual application of brake as they slowed in the snow. At the end of the strip, the pilot had to apply power to taxi off toward the reception committee—a dour-looking group headed by Colonel Arkady Kosokov, whose savage report on the inadequacies of the McNaughton Sidewinder had precipitated Molotov's unprecedented visit to the front.

The rear door swung open, and they could hear the ragged tinny sounds of a pickup military band in the background. Molotov moved slowly down the cluttered aisle; his mind might be indifferent to the cold but his muscles were not, and he almost fell climbing down the short aluminum ladder.

Scriabin stood to one side as the formalities went on. It was strange; all the rituals the Communists had so proudly discarded in 1918—the saluting, medals, and epaulettes, all the signs and privileges of rank, the military ceremonies—were now back in force and with a vengeance. He saw that fighter planes, McNaughton Sidewinders and obsolete Polikarpov I-16s, were tucked into bays thrust among the trees, expertly camouflaged with cut boughs that made them invisible from the air.

Kosokov was introducing Molotov to an ace, Major Ivan Poryshkinov, just back from a mission flown in a grimy bemedaled jacket and a leather helmet too small for his massive skull.

"So, Major Poryshkinov, tell me about the McNaughton fighter."

Poryshkinov, obviously ill at ease and not sure of what was going on, looked in wild-eyed desperation at Kosokov, who nodded impatiently.

"It is a fine airplane, Comrade Commissar, a fine airplane. I just shot up a Fritz tank."

Molotov reached over to Kosokov's chest, pointing to the Order of Glory medal, suspended on its red-black-red-striped ribbon.

"Take that off."

Kosokov stiffened to attention, then unpinned the medal and handed it to Molotov.

"Major, I decorate you in honor of your honesty and of your victory over the German tank." He pushed the medal into Poryshkinov's hand, nodded contemptuously to Kosokov, and walked to the small wooden shack that sat at the side of the runway. He slid in the door and a covey of mechanics and pilots scrambled out, appalled to have been caught keeping warm instead of watching the ceremonies. Kosokov followed him. A moment later the door opened again, and Molotov beckoned to Scriabin to enter.

The room was no more than four meters square. An oil drum, its U.S. markings still visible, served as a stove, while boots and foot wrappings hung on the walls drying, lending their own distinctive stench to the smoky fug of the room. Yet it was a shield against the wind, and the temperature was above freezing, reason enough for the troops to pack it between sorties.

Kosokov was a fighter, and he was obviously not going to let the matter die on the basis of his pilot's comments.

"Don't pay any attention to Poryshkinov; he was still excited from the combat, and he was trying to say what he thought you wanted to hear. Believe me, Comrade Foreign Minister, the McNaughton is shit! We can't keep it maintained, and the ones we get in the air the Germans shoot down. You've read the reports I've sent in. Why can't we have some Spitfires, or even some Hurricanes? Or, if we have to have American junk, let it be P-47s or P-38s."

"Just give me your complaints, and leave the question of new aircraft to me," Molotov said impatiently.

Kosokov was not cowed at all. "I've written all the complaints down in my report, and I'll stand by every word."

Molotov's words were colder than the wind outside. "Tell me, Comrade Kosokov, how did you like our MiG-1 fighter?"

Kosokov now looked apprehensive at the direction of the conversation, but he spat out, "It was a killer on takeoffs and landings. The record shows that clearly."

"Yes, and how did you like our MiG-3?"

"Fast, but a poor fighter—no maneuverability."

"So, and tell me what did you think of our I-16?"

"In Spain, in 1937, it was fine; now it is obsolete, a pig!"

"You really don't like any fighters, do you, Kosokov? Perhaps you'd be better off in a bomber regiment, or in the infantry?"

Perspiration beaded on Kosokov's brow, but Scriabin could see that he was frustrated, not frightened.

"I've lost too many good men to the McNaughtons, Comrade Foreign Minister; your line of questioning is not fair."

"How many?"

"In eight weeks of operation, we have lost thirty-two pilots. Almost four per week, more than one hundred percent attrition for the squadron."

Molotov's voice dropped half an octave. "Thirty-two. My, how tragic." He paused, letting the tension build, and when he spoke again, his voice was savage, chipping at Kosokov's ego like a chisel on marble. "Do you know how many people die in Leningrad *every day* of starvation? Four thousand! And do you know how many we lost last June at Sevastopol? In three weeks, one hundred thousand! That's more than thirty-three thousand a week, *more* than four thousand a day! And you talk about four killed per *week?*"

Kosokov was silent; he knew Molotov's mind was made up, that his own career and maybe his life were over, and that there was little point in pushing him further.

"The problem is not the airplanes, Colonel Kosokov. The problem is you. Certainly you are going to lose men; I would have been happier if you told me you had lost thirty-two hundred; at least you would have been doing something."

Kosokov had fought in Spain. In June 1941, he had rammed his propeller through the tail of a Heinkel; he'd bailed out and was back in combat that afternoon. Since then he had risen to command a squadron and had not even counted his victories. He'd been shot down four times. And he had never been frightened. Till now.

He sputtered, "Trained pilots are in short supply—"

"The only thing in short supply here is courage. You are relieved of your command and confined to your quarters. I'll send you further orders soon. Come, Scriabin, away from this pigsty!"

The flight back to Moscow had been made in silence. Only when they landed did Molotov beckon to him.

"I'm going to confide in you, Scriabin. We have the chance of a great victory at Stalingrad. As it develops, I'll present the report on the McNaughton situation to Stalin. I am going to tell him that the McNaughton is performing well enough, but that Kosokov is a bad leader. He'll be so enthusiastic about beating the Germans that he'll accept my views on this. You're in the clear . . . for the time being."

The severity of his tone told Scriabin just how close to death he had been. Molotov went on: "Try very hard to get other kinds of airplanes from the Americans. If for some reason you cannot, then take the Sidewinders, or anything else they send. I will have instructions sent to the squadrons through the Stavka that casualties are unimportant, but dead Germans are."

"And what if Kosokov complains again?"

Molotov pulled out an ancient stem-winder pocketwatch and glanced at it.

"Kosokov has been dead for thirty minutes."

Stockholm/December 14, 1942

The wrought-iron bridges that connected Stockholm's islands were covered with hoarfrost. Caldwell gazed from his hotel window across the glistening icefield of the bay to the snow-covered turrets of the Royal Castle. The layer by layer frosting of November mists had lacquered everything, castle granite and bridge iron, into a single filmy pearlescence.

The Grand Hotel was painted in subdued tones of gray and yellow, a six-story structure that rambled outward from the small central castellated building into irregular wings built during its ad hoc expansion over the years. In front, a huge striped awning provided protection for the stream of black official cars constantly pulling up, the smooth lines of the Mercedeses, Volvos, and Chevrolets humpbacked with big charcoal-burning gas generators.

A gray blanket of wood smoke hung over the city, mixing with the pervasive dank odor of wet timber and fouling the normally crisp Swedish air. Coal was in short supply, so everywhere, in the streets, the parks, the docks, huge piles of wood were stacked three or four yards high, waiting to be sold for a pittance. The Swedes covered the sides of the piles with posters, and one in particular made Caldwell a little uncomfortable. It showed SOLDATEN 56 KARLSSON, the G.I. Joe of the newly militant Swedes, with his fingers to his lips, saying, "THE SPYS ARE BUILDING A PUZZLE—KEEP YOUR PIECE."

Caldwell had flown in from Scotland in a RAF Dakota, a Lend-Lease C-47, on a long and dangerous route that overflew Norway. Scriabin had come in an Aeroflot Lisunov Li-2. Painted in arctic camouflage, it had flown at night over Finland and the Gulf of Bothnia, vulnerable to any chance interception. Now Scriabin was alone with Caldwell in his hotel room, hunched over a two-kroner glass of brandy, still shivering from the stupefying cold of the unheated transport.

"I'm glad you agreed to meet with me ahead of time, General Caldwell. I'm going to speak plainly because I can't be away from my colleagues for too long. And I'm happy we're having the meeting in Stockholm; it's good for us all to get out of the Kremlin—you can't imagine the climate there. My men enjoy the chance to relax a bit and get a few decent meals."

Caldwell shrugged; it showed how relative things were. Swedish food and drink were patterned along German lines, running heavily to overcooked fish, potatoes, and the ubiquitous dolmas, the stuffed grape leaf delicacy that had made its way from Turkey to Sweden via the troops of Charles XII. Caldwell had lost five pounds on the previous trip. Even in the Grand Hotel restaurant, where Scriabin declined to eat on the basis of its being "too capitalistic," the food was poor by American standards. The one great advantage of the Grand was that there was plenty of liquor—at a price, of course—and for those that fancied it, "taxi girls," who would enter inconspicuously at a side entrance and walk up the stairs to avoid the elevator operator.

"General Caldwell, let me be blunt. The McNaughton aircraft you've sent us under Lend-Lease are inadequate for front-line service. We have the situation under control—at least temporarily—but if things blow up I could be shot."

"You're *not* going to be shot over the McNaughton! It is *not* inadequate. Your air force must not be employing them correctly."

"Not so. We are using them the only way they can be used, as ground attack aircraft against tanks. They are just cannon fodder for the Messerschmitts."

"But—"

"Let me interrupt you. I don't have a great deal of time to spend here. The only thing that has saved my neck so far is that Foreign Minister Molotov has claimed great successes for Lend-Lease, and for the McNaughton aircraft in particular."

Scriabin drank and went on. "Molotov is ignoring our losses in the air, insisting that we use infantry tactics—mass attacks, wave after wave, regardless of losses. That's why we need more airplanes so desperately. We've squandered everything we've gotten so far, killing tanks, but we've made a lot of German aces in a very short time."

"Easy, Giorgi. Our boys are using them, too. One of my best friends was shot down in the South Pacific. But by the middle of next year I'll be able to send Sidewinders with new engines and much better performance."

"It may not be soon enough. What can you send us in the meantime?"

"Well, some P-40s, and more Sidewinders. We can't switch now; we've got the production lines geared up, and the delivery routes prepared."

"I'm instructed to tell you that we'll take what we can get. But when can you give us something decent?"

"We'll try to begin sending P-47s next year. I can't promise anything. But let me show you a sketch of the future."

He pulled out a sheaf of drawings. "This is a turbine jet-powered aircraft, and it will be one hundred miles an hour faster than any plane flying today."

Scriabin was clearly intrigued.

"Where's the propeller?"

"That's just it. No propeller; it's a totally new concept, and McNaughton is ahead of the world on it. You can start getting these in mid-1944, if you want them."

The message was implicit: "You'll get these if you take the Sidewinders." Scriabin understood; he hoped Molotov would understand as well.

After Scriabin left, Caldwell glanced at his watch. He just had time to make it to his next meeting, the real reason for his visit: the reunion with a man who once was a friend. He changed into the workman's coat and hat he'd bribed the hall porter to get for him and left by the stairs.

The lights of the city were already on—the earlier blackouts had caused more accidents than an accidental bombing raid would have. But the energy shortage kept lighting at a minimum, and Caldwell was cautious as he threaded his way through the narrow streets.

Caldwell's map led him to one of the tunnels the practical Swedes had made through the ice-age moraines that divided the islands. As he scurried through the dark passageway, he realized that he felt perfectly secure; crime wasn't a problem in Sweden.

He emerged from the tunnel and found his destination immediately outside. It was the Damberg, the huge, sprawling working man's restaurant selected by his onetime friend as their meeting place.

As soon as Caldwell entered the dingy low-ceilinged room he could see that "restaurant" was a euphemism; the Damberg was a drinking man's establishment, and no mistake. He ordered a Swedish boilermaker—a beer and a *branvin*, and was somewhat startled when the drinks were served with a gray papier-mâché imitation sandwich. Swedish law required the serving of food with drink, and he soon noticed that there was a brisk trade in handing the artificial sandwiches back and forth as drinks were dispensed and replenished.

As he sipped—the pale brown fluid reminding him of the near beer of Prohibition—he thought about the meeting ahead of him. He decided at once that there would be no questions or recriminations; what was over was over. Hafner wanted to do business, and he would just have to see what it was.

It was dangerous business. Hap Arnold had at first refused to let him even think about it—but Caldwell had persuaded him to let him do it at his own risk. A secret meeting with an enemy was a court-martial offense—five years ago he wouldn't have considered it; today it meant nothing more to him than a possible opportunity.

Caldwell was uncharacteristically optimistic, for things were going well. He'd managed to smooth things over with Scriabin, and surely the re-engined Sidewinder would perform better.

A tap on the shoulder caused him to whirl around. There was no one there, and he thought it was a joke until he looked down and saw, barely recognizable through his twisted smile, Bruno Hafner.

"My God, Bruno, you startled me. When did you get here?" The thought that Elsie could never love this grotesque-looking cripple brightened him momentarily; then he felt a savage rush of jealousy that this man could ever have known her, possessed her, made her groan and moan as he had. Hafner had had Elsie in her youth— My God, he thought, this monster took her virginity. Caldwell wanted to reach down and throttle him in his wheelchair.

"Hello, Henry. It's good to see you after all these years. I've been here all along; people tend not to see men in wheelchairs. Some sort of defense mechanism, I guess."

All of the usual polite comments on meeting a former friend

failed Caldwell. He couldn't say, "You're looking well" or "How is your family," for Bruno Hafner was *not* looking well, and he had killed his own wife.

"I was surprised to get your message, Bruno. It's been a long time."

Hafner nodded as the burly man who stood behind him moved down the bar, out of earshot.

"Sergeant Boedigheimer is my combination bodyguard and nurse. Pushes a mean wheelchair, he does. Were you surprised at the messenger?"

"Yes, certainly. I hadn't heard from Lyra Gortchakov since *Kristallnacht*."

"Spare me. We know that you've been in contact with her at least six times. So far I've been able to keep the Gestapo away from her by telling them that she was working for me, not you. I don't know how long I can keep that up, especially if you persist in running those obvious newspaper ads."

Caldwell regrouped—Hafner had him cold. He should have foreseen this, remembering how well the man had always prepared his business dealings. Sparring for time, he asked, "What does her Luftwaffe friend know of this?"

"Helmut? Absolutely nothing. It would kill him. He wants to marry her! And he has such a future—already a big ace, production expert. He'll be a general someday . . . if he lives."

They were silent for a while, sipping and smoking, their eyes searching the room, Caldwell trying to forget that this was Elsie's first lover, concentrating on the bombshells Hafner had dropped. The conversation lapsed into reminiscence. Bruno told him of the fight over Guernica and his long convalescence.

"So you see, you can't get rid of a tough bird like me. Odd, isn't it, that a stepson-in-law almost killed me?"

Caldwell's surge of temper buried his resolution not to comment on the past. "You forget, you were trying to kill him at the time." Unable to check himself, he went on. "You're too easy on yourself, Bruno. It's odder still that you killed your wife."

It didn't bother Hafner at all. "Fortunes of war, Caldwell. I was committed to Germany, and I had to do what I had to do. Besides, you know very well she had always played around. I must say it gave me some satisfaction that the crash got her boyfriend, too."

Caldwell declined to pursue the subject. Hafner obviously regarded murder as a business option.

"Tell me, Henry, how is your jet coming along?"

"Jet? What do you mean?"

"For Christ's sake, do you think I'm an idiot? We know that Bell, McNaughton, and Lockheed are working on jet fighters. We know that Bell and Lockheed are two years behind us and that McNaughton is having problems with both the engine and the airframe. American security is just pathetic."

Caldwell's skin crawled in anticipation. This was the reason for the meeting, surely, and the scent of a bargain hung in the air like the blue-gray smoke roiling up from the grimy crowd of hard-drinkers.

"If you know so fucking much, Bruno, why did you want to see me?"

"Don't be like that, Henry, I'm just trying to get all the cards on the table. I know some other things, too. Like that the Russians are very disappointed in the Sidewinder—they ought to be, our pilots consider them sitting ducks. I know you need to get a jet fighter in the air. And I know there is a lot of talk about you having, shall we say, a 'soft spot' in your heart for McNaughton."

Caldwell studied the bar for a moment, his fingers tracing the scars of initials carved so long ago that their worn edges let the spilled beer pool into little lakes. Be calm, he told himself, you're not here to argue, you're here to get intelligence.

"What are you proposing?"

"First, that we behave like businessmen. You know that the ties between U.S. and German firms are only masked by the war; GM owns most of Opel; Standard Oil works with I.G. Farben, which owns your General Aniline. Patents are shared and profits are pooled, whether in war or in peace. Dozens of companies do it. Boards of directors don't care damn-all about politics."

"So?"

"It happens that we have an interesting interlocking problem. We've got a first-class jet plane, the Messerschmitt Me 262, and the jet engine Junkers is making is coming along. You're having problems with your jets. Maybe you'd be interested in seeing what we have."

Caldwell signaled to the busy bartender, who in two sweeping motions poured *branvin* from a greasy unlabeled bottle, then filled their beer glasses while laying down two of the papier-mâché sandwiches. Caldwell drank the rough-tasting brandy—"burned wine" was the literal translation, probably made in the back from God knew what—and sipped the beer.

"What would it take?"

Hafner looked up at him, weighing his words, lowering his voice to a whisper. "I've always been a conservative investor, Henry. I think it's time I invested in my future."

"Go on."

"There's a joke going around in Germany—'Enjoy the war, the peace is going to be terrible.' Well, if, God forbid, Germany doesn't win this war, I want somewhere to go. I lived through most of one occupation. I'm too old and broken up to try to live through another."

"Go on."

"If Germany loses the war, I want to be able to go back to the United States and live out my life in comfort. I want amnesty, and protection. That shouldn't be too hard to arrange."

"Christ, Bruno, you're wanted for murder there. How could you come back? How could I trust you?"

"I've just put myself in your hands. The Gestapo would kill me in a minute if they knew I was transmitting information on the Messerschmitt jet. . . . And let me raise the ante a little."

Caldwell felt the real subject of the meeting was about to come up. Hafner reached into a pouch tucked beside him in the wheelchair and produced two sheets of paper.

"These are spec sheets in English on what our friend Dr. Goebbels calls "wonder weapons," the revenge weapons. You won't believe what you see, but I can tell you it is factual. Take a minute to read them, and then give them back."

The light was dim in the Damberg and Caldwell had to hold the sheets close to his face. The first sheet was headed A-4 (V-2) and described a liquid-fueled rocket, forty-six feet tall, weighing 26,000 pounds, and carrying a one-ton warhead. Range was over 180 miles. The line that caught Caldwell's eye read: "There is no defense possible against this weapon."

Caldwell felt his chest constrict—there had been rumors of the rocket firings, but no one had any inkling of the potential. At this stage of development, its only use was against England. With five years of development, it could be an intercontinental weapon!

His hands were moist as he turned to the second sheet, headed FZG-76 (V-1). At first glance the V-1 seemed to be a far less impressive weapon—a flying bomb, powered by a pulse jet. This carried a ton of explosives, too, but had a range of only 130 miles and a speed of about 350 mph—less than most piston engine fighters. But the planned production rate of eight thousand per month was terrifying. Firings were supposed to begin in January 1944.

He read the two pages again to compose himself, then handed them back to Hafner.

"Pie in the sky, Bruno. Germany will lose this war before these weapons are ready. Look what's going on in Africa and all along the Eastern front."

"Don't be too sure. We've been in tough spots before. Hitler's pretty clever. We might make another deal with Stalin. If we put enough V-1s across the Channel, there would be no second front. They take only a few hundred man-hours to manufacture—and nobody gets killed flying them. Just think, every month eight thousand of these pounding down on the ports, the assembly areas, the flying fields, and at the same time the V-2s will be smashing London. No, don't count us out yet."

Indecisiveness had never been Henry Caldwell's shortcoming. He discounted the two "wonder weapons," but the information on the jet was valuable enough.

"Okay, we've got a deal. I'll want full data on all three—the jet, the rocket, and the flying bomb. That means full specifications, drawings, everything. In return I'll start work on getting amnesty for you. It's not going to be easy—you don't have many friends in the States."

"Henry, if the going got tough, neither would you. I'll send the material to you through Elsie."

"Elsie? What the hell do you mean, 'through Elsie'?"

"Well, I can't very well send it directly to you, and I don't want the trouble of coming back here. We've got contacts in Switzerland. I'll have the Swiss attaché mail it to her at home."

"Goddamnit, Bruno, you keep Elsie out of this. I don't want you contacting her in *any way*—now, or after the war."

"Don't get excited, Henry. Whatever you say. How do you want me to do it?"

"Have your Swiss flunky contact me in Washington. We can meet at the Willard, and he can give it to me there. You stay away from Elsie!"

Hafner made no attempt to shake hands; he barked a low command and within seconds his bodyguard had wheeled him out through the low door of the Damberg pleased with the deal, delighted that Caldwell had revealed his feelings. It might make things easier later.

Caldwell stood rigid at the bar, aware that he had given Hafner an advantage by overreacting to the mention of Elsie's name. But the deal was almost too good—it could make all the difference for McNaughton with the jet, and the information on the two new weapons would be useful for the next war. Why would Hafner make such an offer? He'd left America because of his "patriotism." Now he was bailing out of Germany, where things were going badly. Hafner had made a fine art of survival.

Pitomnik Airfield, Stalingrad/January 7, 1943

He had done the one utterly stupid thing that everyone joked about, grasping frozen metal. Josten peered closely at his fingers, welded to the corrugations at the bottom of the careened fuselage. He was deep inside the fuselage of an abandoned Junkers Ju 52/3m transport, broken in half and covered with snow for more than a month. A canny supply sergeant had told him that it contained a spare propeller governor, one that he needed badly for the Heinkel He 111 he had flown into beleaguered Stalingrad the day before.

The Russians had set up a flak alley on the route from the airfield at Morosovskaya, where he had taken off, all the way to the diminishing German lines around Stalingrad. No matter how he had thrown the Heinkel around the sky, the gunners had tracked him. He had feathered the propeller on the final approach, and only the grace of God had let him pick his way to a landing between the wrecks strewing the runway.

The Junkers to which his hand was frozen had been looted by passing stragglers, then used as a latrine; the inside was filled with debris and drifted snow, crusted over with the pervasive brown layer of ice that covered the forlorn defensive lines around Stalingrad's last usable airfield. Pitomnik had started out as a fighter strip; now an entire army depended upon it as frantic efforts were made to make another field, Gumrak, ready.

Josten had removed his glove to reach into his pocket for a screwdriver, then slipped on a piece of ice. Trying to brace himself, his hand had pushed against the corrugated aluminum skin, precisely as cold as the thirty degrees below zero weather outside.

Behind him a skinny, gray-eyed giant in a torn fatigue uniform laughed.

"I'm glad you find it amusing, Sergeant Greutzmacher. Now how the hell do I get loose without leaving half my fingers inside this crate?"

Greutzmacher stood above him. "No problem, sir. I've always wanted to do this to an officer."

With a great deal of effort, the sergeant searched within the voluminous folds of his flying suit for a moment, unbuttoned his fly, and began urinating on Josten's hand.

"Pull loose as soon as you can, sir. In this cold I've got a short stack and not much manifold pressure."

Disgusted, Josten pulled his hand away, leaving only a tiny triangle of skin. He wiped his fingers on his fleece-lined flying suit.

"Well, Greutzmacher, I guess you'll enjoy telling this story."

"I will if we ever get out of this place, sir. Unless we get that propeller fixed today, you and I both will wind up with a rifle in a trench, and it won't be only your hand that's frozen."

They searched the wrecked Junkers for another twenty minutes before Greutzmacher triumphantly hacked a box out from a brittle mound of congealed oil.

"This looks like it, sir; let's go back to the shack and warm up for a minute, then I'll get some help to fix our crate."

Like most shelters in Stalingrad, the shack was actually a cave hacked out of the side of a shell-hole in the ground, covered over in this case with a wing from a Stuka. The structure was heaped with frozen clods of earth to give some protection from shell splinters. Inside, three petrol jerry cans had been converted into a precarious stove that impartially threatened asphyxiation and explosion, depending upon the fuel thrust into it. It burned everything from chunks of frozen oil to explosives pulled from land mines and mixed with sawdust, to timber splinters. No one got into the room without contributing something to use as fuel.

The dugout was crowded with stragglers, and Greutzmacher had to use the box as a battering ram to get the two of them space to pull out the prop hub to work on it. Josten backed into a corner, leaving Greutzmacher both room to work and to enlist some help from the starving, apathetic troops seeking a little warmth. One was chewing at the bare white bone of a horse's foreleg. There was absolutely nothing on it, not a shred of meat or gristle, but the others looked enviously at him. It would go into the pot of frozen snow being brought to a boil on the makeshift stove.

God, that the mighty German *Wehrmacht* had come to this! Outside, the wind had died down, and the stove and the bodies were generating a real warmth. Josten sat drowsily watching, his mind going back over the years. He remembered the newsreels of the huge Nuremburg rallies, where thousands of soldiers stood in perfect alignment, row after row, steel helmets glistening, packs perfectly prepared, big, tough-looking men, all fanatically supporting the Fuehrer. He wondered how many of the troops at those rallies had survived all the campaigns—Poland, the West, and now this charnel house of Russia. How many of those steely-jawed supermen were dead, how many had been converted into emaciated scarecrows like those in the hut, men whose jaws now worked weakly at the sight of gnawed bone?

At first it had gone well; everyone had believed in victory when the Army had surged across Russia, almost to Moscow, triumphant everywhere, bagging whole Russian armies. And even after the first dreadful winter, when Stalin had reached into his Siberian stockpile and hurled the hordes against the invaders, even then there had been a recovery. It had looked as if 1942 might indeed be the year of victory. Rommel had chased the British once again across Africa and German troops had conquered the Caucasus and reached all the way to Stalingrad.

When the arms of the Russian trap closed around von Paulus's Sixth Army at Kalatsch in November, the Fuehrer ordered the Army to stand fast, to fight or die in place, and turned for help to Goering, a man no one trusted any longer, not even Hitler himself.

The *Reichsmarschall*, puffed with self-importance, had proclaimed that the Luftwaffe would airlift six hundred tons of supplies a day into Stalingrad, enough to keep the Sixth Army fighting until it could be relieved. Six hundred tons a day was an absurdly optimistic promise, even if there had not been the Russian fighters and antiaircraft. For there was, inevitably, Russian weather, the eternal victor.

A hodgepodge of forces congregated in the loop of the Don, on two large air bases—Tazinskaya and Morosovskaya. Neither base had hangars, billets for air or ground crews, spare parts or supplies, but yet the airplanes came, lumbering squadrons of Ju 52s, Heinkel He 111s diverted from bombing tasks, and later, every ragtag plane that would fly, from the fragile Focke-Wulf Condors, normally reserved for long-distance flights over the North Atlantic, to the trouble-prone Heinkel He 177 bombers. It was in all a perfect example of what had come to be the standard German reaction, the very thing Galland had warned him about, a complete reliance upon improvisation and upon "will." In essence, the commanders asked the Luftwaffe to substitute blood for equipment. Blood was provided in plenty, but blood didn't carry food and ammunition.

The airlift could never have worked—there were not enough operational planes to deliver six hundred tons of supplies a day under perfect conditions. When the weather was really bad—as it was now most of the time—the planes wouldn't even land in Stalingrad but simply dropped the supplies by parachute. Most drifted into the Russian lines.

Josten had heard horror stories about the remaining ones that did make it into the lines. Starving soldiers would break open the canisters to find a supply of condoms or Christmas trees. The latter at least could be burned for heat. But bread and fat, the two things absolutely necessary for survival, were rare commodities. The U-boat fleet had vast stores of dried and condensed foods, perfect for an air-supply mission because of their light weight and portability. Incredibly, none was forthcoming. The soldiers had soon consumed everything edible within the ring.

The day before, shivering with cold and feeling sorry for himself, Josten had watched two *Landsers* creep forward toward the Russian lines. It was unusual—most were content to hole up and stay out of sight unless driven to fight by their officers.

Then he saw why. Incredibly, an emaciated horse, its harness trailing, was pitifully trying to get up an icy incline. The two soldiers stood up and ran for the horse, as Russian machine-gun fire opened on them. They didn't hesitate or dodge—the two of them smashed into the horse simultaneously, knocking it over. Using the twitching body as a shield, the first soldier blew a gaping hole in the horse's skull with his rifle. Throwing the rifle down, he dipped his hands into the skull, pulling out a blob of bloody tissue that he crammed in his mouth. The second soldier moved forward and did the same. Then, very businesslike, as if they had done it often, they put a grenade between the horse's rear legs and dove for cover fifteen meters away.

The grenade exploded, blowing the rear of the horse into pieces and spinning its forward section like a top, intestines streaming out like prizes from a piñata. The two soldiers scampered out and picked up the bloody chunks of meat, cramming them in their coats. They were hurrying until they realized that the Russian firing had stopped. During the entire surrealistic butchering, the Soviets had been methodically covering the area with machine-gun and rifle fire. The two men slowed, picked up the choicest pieces of meat, waved in acknowledgment of the unusual show of mercy, and ran back to their dugouts.

Greutzmacher signaled him, and they moved out toward the edge of the strip, where their Heinkel was hidden between two other wrecks. So far the Russians had ignored it, probably presumimg that it was out of action, too.

They rigged a tarpaulin into a tent over the port engine, and Greutzmacher shaped bits of cowling from two Messerschmitt Bf 109 wrecks to create two cone-shaped stoves, burning gasoline drained from the Heinkel's own tanks. He put the big stove under the engine with the prop hub problem, and the smaller one under the other engine. An oil can rigged with tubing stripped from one of the wrecks was hung on the Heinkel's nose, and gasoline dripped down into the stoves to the bottom of upended steel helmets. Greutzmacher had packed the helmets with rocks, and flames danced from their surfaces.

"Where are you from, Greutzmacher? Nuremburg? I've never seen anybody knock a stove together faster than you."

"Nuremburg it is, sir, but I learned stove-making—and a lot of other things—in this man's army. I just hope we don't blow this crate up before we're done." He left the tent and returned with four men.

"I've promised them we'll fly them out if they help us."

It was interesting to Josten to watch the five of them, all strangers to each other, knit themselves into a little survival family under the pressure of events. Within minutes, Greutzmacher had transformed them into an efficient team who interrupted their work only to hold their hands next to the glowing cowling-stoves. They finished the job by three in the morning.

Josten gathered the men together. "We'll want to get off at first light; as soon as they see our props turning, they'll start shelling.

Don't say a word to anyone else—we can carry only the seven of us and be sure to make it off this short strip."

It was almost eighty-thirty before the glimmer of light crept up on the horizon. Josten walked the length of the field, trying to see where the shell holes were beneath the snow. The wreckage was appalling—six Junkers, four Heinkels, and a dozen Messerschmitts, crashed and abandoned where they lay. Sprawled in the snow like land mines were the remains of supply containers that had been parachuted in. He knew he would have to start his takeoff roll at an angle, gathering speed and then straightening it out at midfield, veering around the wreck of a Stuka that stood like a signboard, straight up on its prop. The dive-bomber had cartwheeled onto its nose, bending its cranked wings into two arms of a distorted swastika, a fitting symbol for this cemetery of an airfield.

Josten walked back along the edge of the field; he had not seen before that it was quarried with empty foxholes and dugouts, a sponge of trenches absorbing filth and despair in equal measure. Pale wraiths, swathed in everything from rags to rugs, scurried from point to point like rats, trailing rifles for tails, red eyes darting at him as if he were the enemy. In one dugout, a group of *Landsers* were wedged around a boiling cooking pot; when he looked in they had, as a man, aimed their Schmeissers at him. He'd moved on hastily; only later did he speculate that they were cooking a comrade. He had only heard of such things—the Italians referred to it as "*casserole de la morte*"—and cannibalism was supposed to be rampant among the Russian prisoners of war. But German soldiers! What had they come to?

He felt a mild relief when he got back to the Heinkel, dingy in its temporary dirty-white winter-camouflage colors. Slow, obsolete and battle-damaged, it was still a beautiful aircraft, the only ticket to freedom. A crowd of soldiers, worse-looking desperados than any gang of Mexican bandits, surged around it—word had gotten out that they were going to try a takeoff.

Josten thought quickly. If he jammed them in the bomb bay like cordwood, he could probably take as many as fifteen along. It was only about an hour back to Morosovskaya; they could stand that. A quick glance showed that there already were more than fifty soldiers, all armed and desperately angry. He pushed among the crowd, then clambered into the belly and up into the cockpit. He forced the cockpit side window out and told Greutzmacher, "Call the men to attention."

The theatrics triggered some ancient rite of discipline within them, and the group stiffened into silence.

"We can take fifteen men this trip, no more. To do even that, I'll need the rest of you to trample out another hundred yards of runway from the snow."

A moan broke through, and Greutzmacher shouted, "Silence!"

Josten went on: "I'll drop the fifteen off in Morosovskaya, and come back for the rest of you, as many trips as it takes. I swear! But you've got to decide right now who's going on the first load. I'm starting engines in five minutes."

Greutzmacher had diluted the engines for a cold start, pouring gasoline into the oil so that it would circulate quickly, freeing the pistons to turn. Josten saw that the propellers were clear, and that Greutzmacher had dismantled the homemade stoves that he hoped had brought the engines to a temperature where they would start. Deliberately, anxious to avoid any mistake that would abort the process and condemn them to a rifleman's death, he began the engine-start process. Cold metal ground against cold metal in scraping anguish; then the reluctant propeller blades began to turn with glacial slowness. Rich blue smoke blossomed from the exhausts, raising the hopes of the fifty men staring at the airplane. Josten begged the engines to start. There was a bark, a cough, and then a steady rumble as the first one broke into life. The second engine started more easily, as if encouraged by the vibrations now quivering through the airframe.

He looked out to see that fifteen men were standing in line, the rest now moving out smartly to trample the snow at the end of the runway. Greutzmacher was some talker; he should have been in politics.

"Let's get them on board!" Josten dropped down and began helping to cram the anxious soldiers in every empty space—the forward fuselage, the bomb bay, the rear gunner's compartment. Greutzmacher even pushed some through the rear fuselage bulkhead into the empty aft section.

"That's enough there, Greutzmacher." Too many men in the tail would throw the center of gravity off, tipping the Heinkel's nose up into an irrecoverable stall.

The sound of the engines had brought more soldiers running. Josten ran the power up, and the Heinkel lumbered forward, gathering speed. The cockpit was crowded with bodies; he snarled until they edged back far enough that he could see out of the conical glazed panels of the nose. He had to keep a clear field of vision to miss the forlorn tail of the Stuka-swastika that marked the right edge of his makeshift runway.

As the Heinkel grudgingly accelerated, he saw a figure run out from the side of the field to stand directly in his path. It was a blond young soldier, his neck bandaged; he held his arms up as if imploring Josten to somehow stop and pick him up.

"Get out of the way, damn you!"

The man stood there, arms waving as if he were a motorist asking for help. The Heinkel's speed was 140 kilometers, not fast enough to fly from the clinging snow yet, and Josten had nowhere to turn. He held the wheel forward, lifting the tail so that the soldier could drop to the ground and save himself. Josten watched in horror as the young soldier stood erect until his skull burst on the glazed nose section like an insect on an automobile windshield. The end of the field roared near and mechanically Josten pulled back on the control column, unable to take his eyes from the red smear on the canopy, cracked now, with frozen blood extruding through it like the coxcomb of a rooster.

Flying automatically, he let the Heinkel struggle into the air, unaware that each of its landing gear struts was encumbered by a single soldier clinging limpetlike in the flash-freezing wind, risking everything to leave the hell of Stalingrad.

Josten could sense that the Heinkel was not performing well, attributing it to tired engines and iced wings; he was haunted by a vivid impression of the man he had run over. The soldier's face had registered photographically—and it had been exactly the same face as that of the British Swordfish pilot. Had he killed the same man twice?

Greutzmacher nudged him and Josten raised the gear. Unknown to him, as the two legs of the undercart struggled upward they dislodged the soldiers, who fell, only their unheard screams accompanying them on their lonely hundred-meter drop. Josten felt the airspeed surge as the Heinkel, free of its burden, its gear retracted, flew normally. It puzzled him that German soldiers were firing at him. They were furious that the men had dropped, but Josten assumed they were angry that someone else was escaping the trap.

By the time he'd reached four thousand feet, the accurate Russian flak had ranged him, and he banked the Heinkel wildly, unmindful of the crush of bodies in the rear.

Greutzmacher yelled in his ear: "We're taking hits, streaming fuel out of the right-wing tank. And we've got some wounded in the bomb bay, probably in the back, too. You better get down at Morosovskaya as soon as you can."

It was the longest one-hour flight of Josten's life.

Karinhall/January 12, 1943

The Russian sharpshooters had riddled the Heinkel, forcing Josten to land wheels and flaps up at Morosovskaya. Landing fast, the plane had sprayed a rooster-tail cloud of snow before lurching to a stop, just one more broken bird on an airfield headed toward disaster. Josten had been grateful that the plane had not burned, and that the impact had expunged the bloodstained canopy at his feet.

The exhausted ground crews at Morosovskaya had needed more than twenty minutes to extricate the scrambled *Landsers* from the body of the crumpled Heinkel. Four had been killed by flak on the trip; Josten had felt less sorry for them than for those back in the pocket, whom he had had to abandon. There had been no airplane available for his use for a return flight and Bruno Hafner was waiting for him with orders to report immediately to Goering himself. It had been the "Iron Man" who had sent Josten to Stalingrad to report on airlift operations, and he wanted an immediate firsthand account.

Now, a few days later, the enormity of the slaughter at Stalingrad was still with him as Josten sat in a daze at Karinhall, listening to Hafner yammer, "We've got to come out of here today with authorization for a wing of Messerschmitts, under your command. Understand? No matter what you talk about with Goering, our job is to get him to believe in the 262. You've got to concentrate, Helmut!"

He understood, but glancing around the incredibly luxurious room, he wasn't sure he could stand the contrast of Goering's sybaritic surroundings with what he'd just seen at the front.

They were seated on a huge couch facing a roaring fire in Karinhall's main room, an **A**-framed hunting lodge, decorated with enormous antlers, Gobelin tapestries, Oriental rugs, a marble *Venus of Praxiteles*, and old masters from Cranachs to Vermeers, looted from all of Europe. For a moment, Josten thought he was hallucinating—a lion had walked into the room, gazed without curiosity at them, and padded out.

"Unser Hermann is an animal lover."

Hafner saw the look on Josten's face and pleaded with him.

"For God's sake, for Germany's sake, don't take issue with the man about things like the lion. And don't take exception to what he's wearing—he has some funny ideas about clothes."

An adjutant came in the room, sleek, pomaded, boots glistening in the firelight. He asked if they wanted something to eat or drink, and Hafner had to lay his arm on Josten to restrain him.

"Now, look. Germany has one chance—to get the 262 into production. We've got one chance to bring that chance about—this meeting. You're a soldier, control yourself. You're being self-indulgent. Let me tell you about this man."

Josten had never before heard Hafner speak in an admiring tone of anyone.

"No matter what Goering's problems are now—and I'll tell you some of them—he's the man who got Hitler into power, and he's the man who built the Luftwaffe. He rejuvenated German industry. Never forget that."

"What are his problems?"

"He was shot in the putsch in Munich, in 1923; he became a morphine addict then. He probably still is. But his main problem is that the barbarians at headquarters have cut him to pieces with the Fuehrer. He knows he has no prestige anymore, especially now, after Stalingrad. He's just biding his time, till we lose the war, or until Himmler nails him on some charge and shoots him."

"If that's so, how can he help us?"

"Because he's still Hitler's sentimental favorite, and he still has influence with the manufacturers. And never forget, no matter how much the Luftwaffe complains, no matter how they say they are going to tell him off, when Goering says, 'Jump,' they just ask 'How high?' Don't worry, he has plenty of power for what we need."

"Glad to hear it, Hafner! Sometimes I don't think I have enough power to feed my big cats."

Goering had glided silently into the room to stand behind them. Both men hoped he'd heard only the last sentence as Josten snapped to attention and Hafner painfully pulled himself erect.

"I'm glad to see you are moving about, Bruno. Good. I'll have you back commanding a squadron soon."

Hafner introduced Josten, and Goering began interrogating him.

"Tell me the truth, Major Josten. Were our Luftwaffe people doing everything possible to supply Stalingrad?"

"In one sense, yes, *Herr Reichsmarschall*. Certainly everyone was trying to do the best they could. The casualty figures confirm that. But an air-supply mission doesn't depend just on people and planes. You need warehouses, trucks, handcarts, parachutes, hangars, barracks, field kitchens, a thousand things, and most of all the right kind of supplies—sausage and bread, guns and fuel, ammunition— and these did not exist."

"What chance is there that the Sixth Army will hold out?"

"None whatsoever, *Herr Reichsmarschall*. The men are already starved and exhausted; they won't last more than another three weeks, if that. They should surrender now. It's all over."

"That simply cannot be true."

Goering crumpled into silence, slumping in the huge elk-skin-covered chair next to the couch, staring into the fire with an unbearable melancholy. Josten started to speak, but Hafner signaled him to be silent.

Almost five minutes passed, then Goering suddenly roused himself.

"Come, let's talk of something else. It's my fiftieth birthday today, you know. Let me show you what the people have sent me."

Goering turned on his heel and walked with unexpected speed to a room at the side, motioning them to follow.

The room had been divided into a series of aisles by long linen-covered tables. Each table was heaped with gifts, each one with a card carrying birthday wishes and a prominent identification of the giver.

"Look at this! A golden sword from Mussolini! Can you imagine what this is worth actually? And historically? And this, a twenty-four-hundred-piece set of Sèvres! What a banquet I'll give with this!"

"I saw a man at Stalingrad make a banquet of raw horse brains. The horse's skull was the platter and his hands the spoon, no fancy porcelain for him. I guess it all depends upon how hungry you are."

Hafner rolled his eyes upward as Goering's face flushed red.

"Are you being insolent, Major? Don't pull your veteran's role on me. I fought at the front, too, you know, and in the streets of Germany as well."

"I don't mean to be insolent, Herr *Reichsmarschall*, but men are dying of starvation right now in Stalingrad. If you were there, they would shoot you and eat you without a qualm."

There was a blanket of silence, broken only by the gurgle of Goering's breathing, and the click of his adjutant's holster being opened.

Hafner hissed, "My God, Josten, shut up."

Goering stood, uncertain how to play the next round of this insane game. He could see that Josten was not dangerous, not an assassin; he couldn't shoot every messenger bringing bad news, no matter how insubordinate they were.

"I guess I'd feed a platoon at least. Maybe that is the best thing that I can still do for poor Germany."

His expression changed abruptly and tears poured down his cheeks. Goering slumped into a chair, pale and breathing in shallow gasps. The adjutant raced to bring him some tiny pills. When he spoke his voice was ragged.

"It's a heart condition; not too serious, but I'm not supposed to get too excited. Or too depressed." He glanced quizzically at Josten, adding, "Or too insulted."

Hafner tugged at Josten's arm; mechanically, the younger man bent to listen.

"You've done it now, you idiot. Now you shut up and say nothing else, you understand? Let me do the talking."

More composed, Goering stood and waved them back into the main lodge. He plopped himself down in a huge, oversize chair.

"Bruno, talk to me as in the old days. You aren't here to wet-nurse this insubordinate major. What is it you want?"

"*Herr Reichsmarschall*—"

"No, I'm too tired and ill for formalities. The young man here thinks I have no feeling, that my heart doesn't ache for the people. He has no idea how deeply I feel that the Luftwaffe's failure is *my* failure. Let's relax, and give me a chance to recover. For tonight at least, let it be Hermann and Bruno again."

"If we leave the new jet's development to Messerschmitt, it will be late 1944 before we get an operational unit. I can put an operational unit in the air by November of this year, perhaps earlier."

"And what is your insolent young friend's role?"

"He'll test it and develop the tactics; he'll pick the pilots."

"What's the point? What can you do that Messerschmitt can't?"

"I can get the engines running so that they don't melt down like lead soldiers on the test stand, for one thing. That's something the famous Junkers motorworks can't do. And I can build airplanes without a million changes. Hermann, remember during the last war, when Fokker created the D VII in a matter of weeks? Now it takes five years to get a prototype flying."

"Airplanes were simpler then."

"Yes, but so was the bureaucracy. The goddamn staffs have gotten bigger and more complex than the airplanes." Hafner paused, then lowered his tortured body into a kneeling position before Goering.

"I beg you, Herr *Reichsmarschall*, give me a chance. What will it cost you? I've already got the airframes, discarded by Messerschmitt because of design changes. I can have the engines in just a few months. We can have an airplane that will wipe the British and the Americans from the skies. Without air superiority, there will be no second front—we know that from 1940. And if they can't invade, maybe we can settle with Russia."

"Settle?" Goering looked puzzled.

"Yes—make a deal, get an armistice, do anything to stop the bloodletting. This is our one chance."

"You can say that. I've said it to Hitler, and been thrown out of his office!"

"That was before Stalingrad. He can't hide the loss of the Sixth Army from the world; he can't hide it from himself. If the British and the Americans get a beachhead next year, it's all over."

Goering was silent, his hand thrust into a bowl. It took Josten a moment to realize that the bowl was filled with cut stones—emeralds, rubies, diamonds; he would lift them and let a cascade of faceted brilliance reflect the flames of the fireplace.

"The Fuehrer always says that he *would* negotiate, but only after a victory."

"It would be a magnificent victory to drive the English and the Americans from the skies; it would be a fantastic triumph to repel an invasion. And it would be a Luftwaffe victory, a Goering victory. Things would be as they were in May of 1940."

Goering looked thoughtful. "Perhaps. But I'd prefer the Fuehrer not to know until you're successful. Then we can spring it on him, and he'll force Messerschmitt and the others into line."

"We won't fail you, Hermann."

"You may call me *Reichsmarschall* now; this interview is at an end."

As they were putting on their coats and hats, Josten laid his hand on Hafner's arm.

"Congratulations, Bruno, you got your way. But you are playing Hitler and Goering against each other. Is this how business is done in the Third Reich?"

Hafner, warmed by an inner glow, thought for a moment. Then he said, "Doing business here is like doing business anywhere—you do it any goddamn way you can, just so you get it done."

Nashville, Tennessee/January 31, 1943

A bleak and palpable cold, no mere lack of heat but a fierce thermometer-crunching enemy of life, invaded the city, cracking its windows, bursting pipes, and freezing wandering strays into furry lumps of ice. The winds staggered the few pedestrians still brave enough to troop along Union Street, then whipped chattering on across the hills to sail southeast toward the glow of Berry Field. There, Sunday night or not, the skylights of the new and roughly built factory buildings gleamed against the winter: McNaughton aircraft were pouring off the assembly line, shiny bright and looking deadly as cobras.

Troy McNaughton, enthroned behind a huge Tennessee walnut desk, its polished top ornamented with a glittering onyx pen set, models of McNaughton aircraft, and a four-inch stack of papers worth untold millions of dollars.

"Absolutely amazing, Henry—you've really gotten the goods this time! The 262 is a beauty—we'll scale up the wing a little and put it on our next fighter."

He riffled greedily through the blown-up prints of the microfilm Hafner had sent Caldwell.

"And this A-4 or V-2, or whatever it is, that's the weapon of the future. If we can get development started on this now, we'll have a five-year jump on the rest of the industry. We won't have to worry about peace breaking out—we'll be ready for the next war."

Caldwell sat staring at the floor, roaring earthward on his psychic roller coaster. He knew he should be congratulating himself on a coup, one that could mean U.S. military dominance for the next fifty years. Instead his obsession with Elsie filled him with shame.

He had briefed Hap Arnold on the microfilm in Washington only four days before. It had been the worst meeting in Caldwell's life. Arnold, notorious for his irascibility and his grudges, had leaned on him as if he were humbling a recruit, starting off with a series of reprimands on the status of the B-29 and long-range fighter programs.

"Goddamnit, Henry, you've got the most important programs in the Army Air Forces and you're not delivering. I want to bomb the shit out of Germany and Japan—and I can't do it if your programs don't materialize."

Then Hap Arnold had gotten down to business.

"I'm coming directly to the point, Henry. I hear stories that you're fooling around with a woman who works for a contractor."

"General Arnold, with respect, that's my personal business."

"Goddamnit, Caldwell, I'll tell you what's your personal business and what's not! It's my personal business when one of my key people is accused of favoritism."

"That's not fair, Hap; I've never been influenced by this woman." It killed him to call Elsie "this woman."

Arnold did not look well; his once boyish face was haggard and drawn. Normally crisp in his movements, he was hesitant, as if overwhelmed by the weight of command.

"Henry, I'm leveling with you. You've got to stop seeing her. We can't afford to sacrifice an entire aircraft plant to some middle-age romance. For Christ's sake, you were married for twenty years, weren't you? What the hell are you acting like a schoolboy for?"

Caldwell, bruised into silence, looked at Arnold's choleric face, veins bulging, red-rimmed eyes wide. They'd warned Caldwell that the Chief was surrounded by a whole new group of staff ass-kissers who kept him isolated, playing on his irritability with rumors.

"I'm not giving you advice, Caldwell, I'm giving you an order. You *will* stop seeing this woman. If you were someone else, I'd ship you off to India or somewhere, but I can't do that. I need you. But I can't have people saying you're favoring McNaughton because you're screwing a secretary there."

"She's not just a —"

"At ease! Do you think I've got time to worry about your love life?"

There was a long silence, Arnold twitching, riveting Caldwell with his gaze, as if daring him to protest, so that he could physically attack him. A clock was ticking in the background; Caldwell hadn't heard it before.

Finally, Arnold said, "You've heard me. Say no more about it. What else have you got?"

It was a relief to talk about his triumph, the meeting with Hafner, the inside news on the jet engine and the "wonder weapons."

Arnold listened to him with diminishing attention. Halfway through the briefing he fumbled in his drawer, took out a tiny pill, and placed it under his tongue. When Caldwell, nervous and less convincing than usual, finished, he wasn't certain Arnold was even listening.

Finally, almost as if he wanted to get rid of him, Arnold said, "Your job is to get the B-29 and the long-range fighter going. Don't come to me with all this Buck Rogers crap, rockets and jets. The war will be over before any of that stuff will be developed."

"No, Hap, listen—"

Arnold's tone was less rigid. "We've got all the first-rate manufacturers loaded down. Douglas is overtaxed already, Lockheed and Republic have all they can handle, Boeing is straining to give us B-17s and B-29s; North American is pumping out B-25s and P-51s. We could spare Curtiss, but they're so fouled up I won't even bother. That leaves McNaughton. Why don't you give this stuff to them to see what they can do with it? They haven't helped us much so far in this war—maybe this is more their line. And if it doesn't work out, at least it won't do the war effort much harm."

Caldwell looked at him. One minute he was forbidding him to see Elsie, the next he was thrusting McNaughton back on him.

"I didn't pick McNaughton out of the air, Henry. I'm covering for you. I owe you too much. If the Truman Committee digs into the problems at McNaughton—the Sidewinder is over-cost and under-performance—you're in trouble, I'm in trouble. This way, I can say that we're using McNaughton for research and development."

Caldwell nodded dumbly.

"I know how you operate, you must have some smart young officer you can assign to the plant to get things going. But don't spend any time there yourself—you stay the hell away from that woman!"

When Caldwell brought up the amnesty for Hafner that had been worked out with Allen Dulles and the State Department, Arnold had flatly rejected the idea. "Why are you fooling with that guy? He's betrayed us once, he'll do it again. You're losing your grip, Caldwell!"

With that, he had been shown out of the office.

Caldwell knew that he'd drawn his last ounce of credit with Arnold. One more foul-up and all the efforts of the past would be forgotten; he'd be assigned to command some training base, watching cadets do close order drill.

Now, Troy McNaughton slapped his hand on the table. "Damn-it, General, snap out of it. It's not like you're giving this to the enemy! We'll do a better job on this than anybody else. You're doing exactly what Arnold told you to do, and you're saving time getting started."

McNaughton persisted with his salesman-style encouragement. "We'll get jets over to Europe before Messerschmitt does, and we'll have long-range rockets before anyone else, too. If we don't invade pretty soon, the Russians will push the Germans all the way to the Channel. Then it will be our turn to fight them."

It was an uncanny replay of his own rationalizing—he was actually doing the country a service by getting the data to McNaughton. If he'd turned it in at Headquarters, the material would probably have been sent to Wright Field to be studied until it was obsolete. This way, at least, it would do some good.

His voice was weak and hesitant as he replied. "The little job, the flying bomb, worries me more than the rocket. If they build enough of them, they can stop the second front."

"Well, then, there's your way out! You've got influence with Arnold, and with Eaker, too. Convince them to bomb out the factories building the jets and the flying bombs. If you get me just six months, we'll have our jet ready to go. Just six months!"

Caldwell left, driving his Plymouth staff car down the icy streets and progressively converting his despair into anger with Elsie, blaming her for his situation, hating her because she had gotten him into this mess and because she had once been Bruno's woman.

More furious than the storm outside, he stomped through her front door, tracking snow across the knotted rag rugs, shouting like a madman. She stifled his cries with an embrace and led him upstairs, where he passively accepted the maddening insouciance of her kisses. In the sweetly familiar bedroom of her old-fashioned two-story frame house on the Murfreesboro Pike, he gazed at the $219 mahogany suite he'd given her, her dressing table filled with the perfumes he loved to inhale as he nuzzled her neck. She was wrapping him in breast-soft comfort, drowning his arguments in her mouth. Shaking off her kisses even as he let her pull off his clothes, he flung more accusations at her, telling her that she had betrayed him, that she was a whore.

She replied with more kisses and darting hands; even as he screamed at her, she unbuttoned his fly, pushing him back down on the bed to pull his trousers down, gently amused that he could curse her as he let her undress him.

Caldwell knew how stupid it was and how perfectly it fitted the bizarre pattern of their relationship. He had been faithfully married for twenty-two years to his high school sweetheart, even though Shirley's increasingly religious bent had muted their sex life. When she died, he'd been blessed or cursed with a sudden new adolescent capacity for love. He had fallen for Elsie with a coltish naïveté that made him more vulnerable than a teenager.

Caldwell tried to regain his anger, struggling to his feet, nude, detumescent, and she slipped behind him saying, "Oh, Hank, you can't be mad about Bruno. It was all such a long time ago, I was just a kid."

Her absolute tranquility appalled him. She felt no guilt or remorse; she was kissing and squeezing him as if she had genuinely missed him. Shamelessly, knowingly, without any regard for what had happened in the past or might happen in the future, she pressed herself on him with her always irresistible ardor.

The terrible, untellable part was that he was responding in every way but the one that counted; he wanted her desperately, wanted to settle all the arguments by bolting himself to her and, bucking, spend himself within her, listening to her gasps of pleasure, not caring if they were real or not. But a countercurrent of quietly determined guilt swam upstream against desire, and he was impotent.

"You're acting crazy, Hank. You've been on a long trip, and God knows what you eat over there. Or what you drink." She looked up at him archly, "Or who you screw. Let me fix you a little bourbon and branch water."

She poured him a drink and said, "I loved Bruno, just like I love you. I still love his memory, poor dear. But that has nothing to do with us."

A wiser man might have expected it. He had felt for a long time that Elsie was strangely and genuinely an innocent, as ignorant of sin as she was of what others called virtue. Elsie was Elsie, enjoying life and making do with whatever circumstances provided her.

"I can't believe you'd say that, Elsie. How can you love a man who killed his wife, betrayed his country?"

"Who ever proved he killed her? Lots of people die in plane crashes. And his country is Germany, he's never betrayed it. Besides, look how he used to make planes for the government. You bought them yourself, just like you're buying McNaughtons."

He listened to her nonsequitur nonsense, sadly aware that of all improbable things, he was a romantic. "Tell me the truth, Elsie. Do you enjoy making love to me?"

She looked at him, sweetly patient with the absurd question. "Of course, darling, can't you tell?"

"Did you enjoy making love to Bruno?"

Her smile was the same. "Sure. The one thing doesn't have anything to do with the other."

He was silent and she said, "Look, Henry, you're just mad because little John Henry Junior there is having his temper tantrum. Let me talk a little French to him, and in a little while you'll be all better."

The ghastly thought struck him. "Do you have names for all of them?" It wasn't a question but a confession, a groveling admission of his subjugation to her.

Her expression was blank, fleeting. "Names for all of what?"

It was agonizing to ask, a painful extrusion of his soul through pressing rollers of pride and embarrassment. He spat it out. "Goddamnit, Elsie, did you have a name for Bruno's penis?"

She burst into laughter. "Lord, I haven't thought of that in years. Sure, it was Red Baron; he was an ace, too, you know. I thought it was cute. And Troy, he's Barney Google because he's got a . . ." Her voice trailed off.

"Jesus Christ, you're fucking Troy, too?"

"Don't use words like that, Henry. Especially not with the Lord's name. Of course Troy has made love to me. Wake up and get your belt through all the loops! Do you think I'd have a chance at a job like mine if all I could do was type sixty words a minute?"

He shuddered in revulsion. He had been so willing to believe that Elsie was "his" in some spiritual way. She had done so much for him, made him feel so good about himself—she was always approving.

It hit him like a sudden light in a dark room. That was it, he knew. Elsie had always approved everything he did or didn't do, unlike his parents, for whom nothing was ever good enough, unlike poor Shirley, who always felt he should pay less attention to his job and more attention to church. Elsie approved of him, so he approved of her—and to do that he had had to be blind to everything.

She moved around him, pressing against him, blowing on his neck.

"Come on, sugar, don't be like this. We're all babies at heart; you've just had your feelings hurt." She slipped her arm around his waist, gently grasping him with her hand, rubbing the rough velvet of her pubis against his bottom.

"Now, I can tell that little John Henry Junior is beginning to feel all better already. Why don't you just let me and him work this thing out; we know how to talk to each other. In a minute or two, you'll forget all this nonsense."

Major General Henry Caldwell, advisor to the President, a towering power in the Army Air Forces, confidant of major leaders in the aviation industry, stood transfixed, watching what was happening in the mirror over the bureau. He stood silently as a tiny bundle of nerves, a shapeless white ganglion smaller than a lima bean, disconnected him from reality as it responded mindlessly to Elsie's soft, wet coaxing.

He felt the stirrings, and he thought, I should walk out of here and never see her again. But he heard his mouth say, "Let's go over to the bed."

Elsie went to work busily, aware that she'd have fences to mend for the next few weeks. She was pleased with her comment about "typing sixty words per minute." If Caldwell was stupid enough to think that Troy McNaughton valued only what she could do on a Sealy or behind a Remington, that was all to the good. Even Troy underestimated her. She wasn't an engineer, but she was a manager and she knew what was going on. And she was *not* going to be left penniless when the war was over, when Troy no longer needed her and she'd be too old to work for someone else. No, she was going to take care of herself, and Henry Caldwell was going to help.

Burbank, California/March 15, 1943

The Lockheed plant had disappeared from the face of the earth. Lieutenant Colonel Frank Bandfield, the new silver oak leaves shining on his shoulders, cocked his Douglas A-20 on its wing and circled until he spotted the runway. The year before a Jap sub had shelled Santa Barbara, and Lockheed had covered the entire plant with camouflage netting. Now there was a huge network of false streets, fake houses, and phony trees that turned this part of Southern California into an incongruous slice of the Middle West.

It was the first leg of a two-stage journey to the South Pacific, one that might bail Caldwell out of his growing difficulties. The Merlin-engined Sidewinder was a failure. But because McNaughton had received all the Merlin engines, there wouldn't be any long-range P-51s in England until early 1944—and that meant heavy bomber losses for the rest of the year. In desperation, Caldwell had assigned Bandfield to go to Guadalcanal to fly P-38s, to see if his cruise control techniques and the new 310-gallon drop tanks could make it into the elusive long-range fighter for the European theater.

Patty had been furious. "I know you. You'll go on every damn mission, and you won't be happy unless you do some shooting. It's in your blood."

"Don't say that, makes me sound like a killer."

"You are a killer. You kill me every time you leave."

It was a tough time for Patty. She'd stopped almost all of her outside activities to take care of the children—and Clarice Roget. After complaining about "the miseries" for months, Clarice had finally gone into the hospital for a checkup. The diagnosis had been quick and cruel: Hodgkin's disease, an incurable cancer of the lymphatic system.

Bandfield could tell that Caldwell had called ahead. Lockheed was completely prepared for him, designating their top test pilot, Milo Burcham, to check him out, and scheduling him for a visit with Clarence "Kelly" Johnson, the Chief Research Engineer.

Bandy had flown one of the pre-production YP-38s at Wright Field, but Burcham took him to new ground, a combat-ready P-38G. It was a beautiful aircraft, gleaming silver, the sleek needle-nosed twin booms bulging with the power of the supercharged

Allison engines, the central nacelle packed with four .50-caliber machine guns and a 20-mm cannon.

"It's an easy bird to fly, Bandy. The props are counter-rotating, so you don't have any torque problems to worry about. The only thing I'd warn you about is high-speed dives. It's so clean that it can run into what we call compressibility." Burcham went on to give him his first real insight on the tremendous forces involved when an aircraft approaches the speed of sound.

"How do you recognize it?"

"It's easy! It feels like you're flying through boulders, and the controls stiffen up, feel like they're reversing on you. We've got some dive flaps coming along that may solve it, but for now—don't dive too steep."

Three days later, Bandy had completed the syllabus of ground instruction and flying that Burcham had specially created for him and felt perfectly at ease in the aircraft.

The visit with Kelly Johnson proved to be unsettling. First, he was so young, only thirty-three, and so self-assured. Bandfield sensed he was in the presence of a great man who wasn't too happy with him.

"Would I be too inquisitive, Colonel Bandfield, if I asked if you were following the progress on jet engine development?"

Uh-oh, Bandfield thought, he's heard about McNaughton's problems.

"Not at all. I've been briefed on as much as we know about the German developments. We know that the British have flown an experimental jet, not a fighter. And as you probably know, we've been doing some work on it, too."

Johnson was quiet-spoken, taciturn, but determined.

"Let me show you a few drawings."

He turned the pages of a sketch pad showing a very clean, low-wing single-engine aircraft, air intakes tucked on the side of its nose, jet exhausting from the tail.

"We'd like to get in the jet business, Colonel. General Caldwell hasn't been very encouraging. He says he needs the P-38s and the bombers we make too badly to let us try."

In the end, Bandfield said that he'd press Lockheed's case with Caldwell. He left confident that if the McNaughton jet did fail, Johnson was clearly a man to be depended on to deliver a jet from Lockheed on time.

Stockholm/April 13, 1943

It was truly a world at war. Distant countries as unthreatened—and unthreatening—as Bolivia, Ethiopia, and Iraq had declared war on Germany. In Sweden, the mood was shifting. The German invasion that loomed so large in its thinking in 1940 no longer seemed so imminent, but a balanced decision still had to be made: did Sweden wish to be surrounded by German- or Russian-controlled land? The truth was neither; the unspoken best solution for Sweden was an endless conflict in which both countries bled themselves to death, buying plenty of war materiel in the process.

On the surface, Sweden still danced to Germany's tune. More than 10 percent of Swedish rail traffic was employed in transporting German troops and materiel, and Swedish naval vessels escorted German ships through coastal waters. In the previous March, six hundred thousand tons of Swedish ore had been funneled into German blast furnaces, and dozens of Swedish "fishing" ships had been sold to serve as German mine-sweepers. Most blatant of all, Swedish vessels under contract served as tankers to fuel German U-boats.

Yet Lyra sensed the fundamental change in Swedish attitude toward Germans as soon as she arrived. Helmut's rank and Knight's Cross had entitled him to fly on the previous day's German courier plane. She had been fortunate to be able to get a seat on the Swedish airline Aerotransport's silvery Junkers Ju 52 *Vikingaland*. When they landed at Bromma Airport, she found that the porters were their normal eager selves with the few Swedish passengers but ignored the Germans. The same applied to everyone, from the hat-doffing doorman to the surly taxi drivers. And where in the past the customs officials had been courteous to the point of negligence in their inspections of papers and baggage, they now acted like Gestapo agents.

It was true in the restaurants as well; service was now slow and surly, even worse if a foreigner from an Allied country was sitting nearby.

Nonetheless, she was glad to be in Stockholm working at the German Legation, devoutly glad tonight to have Helmut lying at her side, and glad to be married. It was so bizarre. She was drifting further and further from a man she once had truly loved. Yet when she realized that she was pregnant, everything had changed. Daring enough to spy on her adopted country, she was too conventional to have an abortion or an illegitimate child. When Helmut, touchingly grateful that she was pregnant, had insisted on marriage, she accepted gladly.

It was an emotional paradox. Once she'd been in love with him, reveling in their intimate physical bonding, even after she'd made a decision to work against the regime. But in the last year Helmut had changed dramatically. He was totally absorbed in his work, trying so desperately to win the war in the air that he no longer objected to the methods the Nazis were using. She no longer loved him—but she didn't want their baby to be a bastard.

God knew, she was certainly entitled to be with child, given their tempestuous lovemaking. If she had counted right, the child had been conceived in November, before Helmut had gone to Stalingrad, on the floor just inside the doorway of her flat. When she first knew that she was pregnant she had wondered how she could carry on, carrying the baby of a man she no longer loved and whose cause she hated. Early on, an abortion would not have been impossible; she had friends who had connections and, in wartime, no stigma would have attached. The thought of an abortion was too abhorrent—she couldn't do it.

The real question, of course, was whether she could put her battle against Germany above the baby. Right now she thought she could; when it was born it might be very different indeed. Nothing in her emotional conflict confused her; she was determined to play out the cards she had been dealt, to take what she could from life, and to strike whatever blows she could against the Nazis.

Helmut lay with his hand on her belly, now round as an Army loaf of bread.

"What shall we name him?"

"If it's a him, Helmut, of course."

"No, I've never liked the name Helmut. My mother's family name was Ulrich—let's call him that. If it's a girl, Gunilla. How would that be?"

He realized that she was softly sobbing.

"What's the matter? Did I say something?"

"No, it's just that the times are so confusing. Should we be bringing a baby into the world at all?"

"Of course. Think of all the people who have been killed. We need good babies for the future. And be glad you're here. The bombing in Germany is going to get worse and worse; we've only seen the start of it. It was bad enough to have you in danger before; now . . ." He rubbed her stomach again.

Lyra had been two months pregnant before she gave in to him and agreed to go to Stockholm. Even then her decision was based in part on the fact that she would be able to communicate with Caldwell much more directly. Ironically, Josten had asked Bruno Hafner to pull some strings and get her an assignment in the Legation. Hafner had said he'd tried but failed; Lyra and Helmut weren't sure he'd even tried. Then, at Helmut's insistence, Lyra had requested assistance from Joseph Goebbels. Within a week she had been assigned to be the Propaganda Ministry's representative at the Legation. Goebbels tried to be romantic, even hinting that he might be the father, yet transparently unable to hide his relief at what he termed "an admirable solution" to her problem.

The secret marriage had been surprisingly simple. The Luftwaffe attaché in Stockholm, Captain Kurt von Wahlert, was an old friend of Helmut's from Jg 26 who had been terribly wounded in a night battle with a Lancaster. Kurt had made all the arrangements, bribing a very thirsty Swedish clerk to forge the marriage documents for them, and arranging for a distant cousin, Folke Holmstrom, pastor of the Linkoeping Cathedral, to perform the ceremony. Von

Wahlert assured her that it was all absolutely legal in the eyes of the Church and the law; he'd been given a secret pastoral dispensation for all the usual requirements.

The marriage had been quick and quiet; the pastor was obviously distressed at stretching his authority, but determined. Afterward, there was a small feast—some strange-looking but delicious fish, dolmas, a pork roast with rice and brown beans. Helmut had brought champagne and Asbach Uralt brandy; the pastor's mood improved markedly after a few drinks. When it was time to go, he struggled to his feet for a final speech.

"My children, I hope that I've made you as happy as you have made me. We must remember that the child to come is innocent of all the politics that poison the world today. Before I give a final toast to you and to your child, I want to add one thing, a sad and I hope unnecessary promise."

They were silent; he hesitated and Helmut saw that the pastor's glass was empty; he hastened to fill it, and the priest went on.

"Nothing is certain in this war—we don't know what will come. But if ever the worst should come, and God forbid that this should happen, if you need someone to care for the baby, bring it to me. I have friends in my parish in whom I have perfect trust, and so can you. I promise you that the child will be cared for. May it never happen, and may all be blessed."

Now, tonight, when it was time for Helmut to leave, Lyra asked, "When do you think you will be back?"

"I'm not certain; Galland is sending me on an inspection tour of the night-fighter wings and we are still having some problems with the jet engine. I'd hoped to have eight or nine aircraft ready for training other pilots by now; we have only two, and the engines go out on them all the time."

She felt utterly perfidious. He was her husband, the father of her child, but he had said the magic words "jet engine" and she wanted to find out more.

"What's the matter with the engines?"

"Don't bother your head about that—you just worry about the baby."

The war had surely ruined her; she felt as calculating with

Helmut as she had with Goebbels. With a warmth she did not feel
she said, "No, I want to know everything about you, what you are
doing, what your problems are, everything."

The sudden warmth caused him to respond gladly; Lyra knew he
felt that it was the pregnancy that had changed her so, made her so
indifferent to him.

"I'll tell you, but you won't understand." He sat upright next to
her, his hands trying to help his words, telling her about the turbine
blades overheating, and how Hafner's people had invented a way to
cool them.

"They keep the temperatures down by bleeding air through the
blade—but they haven't solved the blade welding process. Understand?"

"Not really—but do you think you can solve it?"

"I can't, I'm not even working on it. But Hafner has the best
craftsmen in the world, and if anyone can, they can. It's just a
matter of time—and unfortunately that's what we don't have, time."

"Does this mean that the bombing won't stop?"

"I can't say. If he found a solution today, we could have twelve
fighters ready in a month, and an operational squadron trained and
ready by the summer. If we demonstrate to the idiots at Headquarters that the plane is a triumph, we could have it in mass production
by the fall. Then the bombing would stop, and the invasion would
be next to impossible."

She took his hands and put them on her waist.

"Kiss my breasts, please, and make me forget about the war."

What a whore I am, she thought.

En route from Guadalcanal/April 18, 1943

The control wheel burned his hands as the temperature in the
sun-drenched cockpit soared like a runaway sauna. He was glad he
was wearing only his standard khaki pants and shirt. Bandfield ran
his finger around the scar on his face, white against his deep tan,

then reached over to adjust his shoulder holster, which was rubbing him raw underneath the parachute straps. He felt an inordinate satisfaction.

Goddamn, I'm the luckiest guy in the world! Patty would kill me if she knew what I was doing.

Looking ahead he saw that the usual smooth symmetry of the Lightning—twin props, twin booms, twin tail—was marred, made lopsided with the new 310-gallon tank on one side and the standard 165-gallon on the other. Ungainly as they were, they increased the internal fuel supply by two thirds.

He was the tail-end charlie of a sixteen-ship formation, whipping along at wavetop height on a heading of 265 degrees at an airspeed of two hundred miles per hour; the P 38's engines were just loafing, conserving fuel. At sea level the Lightning had a normal range of about six hundred miles; today's mission was over eight hundred miles round-trip—and if things went as planned, there would be the damnedest dogfight ever in the blue skies over the Kahili airfield.

The extra range came from the big auxiliary fuel tank. He felt some pride in it; he'd sketched out the original shape and internal plumbing, then ramrodded a team to get it into production. It did the job—but unfortunately, despite all its advocates in the Pentagon, the P-38 was clearly not maneuverable enough to become the long-range fighter in Europe—the Messerschmitts and Focke-Wulfs would eat it up.

On Guadalcanal, he had made a pest of himself, insisting that he should at least be listed as a spare on the mission because his plane was already fitted with the tank for tests, while the others had to be jury-rigged overnight. They had grudgingly listed him as number seventeen. The opportunity to fly came when one of the mission pilots ran his overloaded P-38 over a jagged shard of pierced steel planking and blew a tire. Fighter Strip 2, northwest of Henderson Field, was torn up by use and mortar fire, and blown tires weren't unusual. He knew the other pilot felt as bad as he felt good. There was nothing like being in the right place at the right time!

It was sweat or freeze in the P-38; at low altitudes the big canopy let in enough solar radiation to fry you; at high altitudes it leaked enough heat to freeze you. He'd suffer both today and didn't give a damn, because this was *the* dream mission, a chance to kill Admiral Yamamoto, the Commander-in-chief of the Combined Fleet.

Glancing at the clock he saw they had another forty-two minutes to fly on this heading, a long time to sweat and to think. The word on the mission had come down through Navy channels, all the way from that old Rough Rider, Secretary Knox himself. The code-busters had received word of the inverately punctual Yamamoto's itinerary for an inspection trip. His death would come in the air over Ballale, a tiny island just off Bougainville. He was due to arrive there at exactly 07:45 A.M. Japanese time—Tokyo time—and as the Americans reckoned it, 09:45. The Lightnings would be ready.

They had departed from the charred and battered palm groves that surrounded Henderson Field and the two adjacent fighter strips, heading out over the small cliff that fell away from Fighter Strip 2 to circle to join formation.

Bandfield was essentially a loner, but he had never felt more isolated before, in part because he wasn't completely accepted by the fighter pilots, knit together by long months on the island and in combat. They had been polite and mildly condescending to him until he began to return from missions with as much as one hundred more gallons of fuel in his tanks than anyone else, the result of his years of study on cruise control. Now they all had adopted his techniques, flying at higher manifold pressures and lower rpms, never wasting a moment in the air, always cutting courses as close to straight lines as possible, and most important of all, using efficient climb speeds.

He reached down from the sweat-slick wheel to pull his gloves from his pocket. God, what a lovely airplane this is! he thought. Two Allison engines, two superchargers, and in the nose the best gun package he'd ever seen. No worries about harmonizing, syn-chronizing, nothing, just hose 'em and go! This is how technology pays off; when they needed to have a plane with the range to get Yamamoto, it was there. You can't afford to be second best, not here, not in Europe. Especially not in Europe.

Low to the water, their formation was remarkably precise, as if they were all proud that the Navy had reluctantly turned this prize mission over to the Army. There had been no choice—the Navy didn't have a plane with the range to hack it. And once it was turned over to the Army, it was a foregone conclusion that the 339th would fly it, and Major John W. Mitchell would lead it.

Mitchell was a short, dark-haired Southerner with a triangular face and a pouting mouth. He was soft-spoken but very direct; he flew with his head and had not left them any illusions about the toughness of their mission. They were going to fly at sea level, out of sight of land, for more than four hundred miles, with no navigational aids other than their compasses; at the end of that time, they were supposed to intercept a Japanese bomber carrying Yamamoto. To think that they could pull off a miracle of split-second timing seemed impossible, particularly in the hurry-up-and-wait universe of the military. Even if they flew their mission exactly right, there was no guarantee that Yamamoto's pilot would. But the bright side was that if Yamamoto were there, he'd almost surely be escorted by a flock of Zeros, so there would be a chance for a dogfight and some victories.

The four hottest-shots of the outfit had been appointed as a hunter flight to go in and get Yamamoto's plane. The other twelve aircraft would act as top cover, breaking up the Zero escort.

Characteristically, Mitchell took the job of attacking the fighters, leaving the glory of shooting down Yamamoto to the hunters. Bandfield knew only two of these, gregarious Tom Lanphier and the businesslike Rex Barber. He was perfectly content to let them go after the bombers; he wanted some Zeros for himself.

There was a pop from his left engine as the 165-gallon tank ran dry; he switched the fuel tank settings and the Allison purred again. It was going to be a long day.

En route to Ballale/April 18, 1943

A crushing sense of guilt overwhelmed him, compounding his fatalistic certainty that he was living his last days. He had not been strong enough to prevent the war nor wise enough to win it.

Everything that he had predicted, from the early victories to the mounting defeats, was coming to pass. And he was responsible. After Midway, someone had asked him, "Who would apologize to the Emperor?" It was a rhetorical question; only he could apologize, and that was not enough, not for the Emperor, not for the nation.

Admiral Isoruku Yamamoto sat dressed in an olive-green fatigue uniform, a drab contrast to the customary formal whites he wore on Rabaul, saluting each arriving and departing flight of aircraft. It was a concession to his good friend Lieutenant General Imamura, who tried to get him to cancel the trip; he had himself been almost shot down on a similar flight. When Yamamoto had politely refused to delay the inspection Imamura had pleaded with him to tighten security and not to wear the familiar full-dress white uniform that was virtually his trademark. Reluctantly, Yamamoto had given in, not out of concern that some American spy would see him, but simply to appear to pay attention to his friend's concerns.

He had no concerns about himself. Death would be a sweet reprieve, far better than watching Japan slide endlessly toward its certain bloody destruction. The signs were already there; at the beginning of the war, at Pearl Harbor and after, one of his pilots had been worth five of the enemy. Now the enemy was equally skilled and enjoyed an endless supply of superior aircraft.

A year ago today there had been the unthinkable raid on Tokyo, not much damage, but an affront. Since then the Japanese carrier fleet had been plucked from him at Midway, and he had suffered the humiliation of the battle in the Bismarck Sea. The truth was that he'd lost any meaningful offensive capacity.

Yamamoto shifted his samurai sword, clasping it tightly in the three fingers of his left hand and threading the blade underneath his right leg. Son of a samurai and a perfect product of the Japanese naval system, Yamamoto was quite small at five-foot three-inches, paunchy at 130 pounds. His was an unlikely physique, given his robust appetites for sweets, cigars, and geishas. Especially geishas. He had close familial relations with two and enjoyed the company of others. He was liked in return. In the Shimbashi geisha district, he even received a nickname from the manicurists. A full manicure, all ten fingers, cost one yen. Yamamoto had lost two fingers fighting the Russians in 1905. There were ten sen in a yen, so they affectionately called him "Eighty-sen."

He was told that his visit would be a "shot in the arm" for the morale of the troops on Bougainville; it was all he could do nowadays. There were no more Pearl Harbors to be planned, no more Midways to be fought—it was now hang on and wait.

Yamamoto's eyes wandered around the immaculate interior of the Mitsubishi G4M1 attack plane; it was factory-new, still shining inside and out, suffused with the harsh smell of oil, fuel, and raw metal. A piece of paper was handed to him from the pilot. It read "Ballale at 07:45." He folded it and placed it in his pocket; out of the cabin window he saw the escort fighters suddenly dive away.

Ballale/April 18, 1943

Bandfield enjoyed the building tension as the minutes ticked away on their water-hugging flight. One plane caught its propellers on a wave, disappearing momentarily in a white sheet of foam, before struggling out the other side. Mitchell had led them through three course corrections, and now they were heading directly for Bougainville, still on the deck. Suddenly, a low controlled voice broke radio silence.

"Bogies eleven o'clock . . . high."

He saw them at once, two bombers, escorted by two flights of three Zeros each. Mitchell's navigation had been magnificent. Bandfield scanned the sky anxiously—this couldn't be all!

"Skin 'em off!"

On command, the drop tanks fell away and they began a hard climb for altitude, everything full forward, the Lockheeds quivering as they hung on their propellers. The Japanese were surprised; they had been expecting any attack to come from above, not below.

Bandfield followed Mitchell and the other Lightnings on their preplanned climb to twenty thousand feet as the four hunters roared

at the bombers. He scanned the empty bright blue sky, unbelieving—there simply had to be more Japanese aircraft in the air;
they couldn't have left their top man exposed like this.

The diving Zeros had reached the hunter Lightnings just as they
began their attack; Bandfield could see one of the Lockheeds turn
into the enemy fighters, while the other P-38s hurled themselves at
the two Bettys, themselves now diving away, one toward the green
sanctuary of the ground, the other out to sea. His earphones filled
with the excited chatter from the four hunters.

Without waiting for orders, Bandfield rolled the Lightning on its
back and dove for the island below, where the fleeting shape of the
Betty was discernible above the tree line. Two Lockheeds were hot
after it, and two Zeros were converging on the Lightnings. A dozen
lives hung on the razor sharp balance of timing; if the Zeros could
fire first, the Americans would go down, or break off the attack, and
the bomber would land safely; if the Lightnings fired first, the Betty
was doomed.

Bandfield ripped straight down, forgetting all the warnings about
compressibility as the controls grew stiff in his hands, ignoring the
unwinding instruments, intent only on solving the elegant three-
dimensional trigonometry, to place himself in a position to knock
the Zeros off the P-38s' tail.

One Lightning had already fired and gone past the Betty, now
smoking and edging lower to the forest canopy, all trees and vines to
Bandfield now, no longer just a green mass against the sea. He was
too low, too fast, and damn near too late; the Zeros were gaining on
the second P-38 as it sat in perfect position, firing now at the fat
fuselage of the Betty. Bandfield used his maneuvering flaps as he
reefed back on the wheel, winching his fighter's nose around,
shooting as he came, his bullets and shells passing between the
other Lightning and the two Zeros. It was close enough; the Zeros
broke off.

Yamamoto had watched the Zeros drop away, then saw the silver
H-shape of a twin-engine American fighter roaring past. He looked

back, almost casually; this was the day he would die, and he was well prepared.

He grasped the sword tightly, then turned again to see another American fighter close behind, to the left, a shark pursuing a fat tuna, its nose lit up with cannon and machine-gun fire.

The Admiral of the Combined Fleet saw shells tear a piece of engine cowling off, felt the thud of bullets entering the fuselage, and died when a .50-caliber slug entered the base of his skull, tore through the brain that had come so close to defeating the Americans, and exited through his cheekbone. Everyone else on board was killed when the aircraft ripped through the jungle canopy to explode and burn. Yamamoto's body was thrown clear. When they found little "Eighty-sen," he was strapped upright in his seat, his sword still clasped in the three fingers of his hand, face still recognizable, his eyes closed as if dreaming of his geishas.

Wichita, Kansas/May 10, 1943

Major Jim Lee strolled in from the rain, almost as wet as he'd been when the crew of a Catalina had pulled him from the water off Guadalcanal. He shivered involuntarily as he walked into the brilliantly lit fluorescent cavern that was the brand new Boeing Plant II, his injured arm beginning to ache from the bulging briefcase he carried. This was just the first increment of a planned 180 acres of covered floor space dedicated to building B-29s in Kansas.

Two years before this had been a wheat field with an apple orchard on one border. Now slim steel columns supported a webbridge structure overhead, which carried all the utilities and the miles of light fixtures. The floor was a sea of aluminum, subcomponents shipped from Seattle and a thousand other places, marching along toward completion on jigs that looked like giant erector sets. There was tooling everywhere, everything from simple drill presses to gigantic *Modern Times* monstrosities from the Cincinnati Milling and Machinery Company that swallowed aluminum ingots and spit out finished parts. At first glance the plant seemed to be completely automatic, free of all workers; as Lee walked through to his new office he saw that there were hundreds of people laboring like army ants under the canopy of aluminum.

The crash of the second XB-29 in February had stunned Boeing and thrown the entire program into disarray. Lee had come back from Guadalcanal in October, his arm almost healed, and was immediately sent back to the McNaughton plant. He'd donned his new oak leaves in January, happy to be test-flying the Merlin-powered Sidewinder and consulting on the new jet. Now Caldwell had temporarily assigned him to Wichita, where Boeing was in the middle of a production crisis. Lee had liked the way things were developing at McNaughton and protested the move, but, as usual, Caldwell had been firm.

As he worked with Caldwell to get Boeing back on track, for the first time Lee began genuinely to understand just how tremendous the XB-29 program was and how much it owed to Caldwell's vision.

Boeing had built more four-engine planes than any other manufacturer in the world and, in conforming to the basic specifications Caldwell had framed, had created an extraordinarily advanced aircraft that could fly higher, farther, and faster, with a bigger bomb load, than any bomber in the world. But, strained as the company was with B-17 production, the mass manufacture of the B-29 on a tight schedule was too much for them. Caldwell had charted the course out of building disaster with his personal system of orchestrated management. Just as he had Lee at Wichita, Roget at Dayton, and Bandfield in the field, Caldwell over the years had handpicked dozens of other bright, independent managers, men who could grasp what he wanted and then make it happen.

The B-29 program was the epitome of the forced draft war effort, demanding an incredible variety of scarce talent in the work force, everything from spindle shapers to rivet buckers, from heat-treaters to crane operators. In a whirlwind ninety days, "Caldwell's orchestra" had created them out of bakers, housewives, schoolboys, by setting up schools to teach women from Kansas farms and men from Georgia cotton fields how to build airplanes. Many of the workers had never even seen a sheet of aluminum before, much less turned one into parts.

Caldwell's people sent recruiting teams into the field to hire engineers, machinists, and unskilled laborers; he forecast where shortages would occur—aluminum, machine tools, fasteners, instruments—and told his managers to forestall the shortages with imagination and money. Like Caldwell, the managers were supposed to use *any* technique to get what they wanted—cajoling, threatening, inducing, seducing, whatever it took. And when Lee looked out the window of his second-story office, there was the result: B-29s being completed, on their way to the Pacific and the skies over Japan.

At nine-thirty a weary General Caldwell strode into the room, followed by the usual entourage of Boeing and Army personnel. Shaking Jim's hand, he asked the others to leave. He gratefully accepted a cup of coffee as he lit up his tenth Camel of the morning.

"Sorry to be late. Give me a rundown on the engineering fixes."

Lee went through the agonizing list of tooling problems, engine fires, fouled-up electrical systems. Caldwell indicated approval or disapproval of proposed solutions with short nods of his head, then snapped more questions, going into details on Boeing's personnel problems, the work force, the local Army people. It was like feeding grain into a mill: Caldwell just kept accepting facts, grinding them up, spitting out ideas he didn't like. At three o'clock Jim was exhausted, but he said, "I've got some ideas for you on some other subjects, General. I wish you'd hear me out."

"Shoot, you've got five minutes."

"I think it's wrong to apply European methods to the Pacific theater. I've studied all the intelligence reports on the Japanese home defense, on their fighters and their radar. They are pitifully weak, and it doesn't make sense to send the B-29s in at high altitude, at the limit of their range, to try to hit the Japanese factories with precision bombing. It would be a lot more efficient to strip them of their armament, load them up with the max amount of bombs they can carry, and send them in low, at night. Drop mostly incendiaries, and just burn the cities out."

Caldwell, in a voice vaguely like Jimmy Durante's, said, "Everybody wants to get into the act." Then, "Is that your strategy for winning the war?"

"Yes, sir."

"Stick to ramrodding production problems. Hap Arnold has his reputation riding on the B-29 as a high-altitude precision bomber—do you think I'm going back to tell him it won't work?"

"If you don't he'll find out soon enough. This thing is close to my heart; I was in China, I studied the Tokyo raid. It's not like I'm some professor talking theory out of War College."

Caldwell thought it over. He'd made a career of getting the right advice from the field—and Lee was smart. "Okay, Major, you've got a point. You've done a good job here; maybe there's a way we can work together on this." He walked to the door and checked the hallway—there was no one in sight.

"Look, this is absolutely top secret; I could get my ass in a sling for even mentioning it. But there is a mission coming up in July that conforms to your theory—we're going to make a low-level B-24 strike from Benghazi at Ploesti, at the Rumanian oilfields. It's too long-range for conventional fighter escort, so everything will depend upon secrecy, and staying low beneath the German radar. I could get you on the mission, if you want."

"Sounds ideal—I've checked out in the B-24."

"Good. I'll send you to Killer Kane's outfit; they've got a lot of guys ready to rotate, and one of them would be glad to see you. You can make the flight as a copilot, and be back in the States by mid-August."

"What about this job?"

"You've just about finished what I needed you to do. We're going through a standby period, getting all the tooling standardized so that we're building the same thing in Wichita that we're building in Omaha and Atlanta. And this will give you a chance to see your theory in practice and give me a first-hand report."

"Okay, you're on. But one more thing. When I come back, I don't want to stay with the B-29 program. I want to work with McNaughton on the jet."

Caldwell was immediately suspicious—could Lee be interested in Elsie? "Jesus, is the rest of the war being arranged conveniently for you? Would you like to see the second front at Malibu, rather than France?"

"Come on, General, you've run me around the world working for you. I'd be of more use to you in Nashville than I would in Wichita, and I'd like it better."

"We'll see." Caldwell grabbed his brass-laden hat and bounded out the door, leaving Jim Lee thinking sad thoughts about how nice it had been working for a creampuff like Claire Chennault.

A chance to test my theory hell! It's a chance to get my ass shot off one more time.

Cottbus/May 19, 1943

Exhaustion lay across his heavily muscled shoulders like stones from a quarry, but Bruno Hafner was supremely content as he methodically went through the shutdown drill of the Messerschmitt Bf 108 communications plane. It was wonderful to be able to fly again, even in a little crate like the *Taifun*. He'd had to tear out the original four-place configuration and replace it with his own special seat, tailored for ease of access. There was a jump seat and a bucket for his faithful but airsick prone bodyguard, Sergeant Boedigheimer.

Hafner relished the popping of his eardrums, the smell of hot oil, and the wheezing sounds of the airframe metal coming to rest, sounds as therapeutic to his broken body as Kersten's massaging fingers. He nodded and Boedigheimer arranged the ladder to help him out. He was strong enough now to pull himself out of the airplane by upper-body strength alone.

In the air, his bad legs made no difference, for he had lost none of his skills, nor any of his enjoyment of flight. He'd probably never fly in combat again, but then he'd been told that he'd never walk. Now he could do a half a kilometer without a cane, and his endurance was building.

He had just looped and rolled through the white clouds dotting the blue sky, embracing the glorious day in an effort to shake off the worries of the doleful war news. After all of Rommel's tremendous successes, the *Afrika Korps* had come to an inglorious end, with General von Arnim left to hold the bag of defeat. And the goddamn RAF had somehow blown up the Möhne and Eder dams with some devilish new kind of bomb, flooding the Ruhr Valley and severely reducing the power and water available for industry. Goebbels's Ministry, in their indefatigable efforts to show a bright side, had made much of SS General Stropp bringing the bloody fighting in the Warsaw ghetto to an end. Some victory—SS troops and tanks against a bunch of Jews armed with homemade pistols.

Hafner glanced at his watch: nine o'clock, time for the damned meeting with Josten. The more involved Josten became with the jet program, the moodier he got. Hafner wondered how he'd be to work with if things weren't going so well with the 262; as it was, he was increasingly ill-tempered.

Boedigheimer grunted as he strained to keep the wheelchair from speeding off down the long concrete ramp to the cavernous underground factory. Hafner always half expected to be met by a flight of millions of bats roiling out of the gloomy entrance below. It was another one of his "follies" turned into triumph. Everyone, from Himmler down, had thought he was crazy when he laid the huge concrete block on top of solid ground, then burrowed out the factory space underneath. But Speer, a man of vision, was excited by the plant and told Hitler about it. Now they were going to build much larger structures on the same model all over Germany. It was the kind of idea that appealed to the Fuehrer, who was already demanding that caves, railroad tunnels, mines, and every other sub-surface area be used; he wanted all of his industry underground by the end of 1944 in a troglodyte world, all craters above and workers below. When Hitler had said, "Give me four years and you won't recognize Germany," he hadn't been jesting.

It wasn't going to be possible, of course, but the Cottbus method was the cheapest and the easiest. And Speer, as arrogant as he sometimes was, always gave Hafner full credit for the idea, an unusual occurrence in the Third Reich.

Always correct to the point of annoyance, Josten stood up and saluted him as he entered.

"*Ach*, Helmut, what is the complaint *de jour*?"

"*Herr Direktor*, what is the progress on the turbine blades?"

"Some good news, for a change. We've finally licked the welding problem. Old Fritz has come up with a totally different approach, and even mechanized it. Let's go next door."

The two men donned welder's goggles and went into the next room, where Fritz was bent over a machine. The turbine blades were being brought in one by one on a slow conveyor belt. Fritz's device, not too different in operation from the claw machines used in carnivals, had a mechanical hand that grabbed each turbine blade and with a blinding blue-white flash, electrically spot welded the clamped edges along the top.

Hafner, a gargoyle with his burnt twisted face and blue-lensed goggles, showed him a turbine blade. "Fritz toughened the ordinary steel by introducing nitrogen into the annealing process. Then he made one side of the blade longer than the other, bent the top over, and spot welded it."

Josten held the turbine blade in his hand. "Looks pretty crude; doesn't the air bleed out between the welds?"

"Absolutely, and that keeps the temperature down. I'm going to have twelve engines built up by the end of this month, and as many as twenty more next month."

Josten was silent, obviously impressed. "With that sort of schedule, we could start training in June and have a squadron ready to go by the end of July."

"Have you identified your pilots?"

"They've all identified themselves; they are either recovering from wounds, been court-martialed, or are persona non grata politically. I've picked twelve, and they are picking their own ground crew, all with the same kind of background, a regular bunch of pirates!"

"Will '*Unser Hermann*' let you have them?"

"He'll never know about it. Galland is arranging for their orders to read Peenemunde—but they'll be amended so they can report to me here."

"How long will it take once you get the airplanes?"

"We ought to have two weeks of ground instruction, especially on engine operation. We're ready to start on that. Then there ought to be two weeks of multi-engine training for the 109 and 190 boys—we can use Messerschmitt 110s and 410s. Then a solid six weeks in the 262."

"Six weeks?"

"It's a totally different animal than a regular fighter—just navigating is a problem, you're going so fast. We've got to work out tactics, do some fighting against captured enemy airplanes. It will take a week or ten days just to learn how to shoot, throwing all past experience out the window."

"You'll have to compress the training. It's important that you're ready in July at the latest, while the weather is still good and the Amis are still coming in force. We want to hit a big formation, knock down lots of bombers, make a big splash. Then we can force Junkers to convert to our methods, and get Messerschmitt to stop fiddling around with development and start producing."

Josten was straightforward as always. "Do you have an interest in those firms?"

"Messerschmitt yes, Junkers no. But I don't see why I can't license the turbine blade design to Junkers—it would only be fair."

"Why don't you offer it to them now?"

"They'd never accept it—not their idea! The last thing they want to do is pay an outsider a royalty on something they think they can develop themselves. Time means nothing to them! We need a big bomber massacre to force Hitler to order them to take it."

"You could offer it to them, royalty-free."

"Impossible—you don't know how their minds work. Or mine."

Josten shook his head. "Strange world—people are dying and companies are worrying about profits."

Hafner looked at him with real surprise, his twisted mouth stretched further out of shape.

"Why, Josten, why do you think we have wars in the first place?"

• • •

After Josten left, Hafner wheeled himself to his refuge, a smaller underground facility at the extreme left of the experimental complex. The only sign of life was the steady stream of *Wehrmacht* trucks driving up to an elevator in the aboveground loading dock.

In contrast to the bright, noisy underground plant, the inside of the building was dimly lit, with a host of whispering Italian laborers working with enormous microfilm cameras. The loudest sound was the rustle of paper as page after page of documentation was fed into the cameras.

This was his escape hatch, his guarantee. The arrangement with Caldwell was all very well, but he might need to up the ante. And it was always possible that he might have to go to Russia. The use of forced labor was becoming widely condemned—it might affect his amnesty agreement. The Russians wouldn't quibble about forced labor—they were past masters at it.

Technical data from all over the Reich—engineering data from Peenemunde, documentation on the atomic experiments, heavy water stations, poison gases, aerodynamics, metallurgy, every product of the engineering genius of Germany, all went before his cameras. It was the single greatest concentration of secrets in the Reich, authorized by Speer and eagerly approved by Hitler, who was intent on preserving the record of his infallible decisions. Speer had authorized the equipment and the film, valuable and increasingly scarce. Hafner was supposed to make three copies of each document, for storage in three different areas. Instead he was sabotaging the program, making only one copy. It saved time, materials, and money—and it ensured that he would have the only copy to bargain with. If, as he still hoped, the Reich should win the war, he could quickly make as many duplicates as he needed.

Benghazi, Cyrenaica/July 14, 1943

He was becoming a connoisseur of sand, a gourmand of grit. In Guadalcanal it had been more granular, dusty enough to become mudlike when the rains came, but still substantial, concrete-mix-quality sand. Libyan sand was a corrosive red talc that invaded carburetors, eyelids, and the inevitably tepid lemonade with equal facility; it filled the tents, jammed guns, and filed away at the enamel on your teeth, a groaning, abrading filth, tasting of fly-specked tombs. Its effect upon morale was bad; upon engines, disastrous, cutting the normal three-hundred-hour life expectancy to sixty or less.

Jim Lee lay in his sack, contemplating a career that had given him enormous exposure yet always cast him in the role of outsider. The iron cot listed in the sand, which quietly, unevenly, swallowed even the empty K-ration cans he'd planted under the cot legs as footpads.

He reached over and tapped his tentmate's arm. Colonel Willie Westerfield had remembered him from the days in Hawaii and was virtually the only man in the whole operation who had been friendly, gladly taking him on as copilot. Westerfield's eyes followed Lee's finger to the duffel bag strung from the tent roof. It contained their emergency food—cans of Vienna sausage, gum, K-rations, packages of cheese and crackers—and swung under the weight of a desert rat busily trying to gnaw through the sand-dusted fabric.

"Those little bastards have seen too many Tarzan movies. That's a six-foot jump."

Westerfield pulled his service .45-caliber out of its holster and fired; the rat looked down and began chewing on the hole made by the bullet, probably thinking that a German officer would never have missed.

To Lee's amazement, Westerfield fired again, blasting the rodent into bloody bits against the tent wall.

"Jesus, that's disgusting, Colonel! You've been out here too long! Besides, you could get court-martialed for firing a gun like that."

"Only for missing him. They'll never hear it in this windstorm, and if they do it only means that I won't have to go on this totally snafued mission."

Outside the powdery khamsin wind divided its efforts between filling the billowing tents and dropping the visibility toward zero, turning the setting desert sun into an ominous red smear. Shaking his head, his ears still crackling from the sound of the pistol, Lee strode out to the nearest "desert lily," the conical urinals fashioned out of gasoline tins and stuck at random intervals around the base. As he relieved himself, thinking about Westerfield's assessment of the mission, he let his eyes wander around the junkyard that four armies had made of a once peaceful desert. Amid the scattering of palm trees were the oil drum privies, burned-out tanks, an international collection of junked aircraft, scavenged for parts and now capable to serve only as wash lines for the minimum laundry that anyone deigned to do. Even this detritus was coveted by the Arabs, who lurked nearby and stole everything they could, whether it was fastened down or not.

Back in the tent he asked, "Why do you say this is a snafu? I'd say the planning was better than usual. They've built an exact scale replica of Ploesti and flown a bunch of practice missions against it. The sand table model is perfect, we all know it by heart; Tex McCrary's training movie showed us what to bomb, and the flak defense is supposed to be light. What's going to go wrong?"

Westerfield sat upright, arms and legs unfolding like the blades of a Swiss Army knife.

"Look, Jim, you're new here, and everybody's been giving you the business, 'cause you just dropped out of Headquarters and you're going on the mission. They think you'll go back and be a hero, and they'll be out here to try to live out the rest of their tours."

"Reasonable enough."

"Yeah, but behind the gruff exteriors are some pretty mean bastards, and they're not getting along. Old Killer Kane, running the 98th, has been here so long he calls his outfit the 'Pyramiders.' He likes this kind of stuff, and he thinks he knows how to run the show. Then they bring us in, guys from the Eighth Air Force in England, and *we* think they know it all. Then we've got some new guys who don't know nothing, no more than they learned on our practice low levels. That includes you."

Lee shrugged. "So what else is new?"

"What else is new is that they're kidding themselves that they can come in low and not get caught. I'll bet the Jerries know where we're coming and when already; if they don't, they'll know an hour after takeoff, maybe before. They can buy information from the Arabs for peanuts—they're the only people that like what the Germans are doing to the Jews. You can bet that when we get there, they're going to be ready."

"Maybe not—Kane thinks we'll do all right."

"Yeah, he would, he's a Neanderthal, a saber-toothed tiger; he wouldn't tell anybody different. You know what they're saying already—that the mission will be worthwhile if we take out the target, even if nobody comes back. When I heard that I figured they were writing us off."

Lee watched him closely and finally concluded that Westerfield wasn't scared, depressed, or even worried—he was just being matter-of-fact.

"Anyway, I believe in low-level attacks. It makes it tough on the fighters to hit you, and whatever flak there is has only a few seconds to shoot. I'll bet we get in and out without many losses."

Westerfield cocked his head and said, "Would you bet your life on it?"

Southwest of Budapest/July 31, 1943

Two gray-green arrow shapes were strung three hundred meters apart, clipping along at 850 kilometers per hour at eight thousand meters altitude, brilliant white vapor trails marking their path across the sky. Helmut Josten leaned his forehead against the cold, crystal-clear canopy to watch. It was a beautiful sight—and it sickened him. Two Messerschmitt Me 262s, the most potent fighter in the sky— and just one sixth the strength he should have had.

Never before had he felt so deeply that fate was against him, that nothing he could do would change the downward course of events, which in the last few days had shaken Helmut Josten more than anything since Stalingrad. He had spent months bringing the special 262 unit into existence, working closely with Hafner—never an easy task—and calling on every resource he had in the Luftwaffe to get parts, fuel allocations, and personnel. Less than ten days ago he was certain that he had succeeded, finally managing to outfit twelve fighters with the special engines built up with Fritz's new turbine blades. A week ago, his handpicked pilots had flown a successful training mission against a B-24 captured in Sicily. Everything had gone perfectly, and the pilots were bursting with confidence.

Then a wayward stream of British bombers, driven off course from the main mission against Berlin, had dumped their bombs on Cottbus. The bombs had walked through the factory site as if they had individually been guided by a malevolent genie, destroying nine of the aircraft dispersed in camouflaged revetments. It had been blind luck—a few seconds delay on the bomb release, a slight difference in airspeed, a shift in the wind, and the bombs would have plowed up an orchard. Months had been spent preparing the aircraft with their hand-built engines—and *nine* were destroyed in a few seconds.

Then, this morning, he'd lost another, this one a victim of the growing raw material shortages. Instead of the standard forged-steel landing gears of the past, the 262 had been forced to substitute hollow steel tubing. The gear was delicate, and as they were taxiing out, the nosewheel of the second aircraft had collapsed, crashing nose-up on the taxiway, cutting his force down to two planes. It made a mockery of the "big jet blow" he and Hafner had sought, the massive bomber slaughter that would have gotten Hitler's attention and forced him to grant the necessary priorities.

Josten's headset crackled.

"Turbo One, this is Turbo Two. I'm losing revolutions on my port engine."

With smooth, easy movements, Josten swung to the right, placing himself below and to the rear of the second aircraft, already beginning to slow.

"Turbo Two, watch the temperatures. If they go up, go ahead and shut the engine down. Divert to Budapest."

There was a momentary silence, then the single word "Scheiss" as Turbo Two's port engine failed completely and the jet banked sharply to the left and dove straight down. Josten watched it until the fighter was swallowed by a cloud layer. He hoped that the pilot would bail out—and knew how improbable it was.

He flew on in stunned silence. It was impossible; all of the monumental effort was now at the point of dissolution. One aircraft left! It was an abomination.

Fighter Command Post, Otopenii, Rumania/July 31, 1943

In spite of all that had happened, Helmut Josten was impressed with the field at Mizil as he supervised the ground crew camouflaging his lone 262. Some twenty miles south of Bucharest, it was a beautiful meadow carefully graded with decent runways. There were fifty-plus Messerschmitt Bf 109 fighters revetted around the field, and first-class maintenance and refueling set up.

A good friend and comrade understood his mood and tried to restore his good humor. Major Douglas Pitcairn of Perthshire—though English named, the descendant of the midshipman who had first seen Pitcairn Island, he was Prussian born and bred—threw a lavish luncheon for him, with roast pig, delicious sausages, local wines, and endless rounds of mind-numbing plum brandy.

Even better, Pitcairn assured him that for once they had good intelligence. Rommel had left a handful of agents scattered about Libya. Three were reporting the activity from Benghazi, covering the number of aircraft, the practice bomb runs on the artificial Ploesti built in the desert, everything. The signs—bomb accumulation, maintenance effort, all the logistical contortions of a major effort—pointed to a raid by two hundred B-24s in the next two or three days.

All through lunch, Pitcairn pumped him on the 262. Josten told him the whole sorry story of the buildup and the decline of his jet force—and felt better for it.

Pitcairn was philosophical. "Look, Helmut, you can't fight fate. You did everything you could—the odds were against you. Tomorrow you'll get a chance at some juicy targets—maybe you can still turn everything around."

To distract him, Pitcairn took him on a tour of Ploesti's defenses. The beautiful town was straight out of a "Strength through Joy"-style travel poster, with lovely colonnaded buildings, pastel stucco homes—many built around a central atrium—and acacia-lined streets. In the square an abstract Brancusi sculpture seemed oddly out of place until Josten related it to the interlocking net of oil refineries that surrounded Ploesti on all sides, a surrealist twentieth-century wall blocking the Rumanian village. They were laid out like refineries the world over, with long, fire-restraining distances between cracking stations, pumps, and storage tanks. From here went the best oil in Europe, half the Axis's needs.

"You know we've been bombed by the Americans and the Russians. Best thing that could have happened to us. *Generalmajor* Gerstenberg used the raids as a threat to pry resources out of Goering. The man's a genius—and no Nazi, either. Let me show you the results."

Their Horch had passed dozens of cars on the streets; Pitcairn noted Josten's curiosity and said, "No fuel shortage here. There is rationing, but nobody pays any attention to it; they just tap into the nearest tank or line, like a brewmaster in a brewery."

Leaving Ploesti, they went under a hugh pipe, supported on stiltlike wood and steel columns.

"It's like a circular highway, a trunk line connecting all of the refineries and storage areas to each other. It's Gerstenberg's idea, as are the flak dispositions. If one area gets bombed, it's hooked up with another."

Just like Hafner's complex of factories, Josten thought.

They drove past a forced labor camp, surrounded by the usual barbed wire fences, guard towers, and roving dogs; the sight had become Germany's trademark. A year ago it would have depressed Josten; now he accepted it indifferently.

Pitcairn, knowing that he was repeating himself, said, "Gerstenberg is a genius. No one could have done more; he's talked them out of fifty thousand troops and more than that in foreign laborers, all to protect his *'Festung Ploesti.'* "

He drove swiftly through the southern defenses. There were conventionally sited batteries, units of six of the marvelous 88-mm guns, good for antitank, antiaircraft, or personnel work, backed up by four automatic 20-mm and four 37-mm batteries. Most had a 180-man German crew to man them, a few were handled by Rumanians. Outside this ring of heavy flak was another, larger circle, of Rumanian- and Austrian-manned light-flak and machine-gun units.

Pitcairn said, "At my last count we had forty batteries like this around Ploesti; some in flak towers, some in church steeples, the rest camouflaged in haystacks and the woods. Then we've got this."

He pointed to an antiquated train on a siding, its old-fashioned cars bearing the scars of long service. "It's a flak train, sort of like a Q ship in the first war. The sides of the cars fold down, and the batteries start firing. Another bit of Gerstenbergia."

Josten felt a black rage consuming him. If he'd been able to get twelve jets here, they'd have given the Americans a hiding they'd never forget, a victory that would have established what he knew so well—that the 262 was Germany's only answer.

They drove back to the Fighter Command Post in silence, each man preoccupied with the coming battle. Inside the windowless two-story building, Josten watched the *Luftnachrichtenhilferinnen,* Luftwaffe airwomen, sitting in front of the gigantic glass map that reflected the entire theater of war. Marked off in a grid, the route of all the aircraft being reported by radar or visual spotters was flashed on the map.

"How many fighters can you muster, all told?"

"We can put up about seventy 109s, and perhaps twenty 110 night fighters. Then our gypsy cousins the Rumanians have a squadron of Messerschmitts, and about sixty of their own fighters, IAR 80s. They're obsolete, but useful for picking off stragglers."

"You'll have to let me call my own shots about throwing the jet into the fight—I use fuel so fast that I'll have to be sure where the bombers are before I take off."

"You run your own show. I'll have my hands full here."

Benghazi/August 1, 1943

A manmade khamsin of wind and sand darkened the sky, tons of the desert shifted by the four propellers on each of 178 B-24 bombers. Jim Lee sat on Westerfield's right, feeling the fat-fuselaged plane tremble beneath them as the Sunday morning heat built, as he ran numbers in his mind. The aggregate fuel load of the bombing force was more than half a million gallons; they would be carrying more than a million pounds of bombs, five-hundred pounders and incendiaries. If they were successful, they could take out the refinery in twenty minutes; it would take a million-man army six months to fight its way inland from some Balkan second front to do the same job—and they might not make it.

Just under eighteen hundred men were poised at their crew stations, each one calculating the odds against them. The padres had had their hands full the night before. Some Christian men went to both Catholic and Protestant chaplains, covering their bets.

A Jeep pulled up in front of their B-24 and a harried-looking major got out. He climbed through the main entrance hatch and crawled forward to the cockpit, shook Westerfield by the shoulder, and said, "Come with me; you've got to fly *Satan's Darling*—the pilot started rectal bleeding, he's too sick with dysentery to go."

"Who's flying my airplane?"

"I guess Lee, here; we're sending a new copilot over. He's just arrived, hasn't got much time, but he'll have to do. We're short-handed, lots of people down with gyppo belly."

Westerfield sat for a moment, face white, then said, "You can do it, Jim."

The announcement didn't go well with the crew, but the mission procedures were rolling like a runaway locomotive and there were no alternatives. The takeoff from the dust-laden runway was uneventful, and Lee was personally comfortable as soon as he was airborne, circling to let the squadron, the 406th, join him. Its Liberators were just off the Ford production line, not camouflaged, their aluminum skin glistening in the rising sun. It was a brand-new outfit, eighteen aircraft strong, and by a quirk of abdominal fate, Lee was aircraft commander of the plane leading it.

All the ships were flying in the unusual **V** of **V**s-formation, just as the old Keystone bombers had flown in the 1920s, going in so low the usual combat box wasn't workable. Lee's group were the tail end charlies, tacked on to the rear and high behind the 98th Bomb Group's pinkish-colored aircraft, the famous Pyramiders led by Killer Kane. They headed out to sea, five miles of jangling airborne nerves. From his elevated position at the end of the group, Lee could see the entire formation; just ahead was Westerfield's new airplane, *Satan's Darling*, tucked in the rear of the Pyramiders' formation.

After the mandatory intercom checks, the earphones fell ominously silent. The crew had worshiped their former leader, only tolerating Lee while they could make broad fun of his landings, confident that Westerfield could always save them. Now Lee was in the left seat, totally responsible for them and for the seventeen other ships in the formation.

He settled in, trying to ignore the frantic activity of the bright young copilot, Flight Officer Hal Nations, whose hands continuously and unnecessarily roved back and forth over every knob, switch, and button in the cockpit. To soothe him, Lee had pointed to a B-24 ahead of them—just as it feathered a prop and turned out of formation, heading for home. Nations turned to him and put up nine fingers—one for each of the aborts he'd counted, well above the normal rate. Was morale that bad?

The first real trouble started three hours out, just as they picked up their initial landfall, the island of Corfu. The lead ship, *Wingo-Wango*, carrying the primary mission navigator, began to waver, oscillating nervously, pitching up and down, the movements amplifying until the nose rose up, up, into a stall. Then, in dreamy slow motion, it turned over on its back and dove straight into the sea like a Mexican cliff-diver. There was no radio call, nothing. Flames and smoke burst from the surface, rising higher than the formation. Against all orders, the number two ship, carrying the deputy mission navigator, pulled out and circled down, dropping rescue rafts, as if anyone could have lived through the horrifying crash into the sea. The stupid gesture was a gross violation of discipline, jeopardizing the whole mission.

The intercom silence was broken by someone saying, "A total snafu." Lee wondered what would happen now that the two principal navigators were gone, for the disobedient second B-24 could never catch up.

As the mission moved on, the formations began to drift apart, as if the personalities of their leaders were opposite magnetic poles. Instead of the stately tight boxes of the European theater, where each ship was protected by the guns of the others, the Vs began to separate. Then, like squibs of toothpaste smeared on a mirror, billowy cumulus clouds appeared over the first geographic barrier, the nine-thousand-foot-high spine of Pindus mountains that ran from Albania down through Greece. The leading 376th group began a climb through the clouds to sixteen thousand feet. Behind them the rest of the formation bored in at twelve thousand, accepting the danger of flying in cloud rather than using the fuel and oxygen that would be needed to climb.

Lee saw the split, remembered that the tailwinds were considerably higher at altitude and would widen the gap between formations, and murmured to himself, "Snafu is *right!*"

Fighter Command Headquarters, Otopenii/August 1, 1943

The first warning came from the Wurzburg-type radar station on Mount Cherin, near Sofia: "Many aircraft, bearing thirty degrees."

As the Luftwaffe airwomen began making their first marks on the glass screen, Pitcairn turned to Josten. "This is it. The bastards are coming. The Bulgarians will have first crack at them, but all they've got are old Czech biplanes. I'm putting everyone on immediate alert."

Josten left to go to the field where his 262 was fueled and armed, just as the second report came in from Mount Cherin. "Lost contact. The aircraft have disappeared." It puzzled Pitcairn until a telephone report came in from a Rumanian ground station declaring that the target had to be Bucharest.

At Mizil, pilots full of an early lunch of soup, eggs, and fried potatoes ran to their Messerschmitt Bf 109s. In five minutes, fifty-two of the spindly-legged fighters had raced across the dusty field, joining formation even as their gear clanked into the wheel wells on the climb toward the incoming bombers.

Josten waited until the 109s made contact, deciding in the process that he would make as many tail-on attacks as he could, then pull out and try to pick off stragglers for as long as he had fuel and ammunition. He talked to himself as if he were briefing a *Staffel*: "Spread the shooting out, try to damage as many as possible. They've got a long way to go back, and if I can just shoot out an engine, they probably won't make it. Don't worry about kills, just cut them up and let the Rumanians finish them off."

The Liberators slid down mountain slopes, like kids on a banister, to race along at ground level, lifting a wing to go over trees, enjoying a *National Geographic* view of neatly laid out villages, beautiful fields, and horse-drawn hay wagons. A cheer went up on the interphone as they swept over a river where girls were bathing; there was instant consensus that they were bare-ass naked.

Lee thought, Maybe it's not a snafu after all; maybe we'll get away clean. The signs were looking good to him as the countryside unfolded beneath, checkpoints showing up on the ground just as they were marked along the red course line on the map he had folded at his side, a contingency in case the navigator, Fred Pola, was wounded. Lee could just see the lead ship of the first formation, miles ahead. He hoped there wouldn't be many fighters; they had lost most of their formation integrity, and things would get worse when the flak opened up.

He ran his finger down the map; the first Initial Point, Pitesti, sixty-five miles from Ploesti, was coming up. Fifty miles after Pitesti was the second IP, Floresti, the final turn point for the thundering thirteen-mile, four-minute charge down the valley to the refineries. So far it was textbook perfect.

He was humming to himself when the lead formation began a turn. He called down to Lieutenant Pola, crouched in the nose of the B-24.

"Navigator, what's going on?"

"They're turning short; that's not the IP, it's a little town called Targoviste. They're heading straight for Bucharest!"

Lee hesitated for a moment and then broke radio silence.

"Mistake. Mistake. Turning short."

The lead bombers raced on.

"What are you going to do, Skipper?"

"We're going to follow orders; we'll turn at Floresti and bomb as planned."

"Roger; it's seven minutes now to Floresti; I'll give you a hack."

The two bomber formations soared majestically apart; Lee hoped his radio call hadn't been picked up by the Germans; they were low, maybe the mountains had blocked it out.

Mistakes even out. The German fighters had climbed through the mixed clouds, dirty gray on the bottom, silvery white on top. They sought the bright piercing sun canyons as they turned around the thunderstorms building up on the mountainsides. Breaking out on top at two thousand meters, they found the heavens empty.

The Messerschmitt fighter leader called, "Hallo, Otopenii, we're in Cancer sector now and there's not a damn Ami furniture van in sight."

"They must be above or below you; you are merged on the radar."

Helmut Josten, monitoring the radio chatter at Mizil, ran to his aircraft to take off.

Below the circling Messerschmitts, screened by the clouds, the lead B-24s looked ahead in confusion as the smokestacks and towers of the Ploesti they were looking for dissolved into the buildings and churches of a major city.

"Christ, it's Bucharest! We must have turned early."

On board the lead B-24 the pilot was suddenly aware of his

ghastly mistake. Without hesitation, he threw his aircraft into a stately ninety-degree turn that gave them an attack heading directly into the teeth of toughest batteries, parallel to the track of the flak train, as if he were following *Generalmajor* Gerstenberg's battle plan. Half of the formation turned with him; the rest thundered on toward Bucharest, adding their little bit to the billowing balls-up.

But at Otopenii, Major Pitcairn watched the course of the plots splitting on the glass map, thinking, Damn clever attack; they're sending one force in a feint on Bucharest, and hitting the refinery from two directions. Marvelous planning!

He turned to a busy *Leutnant* next to him and roared, "Where are the fighters now, damnit?"

"They should be making contact; the plots are overlapping."

Someone handed Pitcairn a telephone; he listened for a moment, then screamed in rage: "It's a low-level attack! Call the fighters and tell them to get below the clouds. Tell them to ignore the flak, to attack!"

The American bombers' propellers were harvesting wheat, the prop blast cutting shimmering waves through the fields. As they raced in, their shadows flashing ahead of them, a furious sheet of flak spewed from the defending 88s, the gunners firing with contact fuses over open sights.

The B-24s, specially fitted with four forward-firing machine guns for the pilot, their turrets trained ahead, dueled with the flak, trying to shoot their way through the defenses to bomb the refineries now just two minutes away. A balloon barrage loomed ahead—the pre-mission briefing had said, "We think the B-24 is strong enough to fly right through the cables." They were, but not strong enough to resist the contact-fused explosives strung like sugar dots on a licorice strip. *Umbriago* was the first to go, a victim of a balloon's cable, the wing blowing off and the fuselage breaking up in its few-seconds fall toward the ground, its crew trapped and immobilized by the centripetal G forces.

More B-24s fell to flak; an 88 shell blew the cockpit out of *Detroit Maid* and the bomber crashed into a field, plowing through a village schoolhouse to drop into a creek, sending blazing gasoline floating downstream. Another 88 shell clipped the rudder of *Pretty Baby*, sending it into a skidding turn that took it into the side of *Oshkosh ByGosh*, both planes vaporizing in a pink-black blast of bombs and fuel.

But most got through, dropping their bombs and pressing on, the roar of exploding storage tanks lost behind them as they dove to the deck, seeking refuge in the scant curvature of the earth, thankful for a copse of woods, a line of hedges.

Approaching on the preplanned course, in the opposite direction of the mixed-up first wave, Lee's throat tightened as the initial flurry of flak bursts, individual black puffs, suddenly roared into a wall of flame and smoke the length of Ploesti.

"They're hitting it from the south."

"Bomb doors open."

Lee held the airplane steady, waiting for the release, heading directly toward the boiling inferno. He started as the mass of smoke was ripped apart by pink and sandy wings as two groups of B-24s plunged out, some with props feathered, some burning, all of them firing. He heaved back on the control wheel to avoid the lead B-24, then plunged back down into the fray.

Ahead, he saw Westerfield's plane, *Satan's Darling*, take a hit in the fuselage; flames erupted from it as his bombs spilled out. The stricken B-24 staggered into a climb, two bodies dropping out of the back, no chance at all for their chutes to open. Westerfield's plane rolled and crashed directly into an oil storage tank, disappearing in flaming, fan-shaped spray.

The call "Bombs away" came as 20-mm flak shattered the cockpit windows of Lee's aircraft. The new Flight Officer glanced at him and signaled a thumbs up as Lee led them out of the inferno, the airplane hurt but still flying. They had been briefed to turn right to escape the target area; there was nothing but fire and flak in that direction and Lee hauled his airplane around to the left, leading the formation toward Campina in the north.

"Crew check."

The men checked in—no casualties.

"Tail gunner, how many airplanes with us?"

"I just counted them, sir, we came out with all seventeen. We really plastered the target, we won't be coming back here."

Lee eased back on the throttles; it was a long way home, and they hadn't seen any fighters yet.

"Anybody else back there?"

"No, sir, nobody here but us chickens."

Always a comedian in the crowd, Lee thought. He cranked his wing down and saw that the smoke and flames were now reaching twenty thousand feet into the air; he wondered how many of the other bombers had gotten through, if the tail gunner was right about not having to come back.

At least it proved his theory: even with a major navigational error, they had gone in low, blasted the target, and all eighteen in his formation had gotten away. He decided to stay low for another hour, hugging the side of the mountains, then begin his climb.

Twenty miles away horizontally and two miles higher, a very frustrated Helmut Josten was talking to Pitcairn on the radio.

"Where are they, Douglas? I haven't seen a damn airplane, nothing but smoke and flames."

"They came in low; our 109s have caught up with them in Cancer sector, course 240, southwest of Ploesti."

A low-level attack; the worst possible thing for Josten's fuel-gulping jet. Even if he found them now, he'd only have time for one or two attacks—he couldn't stay airborne more than forty minutes at low altitude.

As he turned he caught the silver glint of Lee's formation streaking north.

"*Achtung.* Liberators heading off to the north. Attacking."

It was not a pell-mell, hell for leather attack like the old days. The thoroughbred 262 needed careful handling. In a 109 he could have rolled over and pulled back on the stick, letting the airspeed build as fast as possible. Not with the 262—a steep dive could compress the very air, stiffening the controls and perhaps leading to a breakup. Instead he swung around in a wide circle, throttle just slightly retarded, planning to arrive just below and behind the bombers. Still talking to himself, he said, "God, I wish I had the others with me. Can't fire until I'm sure of a hit."

Like a single hound in pursuit of a run of foxes, his 262 gobbled the distance as he went through the ritual arming of his guns.

In the lead B-24, Lee recognized panic in his tail gunner's voice.

"Skipper, we got company. A fighter, fast as anything, coming up behind." He paused and said, "I don't believe it! This bastard ain't got no propellers!"

Oh, my God—it's the jet, at last!

Josten took one last look at his fuel gauges and concentrated on the attack. The B-24s were not beautiful like the B-17s; they had fat bellies and too thin wings, and the big double tails looked vulnerable. He let the first Liberator fill the Revi 16B reflector gunsight and pressed the firing button; the B-24 seemed to break up instantly from the three-second rumble of his guns. It burst into flames, the left gear falling from its well as the wing folded up and back. He skidded to the right, took another Liberator in his sights, and exploded it in a brilliant red ball.

Josten almost felt sorry for the Americans, to be so vulnerable, to fly an airplane so slow and so fire prone! He'd made a steep climbing turn and now dove back to the attack.

One of the Liberators was falling behind. He fired and the B-24 pulled up in a violent stall, then began to break up, parts shredding from it even as it turned over for the last dive.

The rest of the Americans were already diving even closer to the ground, sending a screen of machine-gun fire in his direction. He checked his gauges once again, then dove after the fleeing bombers, now heading for the cloud-masked mountaintops. Good enough—a rock-filled cloud could kill even better than a cannon.

He closed again, firing, walking his shells from the wing root up into the cabin until his guns went silent, out of ammunition. The bomber flew on.

Josten was exhausted. He banked away, thinking, That's enough.
Back to Mizil to refuel.

In the fight, Lee's plane had been slowed by hits in the right
outboard engine and he had slipped back to the number two position, following another B-24 into the clouds, the rest of the formation behind him. The copilot had been wounded, and the navigator
was leaning over him, fastening a compress to his wounds.

They were burrowing along right at the top of the cloud layer, the
barely masked sun filling the cockpit with a luminous in-
candescence. He reached up over the windshield to press the number four engine feathering button; it was going to be a long ride
home.

Wolf's Lair, Rastenburg/August 20, 1943

There was a rare twenty-minute interval between conferences.
Adolf Hitler cradled his head in his hands on his hard camp bed,
waiting for Dr. Theo Morell's injections—Vitamultin-forte, Pro-
stakrinum, and glucose with iodine—to take effect.

A groan slipped through his enveloping weariness. Assailed by
every detail of the war, great and small, there was no longer anyone
to turn to. He was so terribly lonely. Even the indispensable Bormann was just an automaton who could carry out decisions but not
make them.

And there was treason everywhere! Like a dark spot on an apple,
the rot had started with the Luftwaffe's failure over England. Since
then it had spread everywhere, a soft brown canker contaminating
even his intelligence services. How could the *Abwehr* have been so
wrong about Russia's strength if it were not treasonous? This year
had begun with the catastrophe at Stalingrad and, impossibly, gone
downhill since then, one disaster after another, on every front. Even
the U-boats were no longer effective; they were losing almost twenty
a month, the irreplaceable crews gone forever. This last month had

been an endless buffeting by incompetence, betrayal, and sheer misfortune.

He stretched, rubbing where Morell had placed the comforting needles. The problems in Italy had forced the diversion of forces from Russia, even as the Communists surged forward after their victory at Kursk. Germany could have recovered after Stalingrad, but now Orel was gone, and Belograd, and with it the Second Armored Army, wiped out, a year's tank production totally obliterated. And the bombings—Hamburg destroyed, thirty thousand killed, hundreds of thousands homeless—a complete catastrophe. Why had there been firestorms in Hamburg but not in London, or Coventry? No basic difference in construction—must be the mix of incendiaries and high explosives.

The only positive news had been the feeler from Stalin on a separate peace. What an intoxicating thought! It was a difficult decision. The peace could only be temporary, of course, but it would split the Allies, and give the Army a chance to rest and refit. A tantalizing prospect, one only he could pursue.

But it was impossible without a victory first. One couldn't deal from defeats! If he could stop the bombing and repel the inevitable invasion, then perhaps he could come to terms with Stalin, the only man on the continent—in the world!—worth dealing with. The jets were the key to both problems.

His changing mood reflected the effects of the daily injections that stiffened his will and resolve like steel rods in concrete. He rose, his legs only slightly unsteady, to consult the appointment calendar on the desk. Done in "Fuehrer Type," bold-faced and double-spaced, it showed only two more entries. The first was: DINNER/ LEUTNANT WALTER FRENTZ/STAFF PHOTOGRAPHER; the second: HAFNER/PLOESTI/JET AIRCRAFT.

Hitler groaned. No one obeyed orders. The flak had achieved a great victory at Ploesti—more than forty of the bombers shot down, and the damage to the refineries was all repairable. But the jet fighter! How could the idiots have employed it there, and only one of them? Had they never heard of the tanks on the Somme?

Bormann's discreet rap sounded on the door. Time for dinner.

• • •

The mood was distinctly different from their last visit to the Wolf's Lair; the smartly dressed aides always sniffed how things were going to go, serving as weathervanes for the Fuehrer's mood. This time there had been no offer of food or drink: the barometer was clearly falling.

Hafner and Josten sat quietly, lost in their thoughts. Hafner tried to assess what would happen. The lone jet had performed well under the worst possible tactical conditions, a low-level engagement. He'd shot down three of the bombers and damaged a fourth. If he'd had even ten 262s with him, it would have been a slaughter.

The ground defenses had been marvelous, no question, and *Generalmajor* Gerstenberg had received a personal call from the Fuehrer congratulating him on the success of the flak batteries. Josten had sent a coded report directly to Goering on the results of his flight. Instead of congratulations, he'd gotten a rocket from the Fuehrer's headquarters, ordering him and Hafner to keep silent about the battle, and to be ready to report to Wolfschanze immediately. They'd made the trip twice, and each time Hitler had been too busy to see them, trying to patch things up in Italy and on the Eastern Front. Hafner hoped he wouldn't see them again tonight.

Josten's thoughts were of an entirely different nature. Lyra, due to deliver soon, was doing well and, characteristically, not complaining at all. He knew he wouldn't be able to get away to be with her; if he stayed alive, he'd probably be pushing an old Heinkel around on the Russian front. Well, that's the way it was for most German women; the war didn't stop so husbands could go home. Her letters were cold, but she wrote that she was not afraid, that the people at the Legation were taking care of her. At least she was out of the bombing.

The imperturbable, fat-faced Bormann, a classic gray eminence, glided in on eerily silent feet. He didn't speak, only nodded curtly to the door leading to the conference room.

Hitler was leaning over a map examining a sector of the collapsing front, a far different figure than his newsreel image. Wearing unfamiliar spectacles, his right eye monstrously enlarged by the six-inch-diameter magnifying glass, he had the disordered appearance of a cathedral gargoyle. They waited, Josten standing at attention, Hafner sitting straight up in his wheelchair, Bormann silent by his master's side.

The Fuehrer laid the magnifying glass down, sat in his chair, and studied them both carefully.

"You two are really certifiable!" He paused. "Hafner, I can perhaps forgive your young friend; fighter pilots are not supposed to have brains. But how could you, a veteran of the first war, have forgotten the tanks on the Somme?"

Neither man spoke as Hitler lectured. "The British introduced tanks on the Somme in 1916, a handful, and with no plan to exploit them! They failed, utterly, and lost the surprise factor for the rest of the war. That's what you've done at Ploesti with the jet! I wanted to save them, to use them to repel the invasion, but no, you knew better. And you went into battle with only one. How stupid!"

He was warming to his task, his voice rising; Bormann involuntarily edged away.

"A broken wreck of a man and an idiot major deciding how to run the war! Is this the pretty pass that Germany has come to? I should have Galland's neck for this, and yours, too!"

His manner changed abruptly, as he moved bits of paper around on the tabletop. "Two things have saved you. One is that I cannot find it in my heart to be angry with people who want to fight. God knows we have few enough of them left now."

He was silent, seeming to reach within himself for the strength to speak.

"The second is more important. The damage from the bombing at Peenemunde was incalculable; the RAF wiped out the buildings, most of the drawings, and six hundred scientists."

Hitler paused, visibly shaken that the bombing might have snatched his vengeance weapons from him. Then, his voice strong, he said, "Hafner, the only thing that might save us is the microfilming you've done on the plans for the secret weapons. How far along are you?"

"My understanding is that we are almost completely up to date; General Dornberger's men at Peenemunde have been very conscientious."

"Thank God. We've got to get our V-weapons back in production as soon as possible, and you're the quickest—if not the only— means. Now go back and, for God's sake, don't try any more hare-brained schemes like this."

"*Jawohl, mein Fuehrer.*"

"Despite all the mistakes, you've convinced me on the jets. I've already told Speer to give it top priority over everything, even the tank and submarine programs. I will instruct Messerschmitt and Junkers to take your advice on the 262 program—but I want you to concentrate primarily on the reconstruction of the V-weapon program. The jets can save us from defeat, but only the V-weapons can give us victory."

Josten noted that, just as in his speeches, Hitler's voice was keyed to his emotions: coarse and guttural in reprimand, soaring and seductive when talking of winning.

"As for the major, here, let's find a spot for him in some front line unit where his fighting spirit will be useful."

He picked up the magnifying glass again and Bormann muttered, "You are dismissed."

10

Dayton, Ohio/August 24, 1943

More than three hundred mourners were gathered in the red brick Christ Church on Dayton's West First Street.

In the end, the little that was left of Clarice had expired peacefully. Patty and Hadley were with her, and through his tears Hadley observed that it wasn't so much a death as a subsidence. She had really died weeks ago, when the Clarice of old, so formidably vital, had been transformed with appalling speed into a frail mummylike creature whose weak voice spun an unceasing stream of incoherence, until grinding into silence the day before she died.

Surprisingly, it was Hadley who had insisted on a big funeral; Clarice had always said she wanted to be quietly cremated and forgotten. But Hadley was bereft, guilt-stricken over the years that he'd worked too hard and paid too little attention to her and, Patty knew, totally apprehensive about life without her.

The turnout from the base was large; most had never known Clarice, for the Rogets rarely went out and never entertained, but Hadley was a popular figure, and they were there to support him.

Clarice had never gone to church a day in her life, but Hadley had arranged with the base padre, Father Tedesco, to have an Episcopal service in Dayton—the newly built base chapel wasn't quite ready yet. Patty looked around, quietly gratified that the church was filled with flowers, mourners, and the powerful aura of Clarice looking down from above, irritated as hell that her instructions weren't being followed.

Patty's thoughts turned to Bandy, who felt bad that he could not be on hand to support Hadley. He was in California at Muroc Dry Lake, conferring with Jim Lee and getting ready to fly the first production McNaughton jet. Then he was off to Lockheed to try to expedite progress on their jet fighter. He'd had another tremendous battle with Caldwell.

Yet the stress of the last six months—the war, Clarice's illness, everything—had served to cement their marriage. Patty had made the transition from aviatrix to full-time parent and nurse gladly, even with some relief. Her flying career now seemed like an achievement of her childhood, worthwhile, but just a part of the past. Doing double duty with Clarice and the kids was hard work, but in the process she had become more of her own person, less a captive to her flier's image.

Sitting on Patty's left, Caldwell realized that it was a shame that Clarice had to predecease Hadley, who needed her a great deal more than she needed him. It had been the same with Shirley. He wouldn't be a major general if it hadn't been for Shirley's help. And he wouldn't be where he was—in deep trouble over the McNaughton failures—if her death hadn't triggered the wild, late-blooming adolescence he was suffering.

He nodded his head as if in prayer and let his mind run over the file of reports he'd digested that morning. The appearance of the jet at Ploesti was ominous—no one knew how many more there had been, but even one was a bad sign. Lee had managed to struggle back to Benghazi on three engines, and he'd been smart enough to caution his crew not to talk about the attack. The intelligence officer had immediately sworn Lee and his crew to silence and forwarded a top secret report to Headquarters. Both the Eighth and the Fifteenth Air Forces were already shell-shocked from the flak losses; there was no need to introduce a new terror until more was known about it. But the timing had been perfect; Caldwell had just put together a beautiful briefing for both Arnold and Eaker, stressing the importance of hitting the jet factories. Eaker was going to take the matter up with Bomber Harris and get the RAF involved. It would buy McNaughton time, even though Hap Arnold was already asking nasty questions about how the Germans could have jets in the war and the USAAF couldn't.

Arnold wasn't the only one hammering on him. Bandy was being troublesome. They'd had a donnybrook when the performance figures on the Merlin-engine Sidewinder had come in. It was impossible to understand—the plane Jim Lee had tested had shown tremendous improvement, but the production models were deficient. The top speed was up about five miles per hour, but the range was little better than before. Worse, it wouldn't even fly with the big new aux tanks—they tore up the airflow around the stabilizer and made an already marginal airplane completely unstable.

The ugly scene in his office with Bandfield two weeks before replayed in his mind, as it had a hundred times already.

"What the hell is the matter with you, Henry? Have you sold your soul to McNaughton?"

"I've told you before, Bandy, mind your own business. You haven't come up with a goddamn thing on the long-range fighter. You crashed the Curtiss and you tell me the P-38 won't handle it."

"You stupid fucker, you're sitting on the answer. The goddamn P-51 will do the job, and you're sending all the engines to McNaughton. I keep telling you, Henry, people are saying you're either crazy or on the take."

Caldwell smiled despite the pain of the memory. He'd picked up an ashtray and hurled it across the room at Bandfield. Bandy had torn the clock off the wall and tossed it at him—the flailing cord had caught him around the neck like a lasso, damn near strangled him.

They had both been so embarrassed that the argument died. But Bandfield had made his point, and Caldwell had given in, agreeing to divert engines to North American; it looked like they'd have Merlin-engine Mustangs arriving in Europe by January 1944.

The news from his other projects was mixed. Production of the B-29 was finally getting under way. Lockheed was making rapid progress on its jet fighter. But people—the pesky Truman Commission in particular—would ask some tough questions about McNaughton's failures when the word got out. One of the things Caldwell hoped to get from Bandfield's trip to the coast was a positive report on the possibilities of using the McNaughton as a jet fighter trainer. It would be a loophole, a shield against criticism if it was used.

And the secret data on the V-weapons was encouraging. McNaughton had established a "deep black" super-secret study group, operating solely with private funds. The group's preliminary reports indicated that a scaled-up V-2, one with intercontinental range, could be ready by 1948 or 1949, revolutionizing warfare. It would be a perfect encore to his success with heavy bombers—not a bad legacy to leave his country!

There was another bright spot on the horizon. After weeks of effort, his last briefing on the jets had finally persuaded Ira Eaker to let him go on a deep-penetration bombing mission in Germany. They were going to give him a bogus set of identity papers, so that if he were shot down the Germans wouldn't know who they had.

He really needed to go. Building bombers in wartime required firsthand knowledge; you can read all the reports in the world, but unless you analyze them in the context of personal experience, you could draw the wrong conclusions. Eaker understood that, and so did Arnold. They also knew they owed him this.

He snorted to himself. It was a rationalization. He wanted combat as an antidote to this Elsie-madness. The more he doubted and distrusted her the more he loved her and wanted to own her. She had changed, and he was certain that it was because she'd learned that Bruno was alive. He wondered for the thousandth time how she ever could have loved a man like Bruno—and he knew in his heart that she loved him still.

Caldwell didn't know how to please her. He had just bought her a secondhand 1940 eight-cylinder Oldsmobile Custom Cruiser sedan for $800, and now she was talking about a farm. She was always practical about her future. There was an antebellum house with 150 acres of land, outside Nashville, which was on the market for $9,850; she wanted him to buy it for her. He would probably do it—he had never been so hopelessly in love before.

Sitting next to Caldwell, Hadley Roget was sunk in his thoughts, his face drawn and haggard under the new recruit's crew cut. During the long weeks of Clarice's illness, his silver hair had grown longer and longer. The day after she died, he'd gone to the base barber shop and told them to cut it off. No one knew that he'd arranged to have his hair buried with her—it was a foolish gesture, one she would have laughed at, but it meant something indefinable to him.

Now, edged back on the seat, Hadley had a good view of Caldwell, kneeling, head down, lips moving as if in prayer.

They had talked earlier about their common failings—how little they had appreciated their wives when they were alive, how they had essentially exploited them, and how they hoped their spouses would be happier in the next world.

Didn't take him long to find someone else, though, Hadley thought. He's sure hooked on Elsie Raynor. One thing for sure, there's nobody out there for me—not that anybody would be interested.

Roget felt compassion for his friend. In all the Army Air Forces, no one had been right so many times, or had put his neck so far over the line as Henry Caldwell. It took enormous courage to bet all the country's resources on an unknown bomber program like the B-29. No wonder he was praying—if the B-29 program was wrong, then heaven help us! And that was only one part of Caldwell's grand vision of airpower. The fantastic buildup of industry, of the training command, of the combat units all stemmed back to the measures he'd taken years before, often exceeding his authority to do so. The man was a hero.

And, improbable as it seemed, perhaps a crook. There was just too much fishy stuff going on at McNaughton for Caldwell not to be involved in it. The firm had not yet built a fighter the Army would use, yet they got order after order. Their record with the jet fighter was appalling.

Well, I'll never fault him, Hadley thought. It's because he's goofy about that woman; better men than either one of us have had that problem before.

Hadley had his own problems. Not one of the advanced fighters in Operation Leapfrog looked as if it would work out. He'd spent a war failing in exactly the same manner he'd failed in peacetime— and now Clarice was gone, too. Life had little meaning now. He straightened up. Father Tedesco was beginning to speak; Patty had filled him in on all of Clarice's good qualities, and Hadley was ready to listen and agree.

Stockholm, Sweden/August 25, 1943

Ulrich Helmut Josten celebrated the first morning of his second week of life suckling his mother's breast, unaware that the first trauma he would ever know was about to occur: separation from his mother. Lyra was going to go back to work at the Legation, where she painstakingly translated English and Russian publications into German. Her Swedish doctor, Bjorn Walden, had tried to insist on two weeks of bed rest and at least one more week of recuperation, but too many conflicting pressures were driving her back.

The birth had gone easily; the greatest joy she had ever known, messy little red-faced Ulrich had popped out like a shucked pea from a pod after only four hours labor, a healthy six-pound baby boy. A joyous exhilaration coursed through her—even in the midst of a destructive war, even in a godless time, nature had rendered her a beautiful service. It made her even more unwilling to submit young Ulrich to his father's ideas. War or no war, Ulrich Helmut Josten was going to learn decent human values. She'd already resolved that she'd bring him up alone. If she could not do that she would see that he was raised in a Swedish home. This precious bundle of helpless love was never ever going to be a Hitler Youth, a Nazi, a military man like his father.

The man she had adored, the Helmut Josten of 1938, no longer existed. It was obvious that he loved her just as much as ever, but he had changed, not in his treatment of her, but in his basic values.

The war could not go on forever. If he lived, he might be human-ized again. But she was not going to leave her darling Ulrich to chance.

Dr. Walden had arranged for young Greta Raaby to be her housekeeper. She was an unwed mother with a baby of her own, glad to have a job and a place to stay in exchange for taking care of Ulrich while Lyra went back to work. Greta's ample breasts had plenty of milk, and the doctor thought it would be a good thing if they both nursed little Ulrich—"Give him two sets of protection," was the way he put it. Lyra hadn't discussed it, but it was also a hedge against the possibility that she might be arrested or detained, and the baby left with Greta for long periods of time.

When she returned to work she found her office pulsing with excitement. Hans Thomsen, the Foreign Minister, was obviously interested in redeeming his failures as chargé d'affaires in America by bringing off a rapprochement with Russia, and he didn't care who knew. Twenty minutes after she got back to work, she had been called in to see him. She jumped with the same automatic terror that seized her whenever there was a knock at the door or a telephone rang. She immediately assumed he knew about her dealings with Caldwell and others, and that this was the beginning of the end. It turned out to be nothing more than an urgent request for the translation of a Soviet magazine article, which hinted that a separate peace might still yield Polish and Sudeten territories to Germany. Thomsen was obviously excited; he insisted that she write out the translation on the spot, as he went on with a series of phone calls to Berlin, speaking unguardedly in front of her. Much of his conversation dealt with the rapidly changing conditions in Scandi-navia—the increased Norwegian resistance, the signs of Finland's war-weariness, and the growing hostility of the Swedes, all events calculated to add to the desirability of a separate settlement with Russia.

She realized how fortunate she was that the Press and Informa-tion section of the Foreign Office was at once the most and the least Nazi of all the myriad bureaucracies that choked Germany. At the top, the bosses were handpicked, bona fide Nazis, intent upon imposing good Third Reich behavior on everyone. But the middle-level managers were mostly "aristos," like herself, members of a network that the Nazis despised yet could not do without. She knew that she would never have survived a year in Germany if her family had not been noble.

Now the aristocratic network had even extended to the Red Russians in the person of Madame Alexandra Kollontay, the Soviet Minister in Stockholm. The daughter of a Czarist general, she had known Lyra's father and mother in St. Petersburg and Moscow and even visited them at their estate at Alupka, near Yalta. A beautiful woman in her youth, a radical who proclaimed the joys of free love long before the Parisian existentialists, she had become an ardent Communist in 1917. Somehow she had overcome her royalist family background and risen to become a bright and shining star in Stalin's diplomatic bureau, important enough to attract continual attacks in the *Voelkischer Beobachter*, where Goebbels had styled her "the Commissar of all the Prostitutes."

Madame Kollontay had not hesitated to contact Lyra. Her beauty might have faded, but her will had not. She ran her Ministry with an iron hand, certain that no one would dare report her for dealing with a "foreigner." No longer well, perhaps aware that her time was running out, she had summoned Lyra to a private suite at the Grand Hotel. They had feasted on lobster Madame Kollontay had cadged from the British embassy—which bent over backward to please her—then spent an hour talking about "the old days" at court. At the end she bluntly asked Lyra to work against the Nazis.

"We know about your contacts with the Americans, Lyra; we are on the same side. We also know about your husband's relationship with the experimental work this man Hafner is doing."

The familiar terror stabbed Lyra. If the Russians knew, the Nazis probably did as well—when would they come for her?

"What can I do?"

"The Nazis are finished; it's only a matter of time. We hope that we can work with the Americans after the war, but no one is sure what will happen."

"I can scarcely work against the Americans."

"You can scarcely work against your Motherland."

Silence, then, "Your husband's friend, Hafner, is at the center of a gigantic experimental web. We want to contact him; we know you can do it."

In the end, Lyra succumbed to the hard facts of her situation. The Swedes were desperately afraid that the Russians would invade as soon as they'd finished with Germany, paying off the debt of Sweden's support of Germany. If they did, then a promise from Madame Kollontay would be worth a great deal. Caldwell had offered the same promises, too, but she thought that the United States was unlikely to intervene in a Russian invasion of Sweden. For Ulrich's sake, she had to have as many options as possible.

Muroc, California/September 10, 1943

The early desert heat already soaked Bandfield's four-by-eight compartment in the Visiting Officers' Quarters. The warped green pine one-by-six planks of the rough wooden barracks inhaled the sand driven against it by the late summer winds, and everything from his shaving kit to his highly polished brown shoes were filmed over with white dust.

Jim Lee and Troy McNaughton came by his room to pick him up for his first flight in the McNaughton jet, the Mamba. Lee's appearance had changed—he was leaner and obviously matured by his combat experience, a lieutenant colonel now, rumored to be on Caldwell's list for full bird. His cocky, good-humored manner was as agreeable as ever, making it easier to endure McNaughton's relentless salesmanship. In many ways, Lee reminded Bandfield of Hadley Roget—sharper and more refined, but with the gut feel for engineering blessed with more common sense.

McNaughton asked, "Did my people give you a good enough briefing on the airplane, Bandy?"

"Sure did. Jim ran through all the charts with me, then talked me through about an hour in the cockpit last night, figuring out what all the switches are for."

"The Mamba was a little disappointing for us at first, but our drag reduction program has most of the problems licked. My test pilots have been hitting over five hundred miles per hour true airspeed regularly, and we've got some changes planned that will add another fifty, at least. You've got to expect things like that—this is one of the first jet planes in the world to fly."

Lee saw the flicker of annoyance on Bandfield's face and quickly chimed in, "Maybe not the first, but one of the best. It's going to have to be, to beat the ones that shot our ass off over Ploesti. Anyway, it's the sixth type of jet to fly. The Germans have flown three, the Brits one, and even the poor old Italians one."

As they talked, Lee buffered McNaughton against some of Bandfield's sarcasm, going on point like a well-trained hunting dog when he saw Bandfield's dander rising, quickly changing the subject, or poking fun at himself.

They were silent until they reached the airplane, olive drab against the desert sand. Bandfield walked around the airplane with Lee and a McNaughton mechanic. The airplane was just a Sidewinder in disguise. The jet engines had been built into bulges at the side of the fuselage, which now contained almost nothing but fuel tanks. The wings looked as if they'd been pulled off an old Martin B-10 bomber—long, thick, and broad, and there was no question in Bandfield's mind that the lift they generated would be paid for in excessive drag.

After a long, three-thousand-foot takeoff, the flight itself turned out to be totally uneventful. The Mamba was a delightful toy of an airplane, Bandfield felt, just a powered glider really, easy to fly and so quiet that there was a vibrating mechanism built into the instrument panel to keep the gauges from sticking.

In level flight at thirty thousand feet, he applied full power. Acceleration was glacial—four minutes crept as the speed built to a maximum. Spinning the celluloid dials of the E-6B computer with one hand, adjusting the airspeed indicator reading for temperature and pressure, he was surprised to see a true airspeed reading of 510 miles per hour.

510! Pretty good, for such a big airplane.

At thirty thousand feet there was no visual reference to gauge the speed, but it seemed high—the airplane was just too big and drag-ridden for such performance. He rechecked the instruments and the E-6B—same result. It was puzzling. Maybe without a propeller to disrupt the airflow, a jet was simply more efficient.

As he descended to land he realized that the Mamba was a real confidence-builder, something a young pilot right out of flying school could fly. If the performance figures were correct, then McNaughton had really come through—and Caldwell had been proven right again.

McNaughton, face bacon-brown, age-silvered hair flying in the desert breeze, was waiting for him with Lee at the runway's edge, bouncing up and down in the ankle-deep sand. As soon as the jet rolled to a stop he leapt up on the wing and helped open the canopy.

"Well, what do you say, Bandy? Isn't it a winner?"

Bandfield busied himself shutting off a few more switches, still puzzled by the figures.

"Well, Troy, I'll have to admit I'm surprised at the performance. Are you sure these instruments are calibrated correctly?"

"Sure? Sure, I'm sure. Your own man, Lee here, oversaw the job himself. Tell him, Jim."

"Yeah, it's surprisingly fast and it doesn't feel like it, because there's no vibration."

"Well, it's really easy to fly. You could turn an Eagle Scout loose with this airplane."

Lee spoke up. "The Mamba is the best fighter in the world. What did you get out of it, five-twenty?"

Bandfield thought to himself, He's quite the company man now. Then said, "No, a little less than that at thirty thousand feet. I'd like to take it back up with a chase plane, and calibrate the airspeed indicator, then run some more checks."

"Good idea. We've got to pull the engines, though, and check the turbine blades and the combustion chambers. You could do it tomorrow."

"No, I'm due over at Lockheed. But, Jim, will you do it for me? Get a chase plane—a Mustang if you can—and get the airspeed indicators calibrated at ten, twenty, and thirty thousand feet. The

Mustang can probably keep up with it at low altitudes, and you can throttle the Mamba back at thirty. But then do a full-out, high-speed run, and let me know what it does."

"No problem, Bandy. Glad to do it. I love to fly that sucker."

As usual, McNaughton couldn't contain his salesman's instincts.

"You tell old Henry Caldwell that you need about a thousand of these dudes—and maybe five hundred more, two-seaters, to use as trainers. That'll keep us busy until we get our new jet in production."

Bandfield was surprised. "You've got *another* one coming down the line?"

"Oh, yeah, didn't Henry tell you about it? It's really something else—it'll blow the Lockheed jet right out of the water."

McNaughton's sneering greed sent a tide of unreasoning anger over Bandfield. Lockheed had been a tremendous performer all during the war, and McNaughton shouldn't knock them. "The Lockheed isn't exactly our problem, Troy; it's the goddamn Messerschmitt jets that worry me. We're going to start running into them over Germany pretty soon, and unless you concentrate your efforts on the Mamba, we won't have a damn thing to oppose them with. You've fiddle-fucked with this heap so long that we might just lose the war."

The older man responded to Bandfield's open anger. "You think the Germans are going to be able to do something that we can't? I tell you, *Lieutenant Colonel* Bandfield"—he spat the rank out contemptuously—"you'll see McNaughton jets in German skies before you'll *ever* see Messerschmitt jets."

Bandfield had climbed out of the cockpit and shed his parachute. He was standing with his hands pressed into his back, trying to restore the circulation his seat-pack parachute had cut off, unable to curb his suspicions.

"Troy, you're not talking to some cub reporter from Nashville. You've screwed up the jet program royally for two years, and if the Germans get their jets in the air this fall, the bomber boys are going to pay for it. You'll be lucky to have the Mamba operational by next spring, and you know it."

McNaughton bridled, his suntanned face flushing red, his voice dripping with self-assured sarcasm. Lee backed away, uncomfortable.

"Well, now, you're entitled to your junior-birdman opinion, Colonel, but I'm going to have a word with General Caldwell about your attitude. We taxpayers pay your salary, and don't you forget it."

It was like watching an ancient motion picture of himself. Instinctively, involuntarily, his right hand had moved from behind him in an arc, heading toward McNaughton's chin.

Lee grabbed his arm and spun him around.

"Watch it, Bandy, you can't go around belting people."

McNaughton stalked off, enraged.

"What the hell are you doing? You act like McNaughton's puppet."

Lee lowered his voice, shaking Bandfield's arm violently. "I'll tell you what I'm doing, you dumb bastard, I'm trying to save Caldwell's ass. He's in so deep with McNaughton that the only way to get him out is to get some decent airplanes from them."

"What do you mean, 'in so deep'?"

"What the hell do you think? Do you think the contracts on the Sidewinder or on the jet could stand scrutiny? Elsie's leading him around by his dick, and he's dumped forty million dollars into McNaughton's coffers."

Bandfield felt sick.

"You're supposed to be his friend—making this jet successful is the only way out for him, I swear."

He managed to get a line through to Patty that night, telling her all about it from the refuge of the booth in the dingy crowded lobby of the Hotel Burbank.

"He'll probably get me court-martialed for trying to take a swing at him, but it was worth it. I'm just sorry I didn't hit him."

"Thank God you didn't. And I've got something to tell you that will ruin the rest of your day."

"You can't ruin this one; I've done a good job myself."

"Well, just so you aren't caught short, I just heard from Hadley that Jim Lee's been promoted to bird colonel. Can you imagine that?"

Bandfield was silent for a while, annoyed, but trying to be fair.

"Well, he's done a hell of a job, put his neck on the line a lot of times. He deserves it."

"So do you."

Bandfield reproached himself for his human failings—the inability to control his suspicions, his anger, or his jealousy—for hours before dropping off into a fitful doze. But the next morning his mood improved radically as Kelly Johnson briefed him on Lockheed's amazing progress on the jet—they were calling it the XP 80. They had started work on June 23; the first airframe was taking shape, and the production lines were already being tooled up. It was nothing less than an industrial miracle. They had knocked off at noon to go to the Lockheed cafeteria when a young engineer named George Kidd caught up with them.

"Colonel Bandfield, there's some guy from some senator's office in our main conference room. He says he has to talk to you."

Kidd hustled him down the beige hallway, the walls covered with pictures of famous Lockheed aircraft, to the plush carpeted conference room. At the end of a long mahogany table, a tall young man, long black hair brushed back over a high forehead, with a totally disarming grin, sat buried in stacks of paper and briefcases.

He stood up when Bandfield entered, saying, "I'm Steve Chaudet. I work for the Special Committee Investigating the National Defense Program. Senator Truman has directed me to ask you some questions."

Jesus, Bandfield thought, here it starts.

Great Ashford, England/October 14, 1943

Major General Henry Caldwell responded groggily to the three-thirty wake-up call, slumping back on his cot before switching on a light. He stared for a moment at the unfamiliar uniform, then realized that for this one mission he was Major George White, an observer from the Fifteenth Air Force.

Muscles kinked and mouth dry, feeling every one of his forty-six years, he persuaded himself once again that he *had* to be there, had to find out for himself what was going wrong. Air Corps doctrine had been built on precision daylight bombing, and he had geared the entire B-29 program to it. Long ago, the British had told Arnold—and Spaatz and Eaker, too, and anyone else, whether they asked or not—that daylight precision bombing was impossible. Implicitly the message was: "If we couldn't do it, surely you can't." The British felt that they had learned early in the war that daylight raids didn't work, that the bloody losses of the Wellingtons and Hampdens proved that the German fighters and flak were too good. And the truth was that the USAAF was not getting enough bombs on the target. Caldwell hoped to find out why, today, over Schweinfurt.

Coughing, he swung his feet out of the bed and lit a Camel. In similar Quonset huts all over England, twenty-three hundred other Americans were getting ready to fight their way across Europe to the Bavarian city of Schweinfurt. Eleven centuries old, a sheep and cattle town until the industrial age, Schweinfurt was a vital manufacturing center for most of Germany's ball bearings.

The pace of the day picked up—a quick breakfast, a briefing, and then the silent ride in the Jeep to the hardstand. He was flying with Captain Chet Schmidt on *Bonnie,* crewed by young men with the strangely old look of twenty-nine-mission veterans. He had met them two days before and, despite his *nom de guerre,* most knew who he was, treating him with the easy familiarity they knew went down well with visiting brass. The one exception was the brand-new copilot. Major Malcolm McLean was a hotshot feeling his oats, just back from a tour in the Pacific, and replacing Schmidt's regular copilot, who had picked up a flak wound on the last mission.

McLean had spent the previous two days pissing off Schmidt's crew by telling them what an easy war they had in Europe, and how tough the flak and the fighters were over Rabaul. He was at first openly contemptuous of Caldwell's presence, mumbling something about "old guys trying to pick up medals." Caldwell didn't mind that; what he hated was the brown-nosing that started when McLean learned that the "old guy" was actually a general officer.

Feeling better as the day went on, Caldwell was glad to stand by unobtrusively, to help with the loading of gear, to take his place in the special fold-down seat that had been rigged for him aft of the pilots. It was one of those days when nothing else mattered. His whole life had been in preparation for this, husbanding the Air Corps resources, keeping the manufacturers alive, selecting the best airplanes, all for this moment. He wouldn't have missed it for anything.

A routine takeoff lifted them into a cloud layer briefed to be two thousand feet thick. Instead they staggered through six thousand terrifying feet of gray swirling mist filled with hundreds of other bombers and fighters boring upward like blinded swarms of gnats, from airfields all over east England. There was no attempt at ground control, other than spacing the takeoffs at individual airfields. Survival depended only upon luck and the vastness of the sky. Caldwell whistled with relief when they burst out on top of the clouds, the sun glinting off the hundreds of camouflaged B-17s as they wound round and round to get into formation, alerting the German radar even before they left the English coast.

The long lines of aircraft queuing up made for impressive pageantry, reminding him of the coronation films of King George VI. Individual aircraft circled gradually into squadron formation, then squadrons would join into the combat box, aircraft staggered in altitude and azimuth, positioned so that their 540 heavy machine guns had the greatest fields of fire. Then, streaming contrails, the boxes aligned themselves into a majestic ten-mile-long armada. Instead of pennants or flags, there were the proud tail markings of sixteen bomb groups, from the red checkerboard of the 385th, the slash of red and black triangle A of the 91st, to the ominously fitting black rudder of the "Bloody 100th." The planes, of course, had names—*Dry Martini, Cabin in the Sky, Eight Ball, Great McGinty, Gremlin Gus.*

Republic P-47 fighters—affectionately called "Jugs" because of their bulbous shape—milled around above them. The bomber crews had joked at briefing about having fighter escorts all the way—P-47s to Aachen, then Messerschmitts and Focke-Wulfs to the target and back to Aachen. The briefing officer had concluded with, "This is a tough job, but I know you can do it. Good luck, good hunting, and good bombing." A gunner had immediately added, "And goodbye," and the room had broken up in nervous laughter.

Caldwell was glad no one knew how keenly he felt responsible for the absence of a long-range fighter. His conscience told him that if he had put out the same effort on the P-51 that he had on the Sidewinder, there would have been escort fighters in quantity. Now it would be next year before they arrived—and by then the German jets might be dominant. He *had* to do something before that happened.

If he got the chance. The damn Truman Committee was on his tail, not about the jet fighters—yet—but about the unsatisfactory Sidewinders. Bandfield had been allowed to tell him about his interrogation at the Lockheed plant. The committee had received rumors that the Russians were now going to complain formally about the Sidewinder's performance, which made Caldwell wonder what would happen to Scriabin. Members of the committee had gone to Nashville to investigate. It hadn't helped that when they arrived, two Sidewinders had just crashed, gone off the end of each of the two runways. What a stroke of fate; both crashes had been pilot error, but it had naturally soured the committee and set the course for the investigation. Caldwell would be lucky to last another six months before he was court-martialed. Maybe it wouldn't matter—maybe he wouldn't return.

The light flak started at the coast, but opposition was light until Aachen, when the P-47s, at the absolute limit of their range, apologetically dipped their elliptical wings and headed back to England. The Fortresses were now on their own, and the formations, already tight, shrank closer together as if the twenty-below-zero temperature outside was contracting them.

Caldwell chafed at having to sit and watch, unable to fly. On an ordinary training mission, they would have swapped seats to let him at the controls, but this was combat. The radio discipline was good. There had been little chatter on the intercom and absolutely no interplane communication. His unit formed the low box of the lead division, and he could see planes of both the lead and the high box through the right cockpit windows.

The Germans were ready and waiting. The first attack came from a distance, twin-engine fighters—mostly Messerschmitt Bf 110s, with a few Ju 88s mixed in—lobbing their 21-cm rockets into the formation. The first salvo missed, but the second blew off the tail of a B-17, sending it tumbling down, the first of many. Caldwell realized with a twinge just how much the P-51 pilots would love to slaughter the twin-engine jobs, burdened as they were with the stove-pipelike tubes under their wings.

"109s, twelve o'clock, level."

The call was from the lead plane; Caldwell picked them up on the horizon, waves of wiggling crosses, a dozen at a time heading directly into the guns of the lead formation.

Schmidt's voice came on the intercom: "Guns, they'll be diving through the lead formation at us; watch the two o'clock high position."

The Messerschmitts charged in echelon directly into the bombers' guns. Caldwell watched them, their nose and wings alight with cannon fire, admiring their discipline as they closed, fired, then rolled insolently to dive under the first group of B-17s. He saw one Fortress buck, then slowly side out to the left, flames already roaring from its center section as the black commas of the crew, turning end over end, bailed out.

Other ranks of Messerschmitts came on, hitting the lead elements and diving down, ignoring the return fire. They were putting on a first class air show—too bad it was so goddamn frightening to watch!

There was a lull in the attack. From his position he could see that they'd already lost at least four B-17s; how many more were down behind him? The Germans returned to attack, mottled gray-green hyenas pulling down gazelles. They formed up in pairs, sometimes two pairs together, nervously wriggling to dodge the hail of .50-caliber bullets. They bored in from all angles, slicing down to hit the top formation, their cruciform constantly altering as the bank angle and the deflection changed, then suddenly shooting by so close that Caldwell could pick out details: a pilot wearing a white scarf, the streamlined gondolas for the underwing 20-mm cannon, nitrous oxide exhaust stains down the fuselage. Then they were gone, and the next batch was coming in.

He did not see the one that hit them; 20-mm shells suddenly exploded in the cockpit, metal ricocheting everywhere in a cacophony of sound he'd dream about for the rest of his life. It was terrifying to have no job to do, no gun to fire, and at the height of his panic he was surprised, later, to find that his thoughts had been of his wife, Shirley, rather than of Elsie.

No one had been wounded, but now the bomber sang a different note as wind whistled through holes left by the cannon shells. God, those Germans had guts, and they could fly, too.

There was a brief respite and he noted that the sky was filled with terrifying scents, sights, and sounds: rank cordite from their own guns, huge blossoming belches of oil and gas from the exploding B-17s. The worst smoke of all came from the endless, filthy flak-clouds, black deadly puffs studding the sky in a pointillist painting, resonating waves of turbulence accompanied by the rain-on-a-tin-roof patter of shrapnel against the B-17s' aluminum skins. Yet the heavy flak afforded some relief, for it meant the fighters would not attack for a while.

He turned to check *Carolina Cutie*, framed in his right upper cockpit window. It was flying in the number two slot of the lead division and he had checked on it all the way from form-up, neatly tucked into formation, an olive-gray shell with ten bright young men in it, the yellow triangle *K* of the 379th Bomb Group on the tail glinting in the sun. As he watched, an 88-shell scored a direct hit on its bomb bay, the tremendous explosion stopping *Carolina Cutie* in the sky. Caldwell's mouth dropped at the incredible scene. A fifty-thousand-pound aircraft, moving at 160 miles per hour, had been instantly transformed into a splotchy expanding shadow of white, black, and red from which fell debris, no piece larger than an entrance hatch. No parachutes, of course.

Heading on a collision course with Caldwell's bomber, *Oberstleutnant* Helmut Josten tucked the wing of his brand-new Messerschmitt Bf 109G-6 next to that of Major George-Peter Eckerle, *Kommodore* of *Jagdgeschwader* 3.

The B-17s were formed up ahead, stately, almost majestic, silver contrails streaming, thousands of guns pointed at them. Eckerle had devised a new tactic, a hell-for-leather, line-abreast formation that met the oncoming Fortresses head on. Josten heard Eckerle's calm voice call "Attacking," and they streamed in, twelve fighters flying into the steel teeth of the bombers.

Josten now fought with an absolute awareness of the whole situation. Just as a champion billiard player plans one shot to lead to the next, he knew instinctively how much fuel he had, how much ammunition was left, who had been shot down, and from where to make the next attack. And amid this calm comprehension he knew that, for the first time in his life, he was going to funk it.

Ahead the sky lit up with .50-caliber bullets, the tracers leaving an arcing curve, every line seeming to drive directly at him. Fear squeezed him down in his seat, trying to hide behind the thundering Daimler-Benz DB 605A-1 engine, sneaking glances to his right to maintain formation.

He felt his fighter shudder from hits, saw Eckerle begin his roll as they dove through—and he had not even fired!

As the remaining Messerschmitts—there were only nine in their flight now—began to form up, Josten knew why he had failed. It was the baby, of course. He had not been in combat since the jet fiasco at Ploesti. Since then Ulrich had been born. When word had come from Stockholm that Lyra had delivered a baby boy, things had changed. Before he'd gone into combat with a reckless abandon, certain that he would prevail. This time all he could think about was surviving for Ulrich's sake.

As they struggled for altitude he felt sick—if he had fired he might have gotten one of the gunners who had killed his comrades. And what about Lyra? Why hadn't he felt the same way about surviving for her? Was he some kind of freak, that the thought of having a son could suddenly be so important, could affect him so?

The next attack went better. He concentrated his fire on the cockpit of a Fortress and saw it pitch forward, as if the pilots had fallen on the controls, plunging directly into another B-17 in the formation below.

Josten and Eckerle landed at the same emergency field. While they were refueling, he spoke to his *Kommodore.*

"Major Eckerle, sorry about that first attack. I funked it, forgot to fire. No excuse."

Eckerle pulled the acrid wartime cigarette from his lips. "Happens to me all the time. Don't worry about it; you caught an Ami on the second pass, and got two for one."

He flipped the cigarette away, and they leapt back into the cockpits of their fighters, canopies slamming down as the hand cranks spun the inertial starters. Within seconds they were climbing again to the attack, Josten feeling as if he were being sucked up an inverted funnel of danger into another duel with the Fortresses.

Twelve hours later and five hundred miles away, Henry Caldwell woke up from the sleep of exhaustion, the hysterical laughter of his dreams turning into a choking fit. Red-faced, veins purpling, he was barely able to light his cigarette as he tried to recall what he'd been dreaming of—then it hit him and he roared again.

There had been damn little to laugh about on the mission, but whatever there was had been provided by the smart-ass copilot, McLean. Schmidt and the rest of the crew could barely tolerate him.

The man was nervous, no question. Some experimental flak gear had been put on board to see if it would be effective in warding off shrapnel. McLean had managed to secure an extra flak vest to sit on, joking uneasily about preserving the "family jewels," and had put his flak helmet on early in the flight. With a veteran's disdain, Schmidt had laid his own flak helmet between them on the floor behind the control pedestal.

En route the copilot had kept up his jabbering about the rough war in the Pacific, especially the flak over Rabaul. Then, just before they turned in on the Initial Point, McLean had looked ahead at the black clouds over Schweinfurt and said, "Looks like a thunderstorm over the target."

Shooting a quizzical glance at him, Schmidt turned in on the bomb run, saying, "Shit no, Major, that's just the light flak opening up."

McLean, green-faced and unbelieving, scanned the billowing black clouds multiplying like raindrops on a window. He half turned in his seat, picked up Schmidt's helmet, and vomited into it. Then, gutsy enough, he wiped his lips, refastened the A-8B oxygen mask, and went back to his copilot's duties.

Schmidt hadn't noticed. He was concentrating on the bomb run, keeping the airspeed constant, the plane straight and level, and following the bombardier's instructions until the PDI locked in, giving the bombardier control of the aircraft.

The bombardier called "Bombs away," and Schmidt rolled trim in to keep the aircraft from bounding up, lighter by three thousand pounds. The turn off-target took them into an even thicker wall of flak ahead. Schmidt, concentrating on the turn, reached down and put on his flak helmet, letting out a scream of rage as McLean's breakfast cascaded down over his ears.

After landing, Schmidt hurled himself out of the airplane and was wiping himself clean when McLean walked up and said, "Sorry, Captain, about the flak helmet. Must have been something I ate."

Without a word, lines from the oxygen mask pressed into his haggard face, Schmidt punched him in the belly so hard that McLean doubled up on the ground, puking again. Schmidt watched him, then reached back into the plane, pulled out a flak helmet, and tossed it down beside him.

"Use your own this time, you loudmouth son of a bitch."

Remembering, Caldwell wiped laughter tears from his eyes and lay back, now wide awake. Adrenaline pumped, driving him to relive some of the less amusing bits of the raid, assessing the effect of battle on the B-17s. He'd watched too many of them go down, each separate victim's tableau a distorted vector of time and space, as the shattered aircraft turned into freshly minted flotsam slowly decelerating into the void.

The first reports after they landed indicated that sixty planes had gone down over Germany, with another twelve written off after landing. Six hundred dead or captured, many more wounded. No matter how badly they had hurt Schweinfurt, the Eighth Air Force couldn't go on like this without long-range fighters. He'd have to accelerate the P-51 every way he could. The Thunderbolt was never going to have the range it needed, even with auxiliary tanks, and the P-38 wasn't suited for dogfighting in Europe. He had to get Mustangs over here fast, if it was the last thing he ever did for the air force. If they'd had Mustangs today, the Germans would have been beaten to the ground, and they would have lost only a dozen or so B-17s.

He knew he had to talk to Eaker and Spaatz. The only solution now was to concentrate on destroying the Luftwaffe on the ground, to bomb the factories and shoot up the airfields. It was too costly to try to eliminate them in individual aerial combat. As soon as the Mustangs arrived, they'd have to begin smashing the Luftwaffe in its lair, to hold off the jets.

He felt purged by the danger of the mission, realizing that there would have to be a showdown with Elsie. She'd have to admit to what was bothering her—he knew it was Hafner!—or he'd drop her. And she'd have to quit her work at McNaughton—that damn Troy was a bad influence on her. Hell, he made good money! If it wasn't enough, the hell with her. She could go back to her stupid dreams of Hafner.

The thought came to him that if they court-martialed him, he wouldn't even have a general's pay.

● ● ●

A knock on the door summoned Josten to a telephone call from Galland. Aching with fatigue, stomach still upset from combat, he padded down the dimly lit hallway in his stocking feet, confident that he was the senior officer in the building and wouldn't be called down for his informality.

"Josty, how'd it go today?"

"I was off my form personally, but the rest of the *Geschwader* did well—we probably had fifteen heavies among us."

"You'll get back in the swing of it; it's always tough after a layoff. Flying the 109 after the jets is a terrific comedown, I know. But it shows what we can do if we get enough planes in the air at the same time. We've got to have *mass*; it's no different than the cavalry days."

"We had mass today. What's up?"

"It looks like we shot down a total of sixty heavy babies. I want a personal estimate from you, right now, can't wait, of how many bombers we would have finished off if we'd had 262s instead of piston-engine fighters."

Josten thought for a moment. "That's easy. Given the same weather conditions, same number of fighters, we'd have shot down at least two hundred of them, maybe more. But you know that yourself."

"Right—but it'll carry more weight if a pilot from one of the successful units says it. Between us, the idiots at Messerschmitt are going around in circles. Now they've got a dozen different experimental variations of the 262 in the works—pressure cabins, rocket boost, more sharply swept wings—and still no production articles! It's as if Hitler's orders meant nothing."

"You better watch what you say—you know the phones are monitored."

"I hope so—the only way to get directly to Goering is have him read the brown sheets from the *Forschungsamt*, his listening service. With him it's not 'Seeing is believing' but 'Eavesdropping is believing.'"

Josten cringed. Galland might be able to get away with talk like this, but he wasn't sure of his own safety.

"This points the way to the future, Josty. If we can do this with eight hundred fighters, think what we could do with two thousand, half of them jets!"

"*Ein grosse Schlage,* the Great Blow, eh?" They had talked about it often in the past, getting enough fighters concentrated over the path of the bombers, hitting them coming in, over the target and going out, then sending long-range fighters to England to harass them in the landing pattern.

"That's it, Josty; once or twice like that, and our American friends will forget about coming over Germany. Anyway, good luck with Eckerle. He's one of the best. Not many like him left. I'll get you back to the 262 program as soon as I can, just as soon as they get some production prototypes flying."

Josten shambled back to his room, at once elated and depressed by Galland's call. It was always good to talk to him, but it was depressing to have the slow rate of progress on the 262 confirmed. There was no excuse for it; the airplanes he and Hafner had cobbled together at Cottbus would have done the job. How much improvement did Messerschmitt think was needed?

Galland's comment about the 109 being a comedown relieved some of his guilt, partially explaining his poor showing today. The tragedy was that they *could* have had one or two hundred 262s on hand if Hitler had thrown his full support behind them. Hafner could have made fifty or sixty in his factory, and Messerschmitt could have certainly turned out the rest. Instead, both Messerschmitt and Junkers had reverted to their standard work methods, as if there were no war going on. What a day it would have been if they could have had fifty, even! Then the Amis wouldn't have come back, not for months, maybe not ever!

He stood at the dresser, staring in the mirror at his worn face, still grimy after his wash, forcing himself to concentrate on Lyra and the baby. He could see her face clearly, as tenderly beautiful as always. He had not seen the baby yet, not even a picture, but her letters had said that the baby looked like him. It didn't matter who Ulrich looked like, if the three of them could just live through this war. A few more days like today, and he'd have to settle for the two of them living through it.

Washington, D.C./November 20, 1943

Washington in wartime was a hustling, overcrowded combination of working, wenching, drinking, and pervasive good cheer—war was hell, but most people were enjoying it.

It was a good thing that he had a red C-sticker for gasoline rationing. Caldwell spent his days driving endlessly between Fort Myers, Bolling Field, and the Pentagon, stroking, cajoling, and entreating, trying to marshal support for a focused attack on the German aviation industry. He could easily have had a staff car, but having a driver—and a record of all the places he visited—cramped his style.

It was like tiptoeing around a land mine. Billions of dollars and billions of words had been spent on airpower—and the bomber offensive in Europe was at a virtual standstill because of the weather. There was tension in the air, and Caldwell had patiently spent his time trying to find the right man to take his message to Hap Arnold. He didn't want to raise the issue personally with Arnold unless he could choose the exact time to do it. The pressures on Hap were so great—and his health so fragile—that a meeting at the wrong time could have backfired.

But now he had it arranged. Arnold had come to lean heavily on the advice of Colonel Bob Ringman, a bright young West Point graduate who'd already put in a combat tour on B-25s. In the course of two meetings and a dinner, Caldwell had let Ringman know what was needed: a change of commanders and a much more aggressive posture in Europe. Ringman had been cautious at first, but by the end of the meal at Harvey's had looked around and whispered, "General, we need to do this for all the reasons you've indicated, but we need to do it for General Arnold's health, too."

Caldwell knew when to be silent.

"Every time Hap"—it showed how close Ringman felt to Caldwell, to call the commanding general by his nickname—"goes in to see General Marshall, he gets asked, 'What did the Eighth Air Force do yesterday?' Most of the time, because of the weather, he has to say, 'Nothing,' and Marshall gives him that frozen-face, eyes-rolled-up glance. Then Hap comes back and fumes at us."

"I know he's really been tough on Ira Eaker—he's getting an ulcer from all the nasty letters Hap sends him."

"Yeah, but Ira isn't tough enough himself." Ringman was calling them all by their first names now. "He hasn't fired the people who are too chicken-hearted to take the losses."

"I understand they're going to move Tooey Spaatz in at the top. Why not move Doolittle up to take command of the Eighth Air Force? He's aggressive, and he doesn't have any attachment to the present commanders. That's the real problem—Ira's too loyal to his people."

"I think Hap would agree with that. But I've got to tell him in such a way that he's sure he thought of it himself."

"I'm sure that you can do that."

Ringman had gone away with several of Caldwell's markers, knowing that they'd come in handy in the future. It was worth it. Ringman represented Caldwell's last desperate throw of the dice.

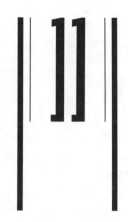

Stockholm/January 25, 1944

Edvard Munch was dead at eighty. The Swedish papers, all Nazi-baiters now, had more praise for the Norwegian's refusal to cooperate with the Quisling government than for his paintings. It was somehow terribly appropriate, for little Ulrich Helmut Josten, fretting with colic, had been giving his multi-decibel impression of *The Scream* all night long, keeping Lyra awake and terribly lonely in the igloo-cold apartment. She took some comfort in knowing that they might be both colder and sleeping permanently now if she had remained in Berlin. The RAF had savagely battered the city on the 20th. Most of the rest of her week had been spent trying to get telephone calls through to check on the families of the Legation personnel.

Berlin was being reduced to rubble, with single lanes hacked through the debris-clogged streets for emergency traffic. By now the air raids were "self-adjusting," the explosions from new bombs filling the craters from previous raids. How long could it go on?

Yesterday she'd had a surprise call from Goebbels, who had taken the precaution of having an adjutant get her on the line. Goebbels had spoken hastily and with some confusion. He had assured her that he was all right and inquired about her health and the baby's, cautioning her to stay inside, out of the cold weather. Anyone listening must have thought the child was his. He certainly knew better than anyone else that the phones were tapped. It was as if he wanted to incriminate himself.

Then, with that eerie insight one has at three in the morning, Lyra realized that it must have been a warning. Goebbels must have some genuine vestige of feeling for her, and he was trying to tell her that her meetings with Madame Kollontay were known.

She pulled Ulrich to her, cuddling him. Were they closing in? No, what nonsense. If she were in danger, Goebbels would never have risked talking to her himself, he could have had someone warn her. And yet . . .

It was all part of the crushing anxiety and guilt she felt. Bruno Hafner was going to visit her apartment tonight. Madame Kollontay was sending a representative, Scriabin, the same man who worked with Caldwell. If the Gestapo knew, they would all die. Her plans for Ulrich were made. Greta had proved to be both an excellent wet nurse and a loyal friend; tonight, she would take Ulrich home with her. If something happened, if Lyra disappeared, Greta knew how to get in touch with the people who were to look after him. As for Helmut, perhaps the fact that she had at last broken with him would help him, deflecting the guilt by association. After all the danger he had exposed himself to, it would be tragic if he died as a result of her actions. But there was nothing else she could do.

At work, she leapt at every ring of the phone; she couldn't eat, and by the time Hafner arrived at nine o'clock that night she was exhausted. He was carried to her door in his wheelchair, murmuring, "I can't climb stairs yet." The two brawny men in shabby civilian clothes with him posted themselves outside her door. At half past, Giorgi Scriabin arrived. She introduced them, and they nodded to the door. She went to stand and wait in the draft-swept hallway, wordlessly freezing with Hafner's bodyguards.

Inside, Scriabin was direct: "Colonel Hafner, first we want *every-*

thing on your atomic bomb project—heavy water experiments, Heisenberg's work on the atomic pile, everything. That is absolutely first priority. Then anything on jet engines and jet planes. Third in priority are the so-called vengeance weapons."

"I have all you need—engineering drawings, correspondence, test reports, photographs—and much more besides. There is material on the new submarines, on the "snorkel," on poison gases. Plus I have data on most of the leaders of the Reich—diaries, records of conferences, letters."

"We'll get it all eventually, but some we want immediately. What do you want in exchange?"

"I need a safe haven, with my security guaranteed—Switzerland, or perhaps Argentina. If my own assets are not confiscated, I don't need anything else. If they are, I want five million U.S. dollars deposited in a Swiss bank account."

"The first part is easy—the money is not."

"What guarantees do I have?"

"What guarantee could we give but our word? And what are your options after the Americans see the camps at Dachau and Buchenwald? Especially when we point out your feeding experiments with slave labor?"

Hafner shook off the impact of the words like a soccer player recovering from a hard hit. "I understand. What are the terms of the arrangement?"

"We want the most important information we talked about as soon as possible—say within thirty days. And we'd want you to stay undercover and keep us informed on German political intentions. We're more worried about Germany making a separate peace with the Allies than we are about any wonder weapons."

Hafner thought rapidly. This might be to his advantage—who knew how things might develop. But he dissembled, saying, "It's riskier for me—the longer I stay, the greater the chance I'll be caught."

"True. But that's the way it is. And you couldn't be safe anywhere, not as long as the Nazis are in power. They'd have ways to get you in Switzerland, or even Argentina."

They started to shake hands, hesitated, and nodded instead. Scriabin called Lyra in from the hallway.

"We've come to an agreement. Colonel Hafner will provide you with some material by one month from today. You will be instructed on how to deliver it to the Soviet minister."

They were gone as suddenly as they had arrived, and Lyra was alone in the apartment, accompanied only by her guilt and her fear, trying to decide what she would tell Caldwell about the meeting. When the hellish war was finally over, she wanted to take Ulrich to the United States—she would not be able to live in Germany as a traitor and was terrified at the thought of going to Russia. She decided she had to tell Caldwell everything.

Castle Coombe, United Kingdom/February 25, 1944

The information from Lyra did not surprise Caldwell. Hafner was on his way to setting some sort of record for treachery. It was probably a simple business precaution to him, like taking out fire insurance. Caldwell was deeply concerned about Lyra's safety— now she was exposed to both the Gestapo and Soviet surveillance. It was time to bring her out of Sweden, along with the baby. She had more than earned it.

But for the moment he had even more pressing issues. He didn't know exactly what Colonel Ringman had told Hap Arnold, but things had moved swiftly. It was rare when things worked out so well and even rarer to be on the spot to see an idea come to fruition *exactly* the way one wished. He'd had a marathon round of discussions with the staff of the new commander of the Eighth Air Force, Jimmy Doolittle, covering everything from the unsatisfactory performance of the P-38 to the delay on the deliveries of the Mustang. One of the meetings had taken place in Brigadier General Bill Kepner's headquarters at VIII Fighter Command. They were all old friends, but in Kepner's office Doolittle saw a sign reading THE FIRST DUTY OF THE EIGHTH AIR FORCE FIGHTERS IS TO BRING THE BOMBERS BACK ALIVE.

The tiny, pugnacious Doolittle had bridled, jaw going tight, veins pumping, but he said only, "Who dreamed that one up, Bill?"

"The sign was here when I arrived, General."

"Take it down, now, and put up one that reads, 'The first duty of the Eighth Air Force fighters is to destroy German fighters.' "

Kepner eagerly agreed. It was music to Caldwell's ears, confirming that all of his manipulative planning had been worthwhile. It was too bad that Ira Eaker had to be one of the eggs broken making the omelette, but that's the way it was in war. The important thing was the end result, "Operation Argument," a week-long assault on the German aircraft industry and on the Luftwaffe. It could be the answer to his prayers.

Caldwell nervously reread the "invitation" from the Truman Committee to testify in Washington the following month on the performance of McNaughton Aircraft. He didn't have much time to prepare, but he'd gotten off some essential correspondence. In the meantime he found once again that it was tougher to wait on the ground for results than to take part in the raid.

Gloom enshrouded Eighth Air Force Headquarters like a throw over a shabby sofa. Everyone was jumpy, convinced that the disastrous October attack on Schweinfurt had cost the Eighth air superiority. There had been no deep penetrations of Germany since.

Intelligence had reported that the Luftwaffe had used the intervening four months to recuperate. Fighter tactics had been improved and the armament of the Focke-Wulfs had been upgraded. The German Air Force could still muster twenty-two hundred operational fighters, and of these, more than fifteen hundred were allocated to the "Defense of the Reich." That meant that across the vast Russian front and the smaller line in Italy there were less than seven hundred operational fighters, perhaps a fifth of the real requirement, and far too few to be effective.

Caldwell had been in the war room at Castle Coombe all week, trying to help assess the results of Argument as they came in. The air offensive had started out brilliantly, with a successful combination raid by the RAF Bomber Command and the American Eighth Air Force on the Junkers factory at Leipzig. Then four hundred B-17s and 272 B-24s had ranged over Germany, striking at aircraft manufacturing plants, just as he had been demanding for months. But the really important news was that almost nine hundred fighters, including a few of the new Mustangs, had overwhelmed the Luftwaffe, claiming sixty-one victories.

By midweek, the Germans had stiffened their defense and American casualties rose. Arnold had said he was willing to accept as much as 25 percent losses, because the U.S. could provide replacements, and the Germans could not. Caldwell was estimating that losses would be less than 7 percent—staggering by prewar calculations, but worth it if the Luftwaffe was hammered to its knees.

The night before Caldwell had gone out to Great Ashford, in Suffolk, to be with the 385th Bomb Group again. He had drinks in the Quonset hut that passed as an officers' club, sitting next to the brick wall with the missions proudly labeled on it—Chateauroux, Wilhelmshaven, Rostock, Leipzig, Schweinfurt—each one more dangerous than the last. In the morning, he'd gone to the briefings, noting the anxiety of the crews, watching as they smoked cigarettes and drank coffee out of thick white china mugs. There was some horseplay, a little joking, but most of the men simply sat locked into their private thoughts.

A bombing operation was an elaborate process that began with a flurry of paperwork, rose in scale to industrial proportions in a furious twenty-four hours, then wound down to a few final actions—tailfins being attached to the bombs, mechanics in a swarm over airplanes for last-minute troubleshooting, Thermos jugs being stowed aboard. A mystic quality attended these last efforts, as if each person was trying to impart his personal strength to the airframe itself, blindly willing it to return.

Caldwell had participated in the ceremony, using a rag to polish the already gleaming landing gear oleo struts of *Bonnie*, the airplane he'd flown in on the Schweinfurt mission.

It worried him that *Bonnie*'s skipper, Chet Schmidt, was haggard

and apprehensive, his hands trembling as he chain-smoked, a totally different man than the one he'd flown with just a few months ago.
His copilot, McLean, had changed for the better, well enough
accepted by the crew to josh Caldwell, telling him. "Wish you were
coming with us, General. We could use an old hand on this run."

"I understand Chet puts his flak helmet on right away nowadays."

McLean blushed, but poor Schmidt couldn't manage a grin,
saying, "General, the way those bastards are shooting over there, we
need a flak helmet over the whole damn airplane."

Now safe on the ground, Caldwell sweated in empathy as the
385th bored implacably toward its target, the Messerschmitt com-
ponent plant at Regensburg-Pruefening. He would have far preferred to have been along, at the controls, but made himself content
that he had planned this particular strike and chosen this particular
target. It was a knife aimed at the heart of the German jet program.
The ULTRA system had reported that the tooling for full-scale
production of the Me 262 was being built at Pruefening. He meant
to destroy it. If he did not, the planes it would build would almost
certainly destroy him and his comrades.

Over Frankfurt/February 25, 1944

A ragged formation of eight Messerschmitt Bf 109Gs of Jg 3, led by
Major George-Peter Eckerle, was being vectored toward Regensberg
on an angle that would intercept the intruding B-17s just after their
fighter escort had turned back.

Eckerle sat in a well of pain. The cold and altitude conspired with
his parachute straps and oxygen mask to torture his aching body. A
pilot with 134 kills, twenty-three of them heavy bombers, he had
been shot down eleven times, suffering seventeen wounds and four
broken bones. Now his aching body cried out for rest. For the first
time he felt his courage ebbing, for he knew there was no one to
back him up, no one to depend upon. If only Josten had been on his
wing! Instead, he had a new man with less than two hundred hours

flying time, only ten in the 109G, a youngster who should have been paddling a *Faltboot* down some peaceful river. It was criminal! The rest of the flight had even less experience—just kids, who had played a few years at being Hitler Youths and then were given the briefest possible flight training.

"*Achtung, Uhrmacher am Gartenzaun.*" Eckerle shook his head and groaned. More bad news. Those code words, "Watchmakers on the garden fence," meant that fighter-bombers were shooting up the home base. Just what they needed.

He saw the B-17s ahead. It would be such a beautiful sight in peacetime, the clouds below, the great regatta of aircraft sailing effortlessly, spaced as carefully as squares on a chessboard. Even the black clouds erupting from the undercast might be considered pretty, were they not the flame-corrupted essence of German towns and German people. He cinched his straps further down into his pain, waggled his wings, and began the dive.

Regensburg-Pruefening/February 25, 1944

At the entrance to the Messerschmitt factory, *Obergruppenfuehrer* Kurt Weigand's scarred face was beaming with pleasure. "Welcome to the club! What a sinister pair you two make. Between Bruno's wounds and Helmut's bandages you look like a hospital ward!"

"Kurt, it's hard not to have one or the other in Germany nowadays."

It was three and a half years since they'd first met at Cottbus to talk about speeding up the 262. Since then Germany had reached the heights of world power and then gone spinning toward disaster.

Hafner pulled himself out of his wheelchair and walked up and down, rubbing his back muscles with his huge hands, trying to fight off the corpse-cold wind whistling across snow soiled with the soot of industry and the ashes of air raids.

"What the hell is going on, Helmut? After months of inactivity, the Amis are at our throats."

The bandages on Josten's arm and head covered the multiple cuts he received when a burst of machine-gun fire from a Liberator shattered his canopy over Brunswick on the previous Sunday. He'd bailed out and spent two hours wandering through the woods, bleeding like a pig, before he could get back to the base for assistance. The aging medical officer sewed him up, then grounded him for a week. Josten was glad for the chance to rest.

"The weather's broken and they've changed tactics. The escorts are not sticking with the bombers anymore. You're more apt to see an American fighter in the landing pattern than one of our own. It's brutal."

Hafner nodded impatiently. "Yes, but I'd rather face the Americans flying against us than some of the idiots who are supposed to be for us."

Weigand nodded in agreement. "We saw that in November when the 'Groefaz' came to see us at Insterburg." The other two stared at him. Things must be precarious if the diehard Nazi Weigand was mocking Hitler with the current joke. Political humorists had dubbed Hitler 'Groefaz,' an acronym for Goebbels's adulatory title, "*Groesster Feldherr aller Zeiten*," greatest strategist of all time. The greatest strategist, impressed by the demonstration of the 262's performance, had decreed that the 262 was to be a "*Blitzbomber*" and not a fighter at all. As usual, the obsequious Goering thundered agreement, and the 262 program was set back even further while Messerschmitt jury-rigged the plane to carry bombs.

Hafner snorted, saying, "Typical Third Reich management! It took a lot of work, but I've got that turned around now—at least they're willing to call it a fighter-bomber."

Hafner settled back in his wheelchair, tucking a blanket around him as Josten trundled him down the glaze of ice covering the red brick sidewalk. The meeting was bound to be adversarial. Both Messerschmitt and Junkers were resistant to taking Hafner's advice on the 262.

"Kurt, what are you going to be able to offer them in the way of manpower?"

"I can deliver an initial shipment of three thousand skilled workers and seven thousand unskilled at the end of this month. After that, I'll provide another five thousand unskilled every quarter. They'll have to be trained."

"How about attrition?"

"All factored in. We'll only be able to feed about twelve hundred calories a day until summer, so you'll lose maybe thirty percent by then. But we should be able to make it up with Italians."

Josten listened dispassionately. Laborers were mere raw materials now, press-gang workers streaming endlessly from a pipeline that began in a round-up and ended in a furnace. He stirred himself to join in the conversation.

"What did you have brought down with you, Bruno?"

"Everything." He pointed to a covered siding, where foreign laborers were busy unloading odd-sized packages. "You can see it right there—three trucks, loaded with enough of the new turbine blades for two hundred engines and the special jigs that old Fritz has created to build them. Fritz came along to teach them his methods."

The wheelchair got hung up on the curb and they struggled with it before Hafner went on. "The rest of the tooling is already stored in the same building. If they do what we tell them, we can have one hundred 262s by March, and five hundred by June! By the end of the year, we can be producing a thousand a month."

Josten had seen Hafner's optimistic production planning charts calling for twenty-five aircraft to be delivered in February, seventy-five in March, then two hundred per month in April and May. If they actually got half those numbers, it could mean a miracle, a reversal of the fortunes of war.

"They'll have to do what you tell them; you've got Hitler's direct orders in your pocket."

"These bureaucrats are experts in evading orders—they use paper-work as a matador uses a cape. If we make them freeze the design on the airplane and the engine and start building them, they'll find every reason in the world why things won't work. But at least they talk to me at Messerschmitt. The Junkers people won't answer my letters, won't return my calls—you'd think I was a leper. They are determined to muddle through with their own design."

The meeting took place in an unheated "administrative office," its unseasoned lumber walls pierced by the February cold. Two low-watt light bulbs, one burned out, dangled from the ends of cords. It had been a storage room, and the empty bins lining the walls made the office a perfect symbol of Germany in 1944. A varnished fiberboard table sat in the middle, adorned with one tablet and one pencil. Everyone was dressed in overcoats, hats, and mufflers, looking more like refugees from the Russian front than business executives.

Sullenly silent, the people from Junkers and Messerschmitt listened to Hafner's exhortations without comment. They showed some interest at Weigand's projections for skilled labor, but quickly lapsed back to their silence. At the first blast of "Goering's Buglehorn," as the air raid sirens were now ironically called, they leapt to their feet and filed off to a special company shelter for executives, taking Fritz and Weigand along, but leaving Josten to manage Hafner and his chair. The two men found their way to one of the employee shelters.

A foreigner—probably a Ukrainian by his accent—had helped Josten carry Hafner in his wheelchair down the steps. They sat him at the entrance door, next to a garrulous old woman. Josten stood beside him, grateful once again the Lyra and Ulrich were safe, desolate because Lyra's last letter made it all too clear that she was abandoning him.

The old woman was clothed completely in black, a bonnet peaked over her dirty gray hair. Blackheads had cratered her lined face, and a steady stream of saliva ran from the corner of her toothless mouth. Her hands moved as if she were knitting, but there was no yarn, no needles.

They ignored her at first, too preoccupied with the violent alternation of pressure-suction-pressure of exploding bombs, a rise and fall that plugged ears and sucked hair upright. In the interval between explosions they heard her say, "Two-hundred-fifty kilograms."

"What's that, mother?"

"Those were two-hundred-fifty kilogram bombs. That's why I

come here rather than a public shelter. It's safer. The concrete is almost two meters thick."

"Are you an expert on bombs?"

"In two wars. I was in the Ruhr in 1918 when the French bombed. Piddling stuff. Even this is nothing like what the RAF uses."

Josten saw that frightened as they were, people around them were listening to her with amusement. He egged her on.

"A bomb's a bomb, isn't it?"

"Not on your young life. The bad ones are the British eighteen-hundred-kilogram bombs—they'd cut through this shelter like it was a cheese paring. But at least you don't hear them coming—just woof, and you're gone."

The groaning ventilator shaft acted as a stethoscope to the outside world. The momentary quiet was broken by a whistling noise, like a flock of doves whirling up through branches.

"Incendiaries," she cackled. "Sounds like the little phosphorus and magnesium sticks. Not too bad—just break the head off and put it in a bucket of sand, then cover the rest with sand. The bad ones have the benzol and rubber—they spread out over a hundred meters, burning everything they touch."

"How did you learn so much?"

"I started in Cologne. My husband was killed there and my son moved me to Berlin. We were burned out there. They killed him, my little Karl. Now I live with my daughter here."

In this interval of quiet, Hafner offered her a flask of cognac. She took it and drank greedily, not forgetting to wipe the mouth of the flask before she turned it back.

"You think I've learned a lot; it's the British who are learning, and the Germans who are forgetting. I was in Cologne during the first big raid—you remember, a thousand bombers?"

Josten nodded.

"The next day, the roads to Cologne were clogged with relief trucks. They set up a hundred distribution points, handed out millions of cigarettes, food, clothing, liquor, everything. Then they brought in workmen; in a few weeks, we had windows again. What happens now? You're lucky to get a slice of sausage or a bowl of soup. Everybody is bombed everywhere, so there's no relief trucks to send."

The conversation was taking an unamusing twist. War damage claims for civilians had grown into so many billions of marks that the country could no longer afford to pay them.

"So you see we have true democracy here, my son. Everybody gets bombed. Even rich *Bonzen* like you, with your cognac and your leather shoes."

Hafner saw that she was wearing the straw-topped, wooden-soled "war shoes," the only kind still obtainable.

When he glanced back her lips had curled into a gummy smile. "It doesn't matter. People will live. As long as there's enough food for today, and a plank to put over a hole, people will live. It won't go on forever. It will just seem like it. At my age, that's not too bad."

As if in reply to her stoic endurance, a tremendous explosion directly above them shook the shelter, showering them with dust and knocking out the flickering light.

Over Regensburg-Pruefening/February 25, 1944

"Steady, steady, PDI centered."

"I've got the airplane."

Chet Schmidt turned the last few hundred yards of the bomb run over to the bombardier, relaxing his grip on the control wheel, but keeping his fingers curled around it, ready to take over at once. The airspeed was locked on 160, the heading indicator on 135 degrees, the altimeter read 24,500 feet. So far they had not been hit by flak or fighters.

McLean was professionally quartering the sky, glad that there were no fighters in sight, ignoring the bubbling wall of flak that flickered around them, black dahlia clouds, creased with obscene red centers. Raw tension compressed the crew's energy into an anxious coil, ready to spring forth at the first sign of a fighter.

Eckerle led his Messerschmitts' attack on a heading of 210 degrees, slanting down from ten thousand meters, cannons blasting at the outermost B-17 of the formation, then rolling inverted to dive away.

As he'd done a hundred times before, Eckerle tugged back steadily on the Messerschmitt's stick, pulling its nose toward the earth, the G forces shoving him into his seat, curving away from one set of flickering guns into the mouths of another. He glanced quickly back over his right shoulder at the B-17 they'd attacked, saw that it was on fire, edging out of formation. The victory cry "*Horrido*" was forming on his lips when, among all the premeditated danger, he accidentally plunged his fighter into *Bonnie's* cockpit. Where in one instant there had been two airplanes and eleven men, there was now just a vaporous explosion and nonexistence.

Washington, D.C./March 21, 1944

The committee was in recess while Senator Harry S Truman attended a roll call. Henry Caldwell sat with his hands folded, thinking for the one-hundreth time that he could so easily have been aboard *Bonnie* and gone to his death with Schmidt and his crew. Two hundred twenty six bombers had gone down during Argument. Yet it had been worth the grievous cost. The targets had been heavily hit, and a decrypted Ultra report indicated that the Germans had lost one third of their single-engine fighters and 18 percent of their pilots during February alone. No army could withstand casualties like that.

Then, on March 6th, the Americans had bombed Berlin for the first time, with Mustangs as the fighter escort. No matter what else happened, no matter who was aware of it, Caldwell knew in his heart that the air war was won. And he knew what he had contributed to that victory.

Being shot down might have been better than being badgered by this obscure senator from Missouri, with his nasal voice and thick glasses. Hick or not, Truman was tough and well prepared. He'd scarcely had any assistance from the covey of aides who sat behind him in the hearing room.

So far the questioning had been ominously innocuous. Truman was simply laying his case out as if it were a jury trial. Hell, I'd be better off if it was, Caldwell thought. This way, he's the judge and jury combined.

The Missouri senator had established that while McNaughton Sidewinders cost about ten thousand dollars more than a P-40 and six thousand more than a P-51, their performance fell far below either airplane. Truman had been fair, pointing out that the P-47 and P-38 were both more expensive than the Sidewinder, and that while better than the Sidewinder, neither were considered to be as effective as the P-51.

Caldwell had been warned that the real issue was the Lend-Lease program. Harry Hopkins had been filling Roosevelt's ear about Russian complaints, and Roosevelt had personally met with Truman on the matter. The last few questions explored the reasoning behind giving virtually the entire production run of Sidewinders to Russia. Truman was no Russia-lover, but he was under the gun by Roosevelt to establish that there was no official decision to furnish substandard airplanes under Lend-Lease.

Caldwell also thought he'd detected the faintest whiff of interest in his personal dealings with McNaughton. He might have been mistaken.

Truman burst back in the room, the million-candlepower grin fading as he sat down and looked at Caldwell.

"Now, General Caldwell, how would you characterize the performance of the Sidewinder?"

"Disappointing, sir. It has not measured up to our expectations."

"No, indeed it has not. The thing that surprises me, though, is that it hasn't measured up to its own test reports. There is a serious discrepancy between the official test report figures and the performance of production machines. Will you comment on that, please?"

"Senator, I've been in England, as you know, and I'd like to ask if

I can provide you with the answer to that question for the record. I'll personally go to Nashville and get at the heart of the matter."

"You'll go personally?"

Was there any malice in the question?

"Absolutely, Senator. It's far too important a matter for me to delegate."

The yellow light from the frosted globes dangling from the ceiling glinted off the flash of Truman's teeth.

"I'm glad you feel that way. Let's return to the matter of Lend-Lease. Are you aware that the McNaughton Sidewinder is regarded as a death trap by Soviet pilots?"

"I don't think that's the case, Senator."

Truman picked up a sheaf of folders. "These are reports from U.S. pilots on the Alaska-Siberia route, ferrying planes to Russia. Everyone states that their Soviet counterparts are openly contemptuous of the Sidewinder."

"There were some initial difficulties with the aircraft, sir. It was much more sophisticated than anything the Russians had used before, and they took a long time to adjust to it."

"Is that your opinion, or do you have some objective proof?"

"Senator, may I give you an original letter from my counterpart in the Soviet Union, Commissioner Giorgi Scriabin? I've taken the liberty to have it translated, but you may wish to have someone look at the original."

Truman read the translation, glancing briefly at the original in Russian, as if to compare them.

"General Caldwell, this makes me very happy. Let me enter the entire letter into the record, but I want to read the last paragraph aloud: 'As we have come to understand the proper employment of the McNaughton Sidewinder, using it in a ground attack role, we have found it to be entirely satisfactory.' "

Caldwell knew what he'd paid in terms of promises to get that letter. And he knew that Scriabin would never have provided it, not for any reason, if the Luftwaffe had not been bled white in Europe. Now the Sidewinders were operating as tank-busters, virtually without interference.

The questioning went on for another two hours, in a much friendlier vein. When the meeting was over, he motioned Caldwell to accompany him to the SENATORS ONLY elevator.

When the doors had closed, he grinned and asked, "Tell me, General, what in hell did you promise Scriabin to get a letter like that from him? You got us all off the hook."

There was no point in lying—Truman was obviously relieved just to have the issue put to bed. "Sir, I said that we would send him P-51s starting in September, Lockheed jets by the fall of 1945, and B-29s in early 1946."

"Remind me not to try to trade horses with you."

Nashville/March 28, 1944

Caldwell felt so devilishly well! He had asked Hadley Roget to come with him to Nashville, to try to figure out what happened to the prototype. And while Hadley was rooting through the mounds of paperwork, Caldwell had finally taken Bandfield's advice and sneaked away with Elsie for a few days in New Orleans.

It had been a glorious round of raw oysters, absinthe-laden Sazeracs in the lush Roosevelt Hotel bar, and riotous lovemaking. He'd been like a sixteen-year-old, ready to go morning, noon, and night. The combat tour had keyed him up, started his juices flowing, given him a love for life that he'd forgotten, a sense matched by her own earthy ardor.

He chuckled at the memory of Elsie's little tribute. One afternoon they were out riding in one of the little horse-drawn carriages, "taking a mattress break" she called it. Elsie had them stop at a florist. Making him stay in the carriage, she rushed in to get a little box, saying only that she'd ordered it earlier.

That night, after they'd reached a pleasant state of excitement, she'd pulled the florist's box from under the bed and removed from it a horseshoe-shaped wreath made out of forget-me-nots, a miniature of the kind awarded to Kentucky Derby winners. On it was a

card saying, "Champion John Henry Junior, March 24–27, 1944."
She'd insisted on trying to make love with the wreath around him,
but it was too uncomfortable. She made life so wonderful with crazy
things he'd never dreamed of!

Her snapping back to her normal, loving self was probably what
made him feel so good. Just as in the early days of their courtship,
she laid care over him like a silken suit. She went on with her
important work at the plant, calling in several times a day. He
enjoyed listening to her swift transition from his consort to the tough
executive, scolding, pleading, encouraging. Troy didn't trust anyone but Elsie to oversee the accounting and purchasing side of the
operation, and when any of the managers wanted something a little
out of the ordinary done, they came to her. She was a marvelous
woman, a champion in her own right.

The joy of Elsie's turnabout was complemented by equally good
news from Europe. Decrypted ULTRA interceptions indicated that
the German jet program had received a massive setback from the
Regensburg-Pruefening raid. The details were scanty, but it
appeared that the 262 tooling was totally destroyed. It gave him
breathing room, a chance to get both the McNaughton and the
Lockheed jet fighters operational.

The Merlin-powered Mustang was working out beautifully, as
more and more of them arrived in England. The young pilots were
going right out on long-range combat missions, knocking the Luftwaffe down in the air, shooting it up on the ground.

Only the B-29 was troubling—another "Battle of Kansas" was
shaping up. Hap Arnold had demanded airfields to be built by the
Chinese by April 15, 1944, promising that he would deliver B-29s
in China on that date. Fortunately Caldwell had sent Lee back to
take charge in February, and he was on the spot directing the
campaign, getting the parts, the subcomponents, the labor.

It was this sort of thing that justified all the risks Caldwell had
taken. As the Sidewinder phased out and the jet production was
building up, McNaughton Aircraft had a temporary surplus of labor
and equipment. Lee had latched on to these, flying back and forth
between Wichita and Nashville almost continuously, working with

Elsie to get parts and tooling built. If he hadn't gambled on McNaughton, the company wouldn't have been there to bail the B-29 program out when it was needed. Picking the right people was the key. Lee was an extraordinary officer; Caldwell had recommended him for promotion to brigadier general.

Hadley bounded into the room, grinning. He tossed a pitot tube, the sensor for the Sidewinder's instrument system, on Caldwell's borrowed desk, saying, "It's right there in front of our eyes. Been there all along. See if you can pick it out."

Caldwell examined the device, a piece of aluminum tubing about a foot long and half an inch in diameter, exactly like that found mounted on the wing or nose of virtually every airplane. Some were built with a ninety-degree angle, some were just a straight piece of pipe. The Pitot tube provided the airspeed indicator with a reading by measuring the difference between the pressure of ram air entering the opening in the end of the tube and the static pressure taken at its base. It seemed perfectly ordinary to him.

"So what?"

"I pulled this off a test aircraft. Look right there."

Roget's gnarled forefinger, the nail lost years ago in a fight with a table saw, pointed at a minor bulge just in front of the openings of the static port.

"I don't see anything special."

"It's this bulge. Looks like a washer was sweated on to the pitot tube, then filed down. Or maybe it was reamed from the inside some way. Anyway, it's just big enough to act like a little airfoil, setting up a negative pressure in front of the static port."

"I get it—the low pressure area gives the airspeed indicator a false reading."

"Roger. We duplicated it on a test this morning, just slid an O-ring on the pitot tube of a production test-flight plane. It only works in the higher speed ranges, but at the top end it caused the airspeed indicator to read fifty miles an hour faster."

"How come no one caught it?"

"I don't know—just too inconspicuous. It's probably a man-ufacturing defect from tooling, probably came from some new manufacturer. It's the kind of thing no one would catch unless they were looking for it specifically."

This was a perfect answer to satisfy Truman, an oddball test procedure anomaly, the sort of thing that happened in the rush of wartime business. It didn't excuse the Sidewinder for being slow, but it removed any appearance of fraud.

"Well, let's get a tech bulletin out to the field to see how widespread the problem is—and to check all the parts in stock. By God, Hadley, you're all right. I owe you one for this."

Hadley's pleasure in his find was transparent. He ran his hand through his crew-cut hair and said, "Yeah, and for a bunch of other stuff, too. How about taking me off this godforsaken Operation Leapfrog and putting me on the jet program? We've done about all the damage we can do with the Leapfrog—we're not going to get anything out of it, not in this life."

Caldwell was feeling expansive.

"Take your pick, Hadley. You want to go to Lockheed or work here with McNaughton?"

"To be honest, I'd rather go with Lockheed. But they're too sophisticated for me—I'd be out of my depth trying to keep up with Kelly Johnson. They need me here. Let me work with McNaughton."

"You're on."

Over Germany/April 24, 1944

Desperate with fear, the Mustang pilot ducked his head down, locked his left arm around the stick and with his right hand pulled the emergency canopy release. The canopy scooped away with a wild rush of wind that jerked his helmet and oxygen mask off and away, whipping red welts across his face and neck with the radio cords. He switched arms, grunting to keep the stick against his belly, and with his left hand first threw the gear lever down and then rolled the elevator trim full aft. The gear doors twisted away, but the plane shuddered and slowed with the increased drag. With the inert reluctance of a boulder slowly being levered from the ground, the Mustang's nose edged toward the horizon, beginning to break the breathless plunge toward the green German earth. It would be very close.

There was nothing more he could do. As the G forces lessened, his vision began to clear. There was a blur of trees ahead, then a town, thatched roofs, a stone steeple, everything growing level, he was going to make it. The nose passed through the horizon and began to rise. With trembling hands he rolled in forward trim and tried to retract the gear. A grinding shudder told him that the gear hadn't come all the way up. Glancing out, the wrinkled upper surface of the wing betrayed the force of the pullout.

The Mustang yawed insistently to the left, and his leg already ached from the full-strength press on the right rudder pedal, skidding the nose to point roughly to the west. Only nine months before a flight school instructor had been screaming at him, "Fly the goddamn airplane, don't let it fly you." He was just barely flying it now, it was screaming to let go and crash; throttling back to save fuel, he felt the creaking warnings of the wind that to go any slower he'd stall and spin forever into the German earth. Panic clawed at his throat—could he nurse this wreck across the Channel, a sitting duck for any flak or fighters?

His instruments spun in a crazy frenzy, the compass points passing in dizzy succession, the artificial horizon tumbling over and over. Only the elusive sun, slipping through the building cumulus, hinted that if he could stay aloft he'd find England.

Damn good thing the jet left—I'd be cold meat, he thought.

The jet had *not* left. *Oberst* Helmut Josten crouched like a hungry lion in the seat of a preproduction 262 just issued to the operational test unit. Now nicknamed the "Turbo," the 262 had for months been the single last hope for the Luftwaffe and Germany, the one instrument that might restore air superiority. Once he had dreamed of leading hundreds of 262s into battle—now he was resigned to working within the jumbled bureaucratic system, aware that no matter what happened, it was too late.

Josten was weary. He had drunk too much last night, but there
had been eggs and white bread for breakfast, with some unbelievable
real coffee, captured months ago in Africa from the Americans. The
bombers going down had raised his spirits. Now he had only to deal
with this cripple.

God, he thought, when the Turbo is right, it is wonderful. The
jet was silkily responsive to his touch, the radical new engines
purring, a thin trail of black smoke tracing his progress. Josten felt
again the long lost sense of command, fluid and powerful, so
different than the crawling anxiety that seized him before making an
attack in the old piston-engine 109s. It was like fighting against
Poland again, or against France, flying invincible equipment
against junk.

Josten's shallow curving dive brought him in level with the
battered Mustang, three hundred meters to its left rear. But what's
the point? he thought. Nothing had gone right since the week before
the Ploesti fiasco. Things had grown even worse with the shattering
raid on Regensburg-Pruefening. The precious turbine blades, the
jigs, and the tooling had all been destroyed. Ironically, so had the
recalcitrant Messerschmitt and Junkers managers, along with Fritz,
all dying when American bombs had pulverized the "exclusive"
company bunker. Kurt Weigand had emerged from the ruins,
physically unhurt but with his nerves shot. In the employees' bunker, the old woman had been killed, but he and Hafner had survived.
For what, he wondered?

The 262 program was still stumbling along; as Hafner had predicted, there were still no planes coming off the Messerschmitt
production lines. The war was clearly lost. Now he was just hoping
to survive to reconcile with Lyra. If there were no war, no politics, it
might happen.

Low on fuel, Josten knew that he had no time to waste. He
couldn't make it back to Augsburg. He'd have to land at Muenster-
Handorf or Vokel—he could get J2 fuel at either place. He searched
the sky above him. With marauding American fighters everywhere
it was deadly dangerous to be low and slow, but he wanted to
revenge himself on this spoiler. He eased his throttles forward,

letting the 262 accelerate slowly. The Mustang grew in size. He had not seen one up close before. Pictures had shown it to be a pretty airplane, but this was a Flying Dutchman, a derelict twisted out of alignment, its left landing gear halfway extended like a broken-legged stork. Something—a gear door, probably—was stuck in the horizontal stabilizer like a cleaver in a round of cheese. The canopy was gone, and the pilot was leaning forward to avoid the wind blast.

Mechanically, Josten checked to see that his guns were armed. This wouldn't take long.

Lyra's last letter had started with similar words—"This won't take long." But it had, four pages of a bittersweet mixture of love and hate. She said as much, that she once loved him, he had changed, that he'd lost the humane quality that had attracted her. "You don't feel anything anymore—you've grown to be like Hafner."

There was some truth in it. The war turned everyone into Hafners. But he still had feelings. He knew how that poor bastard in the crippled Mustang felt, trying to keep his airplane flying, worrying about running into flak or fighters. Why doesn't he look around?

He closed the range, approaching from the left at a twenty-degree angle, dropping flaps so that he could stay behind the Mustang, now flying erratically at about three hundred kilometers per hour. The black and white checkerboard nose of the shiny silver fighter was streaked with oil and exhaust stains. He let the Mustang fill his sights. He could see the pilot, bare-headed, hunched down in the seat, probably pissing in his pants with terror. Just a press of the button, and it would be over.

The American swiveled his neck to the left. The 262 was in so close that he could see underslung jets, the cordite stains around the cannon apertures, the greasy stream of exhaust behind it. Instinctively he'd started to bank into the assailant, then stopped, knowing that if he reefed the airplane around it would stall and he'd spin in. This is it, he thought. At least I'll see it coming.

Josten remembered the August day in Russia when the tough I-16 pilot had forced him to bail out, then come back to shoot him in his parachute harness. The poor bastard is barely flying—he has just got to sit there and take it. I know how he feels.

Josten slid level with the Mustang, staring into the pilot's face. "Damnit, Lyra, I *do* feel."

A sudden blinding apprehension hit him, he was vulnerable, low and slow, and there were enemies about. Without a smile or a wave, he slid back, framed the Mustang in his sights and fired the cannon. The shells tore the cockpit apart, set the engine spinning off to the right, the wings folding together before fluttering down. The aft portion of the fuselage broke away flaming. Within the debris the dead pilot fell toward the earth.

Josten smoothly applied power to the two jet engines, soaring effortlessly up and away, sorry for the American. He whispered to himself again, "Damnit, Lyra, I *do* feel."

12

Omaha Beach/June 12, 1944

Dead men make you feel small, and young dead men smaller still. Henry Caldwell shrank within his brown leather A-2 jacket as he surveyed the only sign of order on the beach, bodies stacked like cordwood in two piles. The American dead were covered with tarpaulins, waiting to make the journey back across the Channel. The Germans lay in stiff embraces in the open, slated for a temporary mass grave scooped out by a bulldozer.

Omaha Beach looked as malevolent as a Salvador Dali painting of an exploding junkyard. The receding tide had bared Rommel's landing obstacles, one triumphantly impaling a derelict LST, the others monuments to the folly of defense without air cover. Like sunken Civil War monitors, the already rusted turrets of foundered tanks poked out, the guns streaming Vs of seaweed. Caldwell wondered if the bodies had been recovered from them yet and had a quick mental image of the poor drowned souls, arms outstretched, blindly bumping about with the tide inside the tanks' dark interiors. A landing craft had rammed a coil of barbed wire into a right angle running from the sea to the beach, changing it from a barrier to a seine for flotsam, snagging rubber rafts, disintegrating boxes, and bits of clothing. The very air was corrupt with the rank odor of war, a nauseating mix of spilled oil, cordite, and burning rubber that even the rolling green sea could not clean. Firing was still steady inland, but the sounds were blotted out by the exhaust-barking trucks lumbering by, stuffing ever more men and materiel on the beach.

He felt a tug on his arm and turned to see Hap Arnold beaming at him.

"By God, Henry, who would have believed something like this back in 1939? Here, have something to eat."

Arnold pulled him aside, handing him a can of K-rations. Just ahead, Eisenhower was proudly showing General Marshall and Admiral King around what he was referring to as "my little realm," the inner core of the hard-won perimeter of land edging out past the bluffs of Omaha Beach.

"We wouldn't be here, Hap, if you hadn't made things happen."

"You mean if I hadn't let you make things happen. Look up there."

Arnold pointed with his mess spoon to the steady stream of Allied aircraft heading for the front. "There's not a goddamn Kraut plane in the sky, Henry, and it stems directly from your hard work in the lean years. I want you to know that I just finished telling Ike that."

His next words were lost in the sharp whistle and crack of shell fire. Water spouts erupted one hundred yards off Mulberry "A," the floating concrete dock where the U.S.S. *Thompson*, the destroyer in which the little group of leaders had crossed the Channel, was tied up.

Looking pleased to be under fire, Hap said, "That's Jerry's twelve o'clock allotment—there's an eighty-eight battery that fires off five rounds every hour on the hour—must be low on ammunition."

"I'll bet their commanders eat their hearts out when they see our materiel. Did you see the crummy clothes on those dead Germans? Their boots were made out of some kind of cardboard! But their equipment looked good. Better sidearms than we have."

"Yeah, it's a good thing they're short of everything now."

Caldwell nodded, mentally thanking God that the Germans were short of jet fighters! It would have been a far different war if the Luftwaffe had had a few hundred jets to put over the battlefield.

London/June 18, 1944

It was absolute hell being away from Elsie this long. The loneliness stoked his recurring depression. He had never been so mesmerized, so enchanted by a woman before. The longer they were together the more intense it became, a yearning offset only by Arnold's warm praise. Maybe all the crazy gambles he'd taken—and was still taking—were worthwhile. He stood gazing out the window toward the Guard's Chapel, gnashing his teeth in frustration as he caught his breath from the fast ten-block walk from his hotel. Now, for the third time that day, he was being kept waiting to talk to some Deputy Twit.

The Wellington Barracks office was the typical dignified anthill of wartime Great Britain—dozens of shabby desks crowded into an area where one glorious desk had once stood in solitary splendor, ashtrays filled to overflowing, tin trays of smudged teacups littering the floor. The acrid tobacco smoke was like a whiplash to his lungs, causing him to salivate in a fit of nicotine hunger. In New Orleans, Elsie had made him promise to quit smoking. It was tough, but she had insisted, and he always gave in to her.

The huge walnut double doors leading into the Deputy Minister's office were open for the stream of smartly uniformed young officers running in and out with sheaves of multicolored paper in their hands, each one nodding to Caldwell as he shot by, as if to say, "What I'm doing is obviously more important than what you are here for."

It was exactly the sort of assignment Caldwell hated—nothing firm, an amorphous agenda, and dealing with the smart-ass number twos of smart-ass number twos, all anxious to impress, but few anxious to work. Two years ago he could have accomplished all he wanted in two days—now it looked like it might take two weeks. The only thing that made the waiting tolerable was the time it gave him to think and plan the rest of his trip.

But this was part of the price Hap Arnold had extracted for the little side visit to Normandy.

"Henry, you don't think I took you to France for nothing, do you?

Caldwell hadn't answered Hap's rhetorical question—the relentlessly busy Arnold always had a motive.

"You heard General Marshall complaining about how unpredictable the Russians were at Teheran. And the British weren't much better at Cairo. Marshall and Ike are both fed up with us making all the concessions. They want to make sure the planners have a firm agenda for the next Big Three meeting. It's supposed to be early next year, maybe in Russia."

Caldwell was spending hours dealing with the Royal Air Force, the Foreign Office, and half a dozen other organizations, sorting out the protocol, pressing not for an exact agenda, but for a format that would require one. He knew it was a losing game—nothing could be accomplished at this level, not even with his contacts.

And it was probably pointless. The last time he'd seen Roosevelt, he didn't look as if he'd survive the year, much less be able to make another trip halfway around the world. The war had sapped the old campaigner's strength and not even the prospective drive for reelection seemed to excite him.

For Caldwell's purposes, it was a perfect time to be in Europe. Miraculously, the invasion had succeeded, despite adverse weather and all the possibilities of its going wrong. On the trip back on board the *Thompson*, Arnold and he had agreed that the turning point was last February with Operation Argument, when the skies over Germany had become a killing ground for the Luftwaffe.

He'd had a chance to visit Farnborough to see a production version of the first British jet fighter, the Gloster Meteor. It saddened him that Gloster had come up with a far more capable aircraft than McNaughton. Using Whittle-designed engines of about the same power, the Meteor was as fast as the McNaughton, but much more maneuverable. Caldwell was going to have to get

Bandy or Hadley Roget give him a report on why there was such a big difference.

On the 15th, the Germans had launched 250 V-1 buzz bombs against England, some seventy of which peppered London. The actual physical damage done was slight, but the threat to morale was tremendous. The winged robots, pulse-jet engines barking along their predetermined course, were as noisy as freight trains until they reached their target. Then, nosing down, the pulse-jet quit, and they would plunge silently and indiscriminately to the ground. Even the most optimistic Englishman of them all, Winston Churchill, took notice and called them "depressing."

Caldwell wasn't as worried by the V-1 as others around him. The value of weapons shifts over time, and the V-1's time had passed. If Hitler had been able to fire them off at the intended rate—some eight thousand per month—during the spring, they would truly have been a wonder weapon. They would have chewed up much of the massed potential of the Allied armies waiting in England, and there would have been no invasion. How close it had been: even sixty days earlier, and the whole course of the war would have shifted. Now that the Allied troops were ashore, the V-1 launching sites would be overrun. He wondered who the German project officer for the V-1 program was—he felt some professional sympathy for him, having a war-winning weapon in hand and then not being able to use it in time. Maybe someday he could compare notes with Hafner about it.

The public knew full well that there were other reprisal weapons in the works, but the true potential of the V-2 had not yet filtered down. No one knew when the V-2 firings would commence, nor how intensive they would be, but Caldwell was betting that they possessed a greater capability to break morale than bombers or the V-1. Swedish observers said that the missile actually left the earth's atmosphere in its flight, then reentered faster than the speed of sound, exploding before anyone could hear it coming! Even if radar somehow managed to pick it up, there was no way to intercept it. The Germans' advance in technology was tremendous; even with the benefit of the microfilmed information from Hafner,

McNaughton Aircraft was technically overwhelmed by the V-2. Yet this was the 1903 of missiles—if they progressed as fast as airplanes, there would be no more manned bombers in twenty years.

He was going to wind up this trip with a visit to Sweden, ostensibly to talk to the scientists who had examined the shattered remains of a V-2 that had crashed there. His real purpose, however, was to bring Lyra and the baby out of danger, to the United States.

Caldwell was confident that she would come. The last time he'd seen her she'd been terribly worried about what would happen to the baby. Elsie was the perfect person to offer Lyra sanctuary, to take care of her until the war was over. It was too sensitive to discuss with her yet, but Elsie was the kindest person he'd ever known—she'd do it gladly.

Lyra was just the start. Intelligence showed that Russia was already gathering up information on missiles, jets, and—God forbid—the German atomic experiments. It was going to be essential to scoop up as many of the German scientists as possible and bring them to work in the United States. Maybe if he got them employed at McNaughton they could make some progress on an American successor to the V-2.

A young aide, terribly tall, terribly thin, and terribly blond, tripped out of the office to announce flutily. "The Minister will see you in five minutes."

Caldwell nodded his thanks and looked out the window. A flight of aircraft—they looked like the new Hawker Tempests from a distance—was peeling off. He followed the line of their dive down and saw a small cruciform at about eight thousand feet, exhaust streaming behind it. The Tempests—big-snouted airplanes with elliptical wings, sort of a Spitfire with a pituitary problem—came down firing, then zoomed back up for another go. They'd missed and he heard the faint popping. It was a V-1 and it was coming his way.

The Tempests were forming up again to dive as the little flying bomb came on, growing louder. Caldwell thought, Must be doing about three hundred miles per hour, straight as a string. The Tempests dove again. Incredibly two of them touched wings to merge in an explosion as the mindless V-1 raced inexorably onward.

It was less than half a mile away when it pitched forward, the engine quitting, plunging almost straight down for the Wellington Barracks, looking as if it were aimed directly at his window. He raced into the astounded Deputy Minister's office yelling, "Get down!" and threw himself under a heavy oak table.

Stockholm/June 18, 1944

The letter in Lyra's hand was, in its own way, as potentially explosive as any incoming V-1. On the surface it was a directive to attend a symposium in Berlin for Foreign Ministry researchers and translators. That wasn't too unsettling—as the war progressed, Nazi Germany had become addicted to meetings, conferences, and symposia, as if talking would somehow solve the increasing difficulties. Despite dozens of official bans on unnecessary travel and explicit prohibitions of "non-essential" meetings, conferences had proliferated.

But people at her level weren't usually invited, for the conferences usually meant tacit perks for higher-ups—trips home, some extra rations, or a chance for some clandestine romance.

It was troubling that the invitation was so preemptive. She had to leave tomorrow, aboard a Luftwaffe transport plane, instead of flying the more comfortable—and safer—civil flight on A.B.A., the Swedish airline to Berlin.

Steeling herself, she went through the by-now automatic precaution of turning Ulrich over to Greta, repeating her precise instructions as to what should happen if she didn't return. She kissed the baby goodbye and embraced Greta, who had given them so much love and support since Ulrich's birth, and upon whom she now depended totally.

The aging Junkers transport was camouflaged for the flight over the sea, with even the black cross insignia on the wing painted in muted colors. It was symbolic. Once the Luftwaffe had ruled the Baltic. Now it had to skulk along at wavetop height to avoid Allied aircraft. There were only three other passengers, men in civilian clothes who nodded to her courteously enough, then returned to their own discussion.

It didn't trouble her when they veered away from Berlin—there was probably an air raid in progress. But her heart plummeted when she realized they were landing at the Focke-Wulf airfield at Cottbus, and that a police van was waiting. So it had come to this.

The largest of the three men escorted her to the van, saying, "I'm Sergeant Boedigheimer. Don't be alarmed, this is for your own protection. You are going to see a friend, Colonel Hafner."

She composed herself on the short drive to Hafner's office. Ulrich was safe, that was all that mattered. She'd done what she had to do, and she'd do what was necessary to survive.

Hafner greeted her with customary directness.

"Countess, I'm sorry that I had to intercept you. The letter you received was a death warrant. Your friend Dr. Goebbels had arranged for you to go to Buchenwald, to be disposed of."

Lyra was wary—this might be a trick, part of an interrogation process.

"Why would the *Reichsminister* do that? I've done nothing wrong."

"Let's not dissemble. He must have decided that he can't afford to have it known that he had a Jewess as a lover."

A sense of helplessness enveloped her. She'd always suspected that Hafner knew all about her.

"What will happen when he finds out that I'm not at Buchenwald?"

"As far as he will know, you've gone to Buchenwald and have been killed and your body cremated. We've arranged for a substitute. No one will ever know the difference."

Lyra laughed nervously to herself—her death was being arranged with false papers, the same way her marriage had been!

"Why are you doing this?"

"I could tell you that it's because your husband is my friend, but I won't. The truth is that you were a threat to me—you knew too much about my dealings with the Americans and the Russians. I don't think you'd betray me deliberately, but you are an amateur and you were being watched. They might have interrogated you, and I couldn't afford that. But most of all, you will be a bargaining chip, either for the Americans or the Russians."

"Helmut will find out and kill you."

"Quite the contrary. Helmut knows and approves. He'll be here this afternoon to collect you. We're going to hide you at Dr. Kersten's country home, about seventy-five kilometers from Berlin. You'll be safe and very comfortable there."

"Am I a prisoner?"

"Not at all. Harzewalde is a large house, with a staff and gardens. You'll eat well. But for your own safety, you will be under house arrest and incommunicado. Do you want your baby brought down to you?"

Panicked, Lyra said, "No. I don't want him to come to Germany, ever. I'll go to him when I can." Recovering her poise, she asked, "Why is Helmut going along with this?"

"He thinks you've been denounced for being a Jewess. That's enough nowadays. I haven't told him about your love affair with Goebbels or that you are a spy. It would kill him if he knew you'd passed on secrets on the jet fighter. And he'd probably kill us both."

When Helmut arrived, he was formal and correct, but terribly hurt that she considered their marriage ended. His blond hair was thinning and the ingrained dirt of combat flying darkened his tired face.

After he was sure she was well, he asked, "Where is Ulrich?"

"I don't *know*, Helmut. Think about it! If I knew, it would put him at risk, and the people helping him, too. The whole agreement to hide Ulrich was conditional on secrecy—they couldn't take the risk, otherwise."

"And what happens now? What if something happens to you or to me? How do we find him?"

"They know to seek us out. They tell me that it will be a religious family, working with a Swedish pastor. I have to trust them. God knows there is no one else to trust."

The answer infuriated him, and they drove in silence to Harze-walde, accepting that the war had made them strangers.

Nordhausen/July 24, 1944

Terror and death, death and terror. That's what Germany's come to today. If we were winning, that might be all right. But we're not.

Bruno Hafner did not dare say out loud what he was thinking, even to poor old Kurt Weigand struggling along beside him. The whole country was drenched in a vengeful more-Nazi-than-thou hysteria after last Thursday's attempt on Hitler's life. Super-patriotism was now the order of the day. No one entered or left a room without an enthusiastic *"Heil Hitler"* salute, especially here at the great Central Works, where the SS had taken over the V-2 program.

What bunglers the plotters had been! There's going to be a blood bath that will make the Night of the Long Knives back in 1934 look like a tea party. God help anyone under suspicion for anything.

Hafner looked at Weigand with concern. He'd been going down-hill ever since being trapped in the shelter at Regensburg-Pruefening. He hadn't been badly wounded, but the experience had stripped him of his drive and energy.

The meeting had been called by Himmler himself. Only God knew what the man wanted, or how he could take time off to come to this colossal running sore called Nordhausen.

The gigantic plant was operated solely on the basis of terror. When Hafner built his underground plant at Cottbus, he had never imagined that subterranean architecture would go to extremes like this. Only 160 kilometers from Berlin, under Kohnstein mountain in the Harz range, a slave crew of human ants had created the greatest underground factory in the world. Two main tunnels, each nearly two kilometers long, had been tunneled out in an S-shaped parallel course (appropriate now, since the SS had taken over) about two hundred meters apart. Joining them, like rungs of a ladder, were forty-three parallel galleries. Almost one hundred thousand square meters of floor space had been hacked out by *Sklavenarbeiter*. More highly skilled slaves were now producing V-2s at the rate of six hundred per month, and still others were building the Junkers jet engines that were at long last streaming off the production lines.

The factory was totally bomb-proof, and there were no limits to its expansion. Plants for producing liquid oxygen and synthetic oil were being built. No attempt had been made to build a runway—they were too attractive as targets—but there was talk of making complete jet aircraft there and catapulting them into the air from the factory entrance.

They had entered via an open elevator, which had clanked down a cool, moisture-glistening limestone shaft. Humidity hung in the tunnels in sponge-like air, stirred periodically by chill gusts of wind that whistled in the skein of electrical wires suspended overhead. Despite the moisture, there was dust everywhere. Hafner had a small cut on his finger, and the dusty air stung it like iodine. Underlying the hollow echoing noises of the workplace was a dull drumming, the hacking cough of the slave laborers. The lights swinging in the gelid draft danced the workers' shadows across the chiseled cavern walls, surrealistic silhouettes waxing large as giants, then waning to nothingness.

"Dr. Caligari's cabinet. Macabre," was Kurt's first comment.

On each side there were endless rows of machine tools, each one served by teams of emaciated laborers in torn striped pajamas. Some wore the yellow patch of the Jew, some the SR for *Sowjetrusseland*, some P for Poles. All wore wooden clogs for shoes. Those at work bent hastily over their tools. Any others stood at a bony attention against the side of the passage, their striped caps doffed, cringing if one of the black-shirted SS *Totenkopfverbande* guards—"death's head" was so appropriate—made a sudden movement. Even in passing, Hafner caught their death scent. They were already decaying, dissolving into the moldy vapors of the manmade cave.

Weigand was agitated, mumbling to himself.

"What's that, Kurt?"

"Look."

He pointed down one of the tunnels to the side. Strung across on a rope, eleven cadavers in advanced stages of decomposition were hanging. A twelfth had rotted and fallen to the ground beneath the rope he had died on.

Hafner couldn't speak. My God, he thought, what are they

doing? Imagine trying to produce sophisticated weapons in a charnel house! How could Von Braun or Dornberger permit this? If they want to kill people, do it decently in gas chambers!

The appalling condition of the Nordhausen slave labor was the reason for the meeting. With six months of back-breaking effort, sixty thousand slave workers from Buchenwald had transformed a small ammonia mine into a monstrous death mill. There had been no power tools, no jack hammers, no blasting—only pickaxes and spades. Despite the disease and the death, V-2 production had started on schedule in January.

In the process, more than twenty thousand workers had sacrificed their "existing stocks of muscle and fat in the service of the Reich." Their skeletal cadavers were laboriously carted by prison labor to the crematorium at Camp Dora.

Someone at Himmler's headquarters had compared this death toll to the number of slaves who died in building Hafner's most recent project, the mammoth V-2 launch site at Watten near Calais. Six miles north of the Luftwaffe field at St. Omer, it was a huge facility, intended to launch fifty V-2s against England every day. More than a hundred meters long by forty-five meters wide, it reached thirty meters into the air. Over one hundred thousand kilotons of concrete had been poured into it by thirty-five thousand slave workers in a six-month period. The project was at least comparable in scope to Nordhausen, but with an enormous difference. Only four thousand workers had died at Watten, and now the SS wanted to know what were the lessons to be learned.

But that hardly seemed adequate justification for a personal visit by Himmler. The fact that he'd leave Berlin at a time of stress like this meant that he was either terribly secure—or frightened.

There was a tap at the door to the little office, a bare cubicle hewn into the side of a gallery, furnished with a table, four chairs, and a field telephone whose wires straggled out the door and up into the rat's nest suspended along the center of the tunnel.

A voice said only, "The *Reichsfuehrer*."

Weigand and Hafner struggled to attention as Heinrich Himmler, Dr. Felix Kersten, and an aide came in. For a moment, the taller Kersten stood immediately behind Himmler, so that their round faces were superimposed like a figure-**8**. The aide immediately went to the field phone, cranked it, and put a call through for Himmler.

Holding the phone in his pale, almost girlish hand, Himmler said, "Excuse me, Colonel Hafner, I must make an immediate call to my train."

Making small talk with Kersten, Hafner recalled an extraordinary meal he had a few months ago on board the train. It was called the *Heinrich*, for obvious reasons, a weird combination of baroque coaches out of a mad King Ludwig fantasy and ultra-modern communication and flak cars. Breakfast had started with a flurry of anxiety when Himmler found that by mistake there were thirteen seated at his table. A hapless colonel was exiled immediately. The food was "idealized SS"—stewed leeks, with mineral water to drink. While they ate, Himmler lectured them on the values of vegetarianism and the evils of hunting "innocent wild animals." Speer had been there, dabbling at the green mess, looking faintly superior. Later he'd called Himmler "half schoolmaster, half crank."

For a man as astute as Speer it had not been a perceptive description. For all his idiosyncracies, Himmler exercised an iron control second only to Hitler over the most efficient of the Party's many organizations. Himmler, now obviously stressed as he talked excitedly into the phone, was not physically impressive. Of medium height and slender build, he had an aura of too-ripe-peach softness, as if his flesh would puncture at a finger's touch. Under his round wire-rimmed glasses, his gray-blue eyes were expressionless, and his thin lips maintained a faint, set smile. Deep creases formed an inverted **V** around his mouth, and his small mustache was trimmed to match, giving him a weak, downcast look.

Since Ploesti, Hafner had often worked with Himmler, finding him shallow as a saucer but hard as steel. The man had no life substance of his own, borrowing his very existence from Hitler. With an inhuman subservience, he had become the Fuehrer's most diligent servant, gifted with a demonic ability to inspire killing.

He hung up the phone and the aide left.

"The assassination attempt has given us all much to do. Thank you for meeting me here. Have you had a chance to look around?"

"No, but I think I've seen enough for our meeting. I can investigate more thoroughly later, if you wish."

"Colonel Hafner, Dr. Kersten is a bond between us. He has quite literally saved my life, and I know what he has done for you. He has also confirmed my belief in you as a human being. And, of course, we have the bond of the work you and *Obergruppenfuehrer* Weigand have done in increasing production."

Hafner nodded appreciatively, as Himmler went on.

"We have two things to discuss. The first is laborer care at Nordhausen. This place is a scandal! Workers are dying at an appalling rate. Two years ago, when we were still capturing huge numbers of Russians, it wouldn't have mattered. Now it is critical. How were you able to do a better job at Watten?"

"Simple, *Herr Reichsfuehrer*. Watten is on the main canal network that connects to the sea. It serves as a runoff drain for the countryside. I assigned one thousand of the laborers, under *Kapo* guards, to use nets to gather food from the canals. They were to touch nothing else, not even if it were on the path beside the canal. They brought in everything, fish, mollusks, weeds, dead animals, birds, frogs, everything. It was cooked in big pots and added to the rations. It stank like shit—I can't imagine what it must have tasted like—but it had calories, and calories meant life. It probably even had some vitamins, from the seaweed and the algae."

"No chance to do that here."

"There are no canals, of course. The prisoners could gather acorns in the forest, pine nuts, bark, even weeds. Anything helps."

"We'll see that that is done. But I have an idea that must not be repeated outside this room. We are wasting an enormous amount of protein and even some fat in the camps. You know what I mean?"

Hafner knew. He had seen and smelled the billowing chimney.

"I'm not suggesting cannibalism—I don't think that would be good for morale."

Whose morale? Hafner wondered. The prisoners? The guards?

"But perhaps there is an intermediate way. Could some animal—rats perhaps—be allowed to feed on the bodies, and then subsequently be farmed as protein for the prisoners?"

Hafner thought about a question that would have been bizarre anywhere but in a cave factory of the Third Reich in 1944. "It's possible. Chickens might be better."

He heard Kersten gasp and realized his gaffe—Himmler had once been a chicken farmer.

It didn't seem to bother him. "Yes, I have some expertise in chicken farming, as you know. But if it got out that we were feeding the prisoners chicken, it would be bad for the troops' morale. The same with pigs. No one would care if the prisoners were eating rats."

"Do you want me to experiment? It would take a few weeks to get some data. I think there would have to be some processing—a grinder perhaps, like farmers use to prepare swill for hogs. Rats probably are the best choice—they could endure the conditions down here better than chickens or hogs."

Weigand giggled. "Certainly better than humans can."

Himmler looked at him with astonishment, then went on to Hafner. "No. Your agreement that it is feasible is enough. I'll put some of my agricultural experts on it. It's more important that you and Weigand give me a complete report on Nordhausen, telling me what we can do immediately to improve the life expectancy of the workers."

Hafner adopted a professional tone. "In my own work, I've developed the phrase 'productive life-hours' as a measure of efficiency for forced labor. After a certain point, life can be sustained but no work results."

"That's the point at which the rats might come into play."

Weigand giggled again. "How strange this is, how sad that we talk about things like this in Germany."

Himmler spoke impatiently. "Nothing is strange if it works!" He turned again to Hafner.

"Let's go to—"

Weigand interrupted. "You could vary the rations, you know. Jews to the rats today, Gypsies tomorrow, Poles the next day." He began to laugh openly as the others stared at him. "The rats might have preferences, so . . ."

Himmler went to the door and spoke in a low voice to the guards standing outside. They came in and led Weigand away. At the door he shouted over his shoulder, "There could be prizes for the biggest . . ."

Embarrassed, Hafner said, *"Herr Reichsfuehrer, Obergruppenfuehrer* Weigand has not been himself since his entombment at Regensburg."

So furious that his hands were trembling, Himmler tried to calm himself. "One must be hard! We cannot risk his talking about this. Why did you bring him?"

"I had no idea he was so ill!"

Shaking his head like a swimmer just out of the water, Himmler went on, his voice now icily cold. "Now to the second order of business. I am well aware of your contacts with the Americans and the Russians. Ordinarily, this would be cause for immediate execution. But these are difficult times. You are able to do some things that I might wish to do—but cannot—because of my unswerving loyalty to the Fuehrer."

Hafner said nothing. A few months earlier, Himmler's words would have been a death sentence for him, as they had just been for Weigand.

Himmler seemed to relax slightly, going on as if he were giving a potentially bright student a lesson.

"The invasion has succeeded. It might at some point be wise for Germany to negotiate a peace. As long as the Fuehrer is alive, negotiations are impossible. He would never permit it—and it is doubtful if anyone would negotiate with him."

Hafner shot a glance at Kersten, amazed that Himmler would speak this way in front of witnesses. But then, Himmler had just demonstrated how he dealt with witnesses.

"Wha . . ." Hafner's voice faded. He composed himself and said, "What is it you wish me to do?"

"Nothing for now. But if Providence removes the Fuehrer at some time—some insanity like this officers' plot, or perhaps if, God forbid, his health fails—I may want you to signal one side or the other that I'm prepared to negotiate as the leader of the Reich. If that doesn't come to pass, then I may wish to make some arrangements for my postwar life, as you have done."

Hafner nodded in agreement. Himmler's eagerness betrayed him. His real concern was obviously escape.

"In the meantime, I'm going to arrange for you to have a large aircraft placed at your disposal—perhaps we might wish to go to Argentina."

Hafner took careful note of Himmler's use of the word "we," saying, "Let me work that out. It might be possible, with some arrangements. I've plotted out the distances more than once. The big Junkers, the Ju 390, has a range of more than ten thousand kilometers. We could probably arrange with Spain to land in the Canaries, or with Brazil to refuel at Natal."

Himmler seemed satisfied, responding, "There is time to see about that. Just come to me with your needs. In the meantime, I want you to carry on exactly as you have been doing."

Himmler and Kersten left, leaving Hafner to ponder his narrowing range of options. There were some precautions to be taken. Poor old Kurt! Not much of a reward for all the work he'd done.

Nashville/August 28, 1944

Caldwell, the pain from a burgeoning ulcer almost twisting him in half, sat glassy-eyed in front of the reports. The better the war news got, the worse things became for him. When he'd gone to Stockholm, he'd found that Lyra had vanished. He couldn't find out if the child had been taken away with his mother or placed in someone else's care. No one, neither the Swedes who knew her nor his German contact in the Embassy, would venture a guess on what had happened. Hafner's got her, he thought. The man is poison.

Now Hadley Roget had summoned him from Washington with disastrous news. The performance of the McNaughton jet was as disappointing as the Sidewinder's had been.

"You remember how Bandfield was suspicious about the flight tests? Well, there's no question about bad parts this time!"

Caldwell hunched over, his stomach contorting with pain.

"You mean this is fraud—not just some production foul-up?"

"Has to be—the mechanism was designed right in from the start. Somebody's built an extra valve into the pitot-static system so that it gives higher readings as the airspeed goes up. Damn clever, and virtually undetectable."

Caldwell, ashen-faced, asked, "How did it work?"

"A relief valve in the system incrementally reduces static pressure. At four hundred miles an hour, it adds about ten percent to the speed."

"Wouldn't it show up on test flights?"

"Not routinely. And it will be a few months before the airplanes get to the field, where pilots will get a chance to check the performance against other equipment."

"Yeah, but sooner or later it'll be evident."

"I think Troy figures he'll have the airplane cleaned up, and he won't need this gadget. If it's like every other airplane, the first batch will go through a modification center—he can change back to a standard system then."

Caldwell asked Hadley to go get Troy McNaughton, then sat with his head in his hands. It was premeditated fraud, pure and simple. But why hadn't Lee discovered it? He was the hotshot engineer and had been here while the production Mambas were being developed. Now he was six thousand miles away, en route to some godforsaken B-29 base in the Pacific.

When McNaughton entered Caldwell almost threw himself at the younger man's throat.

"How in the hell did this happen, Troy?"

Troy sat down, leaned back in his chair and pulled out a pack of Old Golds. He held the pack with precision, the tobacco stains on his fingertips contrasting with the sheen of his manicured nails. With a little pen-knife he slit the revenue stamp, eased the pack open, tapped it smartly on the desk edge, and offered it to Caldwell. Caldwell instinctively reached for it, then declined.

"Jim Lee suggested the modification on the prototype. You agreed, I've got your signature on the approval."

"What modification? I never approved any modification."

McNaughton shoved a sheaf of papers marked TOP SECRET across the desk. It was an engineering change proposal for the pitot-static system. It seemed routine enough, a slight redesign of the static system. The signature on the cover letter was his—but he'd never seen the paper before. A clammy feeling stole over him. The bastards had not only changed the design, they'd made the government pick up the bill for the change.

"I didn't sign this."

McNaughton was patient, reasoned. "Henry, you remember how you used to bring in two briefcases full of correspondence when you came down to visit Elsie? She did a lot of typing for you, on your own Army stationery and franked envelopes. Once some changes had to be made, and you were in a hurry to leave. Elsie had you sign a few blanks for her to retype on later. We saved a few."

"How could she do this to me?"

"She was doing it for *you*, for your own good."

"Troy, I'm going to see that you go to jail."

"If I go, you'll go, Henry. And so will Elsie. She's in it just as deep as Lee and I are. We were all working to help you, to keep everybody off your back until we could improve the airplanes. Your letter from Scriabin took us off the hook on the Sidewinder. We want to look good, and we want to make you look good."

They sat staring at each other, equally aware that Elsie's jeopardy was tipping the balance toward Caldwell's complicity.

Caldwell sat sunk in thought as McNaughton continued. "You've got a way out. You can't lose."

McNaughton took a drink of water, clearing his golden voice for more sales evangelism.

"You can actually make yourself look good, Henry, and refute the gossip about your favoring McNaughton. If we can't get the airplane cleaned up, you come out fearlessly for Lockheed as having the best jet, and buy lots of them. Then you can buy the Mamba as a fighter-trainer, something to bridge the gap between Mustangs and the Lockheed fighter."

His voice dropped to a confidential register. "You know the routine. You penalize us for failure to perform, and we'll drop the price on the Mamba."

He might have been a baker, talking about marking down the price on day-old bread. Caldwell glared at him.

McNaughton went on. "Nobody will ever know about this! We'll route all the affected airplanes back through the mod center, and change the pitot system there. Besides, the way the war is shaping up, they're already beginning to cut back production and cancel contracts. They're even cutting down on the number of pilots being trained. It'll all be over in a year or two, and everybody will be anxious to get back to normal times. Nobody will even remember stupid stuff like this. But, if you want us all in jail, fine. You know they won't put Elsie in the same cell with you. No, some dyke matron would be all over Elsie as soon as she walked in."

Caldwell tried to ignore the image, trying to pump up his anger.

"If that's the way it is, that's the way it is. I've been stupid but I haven't been criminal yet. And I'm not going to be."

McNaughton's demeanor changed from the patient sales-hungry vendor to the boss who's tired of the bellyaching. His face turned livid and his lips curled back in a savage snarl.

"Look, you stupid bastard, the gloves are off! I'm tired of listening to your whining. I've got you nailed dead to rights. You've been shooting your mouth off, now you sit back and listen."

A sickening, inexpressible weariness seized Caldwell. McNaughton was too smart not to have anticipated this. What did he have on him?

"You were very generous with Elsie—gave her a car, made the down payment on the farm for her."

"It was my money, I could do anything I wanted with it."

"That's what you say, Henry, I've got private company records, my own personal accounts, that show cash disbursements to you for amounts that are just about the same as you spent on Elsie, just a few days before you spent it. When I offer that to the court-martial board—and the tax people—your goose will be cooked."

"I never took a dime from you or anybody else."

"No, but the records say you did. You might be able to convince a jury that it's a fraud, but I doubt it. Not after we go into all the times you came down here when you were supposed to be going somewhere else, when you used our guesthouse. We kept pretty good tabs, Henry, we even have some photos. Remember that mirror over the dresser in the bedroom? Well, it's one of those one-way jobs. I hated to do it, especially to you and Elsie, but business is business."

"You rotten bastard. Did Elsie know?"

"Of course not. What do you think she is? She's just a woman crazy in love with you, that's all. Everything she's done has been to help you. I've taken advantage of the situation, but I had to."

He paused dramatically, his manner changing again. "Believe it or not, Henry, I was trying my damnedest to build good airplanes for the war effort. Things didn't go like I planned, but I was trying."

Caldwell groaned out loud. Jesus. What a fool he'd been to trust this con man! And what a fool to play footsie on the Army's time. How often had he signed out an airplane to fly from Wright Field to Scott Field and then "diverted" to Nashville? Everybody was doing stuff like that all the time, nobody cared as long as you got some time on the airplanes, burned up the fuel allotment. But in a trial, it would be presented as defrauding the government, a court-martial offense by itself. And if they knew about that, who would believe that he hadn't taken the money, hadn't agreed to the fraud about the performance? Nobody, not in the government, for sure, and absolutely no jury. He was cooked! The image of Elsie and the prison matron suddenly flared in his mind and he lunged at McNaughton.

"You dirty bastard, you've sold the government a bunch of junk, and you've ruined me!"

McNaughton moved calmly around the desk, aware that he held a winning hand.

"It hasn't been junk. These aren't the first airplanes the government's bought that haven't met their performance figures, and they won't be the last. Look at what Scriabin said. The Russians are glad to have the Sidewinder, and the Mamba will make a great fighter trainer. Don't lose your head."

"Where's Elsie now?"

"She's at home, waiting for you. She's sick about what's happened. Let her tell you herself. She was doing it all for you. It's the war, Henry."

The argument was over. McNaughton had won.

It took almost an hour of fast talking to convince Hadley Roget that the best course was to remain silent on the whole business until "after the war." Roget had agreed only reluctantly, with a sadder-but-wiser look on his face which told Caldwell that they were no longer really friends.

Now he drove recklessly down the dusty farm road, squealing to a stop in the gravel of the circular drive in front of Elsie's new house. She met him with a flood of tears, begging his forgiveness, begging him not to let her go to jail, telling him how much she loved him, how much she needed him.

"Henry, forgive me. And forgive how I look, I haven't slept a wink all night. I only did this for you because I thought it was for the best, like Troy told me. You know I wouldn't do anything to hurt you."

Gratefully, he let her embrace him. As angry as he was, it was heaven to feel her arms around him, to smell her sweet scent.

"Honey, you know how funny I was acting. It was because I was worried."

Amid his anger there was a surge of joy. She hadn't been thinking of Bruno, she'd been worried about him! Yet they argued on, and the more they argued, the more she cried, and the more excited he became. Clinging to him, kissing him passionately, she pulled him with her to the floor. He forgot his anger as they made greedy, forgiving love on the knotted rug.

Later, at two in the afternoon, they were comfortable in her bed, Elsie sleeping deeply, her head on his chest. Caldwell knew that he was hooked on her like an addict on heroin. No matter what happened, no matter how angry she made him, he loved her without reservation. He wasn't going to do anything to harm her, this woman he loved, now lying so trustfully in his embrace. He'd die before he'd let her go to prison.

As for Lee, he'd been a fool—loyal, but a fool. He should never have gone along with McNaughton's scheme to change the pitot-static system design, to fake the test results, no matter how much he believed the airplane's performance could be improved. If he was really trying to save Caldwell, as McNaughton had said, it was still outrageous. Caldwell knew that Lee owed him a lot, but this was too much. He shifted his position and thought that, like most of this mess, it had been his own fault—he'd brought Lee along too quickly. Some people couldn't handle higher ranks.

But at least he'd tried to help. Some people might have stabbed him in the back.

She stirred. It moved him just to look down at her slender body, curled like a child, her full breasts pressed against him and her lovely red hair spilling across his chest. He reached out and, with his fingertip, traced the smooth, melding curves of her body. Her eyelids fluttered and she burrowed against him, stifling a yawn against his flesh, then raising her face sleepily to be kissed. He responded at once, murmuring over and over in a frantic litany, "I love you, Elsie, I love you, I love you."

She responded in a groggy voice, "And I love you." Sleepily, she half-turned to begin kissing his belly, circling him with her hand, moving him gently.

"I love you, and I *really* love little Robert E. Lee Junior here, too—" Elsie sat bolt upright. "I mean, little John Henry Junior." Caldwell was already out of bed. That son-of-a-bitch, Lee!

Isley Field, Saipan/November 27, 1944

With a graceful, unexpected move, the American forces had pivoted and sent a smashing body blow to the Japanese by seizing the Marianas. Everyone—even their Allies—had expected the U.S. forces to chew the Japanese up, island by island. Instead, the Japanese forces at Truk and Palau had been isolated and now offered only the threat of an occasional bombing raid as their ground forces withered on the vine.

The B-29 bomber offensive against Japan was doing its own withering, at the end of an overextended vine of supplies, still unable to justify the mammoth cost that had gone into its creation. Operating out of Chinese bases had proved to be exactly the unproductive nightmare Jim Lee had predicted—it was too difficult to get the fuel and bombs to the bases.

But the worst problem was the poor bombing results. The whole doctrine of high altitude precision bombing was at risk, because the B-29s were *not* getting bombs on the target. And now the horrendous cost in men and materiel for invading the Marianas to establish a B-29 base had to be added to the overall program cost.

Saipan had been invaded on June 15th—a week later, the first American aircraft landed. By the 15th of August, Saipan, Tinian, and Guam had begun the typical American transformation from primitive to wartime-luxurious. It was not until late November that the super bomber operation was at last in place—but it was on Saipan, not twelve hundred miles away beyond the Himalayas. It was from Saipan that Brig. Gen. Haywood S. "Possum" Hansell's XXI Bomber Command would give high altitude precision bombing another chance.

Colonel James Lee, his usually mobile face impassive, sat up on his cot, carefully folded the letter, and put it back in its brown manila envelope.

"Did you read it, Bandy?"

"No—but he's talked to me about Elsie and you, and about McNaughton. Doesn't sound too good, from his point of view, anyway."

"Not from mine, either. Did he send you all the way here just to deliver a goddamn letter?"

"Probably. It's not something he could send through the censors. I've got a day job, of course, same old range-extension stuff, this time for the P-47N. With two external tanks you can get almost twenty-three hundred miles range out of it—if you know what to do."

"Well, I'm gonna tell you my side, whether you want to hear it or not."

Lee tossed the letter over to Bandfield. "You can read that later if you want. And since you're playing postman, I'm going to give you a message to take back to him."

He pointed to the letter. "This just tells me I'm a son-of-a-bitch, that I shouldn't have hurt Elsie, and that if it wasn't for her he'd send me to jail. Also that he's going to punch me in the nose."

"I figured that's what it might be."

The raucous noise of the day at Isley Field—engines running up, trucks pounding by, aircraft flying over—had subsided into the normal buzz of night war in the tropics. There was a continuous murmur from the brightly lit flight line, where ground crews were straining to get the aircraft just returned from that day's mission to Japan—only the second mission from Saipan—ready for the next day's takeoff.

"I'm going to level with you, Bandy. I'm no saint. I probably shouldn't have fooled around with Elsie, but she wanted it."

"Frankly, I don't give a damn about Elsie," Bandy snapped. "It was just an infatuation and Henry's probably well out of it. The business with the pitot tubes is something else again."

"Yeah—that's what I wanted to talk to you about. McNaughton had me convinced there was an engineering fix in the works that would take care of things and make the airplane live up to expectations."

"That might wash once, Jim, even though you're supposed to be an engineer. But not twice."

"Elsie suckered me into it. We got, well, friendly, and she began filling me in. The way she told it, Henry was taking money from Troy McNaughton to give to her. She had McNaughton's books, showed me the disbursements."

"She's the bookkeeper, she can cook the goddamn books any way she wants. That doesn't mean that Caldwell took anything."

"Maybe. But that's not the way I read it at the time. Troy's a hell of a salesman, he convinced me the best way I could help Henry was to keep Sidewinders coming down the line until they got them fixed. And I guess they did. The Russians like them now."

"You're switching tracks—we were talking about Henry being on

the take, and now you're talking about the Sidewinder's performance."

"It's all wrapped together. Troy convinced me that if we could
keep things quiet until after the war, Henry could retire, and
nobody would be the wiser."

"Jesus, if you thought he was guilty, you should have turned him
in. If you didn't think he was, you should have turned McNaughton
in. What the hell do you think an officer's commission means?"

The light from the unshaded sixty-watt bulb dimmed periodically
as more demands were placed on the overstrained generators. Bandfield searched Lee's weary face for some signal that this was somehow just a bad joke, that there was a better explanation.

"Look, Bandfield, you grew up poor. I didn't. I hated it when
Dad lost all our money in the Depression. I want to make it big!"

"Shit, that explains everything. No problem. Anybody would
understand that."

"Don't bullshit me, Bandy, I'm tired. Well, after the Sidewinder,
I was in whether I liked it or not. I really believed I was helping
Henry."

"While you were fucking his girlfriend?"

"We hadn't started anything yet. Then McNaughton came to me
one night with a bunch of papers, showing the high-drag profiles on
the Mamba. Same story. He said he thought they could do some
fixes—better wing/fuselage juncture, smoother skin, the usual—but
that he needed time. I dreamed up the change to the pitot-static
system, and that was it."

"Stop. You could have done that on your own. There was no
need to create the paperwork about Caldwell being on the take."

"I didn't know about that at the time. When I found out, it was
too late. Elsie and I were mixed up together—and I'd accepted a job
offer from Troy for after the war."

Bandfield stood up. "Lee, you really are a shit. If it weren't for
Caldwell, I'd knock your block off and then turn you in for a court
martial."

"Yeah, I figure you would. Why don't you? Don't tell me I was a
patsy for covering for him. You're doing the same goddamn thing

yourself, right now. You want purity and justice, you talk about what a commission means, so you turn me in, and him, too."

The characteristic uneven sound of Japanese engines passed overhead, followed by four sharp explosions.

"Uh-oh—looks like we've got visitors. They sent some Zeros down on a one-way mission the other day."

Both men raced outside the tent as the base defense antiaircraft was opening up. A few searchlights were tracking aimlessly about the sky. Two B-29s on the nearby hardstand were already burning, and the Japs—Bandfield couldn't tell what the planes were, they were too slender-looking to be Bettys—came in at low level, strafing. One swerved as it approached the end of the runway and hit the ground flat. It skipped like a rock, its remaining bombs blowing up on the second bounce, the blast knocking down Lee and Bandfield. The other intruder roared directly overhead, racing out toward Magicienne Bay.

The two B-29s were burning fiercely now, their fuselages collapsed in the center, wings poking up, noses forlornly cast in one direction, tails dumped in another. The blazing bombers were surrounded by a tightly packed ring of B-29s around them, all fully fueled with high octane aviation gas and loaded with bombs for the next day's mission.

Bandfield yelled to no one in particular, "Christ, they're going to go up like firecrackers on a string!" He ran to where the ground crews were frantically trying to push the sixty-ton monsters away, moving the outermost ones to clear a path for the inner circle of planes. Some particularly gutsy mechanics braved the intense heat to climb into the cockpits, trying to get at least two engines started to taxi.

Lee ran in the opposite direction. At the edge of the hardstand, he climbed into a bulldozer left idle for the night and within seconds had the engine running. With the blade lowered, he drove directly at a river of burning fuel streaming toward the next B-29 in line. Scooping dirt as he went, he smashed directly into the center of the first B-29, pushing a section of the flaming carcass off the hardstand into the adjacent gully, away from the other airplanes.

Bandfield had a clear view of him from the cockpit of the B-29 he'd climbed into, amazed that Lee could breathe and function in the firestorm of heat. Lurking like monsters in the raging mass of flame and aluminum were the next day's supply of five-hundred-pound bombs. If they went off, they'd blow the rest of the B-29s to bits—and take Lee and everyone on this end of the island with them.

Twice Lee charged back into the flames, each time scooping the fiery debris over the side of the embankment. The third time he whirled around, he saw that the construction engineers had arrived with three more bulldozers, all heading for the second B-29. Lee turned once again and began packing dirt over the first airplane, still burning, still bomb-laden, riding back and forth until the fires had subsided and the fire trucks were at last on hand, pouring water on the wreckage.

Still unbelieving and more than a little ashamed of his own ineffective action, Bandfield walked over to where a cheering bunch of engineering personnel were slapping Lee on the back, joking and laughing.

A giant of an engineer had grabbed Lee around the chest and was waltzing him around in a circle. "Little Colonel, where the hell did you learn to drive a 'dozer?"

Lee, his red hair singed, skin blistered and totally black with soot, his teeth gleaming in the still glowing fires, replied, "My daddy had a little road construction outfit in Virginia. I worked summers, drove everything. You never know what will come in handy, do you?"

"Well, man, you can fly B-29s during the day for old Possum Hansell, and drive bulldozers at night for us."

Bandfield walked Lee over to the dispensary—his eyebrows were singed away and there were light burns across his face and hands.

"Jim, I got to tell you, that was the bravest thing I've ever seen. Those damn bombs could have gone off any second."

"Hell, I'd never have known it. Stick around. I got a message for you to deliver in person to Caldwell for me."

While Lee was being cleaned up and his burns dressed, Bandfield re-created the scene in his mind, trying to understand how Lee could have been such a bastard to Caldwell—and such an instinctive hero here. It was a cinch that he'd get put in for a Silver Star for this, maybe the Medal of Honor. He deserved it.

How complex people were! One minute Lee had admitted to being a crook poaching his superior and friend's girl. The next minute he was doing the most heroic thing Bandfield had ever seen. It was one thing to be brave in an airplane, in combat—Christ, that's what you were trained for. But to ride that 'dozer into the flames was incredible.

As he waited, he thought about other people and other changes. Who could have believed that iron-ass Henry Caldwell, the real genius of American airpower, could be led around by his dick by a woman who was "No better than she should be," as Clarice would have said. And Hadley, gruff old Hadley, ignoring Clarice all her life, and now pining away for her.

General Hansell came down later to the dispensary, saying, "Lee, maybe after this I'll forgive you for your idiot ideas about area bombing." It was three hours before they got back to Lee's tent, recounting the night, each man nursing one of the clutch of bottles of medicinal whiskey—Four Roses miniatures—the jubilant flight surgeon had given Lee. He didn't get to treat heroes too often, and Lee was clearly a special case.

Now, inevitably, their talk came back to the main agenda. "Look, Bandy, no matter what you think of me, no matter what Caldwell thinks, I've got something to tell him. It's purely professional—and I hope he listens."

"Shoot."

"So far the planning on the B-29 has been brilliant, from the design, to getting coolies to build airfields in China, to capturing this godforsaken rock and stuffing it with airplanes. There's just one problem."

He drank down his whiskey and opened another, tossing the metal cap on the floor.

"The problem is that our bombing isn't worth a shit, and it's not going to get better. We can bomb Japan for the next forty years, the way we've been doing, and they'll laugh at us. With the winds we're running into, the airplanes are coming across the target at maybe four hundred forty miles an hour—too fast for our equipment to drop with any accuracy. The bombs are being sprayed all over. The reconnaissance photos show that we're barely touching the factories, and high explosives don't do much damage to residential areas."

He leaned forward, red hair tousled, the grease from the medication shining in the light, eyes burning intensely. "Now here's what we've got to do. We've got to strip out all the weight of the airplanes, take out the guns and the gunners, load them up with as many incendiaries as they'll carry, and hit Japan at night, at low altitude. We can burn Tokyo out in two raids—I mean every goddamn house in it. But it means that we've got to forget about doctrine, and forget about pride."

"Have you told General Hansell this?"

"Yeah, you heard him in the sickbay. He threatened to take my squadron away from me if I kept pushing it. Hansell's committed to daylight precision bombing. It's a religion with him. He's the most brilliant planner I've ever met—but he's dead wrong about this."

"What can Caldwell do?"

"Christ, he's got Hap Arnold's ear. And Hap Arnold runs the Twentieth Air Force personally—it's the only one that's not under a theater commander. Caldwell's got to get Arnold to let us at least experiment, try it out, see what happens. Otherwise, the mines and the submarines are going to sink the entire Jap fleet and the Navy's going to wind up winning the war."

"I'll do it. I don't expect he'll be receptive to any messages from you, but I'll do it."

"Old Henry doesn't care where an idea comes from if it's good. And about that stuff I talked about—a job at McNaughton. That's just between us, right?"

"Jim, before you got on that goddamn bulldozer, I told you to go fuck yourself, that I was going to turn you in. But not now. I don't approve, not at all. But I figure that anybody with your balls deserves a chance to straighten some of this mess out. I just wish I knew where the hell it was all going to end."

Over Holland/January 1, 1945

By God, there was a sight no one had seen for a long time!

Oberst Helmut Josten lifted his hand and pointed. His wingman in *Kampfgeschwader* 51, *Leutnant* Hans Langner nodded enthusiastically. Dawn was just breaking behind them, the scarlet sun glinting off the wings of the eight hundred Luftwaffe fighters skimming the snow-covered fields to avoid enemy radar. Josten and his precious handful of jets followed the 109s and 190s in great curving arcs, trying not to overrun them. The beautiful scenery below—frozen canals reflecting the sunlight, rows of trees covered with snow—meant nothing to Josten, aware only that the low temperatures meant denser air, which meant his engines would run better.

It was the "Great Blow," at last—a year after Galland had planned for it—and just fifteen days too late for the Ardennes offensive. They'd been ready, but weather had intervened. Now the Luftwaffe, with the biggest force of fighters it had ever sent on a single mission, was going to strike Allied fighter bases in Belgium and Holland. The Allied pilots would all be in bed with hangovers . . . they hoped!

There were no German hangovers—Goering had sent down specific instructions that there would be no drinking at all on New Year's Eve. To compensate, the cooks had come up with a decent breakfast, roast beef, some pork cutlets, and a pudding. Yet the meal at the base at Hespe had been dreary: too many empty chairs. Josten had been with *Kampfgeschwader* 51 only a few weeks, and already Langner was almost the only one remaining of those he started with. The bomber group was another of the Luftwaffe's last-ditch improvisations—using bomber pilots to fly the Messerschmitt Me 262. It was laughable. They thought a steep turn was thirty degrees of bank, a steep dive, eight degrees! The Turbo intimidated them, and many more had died trying to learn to fly it than had been killed in combat. Langner was an exception, quick off the mark and a good pilot.

The departure had been spectacular—twenty-one Turbos ready, lined up to take off across the wide snow-covered field in flights of three. Newsreel cameras, absent for so long, had been there. The radar screens had been carefully checked to see that no RAF intruders were about, then a vast battery of searchlights were turned on behind the waiting Turbos so the camera crews could record the takeoff. Josten had noted how cameras had been placed at different angles—when the German audiences saw the film, they'd think there were five hundred jets taking off! He didn't mind propaganda anymore—it was all that was left to give the people.

Banking slowly back and forth, maintaining his distance behind the formations of 109s and 190s ahead of him, he savored the crisp morning. When the timing was right, he'd accelerate, and they'd all arrive over the targets at the same time. Their goal was to destroy one thousand Allied fighters on airfields in France, Belgium, and Holland in a single precision strike. It was to be a low-level attack, guns only, one pass and out for the jets, as many passes as the piston-engine pilots had stomach for. It all depended upon the intensity of the airfield flak—maybe the gunners would have hangovers, too.

Josten ran his gloved hand lovingly around the canopy railing and across the instrument panel, taking a sensual pleasure from the smoothness, the lack of vibration. What a magnificent machine! The more he flew it the more he knew what it was capable of, the more he grieved that he had not been able to bring it into production earlier. He divided his time now strictly between combat sorties and working at Augsburg on modifications. He was well aware that there was no military point in it—the German grape had been squeezed until only the skin was left. But the Turbo was so superbly responsive that it had become the means and the end itself, his only purpose. He would live for the Turbo—and die in it. It was as simple as that, for everything else worth living was denied him.

First Ulrich, and now Lyra. She was gone, God knew where. Hafner had called to tell him that Harzewalde had to be evacuated, and that he would make sure Lyra was all right. Then he called a few days later and said that she had simply vanished without a trace.

Too bad. It was a pity that she wouldn't survive the war. But Ulrich would, and maybe he'd have a full life, too, without either one of them. Perhaps it was for the best that Ulrich would be brought up by a Swedish family. It had to be better than being in Germany when the Russians arrived.

It was curious—logically he knew how he should have felt, and what he should have done. He should have been outraged, horrified. He should have flown an airplane to Stockholm, deserting if he had to, and found Ulrich. He should have flown to Berlin, searched for Lyra. He should be furious, concerned, devastated. But he felt nothing. It was too late to feel anything. Now he just had his job to do, caring for the Turbo.

The instruments flickered—one engine seemed to be losing revolutions. He checked the throttles and sighed in relief. One had crept back slightly. He adjusted the power and checked the instruments again. It was all right, the engines were running perfectly. He patted the instrument panel approvingly.

A wall of flak erupted ahead, the dotted lines of white and red antiaircraft fire curving up to grab the fighters out of the air. He saw half a dozen explosions, quick black, red, and white splotches against the dark horizon. Christ, no one had alerted the German flak outfits! No wonder they were firing—they'd never seen this many Luftwaffe planes in the air at once. Too bad.

They flashed past the German flak emplacements, edging down to hug the ground even closer. Josten's target was at the fighter field at Eindhoven in Holland, filled with fat juicy Typhoons and Spitfires. A 262 on reconnaissance, equipped with the big Rb 50/30 aerial cameras, had brought back pictures of them lined up like a holiday parade.

His thoughts, as always, swung like a pendulum between his absorption with the Turbo and the pain of losing Lyra. It would be wonderful if she had somehow made it back to Stockholm. She had contacts—perhaps they arranged for it without Hafner knowing. Perhaps she was with Ulrich right now, warm and safe.

It was time. He wiped the thoughts of Lyra away with pressure on the throttles. Twenty 262s followed him, catching up with the mass of German fighters just as they hit the field boundaries. It was a picture-perfect attack on an airfield insolent with Allied riches. There were fuel trucks everywhere, and row after row of parked aircraft, not just fighters as reported, but some medium bombers as well, a B-25, a B-26, and, lined up on parade, a row of transport planes. What a picnic!

He aimed carefully. The 30-mm cannons of the Turbo were slow firing, but the punch they packed did the job. He flashed down the ramp areas, shooting quickly and economically. Smashing the Spitfires gave him a savage pleasure—they'd been such a damnable threat for so long and their pilots were so arrogant. He was over the Spits in a flash, firing at the rows of Typhoons without the same vindictive glee. The Typhoons were tank-busters, easy meat for a Turbo in air combat. They burned beautifully, in the air or on the ground.

The flak troops were asleep at their post during the first half of his run; by the airfield boundary they'd begun to open up. It was all over in seconds. What was it the English were supposed to say—"a piece of cake"?

He was out of ammunition. The others in his flight of jets should be, too, if they'd followed instructions. There wasn't going to be a second pass, the Turbos were too valuable to risk, but he pulled up tight to check the damage—there were fires everywhere, probably fifty aircraft destroyed. If every other unit did as well, it would be the Great Blow, after all.

Josten climbed, then took his formation in a huge circle at nine thousand meters, checking back to see how the piston-engine fighters were doing. He saw them in great gaggles, no formation at all, just herds of planes hurtling back toward German lines. Once again a wall of flak erupted, this time Allied, and he could see planes dropping down, burning, cherry blossom comets in the sky.

Jesus Christ! The escape route led right through the flak alley set up for the V-1s! What terrible planning—to waste those beautiful aircraft like that. It was criminal!

Well, too bad. At least they weren't Turbos. It looked as though they had not lost any jets at all. Langner was still with him on his left. He tried to picture Langner's face and could not. It bothered him—they'd played a game of chess only an hour before the takeoff. He forced himself to concentrate, staring out the windscreen, trying to conjure up his face. No, he couldn't. It was the long training, the repression of feelings, the unwillingness to get involved at any human level.

Back at Hespe, he carefully checked over his own Turbo and saw to it that the other pilots inspected theirs. It was easy to pick up damage on a low-level attack—and the overworked ground crews might not notice it. The Turbo was like a thoroughbred racehorse: it had to be coddled.

A triumphant Goering declared a standdown for the rest of the day, and there was lots of drinking and eating. Langner, jubilant, came over to congratulate him.

Josten stared at him.

"You know, I tried to picture your face when we were coming back, and I couldn't do it."

"No wonder. My face is nothing. Wasn't this a great day? As a pioneer with the Turbos, you must have enjoyed it." He cursed himself as soon as the words were out of his mouth—this would get Josten started!

"They can write the epitaph of the Turbo with just three words, 'Engines and Stupidity.' " Christ, Langner thought, he's launched, and I'm pinned in this chair!

As he went on Langner slid down in the chair, appalled that he had triggered a story he'd heard a hundred times before—the turbine blades, Josten's lonely attack at Ploesti, the raid on Regensburg-Pruefening, Hitler's idiocy. Well, *he* was the idiot—he should never have said the word "Turbo" to Josten. It was a standard *Kg* 51 joke—never mention the Turbo to Josten.

"And then, when they started producing engines in June of 1944, we didn't have the training we needed, we . . ."

Josten droned on, eyes glittering, no longer seeing Langner, talking about all the near triumphs and the great defeats, repeating himself, telling what the situation might have been, then launching into what still needed to be done.

At some point Josten looked at the chair and shook his head. Langner was gone. In the old days a *Leutnant* would never have left while an *Oberst* was talking.

That night they were able to begin to analyze the results. The pilots were claiming eight hundred Allied planes had been destroyed or damaged. Reconnaissance photos showed that less than four hundred were definitely destroyed. Not bad for youngsters. The Luftwaffe losses were known precisely—227, more than half of them by their own flak! Criminal!

Josten went back to his quarters, anxious to be alone. One fact was obvious. The Allies would make up their losses in a week—the Luftwaffe never could.

13

Dayton, Ohio/February 14, 1945

Patty Bandfield heard his footsteps and switched off the bedside radio. "When a Girl Marries" was a private vice, one of the few things she refused to share with the wild ball of energy now pounding up the stairs. He moved as always, a whirlwind bounding off walls, lunging ahead full speed as if someone might be passing him on the way to the top of the stairs. The war had not changed him much physically. Recently, though, he had become a totally different man psychologically, far more introspective. As much as she'd loved him before, she loved him more now—and liked him even better.

"Aha, caught you! Listening to your soap opera again! What am I going to do with you?"

Embarrassed, she said, "Don't you have something better to do than spy on me?"

He swiftly slipped his arms around her, conscious that she'd put on a few pounds, not caring. He kissed her forehead.

"Yeah, lots better. How about slipping into something more comfortable, and I'll slip into you."

"Bandy, you'll never grow up. At least I hope not. But Charlotte's due back from her piano lesson any minute, and Hadley's taken to coming home at odd hours."

"So I'm stuck with the secret bumps in the night, if I'm lucky?"

"If you're lucky. Anyway, you're not serious. I can tell when you're really feeling sexy—now you're just playing the old hotshot pilot role." She pursed her lips and said, "You've either found a used car you want to buy, or Caldwell's setting you up to send you off again."

He shrugged and smiled warily.

"Don't you ever get tired of him running you around?"

He turned serious: "I didn't even think about it until I came back from Guadalcanal. And it didn't really bother me until Jim Lee got promoted to colonel. I finally figured out that I was getting lots of good jobs—and other guys were getting promoted. Bouncing around from one outfit to another is interesting, but it doesn't help your career."

"You don't have a career—you just go where Caldwell tells you to go. What's bothering you?"

He sat down on the edge of the bed. "I might as well tell you. I got a call from that Chaudet guy who interviewed me out in Burbank. Remember, he's with the Truman Committee?"

"Vaguely. What did he want?"

"Well, he's working with the Justice Department now. He went out on a limb for me—told me that they are looking at my role in the McNaughton mess."

She was silent and he went on. "From where I'm sitting, it looks like Lee and Caldwell might both go to jail."

"What are they after you for? You had nothing to do with it."

"No, but I didn't volunteer anything either. Chaudet said that there was some talk about 'obstruction of justice.' Can you imagine that? That's why I'm glad Caldwell's sending me out of the country—they'll stay off my back until I get back, I hope, and by then who knows what will happen."

So this was the cause of the changes in him. Once he'd been eager to go into combat, as if he had a compulsion to put himself in harm's way. He'd been outspoken, impatient, always charging. Now, torn by conflicting ideals, he was often depressed and certainly far more reflective than he'd ever been. She had thought—hoped—that it was just maturity, having to do with what he'd seen and done in the war. It wasn't—it was this Caldwell mess.

"Well, if they're talking about 'obstruction of justice' by you, that must mean they're preparing a case against Henry."

"Yeah, they sure are. He has an old buddy in the Judge Advocate General's office who risked a court martial to bootleg an abstract for him. They've got a charge sheet a mile long, ranging from conflict of interest to taking bribes to misuse of government aircraft. It looks as if they're trying to build a big case, to prove to Congress that the Army will clean up its own act."

"Is he guilty?"

"Not on the bribery charges—he was set up. But he did use government planes to fly down to Nashville to see Elsie. And I sometimes wonder if there isn't some truth to the conflict of interest—he was mesmerized by Elsie, and he let Troy talk him into things he wouldn't have done otherwise."

Patty threw her arms around his shoulders as he said bitterly, "There's a lot of jealousy out there. Caldwell is the only guy on the procurement side to make three star general, and there are lots of people who'd like to see him humbled. And he's been rough when he needed to be, made a lot of enemies."

"Well, what's he got in store for you this time?"

During the early years of the war, Bandfield had religiously observed the protocols of military security with Patty. But mid-way, in 1943, when the problems with the long-range fighter and the McNaughton jets had become overwhelming, he'd begun confiding in her. He was violating security regulations, but it helped him and the war effort. And Patty was too wise ever to trip up.

"This one should be a lot of fun, and not too dangerous. I'm supposed to organize a team of top-notch pilots, guys who can fly strange new airplanes without any check-out, and then follow our troops as they overrun Germany, snatching up German airplanes, equipment, scientists, data, whatever we can get. It's going to be a race with the British and the Russians. My part's called 'Operation Lusty'—great name, eh?"

She was touched as his face lit up with enthusiasm. He could handle challenges like this—the politics of business or of service life had always baffled him.

"When do you start?"

"I'm going to begin picking out the people right away—first-rate pilots and good mechanics. I've got to get some airplanes— Gooneybirds, mostly—and trucks, machine tools, it's like fitting out a safari. But it'll be fun. We'll get to fly the latest German stuff, especially the jets."

"Great. I bet they'll have them all lined up for you, washed and waxed. They'd never dream of booby-trapping them, would they?"

"Damn, that's why I like to talk to you. I'll have to line up some ordnance people, too. I would have thought of it sometime, but this really helps. You're a doll."

"Okay, how about a favor in return?"

"Sure. Name it."

"Don't sink with Caldwell's ship. You've got to protect yourself and your family." She paused. "You've got to protect me. The way Lee is, you could wind up taking the fall for the whole operation."

"Taking the fall"—her *Casablanca* argot. "Well, here's looking at you, kid. Don't worry about it, I won't. Anything else?"

There was a bellow from below as Hadley Roget blew in.

"Anybody home?"

Patty could see from Frank's expression that he'd been expecting Hadley all along.

"Up here, Hadley."

Roget ran up the stairs with an enthusiasm that belied his years, arms encumbered with a tripod and rolled-up drawings. Patty had never grown used to seeing him with short hair, but noticed that, for the first time since Clarice died, his old familiar grin reached from ear to ear.

Oh God, she thought, they want to produce a new airplane. They'll never learn.

Roget's lobster-claw hands fumbled the tripod into place and he put up a series of drawings. The outside page was blank.

"Give me a drum roll, Bandy."

With a flourish, Hadley threw back the first page. Underneath was a pastoral drawing, lots of green fields, trees, a lake, and in fluffy, cloudlike print, the words ROGET ACRES.

The second page flew back, and there was a little house, square, flat-roofed, painted white with windows spaced equidistantly across its front, the door smack in the center.

"Patty, you know we never had much luck building airplanes—and after the war it's going to be very rough for a while. But what's the two things in shortest supply, that all the GIs will be hungry for?"

"Cars and houses?"

"Right. We don't have the money to build cars—but you're looking at a brand new concept—mass-produced housing. Bandy and I've been talking about it for a long time, and it's something we've got the factory and the work force to do. And the land, too!"

Bandfield broke in, excited. "We'll build these little jewels in sections in our factory at Downey, cart them out the door, and set them up on the perimeter of the airfield. 'Roget Acres' first, then the next one can be 'Bandfield Village.' And we can have Charlotte Street, and George Street . . ."

"My God, you guys—"

"Don't say a word, yet. Look at this plat."

He pulled down the third drawing, and the little cube houses marched across the landscape straight as West Point cadets on parade, the parallel streets divided into block-long squares, row after row.

"And look, here's how we'll build them. The kitchen and the bath will be built back to back—simplifies the plumbing, build one unit and install it. All these will be three-bedroom houses, living room, tiny dining room, and kitchen. I figure we can build them for thirty-five hundred, and sell them for sixty-five hundred, lot and all. We already own all the land we'll need at the airfield and in Salinas. The factory's all paid for and we have a good work force. We'll make us a fortune!"

Patty felt giddy at an idea that was, for once, common sense.

"This is brilliant. I'm really impressed. Can I make some suggestions?"

The men looked at each other—they'd expected her to object.

"Don't make the streets so square. Curve them around, break up the lines so that it doesn't look like a tent city or a military parade ground—the guys coming home will have had enough of that. And let's vary the houses a little bit—you know, flip the drawing so that you get a slightly different look. And you'll need some room for playgrounds and stuff—all these young newlyweds are going to start having families right away. Maybe every three blocks, leave one block as a park area? And—"

"Lemme show you something, Patty, it's a detail drawing of the kitchen."

Roget put up another drawing on the tripod. "Straight out of *Good Housekeeping*."

"Straight out of the twenties! You guys should take a trip back East to see what Kelvinator and General Electric have on the drawing boards, and design the new stuff right in." This was it, she thought, a new career, something she could do without damaging the family. "I could do that. That could be part of my job, flying around the country, checking on the new appliances."

"Patty, I got to tell you—"

"Wait a minute. And the colors. You don't want them all white. It'll be no more expensive to have them half a dozen pastel colors—pinks, blues, light greens—and trees, you need to plant trees."

Bandy was beaming. "By God, Patty, I never thought you'd approve of this. I told Hadley you'd come down on us like a ton of bricks because we were getting out of our field."

"No, you guys can build anything, and houses made out of wood and stucco should be easy, because you won't need skilled labor to throw them up. I'm all for it." Am I! It'll be a new life.

Hadley was indignant. "We're not going to build them out of wood and stucco! That's the whole point. We're going to build them out of aluminum! We'll prefabricate the structural stuff, the beams and rafters, and rivet sheet aluminum on the outside. Low maintenance."

"Whoa, guys, listen to me! This is a million dollar idea, but it's a two-by-four and stucco idea. You start building them out of aluminum and you'll have all sorts of problems with building codes, unions, everything. If you want to build with aluminum, stick on some wheels and sell them for house trailers."

Hadley and Bandfield had been bit by unions in the past and grimaced at the thought.

Patty went on. "You guys are making the same mistake you made with airplanes—you're just fascinated with technology. It never occurs to you that simpler might be better."

"She's got a point, Hadley. Maybe we could make stick-built houses at first, and experiment with aluminum trailers. That could be your special sideline."

Disappointment etched the older man's face—he'd already envisioned a metallic countryside gleaming with Roget Aluminum Houses.

Patty saw it and prodded him. "Just think, Hadley, not 'Roget Acres' at first. Let's call it 'Clarice Acres.' She wouldn't care if the houses were conventional—she'd probably prefer it. You know she never really did like airplanes."

"'Clarice Acres.' You're right. She'd be so proud."

"Hadley, you old dear, she *is* proud. She's looking down right now, and she's pleased as she can be."

The two men bounded out of the room talking excitedly, and Patty lay back and switched on the radio, saying to herself, "Of course, if they send Bandy to Leavenworth, we might have to change our plans."

Berlin/February 23, 1945

February's nerve-bludgeoning cold went on forever, endless gray days filled with wet and chilling winds that made the suffering from malnutrition and thin clothes even worse. Lyra could not remember when she had last been warm or taken a bath. Walking was an agony; she blinked back her tears and bit her chapped lips in pain. Shivering, she glanced over the dirty snow that partly covered the ugly shambles of the Berlin Zoo. Miraculously, some animals still survived, calling piteously from their cages, the few remaining zookeepers moving around listlessly. The predators had been killed as a safety measure after a tiger had escaped. That would be ironic, she thought, to live through the bombing in Berlin and then be eaten by a wild animal!

The ragged group of her fellow prisoners looked like peasants in a Brueghel painting, their figures bent, arms thrust within the folds of their coats, feet stamping the ground for circulation. Few faces could be seen among the swathed heads, shielded in scarves or blankets. A few of them had been acquaintances in that far-off past when there was food and warmth and hope.

It was an unlikely crew of prisoners, even in the twelfth year of the Third Reich. Some were aristocratic members of the diplomatic service who had fallen out with the regime. Others were wives of eminent hostages or family members of the July 20th conspirators. There were even a few confused foreign dignitaries from the satellite countries now occupied by the Russians. Some had been riding trains for weeks, aimlessly going from one collection point to another. For some obscure reason they were considered by their captors to be too distinguished to be put in the usual cattle cars, but too dangerous or valuable to be set free. Others, the most frightened and subdued, were straight out of Gestapo interrogation centers. A few, obviously the most well cared for, had been held under arrest in relative comfort at various country homes around Berlin, as Lyra had been until her "escape."

They had all been brought under armed guard to the Tiergarten Tower, a monolithic concrete flak structure brooding over the bomb-blasted remnants of the Berlin Zoo. Thirty-seven meters high and seventy-one meters on the side, it was the apotheosis of Hitler's concrete architecture, a neo-Romanesque monstrosity. Its huge fortress windows were shuttered with steel, and within its clammy walls were combined barracks, bomb shelters, civil defense headquarters, and, in recent weeks, a hospital. On the roof, batteries of 12.8-cm flak guns were manned by sixteen-year-old boys. A near-twin building stood opposite for the radar fire-control systems.

Built early in the war, the towers had appeared to grow in size over the years as the historic buildings of Berlin were flattened around them by the Allied bombing.

The Tiergarten Tower was their collection point for the trip south to Dachau. Lyra was there by accident. After a long run of luck, she had been picked up on the streets of Berlin and forced to join the prisoners. It had begun weeks ago when Hafner had telephoned her at Harzewalde, saying that he was coming to get her. She had slipped away in one of the vans being used to remove Kersten's furniture and paintings. As difficult as transport was to obtain in Germany, six Opel Blitz army trucks had rolled up to the house, and a crew of foreign laborers systematically removed the most valuable pieces under the direction of an officious young SS non-commissioned officer. He told her that the entire lot was being sent to Kersten's home in Stockholm, adding proudly that the orders had come directly from Heinrich Himmler himself.

Hafner's guards had already fled, and when Lyra insisted on accompanying the household goods for "safekeeping," the SS man had reluctantly agreed. The shipment was supposed to go by truck to Neustrelitz, and then by rail to Stralsund on the Baltic. Her heart had leapt. With luck she hoped that she might be able to bluff her way to Stockholm—and Ulrich—with the furniture.

They had left well before dawn, the jolting truck convoy rarely exceeding twenty kilometers per hour, often stopped by the welter of refugee traffic fleeing the Russian advance. At first light a flight of Russian Sturmoviks fell on them, burning the trucks out in two passes before systematically strafing the columns of refugees. Bruised but not wounded, Lyra had joined the trudging refugees as they made their halting way toward Berlin, riding the last twenty kilometers in the back of an ox cart. She rode next to a sobbing grandmother and carried the baby boy whose mother had been killed. She was glad it was not Ulrich; she never wanted him to be exposed to the war or have to live with these bestial Germans. She'd grown to hate them as a people, not only the monsters at the top but the Helmuts who supported them, especially the supine masses who accepted their lot so stoically. Why didn't they rebel? There was a point where suffering should end, where enduring should cease and anger take over. Furious with all things German, she clutched the baby to her as they lay stuffed like rag dolls among the pathetic baskets of household goods.

In Berlin the baby's grandmother took him back, and Lyra began to wander vainly from one friend's bombed-out apartment to another. Her circle of friends and co-workers had simply vanished, dead or evacuated to the south. It was just as well—they would have been too frightened to shield her, and some might even have turned her in. Once she passed the ruins of Goebbels's apartment. The building was demolished, the entire block gone, submerged in the crumpled ocean of brick and mortar in which Germany swam.

After one RAF air raid she'd wandered the smoking, rubble-choked streets, a moistened scarf wrapped around her face. In an alley she had stumbled over the body of a young woman, holding a baby no older than her own, both dead no more than a few hours. Lyra said a silent prayer, then searched the woman's tattered purse. She removed a few marks, the identity papers, and the ration coupons. Ordinarily they might not have helped—you had to deal with a single store, and she would have been recognized as an imposter—but the bombing was so extensive now that ration coupons had become currency. The woman's picture didn't look like Lyra, but like the other bombed-out refugees, she'd become so bedraggled that the differences were obscured. She had been able to get past the checkpoints and the *Feldgendarmerie*, press gangs searching the streets for deserters. They were looking for men to man the shattered regiments on the crumbling Eastern front, but they abused their power freely, checking everyone's papers, including shawled old grandmothers and even obviously wounded veterans, their legs or arms gone, shattered victims hobbling along the shattered pavements.

Lyra hated each interrogation, each threat to her liberty. The military police worked in pairs, strutting as if they were winning the war by intimidating civilians. She slept where she could, in bomb shelters or on the streetcars that were always filled with foreign workers.

She could not even recognize where she was most of the time; Berlin was a nightmare, more a lunar landscape than a city. Mile after mile of gutted buildings stood groaning in the wind, outer walls weaving wearily, interiors collapsed and burned out, a chalky haze hanging like broken souls in the ghostly squares that had once been rooms. Grimy survivors huddled in the wreckage, tunneling into basements, content with a hole in the ground and a plank for a roof as long as the bombers were not overhead. Besides the throngs of desperate foreign workers, the pitifully few men about were elderly or war wounded. The fatigue and pain were egalitarian—the men were all unshaven and dirty, the women wrapped in layers of filthy clothing, often all they owned. Most clutched bags or bundles. With glazed and listless eyes they sat before open fires fueled by the inexhaustible debris of the broken buildings. The lucky ones cooked in fire-blackened pots hanging from makeshift tripods. There was little charity—Lyra lived by bargaining away her ration coupons for short rations from the boiling pots. Infrequently, usually im- mediately after a raid, a sense of solidarity prevailed, and she might be welcomed to share a bowl of soup.

As her strength declined, her hatred grew until she felt it could sustain her without any food or any shelter. It was an illusion. When the blustering militiaman checked her papers closely, then arrested her, she felt an almost perverse gratitude, a desire to put an end to her suffering. By sheer chance, he had turned her over to the police guarding this strangely compatible group, people she might have been arrested with anyway.

She had not been with them long when the old hatred surged back like a tonic, this time for her new companions. She despised them for awaiting their fate like cows. It was a sickness in Germany. People who had been privileged, who should have known better, had tolerated the regime as long as they were unmolested. Now that the Russians were on the Oder River they were protesting the loss of their lands. It was sickening to listen to, and worse to realize that she was nominally "one of their class" and accepted as such.

They were all desperately frightened and fatigued, but invigorated by her anger Lyra moved among them, talking to the few that she knew, checking to see if anyone had enough spirit to fight, to rebel.

Her first success was with a former acquaintance, Countess Ilsa von Heeren—her husband had been ambassador to Bulgaria until 1942. An ardent monarchist, one of the few who were openly contemptuous of the Nazis, the Ambassador had been recalled after some outspoken remarks at an Embassy party. After the Gestapo had interrogated him, von Ribbentrop had intervened on his behalf. He had retained the title of Ambassador and with the Countess was allowed to live a fairly comfortable life in Berlin—but under close surveillance. Even though he'd had no role in the Stauffenberg bomb plot, the Gestapo had used it as an excuse to swoop down and arrest him and the Countess.

Lyra had met the woman at several social gatherings before the war. Countess von Heeren was typical of the German nobility, tall and slender, with an unfailingly icy politeness. Now her figure was stooped, and hunger had etched the flesh away from her bones. When Lyra spoke to her, she seemed totally enervated.

"You know that when we get to Dachau, it's the end."

"I'm afraid so. After all this journeying, too. We've been on the rails all the way from the Brenner Pass to the Baltic, and back again." In her weariness, Countess von Heeren spoke as if the endless ordeal on the trains had been one of those little unavoidable disappointments, like rain on a picnic.

"Where is the Ambassador?"

"Executed. At least I think so. I'm not certain. Nothing is certain anymore."

"Yes, it is! Death at Dachau is absolutely certain. We've got to fight and get out of this shipment. This war can't last forever. If we can survive even a few months, we can make it."

The older woman's voice was lifeless, her dejection total. "I'm really very tired, Lyra. How could I fight?"

"You had three children, did you not? I remember two bright young men and a beautiful girl."

"Of course, the only joy in my life is that they are safe in Spain."

"Well, then, you must fight to live for them."

Color stirred in the woman's cheeks. "You think we might have a chance?"

"Not here. There are too many guns trained on us. No wonder they can't keep the Russians out, half of the German troops are guarding their own people! And we certainly won't be able to do anything if we wait until we reach Dachau. But on the train, perhaps. How were you guarded in the past?"

"Two guards per carriage, one at each end."

"If all of us cannot overcome two guards, we deserve to die. The trip won't be nonstop—there are sure to be air raids. We could kill the guards and make a break for it at the first stop afterward. Who else can we count on?"

Countess von Heeren appeared stricken at the thought of violence.

"How would we kill them? We don't have even a spoon to fight with."

"There's sure to be fifty or sixty of us in the car, perhaps more. We'll kill them with our bare hands if we have to. But let me try another way first."

After hours of waiting they'd been walked to the station to be loaded into a wreck of a third-class car. The windows had long since been blown out, replaced by rough wire netting and pieces of asphalted cardboard that deflected some of the wind. A dim lamp burned at the center and at each end of the car. More than ninety people were jammed inside. Lyra had been able to recruit six of them, three men and three women, who had agreed to escape or die trying. She'd volunteered to get a weapon from one of the guards.

The train moved out slowly in a fitful series of stop-and-gos, grumbling along the bomb-battered railway. It was shunted aside for every passing troop train and stopped repeatedly to avoid the Allied *Jabos*, the fighter bombers. After six hours they were just past Berlin's outskirts.

Lyra edged toward the rear of the carriage. With her fingertips she washed her face with saliva, trying somehow to smooth away the grime, wondering how cats managed the process. She pulled off her scarf and patted her hair into place. Positioning herself near the guard, she waited to catch his eye. He was one of the new *Volksturm* recruits, a stupid *Oldenburger* by the sound of his cackling voice, at least sixty, his once rugged shoulders bent and his pock-marked face a canvas of years of want and deprivation. He sat on an upended trunk, eating greedily, taunting the prisoners, clearly enjoying life. Whatever he had been—a street sweeper, a farm laborer—now he was an armed official of the state, guarding people to whom he would have doffed his cap in civilian life.

The guard placed his rifle to the side and slid his pistol around so that he could sit more comfortably on the battered trunk near the end of the aisle. Holding a dark brown Army loaf in the crook of his arm, he sawed a thick slice off with a serrated butcher's knife. Balancing the bread on his knee, he pulled out a fat sausage—it was obviously real meat and not one of the synthetic vegetable rolls—and cut off a chunk. Smiling, he alternated bites, bread and sausage, bread and sausage, chewing slowly. He swallowed noisily, smacking his lips. Taking a canteen from the clip on his belt, he shook and sniffed it to let them know it was not just water, then drank deeply.

The prisoners had not been fed for two days and, as genteel as they might once have been, those nearby followed his motions like so many Oliver Twists, each person salivating, stomach growling, jaws moving involuntarily.

When the guard looked around, munching, Lyra sent him a broad smile. His glance passed her by, then switched swiftly back. Years of repression stifling him, he put his head down and cut another piece of sausage. As he cut he raised his eyes again to her, then looked away quickly.

Take your time, she thought. Don't frighten him. She forced herself to relax, knowing that she must not fail. This was their only chance. She hoped he wasn't too old or too frightened to be interested.

The air within the car was foul with the odors of ninety dirty bodies, but she forced herself to breathe deeply, summoning her strength and resolve. She edged directly in front of him. He looked at her, flushed, then cut a slice of sausage and passed it under her nose before biting into it.

Lyra ran her tongue over her lips. He glanced around nervously, then lowered his hands so that they were pressed to his stomach. Oblivious to the crowd of people watching, he made a circle of his finger and thumb, and thrust a grime-blackened finger into it in the age-old symbol. She nodded and he stood up, busily putting the sausage and bread into his pack and fastening the canteen to his belt. Wiping the knife on his trousers before thrusting it into a loose scabbard at his side, he shoved his way to the very end of the carriage where a crude storage closet had been fashioned out of boards salvaged from burned-out buildings. As he moved the crowd separated, allowing first him, then her, to pass. From those who were unaware of Lyra's plan there came a disapproving mumble— she was obviously going to do what "wasn't done," and for a slice of sausage!

There was just room inside the closet for the two of them to stand. He pressed himself on her, greasy lips slobbering on her face, his carrion breath foul. He pawed at her breasts through her clothing, then reached down to grope beneath her skirt. She pretended to respond, placing her right hand around his waist and pulling him to her, nuzzling her face in his neck to avoid his mouth as she slipped her left hand to his groin. Moaning, he began undoing his belt. As he did the scabbard holding his knife became free.

Lyra, her heart pounding, reached inside his baggy trousers and began manipulating his penis. There was a quick response. As his breath came faster, she squeezed against him and with her right hand slipped the knife from its scabbard. He squirmed to kiss her again, full on the mouth. She cringed, revulsion at the filth against her face and thrusting in her hand raising bile in her throat.

This is Germany I'm killing. This is all Germans, all Nazis, this evil. The thought gave her strength. Still manipulating him swiftly with her left hand, she slowly brought the knife down. His back moving convulsively, he pressed against her, oblivious to the jolting train or her shift of position. Summoning all of her courage, she brought her hand up in a single swift motion, driving the long blade up under his rib cage directly into his heart, thrusting with all her strength just as he ejaculated. His eyes rolled back and he sagged against her, spurting blood against her chest, semen on her hand.

Quivering with disgust, she let him fall back. Then, deliberately, she washed her left hand in the blood streaming from his wound before wiping it on his shabby uniform.

He was slumped against the wall like a half-empty sack of wheat, his trunk folded forward. Lyra removed his belt and put it around her. Attached to it was the scabbard, the canteen, and an automatic pistol. She searched his pockets, stuffing the bread and sausage inside her blouse, taking the few marks he had kept in a draw-string bag. She discarded his passbook—she didn't want to know his name or think of him as an ordinary human being. He was Germany, and she had killed him. That was enough.

When she emerged, Lyra put her finger to her lips and began to move through the crowd to the other end of the car, the pistol in her right hand, the knife, dripping blood, in the left. It felt as if she had stopped breathing, as if every drop of blood in her body was pounding in her head. Wide-eyed, the others followed her, their mouths dropping open, the babble of their conversation falling with her passage, then rising as she went on. I must look like Lady Macbeth, she thought. She moved effortlessly, everyone now aware of what had happened, quickly stepping aside as she approached, then closing ranks again behind her.

The other guard, a younger man with a deformed leg in a brace, was dozing with his back against the wall, his rifle held between his knees.

Lyra watched him for a moment, feeling a trace of pity for this last scraping from the bottom of Germany's manpower barrel. He was probably a poor farmer pulled from some little village to do a job for which he wasn't fit. She shook off the feeling and shifted the still dripping knife into her right hand. Countess von Heeren stood directly between her and the guard. Lyra nudged her with the pistol and she stepped aside.

It was easier to do the second time. Lyra moved forward, stabbing through the guard's throat with such force that the blade stuck in the wooden wall behind him. He jerked upward, pulling the knife from the wall. She twisted it, dragging him face forward to the floor. There was a single agonized groan of pain as, voiding, he collapsed into a heap, gurgling, legs drumming, a gush of blood spewing from his neck.

The wail of protest from the group surprised her.

An officious middle-aged man, his clothes slack on his once sleek body, yelled, "Look here, young woman, you are going to get us killed!"

Lyra shrugged him off, and as she stripped the guard of his keys and weapons, spoke to her six allies.

"Open the locks now—we may have to jump from a moving train. But if we stop, let's leap out with our guns, ready to shoot. Everybody else will jump out and run. Be sure to scatter—don't bunch up."

The officious man protested, "Don't tell me what to do. I'm not going to cause any trouble."

Lyra looked at him, unable to believe his bovine protest. "Do what you wish. But some of us are going to try to live through this war."

Only twenty minutes had passed when they heard the shrill scream of brakes being applied as the train shuddered to a halt. Before it had stopped the doors were open and the prisoners were streaming out into a driving snowstorm. Lyra stood in the center of the car, alternately urging and shoving as the people leapt out.

There were some shouts and a spatter of rifle fire from guards in the other cars. Then four American fighter planes burst through the low clouds, silver shadows against the gray, red dots winking from their wings. Streams of bullets kicked up lines in the snow before blasting splinters from the wooden cars. Ahead an enormous column of steam roared to merge with the clouds, as the engine blew up. The fighter planes pulled around in a tight treetop-height turn for another run at the train.

Lyra ran through the storm of machine-gun fire, oblivious to the screams around her, plunging forward into the forest, away from the train, away from Dachau.

She blundered straight ahead for almost half an hour, hurtling through the brush, leaping over bushes, branches whipping her face, keeping the pistol in her grasp as she somehow summoned the energy to press on, to fight the overwhelming exhaustion that pulled at her limbs and her lungs. She slipped as she raced down the side of a stream, twisting her knee, and pain swept through her. Bruised and shaken, she was up again, bounding on as if there were no end to her energy, as if she could run forever. A wall of rocks loomed ahead and she turned abruptly to her right to pitch forward down a steep slope, rolling and tumbling. She arose slowly, light-headed and weak. Gasping for breath, she stumbled toward the sanctuary of a huge spruce tree, its lower branches immersed in the snow. Scared and bleeding, she dove like a fox into its burrow, digging under the outstretched branches to the dark shelter of the tree.

Heart thudding, she let her breath subside as she pondered her chances. It was growing dark and it was snowing even more heavily now. Unless they had dogs, it would be difficult to find her. Many people had run away—there would be lots of trails. Most of them were infirm, weaker than she—they'd be found first. And the guards wouldn't be looking for her specifically, not unless some of the fainter hearts tried to shift the blame to her.

If she could stay alive in the forest for a day or two, then find a village, she might be able to hide out until the end of the war. In the meantime, she was free.

Her entire body was stinging from the brambles she had burst through, and her knee was swelling. It pained her even to reach out to gather handfuls of snow. Alternately licking it for moisture and pressing it against her face, she drew comfort from it. When her thirst was somewhat slaked she took a sip from the canteen. It was a raw red wine, rough and sour—and absolutely the most delicious drink she'd ever had.

The spruce tree hung over her like a brooding tent, insulating her from the outside world. She burrowed down gratefully into the many years' accumulation of needles, nesting in their thick bed, lying perfectly still to preserve body heat, trying to ignore the myriad signals of pain being sent from torn muscles and scratched flesh.

She went through the last hour in her mind. Now she understood Helmut's fascination with combat. She had killed and killed with pleasure. If she had to, she would kill again.

Lyra fell into an exhausted sleep; she awoke aching in every muscle but sensed that her strength was returning. Lyra drove the still bloody knife into the bed of pine needles again and again, scouring it until it felt smooth and smelled clean. Then she cut a slice of the sausage off, chewing slowly to let the rich fat pour energy into her. As she chewed she thought, I will survive. No matter what happens, I will survive. I will go to Ulrich, and we will be happy.

En route to Tokyo/March 10, 1945

Colonel James Lee directed the red-lensed instrument light at his wristwatch. It was exactly twelve midnight. A little over an hour to go. The long flights over water in the B-29 were tedious but worrisome. The airplane was a dangerously flawed masterpiece, marred by immature systems brought together too fast and too soon. He ran a constant eye over the engine instruments, watching for any telltale creep-up in temperature or drop in pressure. The flight engineer, Vito Apollonio, was a good man, but with the B-29 you always had to be careful. It was a long way back to the Marianas, a very long way on three engines, and an impossible distance on two. Iwo Jima was available now as an emergency strip, but it wasn't a pleasant alternative.

"Nav, how are we doing?"

"We're right on the button, on time and on course . . . Colonel."

"Colonel," with that period of hesitation, the insufferable skip that said, "I'm being courteous to the rank, not to you." On previous missions the navigator had always used the friendlier "Skipper." It confirmed what he had already sensed—his own crew was freezing up on him, distancing themselves. The rumor mill was running— LeMay was supposed to be ready to fire him. They'd already pulled his squadron from him, booting him up to a make-believe job of "Deputy for Radar Photos."

Lee could still laugh at himself. It was all being done for the wrong reasons. He had been an advocate of low-level bombing for months, taking his ideas to whoever would listen, even though it made him persona non grata with the previous XXI Bomber Command leader, Brigadier General Possum Hansell.

Lee never had a chance to discuss the matter with the new commander, Major General Curtis LeMay, whose gruff style and no-nonsense manner made him virtually unapproachable. LeMay had decided to risk everything on low-level bombing—and he'd arrived at the idea independently. No doubt some "helpful" assistant on LeMay's staff had hinted that Lee felt himself to be the author of the new strategy.

With characteristic bluntness, LeMay had called him in and chewed him out, leaving no doubt in Lee's mind or anyone else's who was responsible for the new technique. He hadn't asked Lee for an explanation—he simply told him explicitly what the situation was.

The darkness hovered in the cavernous cockpit of the B-29 *Virgin Effort*, both a blessing and a curse. It concealed them from the enemy, but reemphasized that each plane was an island, a self-contained entity, isolated in a bomber stream headed for enemy skies. Lee glanced at his copilot, Captain Mauru Nunes, a lawyer in civilian life, cupping his hand over his flashlight as he busied himself over the flight manual, committing the emergency procedures to memory. How nice it would be to be like that, to have only this mission on his mind.

The broad band of instruments on the panels in front of them danced in the phosphorescent reflections of the ultra-violet lamps. Lee sensed a telltale buzzing, a minor disharmony in the propeller synchronization, and he dropped his hand to the controls to adjust them.

They were flying at only three thousand feet, taking advantage of a sixty-knot wind following them from 150 degrees. If they'd had to climb to the old bombing altitudes the winds would have been one hundred knots faster and even more directly a tail wind—great for ground speed but ruinous to accurate bombing. Worse, the tail wind became a head wind on the way home, disastrous if you were damaged or short on fuel.

Unseen ahead of them, eighty-knot winds were racing across the Kanto Plain, knocking down radar antennae and disrupting surface communications. The Japanese picket ships that plotted each passing of the widely spaced B-29 fleet sent back message after message to the waiting Navy shore receivers. But because the Army was responsible for the air defense of Japan, the Navy didn't pass on the news of the coming danger to them.

Virgin Effort droned forward on autopilot, the crew silent at their stations. Lee saw the irony in his situation. He had been dead wrong to line up with McNaughton against Caldwell—but he hadn't been called on that yet. Instead he was in disrepute for something he hadn't done. Although his crew's bombing record was the best in the 73d, they hadn't been selected to be among the pathfinders, to be first over the target and to lay down the strings of napalm-filled incendiaries that would light up a yellow cross in the heart of Tokyo. Instead they were far back in the bomb stream, the fifty-fifth plane to take off on the late afternoon of March 9th. From the Marianas airfields on Guam, Saipan, and Tinian, so dearly bought from the Japanese, the greatest force of B-29s ever launched had grumbled off the ground. Three hundred thirty-four of the very heavy bombers formed a three-hour stream of imminent fiery death pointed at Tokyo. Many had already turned back, most with problems in their temperamental Wright Cyclone R-3350 engines.

He leaned forward and reset his directional gyro. Well, the hell with it. He knew better than anyone that LeMay arrived at his own ideas independently and had never said otherwise. But his swift rise to the rank of colonel had made more than one man jealous. The back-biting was probably just jealousy. If the business with McNaughton would only blow over, he could afford to wait out the war. He'd seen enough combat—they could send him back to the States to be an instructor pilot if they wanted.

There was simply no way to get next to LeMay. The man was a machine. Short, stocky, with a pugnacious jaw that began to bristle with a coarse black beard by mid-afternoon, he was first of all terrifyingly demanding. He had taken command on January 20th. The first few raids he ran were conventional, repetitions of those of the past even as to the results: few bombs on target. Then weather had almost shut the effort down in February. Visual bombing was impossible, and the B-29s' radar sets were incapable of precision bombing on anything but a coastal target.

LeMay found himself in charge of the second biggest armament program of the war—only the supersecret Manhattan Project was more expensive—and it wasn't working. He decided on radical changes, exactly like those Lee had advocated. Against the advice of his staff people—and with only conditional support from above—LeMay ordered the B-29s to go in low, loaded with incendiaries. Precision bombing was out, area bombing was in; he was going to finesse the shortcomings of the bomber with new tactics.

There had been some squawks—some alarmists on the staff feared the Japanese flak and fighters and had actually used the word "murder." But LeMay thought otherwise and Lee agreed with him. The Japanese had virtually no radar-controlled low and middle altitude flak and their night fighter defenses were spotty.

"Apollonio, how's our fuel consumption?"

"We're right on the curve, Skipper. Looking good."

Ah, a loyalist. I'll remember that, Lee thought. Sergeant Apollonio was a tall, skinny blond kid who told rotten jokes as he babied the engines along, nurturing them like a mother hen. Tonight all four were running smoothly, as if they enjoyed the flight at low altitude. So far the USAAF had lost more B-29s to engine failures than to enemy action.

Knowing that the navigator would have tuned in the Jap English-language propaganda station, Lee reached down to his radio junction box and switched to ADF, the Automatic Direction Finder. Incredibly, the Japanese were playing a record of "Smoke Gets in Your Eyes"—he couldn't believe what he was hearing.

"Crew, this is the Skipper. You won't believe this, but switch over to ADF for a minute."

There was raucous laughter on the interphone as he said, "Talk about an omen!"

"Colonel, you got that right."

"Colonel . . ." The pang of pain was foolish. Well, fuck them.

He was still running the airplane. After the war they'd go back to their little jobs—and he'd be at McNaughton, making big money.

They made landfall at the tip of the Chiba Peninsula, and Lee called for climb power as they began the gradual ascent to seven thousand feet, their assigned bombing altitude. They were turning toward their Initial Point, just north of Goi, when a long oblong of yellow flame burst through the black emptiness ahead of them, as if a flaming samurai sword had slashed through Tokyo's belly. It was the first pass of the pathfinder force. As Lee watched, the crosspiece came in, another swath of yellow as the napalm-filled incendiary bombs etched their terrible mark on the heart of the city. He should have been there, dropping the first bombs.

Searchlights suddenly shredded the darkness, reaching high in the sky, frantically searching for them at thirty thousand feet. Flak bursts began to explode well above them in a cascade of white, yellow, and red bursts that streamed away to be absorbed in the light scattering of clouds. Visibility was good, ten miles or better. He felt the familiar palpable rise in tension within the aircraft as everyone became alert, busy about their jobs, no longer joking on the interphone.

Lee concentrated on flying the B-29, listening with pleasure to the competent professional comments of the crew. They were going to drop five-hundred-pound clusters of M-69 incendiary bombs, nasty little six-pound devices that scattered as they dropped. When they hit they spewed a liquid jelly that stuck to any surface and burned like phosphorus for ten minutes. Each bomb created a puddle of fire a yard across, and Tokyo was about to receive an overwhelming flood of fire puddles.

He could see the fires breaking out everywhere, interlocked discs of oscillating flame, undulating together, the shock waves—visible in the pall of smoke—merging kaleidoscopically in overlapping circles that rippled through the transparent layer of low clouds, a quivering patchwork quilt of merging explosions.

Lee's target area was already well alight—there was no point in dropping incendiary bombs into an inferno.

"Bombardier. Don't drop as briefed. Shift the drop zone to the black area to the right."

"That's near the Imperial Palace." The Palace and its gardens
were off limits.

"Damnit, shift the target." Lee knew it was not the Imperial
Palace that bothered the bombardier—it was the old *Appointment
in Samarra* idea, that it was challenging fate to shift from a designated target to another.

An explosion lit up the sky to their left. The flak had finally felt its
way down to the correct altitude. In the center of the red splotch a
B-29 and its crew of ten had been killed. The bombardier came back
on: "I've got the middle of the black area centered. I think we'll be
far enough away from the Imperial Palace."

"Roger."

The wheel jerked in his hands violently.

"Thermals from the fire. I'll hold her as steady as I can . . ."

Lee's words were drowned out in the blast of the flak explosion
that tore into the left wing root and the fuselage of *Virgin Effort*,
tearing a gaping hole in the fuselage and ripping open the wing. The
violent explosive decompression in the forward pressure cabin
sucked charts, checklists, and dirt out of the airplane before a rush
of smoke filled the cockpit.

"Everybody go to one hundred percent oxygen."

"We're hit bad, Skipper. The whole left wing is burning."

"Skipper" now, huh, now that you need me?

Apollonio's voice was calm. "We've lost number two, and the
number one propeller is surging."

"Feather number two, keep number one in limits by tapping the
feather switch."

"Feathering two."

Lee felt the old incisive thrill of combat and command. "How
long until bombs away?"

"Three minutes. But shit, drop them here, let's get out of here,
make for the coast."

"Negative! You drop on time!"

Lee had the right rudder jammed all the way, cranking in trim to
keep the airplane on course. *Virgin Effort* was staggering, flames
roaring out of the fuel tanks in the left wing.

"Damnit, let's bail out, Skipper. This thing is going to blow."

"Get ready. Let's get the bombs off and make for the coast, see what we can do."

Just as the six thousand pounds of bombs left, the stricken B-29 flew into a towering thermal from the fires raging below. *Virgin Effort* bounced crazily upward into an intersecting beam of searchlights whose glare turned the smoke-filled cabin incandescent. Lee racked the airplane to the left, desperate to escape the clutching searchlights, but they followed him tenaciously. He leaned forward, low, sheltering his eyes with one hand, concentrating on the flight instruments, desperately trying to escape from the lights. His head was down when the fuel tanks exploded, blowing the left wing off at the root and sending the *Virgin Effort* into a vicious flaming spin trapping everyone inside. At three thousand feet the empennage broke away, carrying the tail gunner into the black void of night to a lonely death. The rest of the B-29 plunged down erratically, striking the earth on its right wing, then cartwheeling through the flimsy homes of workers at the Nakajima plant. High octane gas spewed from ruptured tanks like a Fourth of July pinwheel, adding fuel to the already leaping flames. The gale force wind from the Kanto plain crossed the city, stoking the fires and spreading them over the fire breaks, jumping canals, turning the wood-and-paper houses into instant torches. In the middle of the flames, the shattered remains of *Virgin Effort* and its crew were totally consumed, resting on the ruins of a house where an entire family—mother, grandfather, and two children—perished. It was one house out of 272,000 houses that burned that night; they were four out of 83,000 who would die. Thirteen other B-29s were lost.

Nashville, Tennessee/March 18, 1945

She was standing at the head of the stairs in a tattered white robe, her hair down, her face puffed and swollen, raging at the top of her voice, "You did it, you killed him, you sent him over there to die. You filthy old man, I hate you."

Henry Caldwell stood penitently, his head hung, his hands folded behind his back. What did his promotion to lieutenant general mean now?

"Get out of here. You killed him."

"Now, Elsie, don't say that. Jim Lee was a fine combat officer. He was doing exactly what he wanted to do."

"Damn you, he was not! He wanted to be here with me. We were going to get married. Jim and I would have been happy together. You sent him away to be killed, you bastard. Now he's dead and you killed him as surely as if you'd shot him yourself."

I should be angry, he thought, and all I can feel is love for this poor woman. Maybe she's right. Maybe I did kill him.

"Get out of here. I can't stand the sight of you. I never could stand you, your stinking breath, your tobacco smell. Get out of here with your dried-up old body. You killed my angel!"

Her words drilled into him, each insult a jab of pain.

"Come on, Elsie, pull yourself together."

"I know why you did it, too! You wanted him dead, so he couldn't testify against you. Well, don't you worry, I'll do it for him. I'll get you sent to jail! I don't care if I have to go, too, I'll get even with you."

Shaken by her fury, it took him a moment to understand what she was saying. From the moment word had come to him that Lee had been killed, he'd been overwhelmed by a concern for Elsie. It had not even occurred to him that Lee's death might benefit him, but he could see that it was true. With Lee dead, he stood a far better chance of being believed. It would be his word and his reputation against Elsie and McNaughton.

"Get out of here! I don't ever want to see you again. But I'll see you in jail. I'll go to the FBI, I'll go to the President, I'll do whatever I have to do to get revenge."

He stared up at her. She grabbed a vase from a tabletop and threw it at him, the water splashing over his uniform before it shattered on the floor. Then she picked the table up and hurled it down the stairs.

Afraid that she'd hurt herself, Caldwell fled in shame to the

Cadillac outside where Troy McNaughton sat waiting. Humiliated, broken-hearted, Caldwell felt a leaden anger with himself for still caring for this woman who had destroyed his life, who now hated him—had always despised him!—and who had made such a fool of him.

McNaughton drove slowly, watching Caldwell out of the corner of his eye. He entered a gate in the enormous fence that had been built around the McNaughton plant property, then drove slowly up a back road that led to an overlook from which the entire field could be seen. There were Sidewinders parked everywhere, with a dozen aircraft climbing and descending in the traffic pattern. McNaughton knew that there was no balm for a pilot's soul like watching aircraft land and take off.

When he saw that Caldwell was beginning to compose himself, he said softly, "I've never ever seen her like this. Underneath that Southern-comfort charm, she's always been such a calculating bitch—"

Caldwell interrupted. "Don't bad-mouth her, Troy! I wish I had someone who cared for me as much as she must have cared for Lee."

"Christ, Henry, you did. You had Shirley. Pull yourself together and don't be such a patsy so late in your life. This woman has screwed you royally, she's threatening to send you to jail, and you're defending her? You must have bats in your belfry."

Caldwell stewed at the truth in the remarks. Shirley had loved him unreservedly, in her own way. But it was different with Elsie— she had him enthralled in a way he never would have believed possible. Finally, he said, "You're just worried because you'll be going to jail, too."

"You're goddamn right I am. Lee's death has changed everything! We've got to get her to shut up some way, somehow, and we can ride out whatever they come at us with. I've talked to my lawyers— we can both blame the whole damn thing on Lee. We'll say that he was a careerist sucking up to you, that he wanted a job from me, but that we didn't know anything about the business with the pitot tubes."

Caldwell's voice was resigned, almost academic. "Troy, I never did anything wrong. Why should I run the risk of covering for you? We'll just let the thing come to trial."

"For a smart man you've got a short memory. If it goes to trial, Elsie will go to jail, sure as hell. You might get off, but Elsie would go to the pen."

Caldwell thought this over. He knew he shouldn't care that Elsie hated him. And if she had always hated him, if she'd always been pretending, what difference did anything make? He tried to summon an argument against taking any action.

"How can you stop Elsie from talking if she wants to? She's a determined woman, and bright, too. I just wish she cared for me."

McNaughton didn't try to conceal his disgust. "Henry, stop acting like an overaged Romeo! It's bad enough for you to hurt yourself, but I'm not letting you take me with you. There's got to be some way short of killing her to shut her up."

Caldwell whirled in his seat, emotions stirred by other than sadness for the first time in days. "By God, don't even talk about killing her, or even hurting her, because I swear if anything happens to her, I'll strangle you with my bare hands."

McNaughton looked at him and smiled. "I believe you would, Henry. You are an old fool and a mean one, too. But we've got other problems."

Caldwell looked at him contemptuously. "What could that be?"

"The microfilm you brought back from Hafner on the V-2 is not complete. The material dealing with the guidance systems is not up to date with the rest of the drawings. My scientists tell me that there's no sense in even trying to build a copy until they get the rest of the data. They're working on it themselves of course, but there's no chance that they'll be able to duplicate in a few months what the Germans did over ten years."

Sagging, Caldwell shook his head. "It's that fucking Hafner again. He's a Borgia, everything he's connected with is poisoned somehow."

They were silent for a moment and Caldwell continued. "I got the State Department's agreement to arrange amnesty for Hafner, *if* he comes across with the rest of the material on submarines and poison gas and the other stuff. But he's disappeared. I can't get in touch with him."

"How about your contact in Sweden?"

"She's disappeared, too. He's probably had her killed. Eventually he kills everyone he comes in contact with."

"Well, you better pray that the Russians don't grab Hafner, or even the British for that matter. What's happening with this so-called Operation Overcast?"

"You're not even supposed to know about that, Troy. I can't tell you anything."

"No, but I can tell you plenty. There's a hotshot Army colonel who already has a firing range being built down in New Mexico, and he's got a request in to have captured V-2s sent there for tests. We'll be sucking hind tit if that happens before we get going on our own missiles."

"So what?"

"And I can tell you about Bandfield going off to pick up jet airplanes with this Operation Trusty."

"It's 'Lusty,' not 'Trusty.' Where do you get your information?"

"Hell, I pay for it, just like you do. Only I pay in money and you pay in jobs and perks and promotions. Why don't you have Band-field concentrate on picking up Hafner? He's bound to be running into people who will know him."

Caldwell stirred. If they picked Hafner up, he could smash his face in, kill him.

"Not a bad idea. Maybe I'll go myself. He is totally evil."

"Right! Don't forget the spot we're in. If you come back with a bundle of first-rate information, you'd be in a hell of a lot better position if Elsie causes some trouble. Why don't you see Arnold and try to get control of the whole operation?"

Lethargy returned to Caldwell's manner. "I can't. He's recovering from a heart attack, a bad one. I wouldn't need him anyway. I'm sending Bandy over—I could just go with him. At this stage of the war everything's looser than hell, anyway. People are spending more time jockeying for position in the Pacific war than worrying about what I'm doing."

"You do that. And I'll take care of Elsie on this end." He saw the look in Caldwell's eyes and added, "But nicely, never fear."

Munich-Reim/April 24, 1945

Early morning fog nestled down around the ring of hills circling the horizon. The two old friends sat under the just budding trees that surrounded the makeshift dispersal pens. They were dressed alike in gray leather flying suits, their pockets bulging with the miscellaneous necessities of flight, misshapen officer's caps pulled down so low that the brims touched the rims of their sunglasses. A few chairs, a table made out of a door and fuel drums, field phones, and a ration can ashtray for Galland's black Brazilian cigars constituted the "operations area." They were drinking ersatz coffee out of thick *Wehrmacht* cups and chewing slowly on pieces of damp Army bread smeared with a thin red substance that smelled not unlike the noxious J2 fuel being pumped into the Messerschmitt Me 262s of *Jagdverband* 44.

The airfield was a ragtag mixture of runways and battle damage— some real runways with fake damage, some fake runways with real damage. Few buildings were still whole, and all maintenance was conducted outdoors. But it was spring, the war was nearing its end—and *Ju* 44 was the world's most elite fighter unit.

"Well, it's full circle, Josty. I started out in 1939 as a *Staffel* commander. Here it is 1945, and I'm a *Staffel* commander again."

"Yes, but then you were an *Oberleutnant*, flying Henschel biplanes. Now you're a *Generalleutnant* flying 262s! Quite a difference."

Galland snorted with rage. "The biggest difference was that then *we* were winning the war! Now the Americans are past Aachen and the Russians are swallowing up Berlin. We'll be lucky to last another week."

His words didn't seem to faze Josten, preoccupied as usual with the technical details of the next mission.

"How many 262s can you put in the air today?"

"Exactly six. We're not ready for another 'Great Blow' yet."

"Make it seven. My own airplane is back in service."

Josten, still working directly with Messerschmitt in Augsburg, had begun testing the new developments in combat, bypassing the normal Luftwaffe red tape. Everyone, himself included, knew that it was futile, that it could have no effect on the war, but he persisted just as the Messerschmitt plant did. It enabled him to deny what was happening, to focus so sharply on an instrument of war that the war itself was forgotten.

Calland went on. "It's incredible that the mighty Luftwaffe could fall so low. Imagine, if you hadn't been bombed out, you'd have had a *Staffel* of 262s at Ploesti in August of '43. Now, more than a year later, we're still only able to put up six today! How the hell did we get ourselves in this position?"

Josten stretched and yawned. "It took the 'Groefaz' to do it, Dolfo. We always said technology would win the war—we just didn't know it would be American technology."

Galland laughed mirthlessly, saying, "You and your technology! It's always just brute force, one set of animals clubbing another set to death." He ground his cigar into the ashtray and said, "But at least in the beginning, we had the clubs!"

They were quiet for a while, then Josten asked, "How are things with you?"

"All right until this morning. Headquarters usually leaves us alone. We're getting more airplanes now—the other bases are being overrun and there's nowhere else to send them. And we're finally getting the R4M rockets issued. If we'd had them in 1943, things would be very different now. They are lethal."

"What happened this morning?"

"They told me that Bruno Hafner is coming in to commandeer my two last transport aircraft. I need them to fly parts in to keep my aircraft in the air, and he's pulling them out from under me. What's worse, we're supposed to escort him in our jets!"

"On whose orders?"

"Hitler's, no less! The worse the war gets, the better it goes for Hafner."

"I don't want to talk to him. I know he was trying to help Lyra, but if it hadn't been for him she might still be alive."

"Too late. This must be him now."

A Mercedes staff car, closely followed by an Opel truck, drove up. Struggling by himself, refusing any help, Bruno Hafner wriggled his twisted body out the back door like Houdini escaping from a chained trunk, then pulled himself upright and saluted Galland. In the interval, Josten moved out of sight behind the sandbagged revetment.

"General Galland, you received the orders from OKW on escorting my aircraft?"

"Yes, Colonel. I protested, but they confirmed the orders. The two airplanes are ready." He nodded toward the field's edge, where the two Junkers had been prepared for flight. Hafner's crew members were already on their way over to them.

Galland pulled the cigar from his mouth and jabbed at Hafner with it. "Do you realize that they are the last I have and that I desperately need them to collect parts to keep my combat aircraft in commission?"

"That may be so, General, but I have my orders, too. Directly from Heinrich Himmler. I've got to get these planes to Leipzig this afternoon."

Hafner, still charged by Himmler with the responsibility of "saving the Fuehrer," had lost his big six-engine Junkers in an Allied strafing attack. Now he was collecting a smaller four-engine Ju 290 and one of the old reliable Ju 52s.

"Can't you wait until tonight? You're sure to run into enemy fighters if you try to fly now."

"No choice. It's Himmler's timetable. And I've got to be in Flensburg tonight."

"Well, no matter what the orders are, we can't escort you. You'll be flying at treetop level at two hundred fifty kilometers per hour. We'll be at eight thousand meters, flying nearly four times as fast. Who in God's name suggested that we could fly cover for you?"

"Hitler. Who else? I told him the same thing—discreetly, of course—but he's buried down in the bunker, divorced from reality. He just waved his arms and told me to get on with it. He said that if you could get three battle cruisers through the English Channel you could get two airplanes to Leipzig."

"We'll get on with it, but with some sense. I've managed to get a flight of 109s assigned to the mission. They'd be better employed elsewhere, but we'll follow orders. We'll act as high cover for them, and they can protect you. But God help you if you get caught by Mustangs—we won't be able to."

Hafner nodded, then walked slowly toward the Junkers Ju 290. He still limped badly, but he hadn't used his wheelchair since early March.

Josten reappeared and nodded toward the receding figure. "A monster! But an indomitable one."

"I told you he was a monster and you wouldn't listen. What do you think he's supposed to do with these airplanes?"

"Probably try to fly Hitler somewhere."

"You're still a dreamer, Josten. There's nowhere in the world for Hitler to go. The Allies would track him down like a mad dog, and if they didn't, we would. No, Hafner wants those airplanes for Hafner, make no mistake about that. He's one of the few who have fooled both Hitler and Himmler."

"It doesn't matter to me anymore, Dolfo. We've got a few more weeks of flying before the American tanks get here. The only thing that matters is keeping these Turbos running. There's still much to learn about jet aircraft."

"You're incorrigible. Other people are here fighting for the sheer hell of it, or because they hate the thought of losing. You are fighting for a piece of machinery."

"I know that it's stupid. But it's as if I've transferred all my human feelings to the airplane. I can't help it—I don't have anything left. It's the only way I can go on."

"What about your wife and child, for God's sake? You don't know whether they are alive or dead. You ought to be worried about living, to protect them."

"Lyra's dead, I know. I would have heard from her otherwise."

Josten's voice trembled with emotion. "And the child is in good hands, better off than he would be in Germany. I don't even know if I'd be good for him—I'd ruin his life just as I ruined Lyra's."

Galland pulled on his cigar for a moment. "Don't talk like this. There was nothing you could have done."

"Yes, there was. And you, too. Before the Stauffenberg fiasco, either one of us could have shot Hitler. We saw him a few times— we could still wear sidearms in his presence."

"We're not assassins."

"No, we just should have been. We've spent a war trying to kill young Englishmen when we could have solved the problems of the world with a single bullet in Hitler's head. And now we've got to escort Hafner to safety, when what I ought to do is shoot him down."

Exasperated, Galland sneered, "Don't destroy an airplane and kill his crew. If you want to shoot him, take your pistol over to the airplane and do it now. Damnit, Josten, you wouldn't even shoot a partridge. I can just see you murdering Hafner, or Hitler for that matter. That's just talk."

Angry with each other for the first time in years, they turned away to watch the big Junkers Ju 290 lifting off to hug the treetops, setting course for Leipzig. The Ju 52 followed it just as the flight of escort Messerschmitt Bf 109s appeared overhead.

Josten felt embarrassed. Galland had enough on his mind without arguing with him. "Sorry, Dolfo, I didn't mean to lose my temper."

"It's all right, we're just tense, like we were during the Channel dash. Hafner said Hitler mentioned it."

"A capsule history of the Third Reich! Then it was three great capital ships; now it's two old Junkers."

Galland grinned. "Well, we did it then, we'll do it now."

The armorers were swarming around three Turbos, installing the twelve R4M rockets on wooden racks under each wing. The 55-mm rockets had the same trajectory as the 30-mm cannon shells, so they were able to use the same gunsight. All twenty-four rockets were fired in a salvo from three hundred meters out, beyond the distance of the bombers' guns. They blanketed a hundred-meter-square area, and a hit from just one was enough to destroy a B-17.

The speed of the Turbo had made the old *rotte* and *schwarm* formations that the Luftwaffe had used since Spain obsolete. Now they took off and flew in a loose V-formation of three planes. The other pilot in their trio, *Leutnant* Karl Rademacher, a veteran from the Eastern Front, walked up as Galland began his short briefing.

"This makes no sense, as you know. We can't fly at their altitude and speed. So we'll do this for show. We'll climb to eight thousand meters and do S-turns above them. If they get in trouble, we'll drop down and try to help. When they get to Leipzig, we'll return here, if we can. If not, we'll go to Prague. Agreed?"

Rademacher asked, "What if we see some *Viermots?*" He was a four-engine specialist, having shot down fourteen of the big bombers. A dour little man, lean as a whippet, he was as focused on combat as Josten was on the Turbo.

"It depends. If I think the 109s can get the Junkers into Leipzig, we'll attack."

The jets burned fuel so fast that they were routinely towed to a starting position at the edge of the field and screened with camouflage netting until the last moment. Galland was in the center aircraft, Josten on his left wing and Rademacher on his right.

At Galland's signal they rolled forward, accelerating slowly. The tricycle gear had vastly improved the takeoff handling of the aircraft, and Josten was soon absorbed in the sheer pleasure of jet flight. He was sure that the other two were caught up in the sense of superiority the airplane gave. What did it matter if there were fifty American planes in the sky for every one of the Luftwaffe's? *They* were flying Turbos, and that's all that counted.

The three 262s climbed rapidly to eight thousand meters, then began curving in great wide arcs above the escort Messerschmitts so far below them. The weather had been miserable on the two previous days but now only half the sky was filled with cottony patches of cumulus clouds, sunlight glinting on their rounded tops. The clouds obscured the planes they were supposed to be escorting but served equally to hide them from any marauding Allied fighters.

Josten divided his time between maintaining a loose formation with
Galland and recording his instrument readings carefully on a tablet
strapped to his knee. He was flying a specially modified aircraft,
equipped with an automatic throttle control designed to prevent
flame-outs. There was also a new auxiliary tank installed behind his
seat to provide some additional fuel. The extra weight moved the
center of gravity to the aft limits, making the aircraft as uncomfortably unstable as a marble balanced on a needle. He needed to use as
much fuel from the aft tank as possible before they engaged in
combat.

Forty minutes later they heard Hafner's transmission: "QFU
Leipzig," the standard code inquiry for landing directions. They had
made it. At the same moment Rademacher's excited voice came
crackling through the headset: "Marauders five thousand meters
below, straight ahead."

"Attacking." Galland's voice carried the same crisp authority it
had five years before over England—it was as if nothing had
changed.

The three Turbos slipped down in a wide arc, the airspeed
nudging nine hundred kilometers per hour. Josten noted with
approval the way the automatic throttle control kept the engines
within limits, the "Zwiebels," onion-shaped cones in the jet exhausts, moving in and out to match the changes in thrust.

The twin-engine Martin B-26s were ahead and to the left. They
were old friends, extraordinarily rugged aircraft filled with heavy
machine guns, much harder to shoot down than either a B-17 or a
B-24. Through the holes in the clouds, Josten counted eight of
them, a group of five and a V of three off to the left. All silver, he
thought, the bastards don't even bother to camouflage their airplanes anymore. They think they own the skies.

The three Turbos spread out to approach from the rear. The
standard tactic was to dive below the enemy's altitude, pop up level
and fire off the rockets, then close in to use the cannons.

"Take the group to the left, Josty; Karl and I will take the big
formation."

Josten's fingers caressed the stick and the 262 curved slightly, closing swiftly on three Marauders packed so tightly in formation that their wings were overlapping. He decided to get closer, to fire the rockets from a hundred meters so that their pattern might cover all three enemy planes. He'd be closing on the Marauders at a rate of four hundred kilometers per hour—just time to fire the rockets, then shoot.

Josten approached cautiously, switching his attention back and forth from the target to his engine instruments, where a slight rise in temperature worried him. At one hundred meters out he pressed the firing button.

Damn! Nothing happened, he'd forgotten to arm the rockets. A silver Marauder filled his windscreen, bullets streaking out from its turrets. Mashing the cannon button, he saw the Martin stagger from the hits as he hurtled up in a wide left turn. A quick glance showed him that Galland or Rademacher had scored against the others, but his own target was flying on, streaming smoke from the right engine.

Deliberately shoving the throttles forward to test the automatic regulator, he noted the calibrated engine response with approval. In an ordinary Turbo, mishandling the throttles like that could have caused a flame-out. Reaching down to arm the rockets, he again checked the engine temperature and revolution instruments to see if there were any changes.

All of them changed before his eyes into a shattered mass of glass and aluminum as .50-caliber bullets stitched through the cockpit, wounding him in his left arm and leg, shattering the instrument panel and blowing up the left engine. The Turbo rolled violently to the left, its aft center of gravity throwing it out of control and setting the earth to spinning wildly.

As the airplane snapped he saw Thunderbolts pass on either side of him. He pulled the throttles back and let the Turbo spin through two turns, then popped the stick forward and pushed the right rudder pedal all the way forward. The airplane shuddered as if a hand had grasped it, breaking the spin as he passed through eight hundred meters height. Raising the nose he saw the tracers from another Thunderbolt's guns passing ahead of him. He stuck the nose down, diving into the cloud cover below, adding power to the right engine, fighting to keep control of the bucking 262.

They were near Brandis. If he could shake the Thunderbolts he could land there. He looked down, surprised to find that there was an ugly red-rimmed hole in his leg the size of his fist. There was no pain, but now he felt blood coursing down into his boot. He had to land, soon, before consciousness drained away. The altimeter showed only two hundred meters.

Magically, the camouflaged field at Brandis appeared on his left, its pockmarked runways barely apparent against the forested green and brown backdrop.

Radio's shot away, he thought. I'm just going to plant it on the runway and pray. Josten slowed his approach to the field to two hundred kilometers per hour before dropping his gear. Behind him, six Thunderbolts were jockeying each other for position to shoot, anxious to claim an aerial victory over this cripple. Josten touched down as multiple lines of American machine-gun fire created a musical staff down the runway, the notes the puffs of powder rising from the bullets. The Turbo slewed to the left, catching its wingtip on an earthen mound. The 262 bounded upward again, as if it had to make one last flight, a final trip through the air. The seamless steel tubing landing gear sheared off as the masterpiece of technology touched down again, shedding the port wing as it skipped along the runway like a flat rock on the water. Josten rode with it, futilely pushing stick and rudder. The fuselage rose again and then slammed down, flame bursting from the ruptured tanks. As he glanced out of his shattered canopy through the flames he saw one of his wheels bound by, arcing over the debris of the fuselage seemingly in slow motion. There was a hissing sound, and long streaks of ragged fire began bursting past him, snaking over the ground to explode a hundred yards away.

Groggy, he talked to himself. "My left wing is firing at me. The damn R4Ms wouldn't shoot when I wanted them to; now they're going to shoot me down on the ground."

Josten unbuckled his harness and heaved upward on the canopy. It swung heavily to the side as flames began to reach up around the cockpit section. There was no strength in his left leg; with his arms he pulled himself out of the cockpit and to the ground where the wing should have been. Searing flames plucked the oxygen from his lungs as he crawled away from the wreckage. He didn't see or hear the Thunderbolts' next firing pass.

14

Plon/May 2, 1945

Hitler was dead, his ravaged Germany expiring like a wounded wolf, teeth bared even as life emptied from a thousand wounds. Organized resistance was almost over. There was no longer any grand strategy or central direction. Individual battle groups fought bravely if their leaders demanded, surrendered gladly if they did not. Yet at the provisional headquarters at Plon, life went on at an almost placid pace.

Hafner's presence at the first meeting of the Doenitz government was an accident. The designated Luftwaffe liaison officer, the great bomber pilot Werner Baumbach, had not yet arrived, and it had fallen by chance to Hafner to supervise the pitiful rump that remained in North Germany of the once feared Luftwaffe. As far as he was concerned, only one aircraft was important—the one for his escape.

Choking back his impatience, he watched the bickering for position with concealed contempt. It reminded him of pampered apartment house dogs consecutively marking the lobby potted palm as exclusive turf. They kept up the trappings—the Reich battle flag was raised each morning, wherever they were, and the grand admiral was chauffeured in one of Hitler's own Mercedes limousines. Himmler's menacing personal guard was turned out in immaculate uniforms. Yet they were arguing without embarrassment for precedence in the convoy that was leaving that night, its destination Flensburg. Undoubtedly it would prove to be the last capital of the Third Reich.

Once they had been Hitler's paladins, masters of Europe. *Reichsminister* Albert Speer had galvanized the German economy to unbelievable heights of production—now at the last moment he was accepting blame, and calling for a corporate responsibility for the Nazi excesses. *Reichsfuehrer* Heinrich Himmler had terrorized the world with ruthless killing camps. Now he saw himself at the peace table, negotiating the fate of Germany. Yet, the two men, always cautious, were carrying on a surreptitious dialogue on the prospect of escaping to Greenland and hiding there, a fantasy escape for this fugitive government.

Since the fateful word from the Bunker, there was a new Fuehrer, Grand Admiral Karl Doenitz, the dour fanatic whose submarines had almost brought Great Britain to its knees. Small and wizened, his uniform always seeming to be two sizes too large for him, he had been as surprised as anyone to have been selected as Hitler's successor. Now he seemed torn between a desire to honor his oath to the fallen Fuehrer and a heartfelt urge to end the killing by surrender. He knew about killing. His U-boats had sunk millions of tons of shipping—and of his forty thousand submariners, thirty thousand had drowned.

Perhaps the thought of their deaths had given Doenitz the early morning courage to inform a shaking and unbelieving Himmler that there was no place for him in the new government. It was a crucial decision that affected Hafner directly, for the two Junkers escape planes he had waiting at a small field outside Flensburg were guarded by loyal SS troops. There was no way he could use either airplane without Himmler's permission.

Doenitz and his cabinet had spent the day making meaningless decisions and issuing hollow statements solemnizing Hitler's death.

Now the meeting was breaking up for the one-hundred-kilometer retreat to Flensburg. The shabby Doenitz government, moving in a ragged convoy, was going to run the gauntlet of British fighter bombers, fleeing north of the Kiel Canal to the naval cadet school at Murwik. Himmler, refusing to believe that Doenitz could operate without him, had insisted on hanging on. Doenitz had acquiesced, but insisted that they not travel together. Abashed but quietly defiant, Himmler agreed that his own convoy of Mercedes staff cars would follow the Doenitz party.

Hafner waited patiently in the gathering dusk, standing quietly by Himmler as the last Mercedes was being loaded with the *Reichsfuehrer*'s personal papers.

"Ah, *Herr Reichsfuehrer*, it is times like these when the services of our friend Dr. Kersten would be invaluable."

Startled, Himmler turned his owl eyes upon him, clearly unaware of his presence until that moment.

"Oh, it's you, Hafner. Yes, Kersten is a magician. He has done well for you, I see."

"*Herr Reichsfuehrer*, may I ask you a question?"

"Not now, Hafner, I'm preoccupied. Get in the car with me. We can talk en route. Right now I have to think."

They sat in the back of the Mercedes as Doenitz's caravan pulled out. Himmler watched his wristwatch steadily for ten minutes, then curtly nodded his head. His own convoy followed.

The road to Flensburg was crowded with refugees moving slowly along the sides of the road while untidy detachments of troops, using any sort of conveyance, retreated in disorder, as much afraid of the brutal execution of summary court-martial squads as of the Russians. The roadsides were littered with burned vehicles, corpses, and dead horses. Among the martial debris, strange mixtures of destroyed domesticity hinted at an earlier, saner life. There were baby carriages loaded with clothes, broken bottles of wine, torn paintings, an open family album with photos staring blankly at the passing parade, dolls, a dead puppy, a harp. All had been at one moment the most important thing in the world to their owners, selected from all other things to flee with. And now they were abandoned forever.

Himmler stared straight ahead, his hands positioned on his knees in the position of a cadet sitting at attention, his lips occasionally moving soundlessly. Hafner noticed that Himmler's usual military luster was dulled—his uniform had not been pressed, and it was without the usual array of medals.

Drumming his fingers on the cushion beside him, Hafner waited to speak. He had left his own car at Plon, but it didn't matter. If he reached Flensburg with Himmler's permission to take off, he'd walk to the airfield if he had to.

In the red haze of the deepening dusk they saw the all too familiar British Typhoons attacking the road ahead of them, a sight as common in Germany now as marching Hitler Youth once had been. Their driver pulled off the road to shelter under some trees.

Himmler turned to Hafner and smiled.

"Our new Fuehrer"—the word "Fuehrer" sounded as if his tongue was handling it with tongs—"is tasting some of the problems of office. I'd volunteered to precede him, to make sure things were safe. Now the Tommies are giving him a little lesson."

Hafner nodded, and Himmler peered intently at him, his eyes growing large behind the round lenses of his glasses.

"What is it you wanted to ask me?"

"*Herr Reichsfuehrer*, I owe you a great deal. If you had not allowed Dr. Kersten to work with me, I never would have walked again. Now, I implore you to allow me to fly you to freedom. We have two Junkers aircraft at Flensburg. I could fly you to Spain in the larger airplane, the 290. You could go incognito, and perhaps escape to South America." Hafner had no intention of flying Himmler anywhere—if he boarded the aircraft with him, he would take him to Russia as a present.

Tears misted Himmler's eyes. He had always been sentimental, sensitive to his own feelings, and the nearing end made him more so.

"Ah, Hafner, there are few left like you. Even in my own SS there are traitors. But I can't go. I'm the only one the Allies will deal with. Doenitz doesn't realize this yet, but he will want me to become the Chancellor. No—but you go. I'll authorize the release of the aircraft as soon as we reach Flensburg."

"Thank you, *Herr Reichsfuehrer*."

Hafner felt relief sweep through him. He had been convinced ever since that meeting at Nordhausen that Himmler's almost paternal benevolence toward him masked a raging suspicion. Now things had so shifted that he no longer cared what Hafner did.

But Himmler's previous reluctance to provide him with an aircraft had forced Hafner to take risks, forcing him to set the date of his defection early. His last contact with Scriabin had been his easiest—the Russian advance had been so swift that they had captured town after town with the telephone lines intact. Scriabin had simply rung him up at his Cottbus office. Now he was just going to make it. He had arranged with Scriabin that he would arrive off the Baltic Coast near Peenemunde just after dawn on the 3d, 4th, or 5th of May. The Russians would have a fighter escort on station each day for one hour, waiting to escort him in to his new fatherland.

They drove in silence for a while and Himmler turned to him.

"Tell me, Hafner, who made the best offer, the Americans or the Russians?"

Munich-Reim/May 2, 1945

"I was here before, you know."

Caldwell grunted apathetically.

"Back in 1936, when you told me I was going on a boondoggle."

As usual Caldwell didn't reply. At least he wasn't drinking anymore. Bandfield had initially been pleased when his old friend had said that he was going to join him on Operation Lusty. But he'd started drinking on the C-54 flight across the Atlantic and didn't stop until what Bandy was mentally calling the "Miracle in Frankfurt."

If they had been in any sort of regular outfit, Caldwell would have been brought up on charges long ago. But because they were operating independently, Bandfield was able to keep his old friend under cover most of the time. It had been a strain caring for him, protecting him from himself. He'd spent most days passed out in the back of the Douglas C-47. The tragedy was that it was exactly the sort of irregular, free-lance work that Caldwell ordinarily enjoyed. Their original charter called for them to "closely follow" the advancing American armies, but the Germans were now so eager to be in American custody that they had twice landed behind German lines to accept the surrender of an airfield themselves. It was laughable— the C-47s they flew were normally unarmed, but Bandfield had had two .50-caliber machine guns installed in flexible mounts. One was fixed so that it would fire out the big door on the left-hand side, the gunner restrained by a makeshift harness of safety belts and parachute lines. The other fired through the aperture of an escape hatch on the right. They'd been afraid to test-fire them, for a huge long-range fuel tank was rigged in the center of the cabin, and it gave off fumes continuously. Caldwell had requisitioned a small arsenal of captured German weapons—rifles and submachine guns—but they'd lain inside under a canvas cover for the whole trip.

It didn't matter to the Germans that they were virtually unarmed; there was no question of protocol or rank, or of marching out with flags and arms—they just wanted to surrender to the Americans.

"Let me show you something eerie, Henry. All Germany is in ruins, and this place has survived everything. Come on."

They went down a flight of stairs of the Luftwaffe's officers' mess, abandoned by all but its white-liveried staff. Bandfield led the way down a hallway lined with framed paintings of *Staffeln* insignia to a white-tiled lavatory, immaculately clean.

He pointed to large white basins fitted with large drains in the center, equipped with handles at the sides. Above each basin was an enormous faucet, more the size of a fire hose than a bathroom fixture.

"Look at these, Henry."

"Brother! What the hell are they?" It was the most emotion he'd expressed in days.

"Vomitoriums. The Krauts would drink all the beer they could hold, then come down here and throw up."

The uniform Lieutenant General Henry Caldwell had worn on

the Schweinfurt raid when he posed as "Major White" hung loosely on him, disheveled and spotted with cigarette burns. He was chain smoking again.

Caldwell sighed, saying lugubriously, "They're strange people, Bandy."

Bandfield wanted to encourage the little glimmer of interest.

"Yeah, like when I landed at Leipheim. I taxied in and told the old captain running the field that I was taking off in one of the jets he had parked on the line. He was agreeable as hell—*if* I signed a receipt for the airplane! As long as his ass was covered, he didn't care who took it."

Caldwell reverted immediately to his idée fixe. "But nobody knows where Hafner is! He's my only chance, Bandy. If I could get to him—or at least get to the material he has on microfilm—I might be able to beat the rap."

Bandfield nodded, even though he didn't agree. If the Judge Advocate General was out to hang Caldwell, some captured data wasn't going to save him. But as long as it gave Caldwell something to cling to, it was fine with Bandfield.

"You'd never recognize him, Bandy. You remember what a handsome devil he was in the old days? All the women used to throw themselves at him. Well, you fixed him. His face is twisted and burned, and his legs are atrophied. He's built up his arms and shoulders, though."

"If I see the son-of-a-bitch, I'll recognize him. He did me enough harm to remember him no matter how he looks."

They walked back upstairs to the deserted dining room. Their crew chief, Vince Lowe, was tired of living out of cans and had talked the German cooks into preparing a meal. The Germans had gone full out, delighted to have the American rations, and the table was glittering with white linen, crystal, and formal Luftwaffe dinnerware. Caldwell picked at the food, the highly prized C rations and a can of Spam, nicely presented, with German Army bread on the side.

"Damnit, Henry, you can't go on like this, never eating. What the hell is the matter with you, anyway?"

"There's nothing the matter with me that a shot from a forty-five-caliber pistol wouldn't cure. Anyway, who knows what will happen over here? Some Kraut might put me out of my misery. Or we might land at some field, and up would pop our friend Bruno."

Bandfield nibbled at his food, conscious that he was watching the death of a career and perhaps the death of the man. Caldwell had spent his life doing things for the Army that no one else could have done. It wasn't an exaggeration to say that he had laid the foundations for victory. But in the process he had made enemies—and some big mistakes. Now they were going to destroy him.

"Remember that meeting back in Yankee Stadium, Henry? You told me we'd get to fly everything, but I never thought we'd be flying stuff like this."

Caldwell agreed. "Some of it makes old Hadley's Operation Leapfrog look pretty tame."

So far they had collected half a dozen 262s, two of the strange Dornier Do 335 twin-engine "push-pull" fighters, an Arado reconnaissance jet, and a single-engine Heinkel jet, a 162. In the process they'd taken far more prisoners than they could handle, content to send most of them marching back without an escort, retaining only the best of the German mechanics. Bandfield had run the selection like a dockyard shape-up. He tried to figure out who had the most talent and sent the rest along on their own.

The most important catch of all came to them voluntarily, in the "Miracle in Frankfurt." Karl Hoffman was a mountain of a man who'd served throughout the war as a civilian production test pilot for Messerschmitt. He'd flown in a rare two-seater 262 to the bombed-out airfield at Frankfurt am Main. Bandfield had grabbed him, and Hoffman gladly agreed to teach them to fly the 262 and anything else they captured. He spoke English well enough to get by and had been with them ever since.

The "miracle" had been Caldwell sobering up for a demonstration ride in the two-seat 262 with Hoffman. He came down boiling with enthusiasm, looking more like an eager cadet than a tired and frightened old man. He stopped drinking on the spot, and the next day Hoffman sent him solo in a single-seat 262. Since then there had been increasing signs of life in Caldwell—and he had stayed on the wagon.

"Look who's coming, our newest recruit."

Hoffman bustled in to stand at rigid attention beside the table.

"I have some information for you. One of the most important pilots in the 262 program, *Oberst* Josten, is in the Oberfoehring Army Hospital in Munich. He is badly burned from a crash but conscious. You might want to talk to him about the airplane."

Caldwell was on his feet. "Airplane hell! I want to talk to him about Bruno Hafner."

Hoffman, frightened that in his fractured English he had said something offensive, began to apologize.

"Take us there right now, Karl. We've got to talk to this man."

As they rushed out Caldwell grabbed a piece of Spam from his plate and stuck it between two slices of German Army bread.

"This is the break we've been looking for, Bandy—he's bound to know where Hafner is."

Bandfield hoped that it was not just a forlorn whistle in the dark.

They were treated like kings by Major Pingel, the harried head of the hospital. As soon as they'd entered the hospital grounds, he materialized, all smiles and wringing hands, bowing and scraping.

"*Oberst* Josten is recovering better than we could have expected. He's in considerable pain and we've kept him under sedation. He's been taking Dolantin, and we're beginning to reduce the dosage. His face and hands were badly burned, and he has two bullet wounds and a fractured hip."

Caldwell asked impatiently, "Will he be able to talk to us?"

"Yes, it might even help him. He needs to get his mind off the crash. Conscious or unconscious, he complains continually about having wrecked his aircraft." The major laughed heartily, as if he were sharing a rare joke with them. "As if it mattered anymore."

Bandfield spoke quietly to Caldwell. "Strange how easily they've gone belly-up, now that it's almost over. He's acting as though they just lost a rubber of bridge."

"Churchill was right—the Germans are either at your feet or at your throat."

The hospital was overflowing with the wounded, civil and military; patients were jammed into every room and beds lined the hallways. One entire wing was open air, the walls and roof gone. Yet the floors had been swept clean and the beds were lined up at regular intervals, patient charts in metal holders at the end, just as if it had been planned that way.

"We have a few rooms reserved for special cases." Pingel pointed to a heavy oak door and the two Americans went in.

There were only two beds in the room, and one was vacant. Josten was asleep, his arms and head covered with thick white gauze, his left leg in a hip-high cast.

"Can we wake him up? It's urgent."

"No problem at all!" Pingel seemed genuinely pleased to have to disturb Josten for them. "We have to awaken patients at all hours for their medication, they're used to it." He leaned down and shouted, "*Oberst* Josten! You have important visitors."

"Thoughtful fucker," Caldwell muttered.

Josten, hearing strange voices even before Pingel shouted in his ear, had already begun the long swim upward through the opiates to painful consciousness.

"Who is it?"

"Some old friends of yours, Helmut. I'm Henry Caldwell—we knew each other in Berlin before the war. And you met Frank Bandfield in 1936."

"1936?" Josten's voice was fuzzy. It took a moment for the names to register.

"Americans. Is the war over?"

"Almost. A few days more, at most. We need your help. Perhaps we can help you in exchange. You'll remember that I knew Lyra before the war. Can I be of assistance to her now?"

A low sob, more a rattle than a cry, came from the bandages.

"I don't know where she is. If you can find her, bring her to me. I need her."

"And what about your child?"

"Ulrich's in Sweden—I may need help to find him. But first, find Lyra and bring her here."

"We'll do that if we can. First we need some information. Do you know where Bruno Hafner is?"

"Of course. Or at least—" His voice choked and Pingel thrust a glass straw through the slit in the bandages over his mouth. Josten slurped water noisily.

"At least I did. He had positioned two airplanes at Flensburg in Schleswig-Holstein. Near the coast. But he may be gone. I suspect that he has an arrangement with the Russians."

The expressions on Caldwell's face were changing like an electric sign, registering hatred, hope, anger, and hatred again in rapid succession. He jerked his head to the door and said, "Helmut, we've got to leave, now. We'll be back, and if we can find Lyra we'll bring her to you. Thanks for your help."

There was no reply as Josten slipped back into unconsciousness.

Caldwell turned to the hospital administrator. "Major Pingel, I must swear you to secrecy."

Pingel drew himself up. "You have my word as a German officer."

"I don't want your word as a German officer. I want your word as a human being, one who knows I'll shoot you if you break my confidence. I'm Lieutenant General Henry Caldwell, here on a secret mission. I'm charging you *personally* to see that Colonel Josten is taken care of—get him anything he wants or needs, and keep him safe. When I come back, I'll see that you are rewarded. If you fail, you'll regret it. And you will mention my name to no one."

Beaming, Pingel drew himself up to full attention. "*Jawohl, Herr General.* I did not think you looked like only a major. I will not fail."

When they reached the commandeered Mercedes where Hoffman was waiting, Bandfield asked, "How the hell did they make the war last so long with pussies like that?"

Outside Flensburg/May 3, 1945

The ground crews had been working all night, transferring the microfilm material from the larger Junkers to the Ju 52. The week before the old tri-motor had been sprayed white, large red crosses painted on its wings. Hafner doubted if it would deceive anyone, but if he were intercepted it might be the only chance he had.

The Ju 290 was still on reserve. Himmler, aware that he might need to flee, had changed his mind and authorized only the release of the Ju 52. Hafner smiled to himself. Himmler didn't know that only one pilot was available. It would be wonderful to see the look on Himmler's face when he rolled out to the field to fly away in his 290—and found no one to fly it.

He was running late. He had planned to take off an hour before dawn, but yesterday afternoon the starboard engine had failed to start on a routine run-up. The mechanics had worked all night on it. He had tried to sleep in the Gluecksburg Castle, but it had been turned into a hospital. He'd come back to the field to rest under the wing. It wasn't until just after dawn when his pilot, Sergeant Alfons Holzamer, came toward him.

"We're ready to go now, Colonel Hafner. Did you wish to fly the airplane yourself?"

"No, Holzamer, thank you. I'll man the upper turret, just in case we run into something we can defend ourselves against."

"*Jawohl.* Would the Colonel object to telling me where we are going so that I can plan the flight?"

"No, Holzamer, not until after we take off. Then I'll give you a sealed envelope. Those are my orders. Stay low, at treetop level. We'll be going down the Fehrman Strait, to the Baltic, and I want you down right at surface. Done much low-level flying?"

"Enough, Colonel. Don't worry, we'll be all right as long as the Mustangs don't catch us."

Hafner nodded and turned away to supervise the last of the loading. Holzamer watched him limp away, reckoning that Hafner would want to go to Sweden. That would be all right. Anything would be better than being caught by the Russians.

Approaching Flensburg/May 3, 1945

It had taken Caldwell three hours to get permission to fly from Munich to Flensburg, and it took another two hours after that to get confirmation that all the Allied fighters and antiaircraft units had been notified. It would have been suicide to fly without permission—the hungry night-fighters were running out of targets and the antiaircraft usually shot first and identified later.

Their route had taken five hours to fly, and they had rotated cockpit duties, the third man grabbing a little sleep in the back. Hoffman was a gifted pilot, as at ease now in the C-47 as he was in the 262. It was dawn, Bandfield and Hoffman were flying, and the spires of the church of St. Nicholas were glistening above the shadows of bombed-out, blacked-out Flensburg. Even this remote port was a shambles of sunken vessels and gutted warehouses.

Henry Caldwell stood between them, eyes searching the horizon, head swiveling on his long neck. He spoke into the interphone.

"Too bad Josten didn't know where Hafner was hiding out. There's an airfield south of town, but it looks like it's been bombed to bits."

Hoffman came on: "He probably went to the emergency fighter field past Murwik on the way to Gluecksburg." Hoffman sliced his ham-sized hand toward the northeast.

Bandfield turned the C-47 sharply, slowing down to 130 miles per hour and reaching down to switch tanks. "We've only got about another hour's flying time, gents—I'm going to go at economy cruise until we see something."

They had flown for only four minutes when Gluecksburg Castle swam into view, suspended like a toy ship on the mirrored surface of the lakes surrounding it.

"The field is on the left. See it, right where—"

Bandfield's voice broke in excitedly. "At ease, Hoffman. Look to your right, low on the horizon. That's a Ju 52, isn't it?"

"That's got to be him, Bandy. Let's go get him."

"Henry, do you want to get in Hoffman's seat?"

"No, let him fly. I'll go back and see what I can do with the machine guns, if we need them. We're faster than he is."

Bandfield shoved the mixtures, props, and throttles forward and put the C-47 in a slight dive toward the tiny dot on the horizon. "We're gaining."

Caldwell had swung the cargo door back and buckled himself into the harness by the .50-caliber Browning machine gun. He plugged in the intercom and said, "Go get him, tiger."

Hafner's bulky shoulders loomed from the dorsal gun position of the Ju 52. He was both comfortable and content. Squeezed into the ring turret, his bulk was supported by his arms and shoulders while his legs dangled on either side of a leather strap. He'd had a special interphone cord rigged to run to the pilot—most of the 52s coming out of the factories now didn't have them installed.

It's a good thing we didn't have a bigger airplane—it would be much more obvious. This way we'll sneak down the coast, pick up the escort, and be home free.

He scanned the sky as he used to on the Western front, quartering it systematically, methodically checking every sector, high and low. He started when, low on the horizon, he saw the glint of wings in the sunlight.

He pressed the intercom button and said, "Holzamer, put on full power. We're being followed. I don't know what it is. Looks like a twin-engine bomber of some sort, but whatever it is, he'll be faster than we are."

Hafner methodically checked out the two 13-mm MG-131 machine guns mounted in the swiveling ring. Only fifty minutes to the rendezvous point, he thought. Damn. If we can evade for a while, perhaps the Russians will see us coming.

Hafner swung the guns around and warmed them, sending a burst out into the sea.

I should have arranged to have the fighters meet us halfway.

The old warrior, broken but unbowed by three wars, forced himself to scan the rest of the sky, to tear his eyes from the slowly growing dot that had transformed itself into the silhouette of an oncoming Douglas C-47.

"It's a Douglas, Holzamer. He'll be fifty kilometers an hour faster than us."

There was a double click of acknowledgment.

Hafner reached down into the navigation bag he had stowed in the lower part of the turret. In it was a white flag he'd planned to use with the Russian fighters.

"Holzamer, let the American plane come alongside. He's probably not armed."

Again the interphone clicked, and Holzamer reduced power.

"Not too slow, Holzamer. Just ease off and let him come up on us. The main thing is not to have him call in any fighters on us.

What a joke it would be to spend the war developing a jet fighter and wind up dying in an old crate like this.

The gray outline of the Junkers suddenly blossomed in the sunlight, its white colors and red crosses gleaming. When Bandfield had fought in Spain, the Ju 52 had been a bomber. As clumsy as it looked with its fixed gear, corrugated skin, and the oddly canted wing-mounted engines, he knew the Junkers was nimble.

He spoke into the interphone. "He's slowing down, Henry. Looks like a hospital plane, all white with red crosses."

"You believe that, and I've got a bridge I want to sell you. What the hell would the Germans be doing risking a flight east when the war is almost over? Is the turret manned?"

"Wait a minute."

The C-47 was straining at an indicated 190 miles per hour. Hoffman reached down into his kit bag and handed Bandfield a small pair of field glasses. Bandfield nodded to him that he had the airplane and Hoffman shook the wheel.

It took a minute for Bandfield to adjust the glasses to his eyes, and almost thirty seconds to acquire the Junkers in his visual field. When it loomed up he murmured, "Holy shit!"

He had trained the glasses on the cockpit of the Junkers, then moved it slowly back to the ring-turret. There, wearing goggles but bareheaded, his hair more silver than blond over his scarred and twisted face, was the unmistakable looming presence of Bruno Hafner.

"My God, Henry, you were right. It is Hafner. He's waving a white flag."

"The bastard must be heading for the Russian lines. Let me warm up this machine gun and you make a pass alongside him. Any way you can talk to him?"

"No, the radios aren't compatible, and we don't even know what frequency he'd be on. I got my doubts about this—Bruno won't surrender. He's got two guns in that turret, looks like thirteen-millimeter. I don't want to get our ass shot off right when the war is ending."

The voice that came back on the interphone was not that of his old friend Henry. Instead, suffused with excitement, but unmistakable in his authority, Lieutenant General Caldwell said, "Colonel Bandfield, I'm not interested in your fucking opinions. You bring this airplane alongside the enemy. Approach so that I can shoot from the left side. Get within two hundred yards at the most."

"Jesus, Henry, think about it. Our fuel state is lousy. If you don't nail him first, we'll be swimming home. Let me call back to get some fighters sent up. We can just shadow him till then."

"Call up the fighters, Bandy, but I want this airplane placed alongside the enemy."

Bandfield thought, The fucker's playing John Paul Jones with me—but he banked in toward the Ju 52. In the right seat the usually cheerful Karl Hoffman went white-faced as he realized what was about to take place.

"I've *got* to try to get him to come back to American territory, Bandy. I'll stand in the doorway and signal him to return. If he doesn't, I'll shoot his ass down."

"What if he shoots first?"

"That'll be your problem, Colonel. Make sure he misses."

On board the Junkers, Hafner stowed his machine guns and continued to wave the white flag, watching the C-47 come closer.

"Holzamer, it looks like they've got a machine gun mounted on the left side by the door. There's a man in the doorway . . ."

Hafner's tone changed as he recognized him. My God, it's

Caldwell. I'll bet that Bandfield is flying the airplane. The old bloodlust surged within him, a hot burning like a youthful awakened sexuality, filling him with passion to revenge the battle over Guernica, to make the two of them, old friends and ancient enemies, pay for his years of suffering.

He tried to keep his voice calm.

"Ah, Holzamer, he's signaling us to turn back to land. I want you to start a gentle turn to the right, as if to comply. Turn about thirty degrees and level out—then I'll start firing."

Bandfield watched the Junkers, one hundred yards away and no more than fifty feet above the mirror-smooth surface of the sea. It began a shallow bank to the right to the pebble-studded beaches of Germany's coastline. Preoccupied as he was, Bandfield was struck by the idyllic peacefulness of the scene, the waves curling on the beach, the little silver lines of streams running down to the water, beach houses, a small village. Who could believe that a world war was raging to a close just a few miles to the south?

"He's turning, Henry. I'm going to stay outside, about one hundred feet above him."

Just as Hafner had planned, the C-47's nose turned in toward the Junkers, narrowing Caldwell's field of fire. In a single fluid motion, Hafner raised the machine guns, fixed the C-47 in his sights and fired. The first burst slammed into the starboard engine, danced along the leading edge of the wing and into the cockpit, smashing the windscreen and tearing Hoffman's head into a bloody pulp, then pulverized the hydraulic system. The wounded airplane staggered as Bandfield jerked it into a climbing turn to the right.

Henry Caldwell swore as he aimed the .50-caliber machine gun down at the Junkers now in a steep left turn, passing under the C-47. He fired and missed.

"Bandy, turn left."

Bandfield shoved the throttles forward as he sensed the number two engine losing power. Glancing to the right past Hoffman's lifeless body he saw the needle of the hydraulic gauge fall to zero, just as he felt the lurch of the landing gear free-falling to the down position. The control wheel hammered in his hands, frantically signaling that the plane was edging toward a stall. There was only one sane course of action, to break off combat and head toward shore.

Hafner, fevered with the combat lust that had been denied him for years, watched the C-47 stagger into a turn, its landing gear partially hanging down, smoke streaming from the right engine. His killer instinct came boiling to the surface. He would not let Bandfield get away this time.

"Turn around, Holzamer, I want to finish him off. Approach him from the left so that I can get a shot at the pilot."

In the Junkers cockpit the grim-faced Holzamer shrugged and applied full power, maintaining the steep left turn, his wingtip almost touching the water.

"He's slowing down, Colonel, we'll be able to catch him easy enough."

Caldwell, exhilarated, combative, called, "Bandy, he's coming at us. Make a sharp ninety-degree turn to the right, now!"

Without hesitation, Bandfield turned, pouring power to the left engine, ignoring the sound of Hoffman's crimsoned body flopping against the side of the cockpit.

Like two battered ships of the line the transports moved toward each other, the radius of their turns edging ever nearer to tangency.

Holzamer struggled to keep the fear from his voice. "He's turning into us, sir, it's going to be close."

Both pilots leveled their wings to avoid a head-on collision, and the two old transports turned warplanes passed level, Hafner and Caldwell firing simultaneous broadsides.

Bandfield eased into another right turn, conscious that a stall was imminent, that when the air burbled and the wing lost lift, the drag of the hanging gear would snap them inverted into the sea. The stubborn Holzamer, an old campaigner caught up in the battle, pulled hard in a near vertical bank to position the Junkers to the C-47's left rear.

Hafner was firing up at them, over his right wing, the lines of his bullets stitching through the rudder and dancing down the length of the cabin.

"Bandy, turn hard left and roll level. I've got to get a shot off at this guy."

"We're barely flying now, Henry. I'll probably stall this sucker out."

"Turn now!"

Bandfield racked the C-47 up into a protesting ninety-degree turn, felt the pre-stall trembling, and popped the nose forward as he rolled level. Caldwell fired a long muzzle-burning burst that reached into the cockpit of the Junkers to kill the pilot. He traversed his gun, running the line of bullets back to hammer Hafner, still maintaining his vicious fire into the rear of the American plane. As Hafner fell forward in his turret, killed instantly as Caldwell's bullets tore through his head and chest, Caldwell slumped in his harness, blood flowing from a dozen wounds.

The war-weary Junkers hesitated for a moment, then dove straight down into the sea, disappearing in a wild ring of white water.

Bandfield, wounded in the right arm and covered with Hoffman's blood, gazed back at the shambles of the cabin. Hank the Hawk, suspended in his makeshift harness like a fly in a spider's web, hung over his machine gun, his head pointed toward the cockpit, looking strangely at peace.

Even with all the trim rolled in, it took all Bandfield's strength on the wheel and rudder to keep the C-47 airborne. He wanted to go back to Caldwell, to help him if he could, but it was impossible. With the gear down and the engine out, he struggled to keep it flying straight and level. If he'd relaxed an instant, the battered C-47 would have stalled and spun in.

He headed for land, miserably aware that if Caldwell was not already dead, he would be before they landed. Saddened as he was, he knew that it was the ending Caldwell wanted. Now there would be no court martial.

EPILOGUE

Muroc, California/September 18, 1947

"Good God almighty, would you look at that!"

Hadley Roget pointed up at the huge Consolidated Vultee XB-36 droning overhead, the roar of its six pusher engines rising and falling like waves on a beach.

Charlotte Bandfield squealed and put her hands over her ears. George, clutched in Bandy's arms, waved frantically as the enormous airplane wiped its shadow over the crowd, then began a slow climbing turn to the left.

The XB-36 was just one in a succession of marvels passing in review at the ceremonies marking the first day of existence for the new United States Air Force. Similar ceremonies were going on all over the country, but Muroc was the place to be, because the leading edge of aviation was assembled in its dusty hangars. Now they were watching the fly-bys. The first had featured the stalwarts of the past, the war-winning Mustangs, Thunderbolts, and B-29s. Then a flight of Lockheed P-80s roared by on the deck, their shimmering exhausts churning up dust from the salt flats.

"Hadley, we were born twenty-five years too soon. The next ten years are going to be the most fantastic ever."

Roget ran his fingers over the stub of his crew-cut, as if he were searching for the lost glory of his hair. "Boy, I know it. They gave me a briefing this morning, then took me on a tour of the hangars. They've got jet fighters and bombers coming down the pike that would make your eyes water."

"What do you think young George here will get to fly?"

George Bandfield was almost eight, and was too preoccupied to give more than a passing glance at the airplanes flashing past him. The desert sun was melting his Eskimo Pie, sending vanilla rivulets down his uplifted arm.

"Rocket planes, probably, and maybe by then they'll be letting women in, and Charlotte can be his copilot."

Charlotte, a dignified eleven, looked up and said, "If I fly with Georgie, *I'll* be the pilot and Georgie will be the copilot."

Patty nodded in agreement as they strolled to a halt at the western edge of the swiftly growing air base. She was as absorbed in their new house-building business as she had been in aviation, and she surveyed the matrix of streets, still void of buildings but a clear forecast of the ultimate size of the base. She was mentally laying out the buildings, computing the square footage, mentally putting a bid together. She let her eyes wander around the crowd standing with them near the cluster of five parachutes being used to cover the massive memorial being dedicated to Lieutenant General Henry Caldwell. She wondered if it would be as imposing uncovered as it was now, with three huge cargo parachutes draped over what was obviously an aircraft, mounted on a pylon. Another covered a statue. The fifth, a smaller one, was fifty feet away at the intersection of two streets, both empty of buildings for as far as she could see.

She really shouldn't have come. She was missing a meeting with the Weyerhauser executives on getting priority delivery of more lumber, and some people from the San Jose city government were coming down in the afternoon to talk about creating a plant to build Roget houses up there. But she couldn't miss the dedication ceremonies, not after all they'd been through with Henry Caldwell. Suddenly, she stiffened and drove her nails into Bandy's arm.

"Ouch, watch it, that's where I was wounded. What is it?"

"Look over there, talking to that big three-star general. It's your old pals, Troy McNaughton and Elsie Raynor."

"God, what gall! She drove the man to his death, and now she comes to his dedication ceremonies."

Bandfield was outraged, remembering all the bitter conversations with Caldwell in Germany. The man died as Elsie's greatest defender, even though she had sworn to get revenge on him. Caldwell had never had much faith in Troy McNaughton's promise to "take care of her nicely." Instead, he had been desperately worried that McNaughton might somehow harm her. But here she was, appearing as happily unconcerned as she had been when they'd watched the Yankees beat the Cubs in the 1938 World Series.

Mercifully, the whole business of Caldwell's involvement with McNaughton Aircraft had died a quiet death in the convulsion of demobilization that had come with the end of the war. Instead of a court martial for lack of judgment, Henry Caldwell had received a posthumous Medal of Honor. The citation for the medal talked about his last, valorous combat with Hafner, but the real reason for the award had been his monumental contributions to airpower.

McNaughton, his skin deeply tanned and hair now totally silver, led Elsie away by the hand. Still unrelentingly flirtatious, she left reluctantly, casting one last look over her shoulder at the smiling Air Force general.

Bandfield whispered, "What an actor."

McNaughton was pretending to be delighted to have seen them and was waving broadly as he made his way through the crowd toward them, Elsie lagging behind.

"Patty! You're as beautiful as ever." He grabbed Bandfield's free hand and pumped it, then slapped Roget on the back.

"Hadley, you old dog, we hear you're making a fortune from your houses! Why don't you come down to Nashville and set up a factory in my shop? We've got a lot of excess capacity."

Before Roget could think of a reply, Elsie bounded up, dressed in a filmy blue silk dress, wearing a pillbox hat. The red nails gleaming through her white open-toe shoes confirmed that she wasn't wearing hose. In spite of his genuine distaste for her because of the harm she'd done Henry, Bandfield had to admit that her flashy beauty was undeniable.

Bubbling with enthusiasm, she shook Bandy's hand, saying, "Hi, y'all. Isn't this thrilling? I just wish old Henry could be here to enjoy it."

There was a brief silence. Of all the things she might have said, this was the least expected—yet the most Elsie-like. Bandfield almost said, "Yes, and Bruno, too," when Troy capped her remark.

"We wanted you to be the first to know—we got married last week. Meet Mrs. Troy McNaughton." He beamed as if he were their oldest family friend letting them in on a secret they would all cherish. Bandfield realized now how Troy had "taken care of her." She probably owned a big chunk of McNaughton Aircraft.

Elsie nodded vigorously but clung to her opening remarks. "Old Henry, he'd have liked the airplanes, but hated the waiting around for the ceremony. Have you seen his statue? Troy commissioned it. It looks just like Henry when he was younger. It's really good."

Bandfield began to recover and realized that he was still holding Elsie's hand.

"Wonderful. Best wishes to you both. No, we haven't seen the statue. It's really quite a day for you, isn't it?"

"Sure is." McNaughton glanced at his watch. "You know, they've asked me to make the remarks at the dedication, after General Orr's introduction." He added, "Wish I had time to take you over to our hangar to show you our X-plane. It's top secret, but I could get you in."

"What's that, Troy? I thought most of McNaughton's effort was going into missiles."

"That's our San Diego branch. Back in Tennessee, we've built a research plane. We're working for the Navy, can you believe it? We're competing with Bell to see who'll be the first to break the sound barrier. Once we've done that, we've opened up a whole new frontier."

Roget turned away and shrugged. The whole thing was incomprehensible to him. After failing to produce a single first-line fighter during the war, McNaughton Aircraft was riding higher than ever, and Troy McNaughton was clearly as much in favor with the military brass as he had ever been.

Hadley saw that Bandfield had also edged away. They both watched McNaughton closely as he spoke to a group of field grade Air Force officers who had wandered over, attracted by Patty and Elsie, but pretending to be interested in the parachute-veiled memorial.

Bandfield whispered, "Hadley, he doesn't look much different than when we saw him in New York."

"That was nine years and one war ago, Bandy, and the son-of-a-bitch looks as young as ever. His hair's gone silver—better than yours, it's just going."

Bandfield flushed, irritated for the millionth time in his life with Hadley's nerve-prodding sense of humor. It was true. He had aged visibly during the war, his hair was thinning, and here was McNaughton, except for his hair almost as young-looking as ever, and even more confident, more intense. Only his eyes had changed, grown still colder in contrast to his smiling face. They walked back toward the newlyweds to hear McNaughton announce, "You folks are going to have to excuse me. They've asked me to do the honors at the dedication, and it's almost time. At ten o'clock sharp, I'm having a flight of Sidewinders come over, followed by a flight of Mambas. Then I've got a surprise for you. After that I'll say a few more words, we'll pull the parachutes off, and that'll be it!"

General Orr started the ceremonies with a muffled curse when he found the microphones weren't working. A harried lieutenant bustled to the stand to push some buttons. Orr had an unfortunate speaking voice, a shrill, high drone that made listening torture.

"We're here today to dedicate a memorial to a great man, a combat hero in the greatest American tradition, Lieutenant General Henry Caldwell." His voice dully screeched on, as if he were reading an efficiency report, talking about Henry Caldwell's dedication, vision, attention to duty, stripping him of vitality and humor, painting a portrait of the man as lifeless as the statue about to be unveiled.

Bandfield thought back to the last battle, when all of Henry's pugnacious love of combat had surfaced. He'd directed the battle like an old-time naval captain. And Bandfield fought away the last memory of Caldwell. Perilously close to crashing the whole way, he'd managed to fly the battle-ravaged C-47 back to crash-land on a Luftwaffe auxiliary field. The officer in command, a surly major, had refused to allow his men to help until Bandfield had accepted his formal surrender. The rear of the C-47 had been awash in Caldwell's blood. One arm useless, slipping on the bloody aluminum floor, Bandfield had worked with two black-clad Luftwaffe mechanics to take Caldwell's cold body down from its gory harness.

". . . and now I'd like to introduce a pioneer in his own right, one of Henry Caldwell's closest friends, Mr. Troy McNaughton, who will unveil the memorial."

McNaughton was as good as Orr had been bad. He started off with a few funny stories about Caldwell that rocked the crowd with sympathetic laughter, then turned on the tears with a somewhat exaggerated tale of Caldwell's devotion to his wife. He surprised Bandfield by talking expertly about Caldwell's true accomplishments—the careful spending of funds before the war, the preservation of the aircraft industry during the Depression, and his prescient vision in bringing about the B-29 and the long-range fighter.

Bandfield felt Patty's nails dig in again as McNaughton went on more true to form. "Henry Caldwell had the guts to encourage me when I wanted to quit. He took a gamble on McNaughton Aircraft that paid off handsomely on the Russian front—some say it won the war there. And now, first you'll hear, and then you'll see, some of the results of his confidence."

A flight of three Sidewinders swept over, the crackling of their Merlin engines sounding like ancient history against the rumble of the three Mambas that followed, black smoke pouring from their jet exhausts.

After a brief delay, McNaughton interjected: "And here's one that I wish Henry could be with us to see, the latest member of the McNaughton family."

Patty saw it first, a tiny cross that grew as rapidly as if it had been fired out of a cannon. It flashed over them, a silver shark with swept-back wings and a triangular swell to its fuselage. It was past the airfield boundary before the rounded thunder roar of its exhaust rolled over them.

"That's the new McNaughton Copperhead—fastest jet in the world."

Bandfield watched the airplane pull up in a sharp right turn, reverse, then head back down the field to repeat the pass in the opposite direction. He shook his head in disbelief. It was basically a single-engine Messerschmitt Me 262! In his missiles and his airplanes, Troy McNaughton still lived off the work of others—especially the work of Henry Caldwell.

"And now, let me show you a fitting memorial to a great man."

When the reverberations of the Copperhead's engine had finally gone silent, McNaughton signaled and a team of enlisted men pulled at the shroud lines. The big cargo chutes came off, revealing a gleaming McNaughton Sidewinder on a pedestal, its wing tilted in a right bank. Then the center chute was removed, and there was Henry Caldwell bigger than life, his left hand reaching down as if to steady himself on the lowered wing of the Sidewinder, his right holding a superb model of the Boeing B-29 as if he were launching it to fly.

A burst of applause rippled through the crowd. It was a good likeness. The artist had captured Henry Caldwell in his prime, dynamic, filled with energy, and looking to the future. The strength portrayed in the statue's uplifted arm looked fully capable of launching the fleets of B-29s that had won the war against Japan.

McNaughton spoke again: "Now look at the remaining parachute, ladies and gentlemen."

They turned and two sergeants pulled the parachute away. It was a standard street sign at Muroc, and it read CALDWELL BOULEVARD.

Exultant, McNaughton said, "In a few ten years, this will be the center of the base, and Caldwell Boulevard will be one of the main thoroughfares. I've seen the plans, and this is the place Henry ought to be!"

There was a long burst of applause as McNaughton turned and

saluted the statue of Henry Caldwell. General Orr, clearly irritated by the masterful performance, said, "This concludes the ceremony, ladies and gentlemen. There are refreshments in the big tent."

As the crowd began to move away, Elsie stepped between Patty and Bandy and took them by the arm, leaving George and Charlotte to trail along.

"I want to show you something."

They moved a few feet and stopped at the street sign.

"My God!" was all Bandy could say. They were at the intersection of Caldwell Boulevard and Lee Street.

"It was Troy's idea, and since he was donating the memorial, they let him have his way. I think it's nice. Jim Lee was a hero, too."

Shocked by her blithe insensitivity, the Bandfields pled their children's fatigue and walked toward the parking area where Hadley was waiting in his new Frazer Manhattan.

"My God, Bandy, did you ever see anything like it?"

"No—but somehow it's the way life always works out. It's a wonder it didn't turn out to be Lee Boulevard and Caldwell Street, the way Elsie felt about them."

"They should name a street after you! You were a hero, too, right from the start."

"Honey, I don't want them naming any streets after me for a long time—they generally do it for dead people!"

"Doesn't it bother you at all? And how about McNaughton? Why do you suppose he donated the memorial, or arranged to have the streets named that way?"

"I don't know, Patty. Guilty conscience, maybe. He'll probably charge the government for it some way. The one sure thing is that they both would have gotten a laugh out of it."

He was silent for a while, then said, "And we might as well, too. I've got an idea we'll both be back here at Muroc before too long, maybe walking down Caldwell Boulevard toward a new airplane."

She glanced at him. "Maybe a new airplane. But surely some new buildings."

Author's Note

This work grew out of years of study, interviews and correspondence with a wide variety of talented people. Among them were famous military leaders and/or legendary pilots like *Generalleutnant* Adolf Galland, General Jimmy Doolittle, Major General F. O. Carrol, Lieutenant General Laurence Craigie, Sir Douglas Bader, Hans-Ulrich Rudel, Tony LeVier, and Slick Goodlin. Some were great engineers like Dr. Hans von Ohain, Sir Frank Whittle, Dr. Anselm Franz, Dr. Ludwig Bolkow, Ezra Kotcher, and Don Berlin. Many others were less well-known but enormously capable people like Opie Chenoweth, Dr. Guido Mutke, Brigadier General Benjamin Kelsey, Vance Breese, Tom Lanphier, C. V. Glines, Waldemar Voigt, Archibald Hall, Robert Rummell, Gene Odekirk, George A. Page, Payton Magruder, Russ Schleeh, Bill McAvoy, and Sam Shannon. There were literally hundreds of others, and all added to my general store of information. I've synthesized much of the factual information in this book from these sources, and of course added to it the fictional elements necessary to compress so much time and so many events into so few pages.

I want to express my deep gratitude to my editor Jim Wade, his able assistant Victoria Heacock, and my agent Jacques de Spoelberch for their invaluable guidance. Thanks, too, to Henry Snelling and DeWitt Copp for all their insight and patient help.

The ardent buff will note some minor fictional liberties taken with the actual chronology of technical development, but everything that happens *could* have happened if human frailties had not intervened.

Walter J. Boyne
Reston, Virginia